Tierney Page is a contemporary romance author and content creator based in Melbourne, Australia. At thirty-two, she crafts stories filled with relatable characters, swoon-worthy MMCs, heartfelt connections and spice that keeps readers turning pages late into the night.

When she's not writing, Tierney enjoys travelling, doting on her fur babies and indulging in a good book. Most days, you'll find her curled up on the sofa in cosy fluffy socks, a steaming cup of coffee in hand, a cat on her lap and a spicy romance novel keeping her company.

VISIT TIERNEY PAGE ONLINE

◉ tierney.reads
♪ tierney.reads

LONDON HEARTS SERIES
BOOK TWO

THE
SUITE
SECRET

TIERNEY PAGE

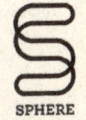

SPHERE

SPHERE

First published in Great Britain in 2025 by Sphere
First published in Australia in 2025 by Hachette Australia

3 5 7 9 10 8 6 4

Copyright © Tierney Page 2025

The moral right of the author has been asserted.

*All characters and events in this publication, other than those
clearly in the public domain, are fictitious and any resemblance
to real persons, living or dead, is purely coincidental.*

All rights reserved.
No part of this publication may be reproduced, stored in a
retrieval system, or transmitted, in any form or by any means, without
the prior permission in writing of the publisher, nor be otherwise circulated
in any form of binding or cover other than that in which it is published
and without a similar condition including this condition being
imposed on the subsequent purchaser.

A CIP catalogue record for this book
is available from the British Library.

ISBN 978-1-4087-2668-6

Printed and bound in Great Britain by
Clays Ltd, Elcograf S.p.A.

Papers used by Sphere are from well-managed forests
and other responsible sources.

Sphere
An imprint of
Little, Brown Book Group
Carmelite House
50 Victoria Embankment
London EC4Y 0DZ

The authorised representative
in the EEA is
Hachette Ireland
8 Castlecourt Centre
Dublin 15, D15 XTP3, Ireland
(email: info@hbgi.ie)

A Hachette UK Company
www.hachette.co.uk

www.littlebrown.co.uk

*To anyone who was made to feel their heart
wasn't worth holding.
It was. It always will be.*

Disclaimer

This book is intended for adult readers and contains sexually explicit content, graphic language, and mature emotional themes. It includes workplace romance, complex family dynamics, mention of divorce, brief references to stalking and harassment, and emotionally intense situations. Please read with care.

Chapter One

Gemma

I detest the Tube at peak hour.

"Are you right?" I say, turning to glare at the person jabbing their elbow into my ribs.

"Sorry," mutters an older man beside me, busy scrolling through his phone.

We're crammed into the train carriage like sardines, and unfortunately, it smells just as bad—like a blend of yoghurt left out too long and body odour.

The joys of living in a city with a population of nine million.

With a huff, I turn back to the window, my reflection mirrored back at me thanks to the pitch-black tunnel. I push my glasses further up my nose, watching as the occasional light flashes by. In the glass, I spot a tall man behind me, his back turned with his phone pressed to his ear, barking orders at whoever's on the other end.

His voice is delicious—smooth and rich, like aged whisky, and I lower the volume of my music to eavesdrop.

"What? No, I can't hear you properly. You're cutting in and out ... I'm on the bloody underground!" the man says. He pauses, adjusting his stance. "I know the meeting's at nine.

I'll be there as soon as I can." And with that, he hangs up, muttering a quiet, "Jesus, I should have taken the car."

Snob.

Returning to my little bubble, I tap my foot to the beat of the music.

Upon a sudden lurch of the carriage, the tall man crashes into me.

"Ouch!" I cry. Pain explodes through my back as the train suddenly slows down and passengers sway unsteadily. I yank out my headphones, shove them into my trench-coat pockets, and rub the sore spot on my back. I whirl around to deliver a scolding. "Oh, for God's sake. Just hold on to the strap. It's not that bloody—"

The man turns and I halt mid-sentence, not by choice, but because words escape me.

"I tried to grab the strap, but the crowd pushed me before I could," he says. "Are you hurt?"

For the love of all things holy.

He's at least six foot two, clad in a perfectly tailored dark grey suit. The fabric is undoubtedly expensive—vicuña or cashmere—and it clings snugly to his bulging biceps and thighs.

It's obvious the bloke works out.

I'm captivated by his pale blue eyes—cool and clear, like aquamarine. His hair is dark brown, flecked with silver at his temples. It has just the right amount of product to give that *I woke up like this* look. His fair skin is flawless, even under the shitty carriage lights. He has a smattering of freckles dusted across the bridge of his nose and the apples of his cheeks, while faint stubble peppers his jawline, which is so sharp it could cut glass.

Something about him is vaguely familiar, but I can't place it.

Have I seen him in passing? Surely, I would have remembered him had we met. You don't forget a face like *that*.

There's a casual confidence in his stance. While the rest of us are packed together, he somehow commands his own space. My brain turns to porridge because this stranger is radiating a serious case of Big Dick Energy.

Which just so happens to be my favourite kind of energy.

I don't get my kicks from running or reformer Pilates. To be honest, I'd rather sit on a pineapple than exercise. However, sex—that's a form of physical exertion I'm more than willing to engage in, and it definitely keeps my energy levels up. And I've become rather good at it, if I do say so myself. Honestly, I deserve a bloody medal. Considering I don't work out, you'd swear I was an Olympic gymnast.

My favourite kind of sex, however, is the kind where I can sit back and enjoy myself. I like being in control—of course I do—but after years of taking charge in the bedroom, sometimes I just want a well-equipped man to take charge of *me*. And this man looks like he's capable of doing precisely that.

Powerful men in powerful suits with powerful penises make me very happy, and unfortunately, appear to be few and far between.

Trust me—I've done extensive research—this man intrigues me.

He clears his throat, pulling me from my daze.

"Huh?" I ask, still rubbing my back.

He huffs a low laugh. "I asked, *are you hurt?*"

His accent is Londoner, but somewhat muted, softer.

Where have I seen him?

I mentally flip through places I could've met him, scanning faces and voices—anything that might spark recognition. Without thinking, I brush my hair back from my shoulders and arch my back slightly—just enough to draw attention where I want it. The girls have never let me down.

His gaze follows the movement, trailing from my face and lingering where my body nearly brushes his chest.

Even in the winter chill, I chose my outfit carefully. The neckline of my silk shirt dips beneath my open trench coat, just low enough to show my silver infinity necklace against bare skin. My skirt walks that perfect line between professional and sexy—a modest length but fitted enough to hint at the curves beneath.

The silence stretches and I realise I've been staring at him, completely lost in thought.

He tilts his head, studying me with an amused expression. "Right," he says, his tone shifting to something I don't quite like. "Perhaps I'm not being clear enough."

He bends at the knees, bringing himself down to my eye level, as if I'm a confused child.

"I asked"—he pauses, his words dripping with condescension—"are you hurt?"

And just like that, the urge to knee him in the balls is overwhelming.

Jesus. Does he think I'm an idiot?

A trail of fire burns through my chest.

"No," I say, my tone clipped.

"See?" He straightens to full height, an infuriating hint of humour dancing in his eyes. "Wasn't that hard, was it?" The wink he gives me makes my eye twitch.

I scoff. "Excuse me?"

"You were just a bit slow on the uptake."

He's so patronising, I want to kick him.

I recoil at his audacity and stumble straight back into the arms of whatever unfortunate soul is contributing to that god-awful body odour wafting through the carriage. Brilliant.

"I beg your pardon?" I demand, my voice rising.

His smirk widens. "You seemed a little ... overwhelmed. I wasn't sure if it was because you were hurt, couldn't quite follow along, or maybe"—his eyes are pure mischief—"you were struck by my devastating good looks."

The Suite Secret

Arrogant prick. If his head were any further up his arse, he could lick his nostrils clean.

"Did you just suggest I'm stupid?" My voice drops, more threatening than friendly. I ignore the remark about his good looks—because he's absolutely right, the smug turd, but I refuse to give him the satisfaction.

He chuckles, clearly enjoying himself. "I said you were slow to respond, not that you *are* slow. There's a difference."

His gaze drops to my chest before snapping back up to meet my glare.

"Did you just look at my breasts?"

"Well ..." He shrugs. "To be fair, you are shoving them in my direction."

My mouth drops. The nerve of this man.

"I most certainly am not shoving my breasts into you."

I absolutely am. Anyone with a set of eyes in their head can see exactly what I'm doing, but I'm not about to admit it. He knows I'm full of shite, but I won't waver.

He raises a hand in mock surrender with an insufferable grin. "You're right. My apologies. I'd step back to give you proper space, but there's a pram lodged up my backside."

I scrunch my brow and crane my neck to peek behind him, only to be assaulted by the sight—and smell—of someone's rancid armpit. Sure enough, there's a pram wedged between his arse and another passenger.

"Good," I mutter, fishing my AirPods from my pocket and slipping them into my ears.

Turning back to the window, I watch his reflection, catching his soft scoff and the slight shake of his head as he turns away from me. Instead of music, I resume my latest audiobook, letting the narrator's soothing voice drown out the sounds of sneezing, coughing, and—my personal favourite—crying infants.

Two stops later, we finally crawl into Leicester Square station. As I get ready to step off, I notice my charming new acquaintance is also disembarking. I find myself trailing behind him as he weaves through the crowd, heading for the escalator.

Women stare as he passes—of course they bloody do. But my attention is on the way his trousers hug his firm, spectacular arse.

Glorious. He might be totally up himself, but credit where it's due.

By the time I reach street level, he's disappeared into the sea of morning commuters.

Another manic Monday begins.

Chapter Two

Gemma

The wind bites at my exposed skin, leaving a trail of gooseflesh in its wake. I bounce on the balls of my feet, alternating between rubbing my gloved hands together and tucking them under my arms to stay warm.

Around me, people dart between the criss-cross pathways of Soho Square Gardens, heads bowed against the cold.

Lance's Kiosk stands at the edge of the gardens, chipped brown paint peeling from the worn timber and revealing patches of bare wood. The smell of coffee and hot food drifts into the cold air, making my stomach grumble as I step forward to order.

"Morning, lass. How are you?" Lance booms in his thick, northern Scottish accent. I order my usual, double-tapping the button on the side of my phone to pay.

"Ecstatic, thanks, Lance," I reply, flashing him an exaggerated grin.

He chuckles, the corners of his eyes crinkling as he slides over my apricot Danish and latte. "Thirteen pounds, love."

My jaw practically hits the floor. "What the *hell*, Lance? That's daylight robbery! It was ten pounds on Friday!"

He sighs, adjusting his woollen rounded cap. "Council's hiked up their rates. Sadly, it's me and my customers taking the hit. I've already lost four regulars, and it's only Monday. I was hoping to upgrade my coffee machine and replace the display cabinet, but it doesn't look like that'll be happening anytime soon. In fact, it's all looking a bit grim."

My shoulders slump in defeat. "Bloody hell, Lance. I'm so sorry."

Lance's gaze drops to the ground before returning to meet mine. He forces a small, weak smile. I can barely stand it. He's the sweetest man.

I've been frequenting his stall ever since I started working at Prestige Partners, stopping by for my daily Danish and latte every morning on the way to work. Rain, hail, or shine, Lance has always been here.

"Twenty-five years I've run this kiosk. Back then, a coffee was barely a wee two quid." He removes his hat, scratching his bald spot. "I don't know how you youngsters do it."

"Honestly, Lance? Neither do we. Half my pay cheque's gone before I've even paid rent."

He nods, leaning in and crossing his arms over the counter. "But we don't have a choice, eh? Can't just stop living."

"Exactly. Bastards." I gesture to my latte. "Though I might have to start rationing my coffee addiction."

Lance laughs, but it's a tired sound. "You'd think with all these clever new gadgets, life would be easier. Cheaper. But it's just more expensive, and no one's happier."

I shoot him a smirk. "I don't know about that. Your coffee and pastries make me pretty happy."

He reaches forward, gently holding my hand around my pastry. "As long as I get to see my regulars—well, for now, anyway."

Pressure builds in my chest. Lance's Kiosk is a large part of why people visit Soho Square Gardens, and I couldn't bear seeing it go. It's not just the coffee—it's him. There's a comfort in knowing that, even if you're not looking forward to sitting at a desk all day, he'll be there every morning to greet you with a friendly smile. The area without him would feel emptier, colder, *barren*.

"Hang in there," I say.

He offers a slight shrug. "I'll fight it as long as I can, lass. But if it's not meant to be ..." He doesn't finish his sentence. He doesn't need to.

I place my coffee on the counter, delicately covering his hand with mine. I can feel him tremor. "You'll be okay," I say, squeezing a little tighter.

"Enough of that," he says, releasing his grip. "How'd that date go then, lass?" Lance changes the subject.

I shake my head. "Disastrous."

His face splits in a grin. "You don't have much luck with the fellas, do you?"

I take a tentative sip of my coffee. "Oh, I get *lucky* plenty, but no, when it comes to finding someone who isn't a complete tosser? My track record is spectacularly shit."

He points a finger at me, his eyes twinkling. "Don't you give up hope yet, lass. There's a good man out there somewhere for you."

I scoff. "I'm not looking for a relationship, Lance. I just need someone to shag—someone who can keep up with me. They're either intimidated by me or completely selfish."

He laughs. "Aye, you need someone with a backbone. You deserve someone who appreciates that fire in you, not someone trying to put it out."

I raise my coffee in cheers. "See?" I nod. "You get it."

He plants his palms on the counter. "Aye. My Everly was just like you back in the day. See, when we were young, we had the sexual appetite of a—"

I nearly choke on my coffee. "Christ, Lance! Too much information!" I hold up my hand to stop him. "Right, that's my cue to exit before you scar me for life. Bye!"

"Aye, but I was just getting to the good bit!" he calls after me, chuckling to himself.

* * *

The revolving door opens into the lobby where blasts of heat wrap around me, thawing my cheeks. My heels click against the polished tile floors as I head toward the lift, sipping my latte.

"Morning, Gemma!" Tab, our receptionist, greets me with a bright smile and wave from behind the desk.

"Morning, Tab." I beam.

I've been at Prestige Partners for nine years, starting as a fresh-faced creative intern straight out of London College of Communication. Henry Matthews, our chief creative officer, saw potential after viewing my grad portfolio and took me under his wing. Henry and I make a great team. What started as small talk and stiff work conversations quickly turned into after-work vinos and the occasional Sunday brunch.

Henry's become a real friend, not just a colleague. Miraculously, he's the first gorgeous man I've maintained a purely professional relationship with—though I suspect his boyfriend might have something to do with that.

I've never been one to shy away from sexual adventure, especially after my last long-term relationship. I made it my mission to experience everything I missed out on while being tied down to Todd.

The thought of two gorgeous men and me, focused entirely on joint pleasure, is *very* appealing, but I'd bet good money that if I ever had a crack, I'd be up shit creek without a paddle, and I value my position here far too much to jeopardise it.

I didn't claw my way from junior intern to associate creative director to throw it away now. I might play around outside these four walls, but at work, I'm strategic about everything.

It wasn't all glamour at the beginning. I started off managing social media content for smaller boutique hotels and crafting email campaigns for luxury hotel spas. I spent countless late nights tweaking presentations to ensure my pitch was the best, and it paid off. Now, at thirty-four, I'm the youngest creative director in the agency's history, leading our biggest luxury hospitality accounts. Today, Henry and I are gearing up to pitch our campaign for what's set to be London's most talked-about hotel in decades.

Ping.

A notification chimes.

Balancing my pastry and coffee in one hand, I bite down on the finger of my glove, tugging it off before pulling my phone from my pocket.

Declan: *You busy tonight?*

"Ugh," I groan, rolling my eyes as soon as I see the name.

Declan was last night's mistake, courtesy of KinkApp. I used to use the mainstream dating apps but deleted them when I realised most of the men on there are painfully vanilla and actively looking for marriage and babies—*so* not my vibe.

I matched with Declan last week, drawn in by his silver-fox looks and the promise of experience. Sure, he might be forty-three, but I've always had a thing for an age gap. I thought, *What could go wrong?*

Well, it turns out plenty can go wrong.

He rescheduled the date twice. At first, I suggested coffee and a walk on Sunday morning, but unfortunately, Declan doesn't "believe in waking up to an alarm", so he never commits to morning plans. That should have been my first red flag, but I decided to give him the benefit of the doubt and meet him for dinner instead.

This is when I finally learnt that giving someone the benefit of the doubt never benefitted me.

Throughout the entire meal, his eyes never made it north of my tits—which, if I'm honest, I can't blame him for, they are phenomenal. But then came the speech about his journey of "self-discovery" and how after four months of celibacy, he's "finally ready to honour his body with release".

That should have been where I drew the line in the sand. But what can I say? I'm not one to turn down the opportunity for a good shag. Plus, I was horny and stupidly optimistic—a dangerous cocktail. I hoped that he might actually be able to put his money where his mouth is and deliver in the bedroom. So, I went back to his flat, hoping he'd prove me wrong about being a complete waste of my time, and wouldn't you know it? He came inside me after two disappointing pumps, then proceeded to tell me that our souls had just intertwined on a higher frequency.

I don't think I've ever dressed and legged it out of a building so quickly. I scrubbed my skin raw as soon as I got home.

I cringe, tapping out of the message. *I must remember to unmatch him.*

"Ooft." A deep sound reverberates through the space as I walk straight into something—no, scratch that—*someone*. My glove slips from my mouth and the lid pops off my cup, sending coffee splattering all over my victim's shirt. My Danish and phone clatter to the floor, both covered in coffee, and the screen cracks on impact.

"Shit!" I say. "I'm so sorry!"

I look up, freezing as I come face-to-face with a pair of familiar crystal blue eyes.

My eyes narrow to slits as they land on the jerk from the train.

"You," I say, accusatory.

He wipes his hands down the front of his shirt.

Oops, I've completely ruined it.

He flicks his fingers and droplets of coffee fly through the air, spattering onto my cream trench.

"You," he replies, his voice equally low and cutting.

"Perfect," I say, inspecting the brown dots on my coat. "There goes my bloody breakfast."

"I know. I'm the lucky prick wearing it."

I dramatically sweep my eyes over the foyer. "What happened to the pram?"

He cocks an eyebrow. "You mean the one I had lodged up my rectum on the Tube?"

I click my tongue. "That's the one. Did you manage to get it all the way inside this time? I imagine that would have been a difficult feat, considering how tight I'm certain your arse is."

He releases a deep chuckle.

Shit. Even his laugh is hot.

No, traitorous vagina. You do not have a say in this.

I look up as his gaze drops to his shirt. It strikes me that he's lost the suit jacket. The damp, stained fabric clings to his flat, taut stomach, accentuating a dusting of dark chest hair beneath.

Out of all the offices in the area, he had to be at *mine*. Why?

My stupid heart stutters, which is bloody annoying, because this guy is magnetic. It doesn't happen often, but every now and then you lock eyes with someone and feel that pull—like gravity itself shifted and suddenly you're the only two people in the room.

That's exactly what this feels like.

I don't know him, but he affects me. And I've just gone and spilt half my latte all over him. I didn't get more than a few sips from it, so I'm also pissed—that latte cost me half of my thirteen-pound breakfast, the rest of it currently swimming in a puddle on the floor.

I never lose my cool in front of a man. If anything, it's the other way around. I'm confident and go after exactly what I want. And I'll be damned if this stranger, just because he's handsome, is the one to throw me.

I squat to collect my phone and soggy Danish. "Fuck," I mutter, trying to hide the phone cover as I wipe the liquid off the screen, inspecting the damage.

"Is it broken?" he asks.

I angle the phone to show him, and he scrunches his nose when he spots the labyrinth of cracks.

"What are you doing here, anyway?" I say, dabbing my sleeve over the coffee stains on my coat as I straighten to full height.

"I'm here on business. I'm assuming you work in this building," he says, bending down to collect my glove. I snatch it from him, shoving it into my pocket.

"Got it in one, Sherlock," I reply, my eyes trailing over his frame. "Hope that shirt wasn't too expensive."

"Only Tom Ford."

"Shame."

"I can tell you're really cut up about it." The corner of his lip twitches.

"Naturally."

Behind him, I see Tab spring into action, grabbing paper towels and cleaning spray from under her desk. She walks toward us.

His brows pinch, eyeing me with way more interest than I'm comfortable with after making a complete tit of myself. "What's your na—"

"It's okay, Tab," I say quickly, interrupting him as I lift a hand to stop her. "I'll clean it up."

"No, no. I insist!" Tab says, dropping to her haunches, mopping up the coffee puddle and wiping his shoes.

"Oh," he starts. "That really isn't necessary—"

"Exactly, see? He's happy to clean his own shoes."

Tab's cheeks stain pink before she ducks her head and darts back to her desk.

I fix him with a pointed look. "Well, this has been nice. But I have a very important meeting to attend, so if you'll excuse me."

Before he can respond, I sidestep him, darting toward the elevator.

"Apologies about the shirt," I call over my shoulder.

Once I'm inside, I turn back to find the stranger rooted in place, watching with a smirk as I jab at the buttons, willing the doors to close. As they finally shut, I release a deep breath, inspecting my ruined coat. "Damn it."

Chapter Three

Max

Six companies occupy multiple floors of the building.

I watch the elevator numbers ascend to see which floor she gets off at. I turn away when I see she's reached the upper levels.

Bingo. Exactly where I'm going.

I noticed her the moment I stepped onto the Piccadilly line, trying to get as close as possible in the crammed carriage. As luck would have it, some mother wedged her pram against my arse, trapping me in place. Between that and being sandwiched amongst other passengers, I couldn't have moved even if I'd wanted to.

She's of average height, maybe five six, with a slender build and curves in all the right places. Even with her trench, I could clearly make out the dip of her waist. Her coat hung open, teasing the fullness of her chest and the delicate infinity necklace resting against her creamy skin. Her dark blond hair brushed just past her shoulders. Cute wire-framed glasses perched askew on her button nose. Her ivory skin was make-up free, except for a flick of eyeliner, and glossy lips that begged to be touched.

Most of all, I was intrigued by her sass—she didn't speak

to me the way some women do. Not that I'd expect her to swoon, but I'd be lying if I said other women didn't.

Venom and sin wrapped in a delicious, unassuming package, and I can't help but crave her bite.

I run my hand down my front. Lukewarm coffee has seeped through the expensive fabric, plastering my shirt to my skin. It feels revolting, but I can't even bring myself to care—I had too much fun watching the little live wire panic.

I'd been heading out to grab a coffee before my meeting, but looks like I'll be wearing it instead.

I glance at my watch and sigh. Five minutes until the meeting.

I wonder if she'll be there.

I pivot, catching the receptionist's gaze again. Tab, I think her name was. She blushes.

Her cherry-red lips curl into a shy smile, and when I return it, her cheeks flush an even deeper hue.

I straighten my posture and head toward the elevator, passing inquisitive eyes.

I press the button for the top floor marked Prestige Partners—Executive Suites.

A chime sounds as the elevator doors slide open to reveal a bright, airy space with a modern layout.

A secretary's desk sits front and centre in a spacious foyer, flanked by corridors leading to several offices. Right there, leaning casually over the desk with arms crossed, is Grayson Livingstone—CEO of Livingstone Hotels. He's doing what he does best, if his easy smirk and the secretary's insufferable giggles are any indication.

Classic Grayson.

He runs the prestigious New York luxury hotel empire passed down by his late grandparents, shared with his two brothers, Cole and Noah.

We met back when I decided to complete my MBA in New York. What started as after-class drinks and attending lectures together quickly evolved into a close friendship I'm extremely grateful for.

I roll my eyes as I watch Grayson work his usual charm. Women turn their heads—and drop their knickers—wherever Grayson Livingstone goes, the lucky bastard. Not that I can talk. I don't exactly have trouble in that department either, especially following my divorce four years ago.

Like Grayson, I've got zero interest in entertaining anything more than a quick fuck. Four years of freedom since my divorce have taught me exactly how I prefer to keep things: uncomplicated.

Stepping forward, I clap Grayson on the shoulder. He jolts, standing upright as he tugs at the lapels of his jacket.

"Sorry, ma'am. Is my boss here keeping you from getting anything done?" I ask the secretary.

She spins a biro between her pink-tipped fingers, biting down on her lower lip.

"Not at all, sir," she says, fluttering her lashes. She pauses when her eyes zero in on the stain marring my shirt.

"Just call me Max, please," I insist.

"I'm Molly," she says.

"Molly," Grayson repeats with a sly smile, like he's testing her name on his tongue.

Grayson raps his knuckles against the smooth mahogany desk. "Right, better let you get back to it, then. Do feel free to call me." He grins, sliding a sleek matte-black business card out from his jacket—the one with his direct number printed on it.

His fingers brush hers as she takes it, and sure enough, it earns him another giggle.

He turns to me, scrunching his nose as his gaze trails down my wet shirt. "Jesus, you smell like sour milk. What happened to you?"

"Some bird spilled her coffee all over me."

"Obviously," he says, chuckling, checking his watch. "Shit. We don't have time to get you a new shirt." He looks up. "Can you throw your jacket over the top?"

I nod.

Working closely with Grayson these past few years has changed my life in ways I never could've imagined. I had spent years in investment banking at a property firm in Canary Wharf, where my focus had been on hotel acquisitions and developments. I oversaw the details that determined whether a luxury property would thrive or fail. I structured deals for renovations and new builds, worked on expansion strategies, and analysed high-profile portfolios—learning the business side of an industry I'd grown up loving.

I received a desperate call from Grayson two years ago. His grandfather had just passed away, leaving him and his brothers an empire they weren't quite ready to inherit, regardless of how hard they all worked. He needed someone beside him who he could trust implicitly and understood business the way he did. His call couldn't have come at a better time. The divorce from Casey had been final for a year by then, and I was itching for a fresh start, away from her and the constant phone calls.

Seventy-two hours after Grayson's cry for help, I was on a plane to New York, stepping into a new chapter as chief development officer for Livingstone Hotels.

For two years, I helped Grayson lead Livingstone's global expansion, acquiring twelve new luxury properties and boutique hotels worldwide. Now the role has taken me back to the city I grew up in.

Touching down at Heathrow yesterday awoke something unexpected in me. Knowing that my parents and my sister Anna were a few suburbs away again brought a comfort I hadn't realised I'd been missing. The tooting of cab horns, grey skies, and row after row of white terraced houses reminded me of everything good I'd left behind, instead of dwelling on the negativity I'd associated with this place because of Casey.

I started to feel slight remorse. The deeper I descended into the belly of London, the more homesick I felt. But I'm not back here to settle into my old life or to share Sunday roast at Mum's, I'm only here for two months. This isn't a homecoming—it's business.

I'm launching Livingstone Hotels' boldest venture yet: Gray Hotel. Grayson's idea, naturally. It's a sleek new luxury hotel brand, blending old-money elegance with a modern edge, set in London's affluent Mayfair. Picture penthouse suites and infinity pools overlooking Hyde Park.

It'll be the kind of place that draws in the young, hungry, and wealthy. A hotel where every Instagram story promises FOMO and every check-in feels like guests have finally made it. Guests will come to see and be seen. To flaunt their wealth.

It's exactly the sort of project that made me fall in love with this world.

Growing up, I watched the elite from the inside as my father moved us between cities for his role as regional manager of luxury hotels. I saw how the rich lived, how they travelled, and the way they moved through spaces as if they owned them. While other kids were home watching television and playing Pokémon, I was listening in on board meetings from the corner of my father's office, amazed by the million-pound decisions and power plays.

I couldn't believe how much sway money and status could carry, and I wanted a taste of it.

The grandeur of it all got me hooked early, and it's allowed me to follow in my father's footsteps. I'm not just observing the elite anymore; I'm a major part of creating the world they want to live in. And this new project? I see a chessboard, except this time I'm the one orchestrating the next moves and shifting the pieces.

If Gray Hotel is a success, then we'll expand our reach to other global hotspots. I can see it now: Tokyo, Sydney, Hong Kong, Dubai, Paris, Singapore, Barcelona—the possibilities are endless.

To turn this vision into a reality, we've come to Prestige Partners, the global leaders in luxury marketing campaigns.

What a mouthful. But we want the best of the best when it comes to developing a viral campaign tailored specifically to launch Gray Hotel.

"Gentlemen," greets Henry Matthews, chief creative officer of Prestige Partners, as he steps through his doorway, gesturing for us to enter his office. "Sorry to keep you waiting."

We met with Henry informally earlier this morning to get the preliminaries out of the way before he sat us down to discuss the agenda for today's meeting.

We're here to meet the team bringing the Gray Hotel to life. Henry's creative director is supposedly some marketing genius, having delivered several viral luxury hotel launches. Ironically, she's running late, which usually means unreliable, but I figured I'd use the time to grab a coffee to fight this jet lag. That bright idea backfired spectacularly.

Stepping inside, I make for my suit jacket flung over the armchair opposite Henry's desk. I slip my arms into the sleeves, buttoning it up to hide the coffee splodge.

"I understand we'll be working together for a while, so I've had our secretary set up a spare office for you on this floor. I expect you might have your own arrangements with Livingstone Hotels, but we've made one up here just in case. You're welcome to come and go as you please," Henry says.

"Thank you," Grayson replies. "I'm staying at the Livingstone Hotel and Max has made his own arrangements, but we appreciate the thoughtfulness. Having a workspace here could be convenient for collaboration, so we'll most likely alternate between working from home and coming in, if that's alright."

"Perfect. It's yours to use whenever suits. I figured that since you're both here in London, you might appreciate a change of scenery, to see some of the city," Henry says.

"Thank you," I reply.

Henry picks up his phone from the desk, frowning at the time.

While Henry fires off a text, Grayson claps me on the shoulder. We exchange a glance, a silent nod of understanding passing between us.

We're ready.

After a year of preparation and countless late nights perfecting this project, we can't wait to share our concept and ideas with the team.

I always get excited to meet the professionals who'll be working alongside us; it's one of the best parts of the job.

Henry's phone chimes, his thumbs swiftly tapping across the screen as he checks the message.

"Alright, everyone's already down there. We'd better not keep them waiting. I'm so sorry about my colleague, Gemma—she's usually very punctual. I can assure you this is most unlike her. She's messaged to say she'll meet us there," he says.

Gemma.

Why does that name ring a bell? I'm sure I've heard it somewhere recently.

It finally clicks—Anna had mentioned her friend works here. That must be her.

We rise and follow Henry to the elevator. As the doors close, he scrunches his nose; his brows pinch and his nostrils flare.

"Does something smell like sour milk?"

Chapter Four

Gemma

These guys are the big players. *The* Grayson Livingstone, from Livingstone Hotels, and his chief development officer, who I'm told is absolutely brilliant.

Henry and I have been burning the candle at both ends to craft the perfect pitch for Gray Hotel.

Luxury hotels are my specialty—my bread and butter—so it was no surprise that Henry's boss picked us when Grayson Livingstone reached out about collaborating. Some of my colleagues were absolutely fuming. Every marketing agency in the UK wanted this campaign. Louise and Theo, our colleagues, have been shooting daggers at Henry and me ever since we were announced for the pitch.

Louise hates me with a passion. We both started at Prestige together, but my career has progressed much faster than hers, and she's never forgiven me for it. I was promoted to creative director while she stayed stuck as marketing strategist, and where Louise goes, her loyal minion Theo follows. She's only gotten more bitter with time. Not that I care—I find her about as appealing as a colonoscopy. The vindictive cow reached peak evil last year when she nearly cost me an entire account.

She went behind my back and told them I was "difficult to work with" and had a drinking problem, all because she couldn't stand that I was chosen to be promoted, not her. I'm lucky HR didn't performance manage me after her wicked lie.

Now that Henry and I were selected to pitch for this project, she's dropped the two-faced facade entirely. She openly mutters insults as I walk past—mainly about the way I dress—gives me filthy looks across the office, and has even stooped to petty pen thievery, the little shit.

Having your pens go missing? It's bloody annoying. I know it's her because I can *feel* her eyes follow me from my office (she's in a cubicle) all the way to the supply closet. Every. Single. Time.

So yeah, Louise can suck on my big, fat, metaphorical balls.

Waving my hand under the sensor tap in the ladies' bathroom, I attack my trench coat with damp paper towels, attempting to save it. The coffee stains have set into the cream fabric, and my blood pressure rises with each useless dab. At this point, I'm just diluting and spreading the stain even further.

Giving in, I toss out the paper towel. The hand dryer roars to life, blasting hot air over my ruined coat to dry the wet patch. I watch in horror as the expensive fabric stiffens under the assault, setting the stain deeper.

Perfect. Just bloody perfect.

My phone chimes and I dig it out of my pocket, swiping across the chipped screen to open Henry's message.

Henry: *Where the hell are you?*

The glass snags my thumb and a small bead of blood blooms on my fingertip.

My eyes dart to the time: 9.00 am.

Shit. I need to get to this meeting. My blood smears over the screen as I hurriedly type out a response.

The Suite Secret

Me: *On my way! Go ahead and I'll meet you in there.*

I bolt into my office, sweeping my hair out of my face and adjusting my glasses. I snatch my folder, and then, unusually for me, I'm running—as much as one can in heels—toward the boardroom.

Ping.

I flip my phone over, reading the message banner as my legs propel me toward the end of the corridor.

April: *Are we still on for drinks tonight?*
Anna: *Yes! Come to mine, I picked up some cheeses.*

My fingers fly across the screen.

Me: *I'll bring wine.*
Anna: *Fab.*

Another message comes in.

Henry: *I'm starting without you.*

Crap!

I lurch to a stop when I reach the end of the hallway. Taking a deep breath, I steel myself before pushing open the double doors.

Henry stands in front of a large projector, preparing to begin the pitch without me.

Sorry, I mouth. All chatter ceases as his eyes bore into mine, horror etched across his face. His gaze slowly peruses from my head to my toes, and I gulp, dropping my folder onto the table and shedding my coat. As I lower the trench off my shoulders, the worst imaginable thing happens.

My top button gives way, popping off with dramatic flair. It gets some serious air behind it and I watch, helpless, as it arcs across the room in slow motion, only to strike the left eye of one of the most beautiful men I've ever seen.

Grayson Livingstone.

"Ah! Fuck!" he yells, clutching at his eye.

Fuck, indeed.

My heart slams against my ribs as I cover my mouth with my hand, totally mortified. Did that just happen? I glance to Grayson's left, where his chief development officer must be seated, only to freeze when my gaze latches onto a familiar pair of ocean-blue eyes. A dark eyebrow arches as he leans back, crossing his muscled arms over his chest, a smirk on his face.

You're shitting me.

"I'm so sorry!" I say.

Henry sidles up to me, his voice strained. "Gemma Clarke, meet Grayson Livingstone and his chief development officer, Max Browne."

Ah-ha! I knew the handsome bastard looked familiar.

Max Browne. As in my best friend Anna's older brother, Max Browne. The one I've somehow managed to avoid meeting for thirteen years of friendship with Anna.

Not only have I potentially blinded one of the most important men in my professional career with wayward haberdashery, but not ten minutes ago, I told his partner—my best friend's brother—that I was certain he had a tight arse.

Bloody brilliant.

Chapter Five

Gemma

The pitch flies by in a blur. I utter a silent prayer as soon as the meeting finishes, and I can't escape fast enough. I burst through the double doors equal parts flustered and humiliated.

Louise couldn't take her eyes off Max *or* Grayson. If she wasn't staring daggers at me, she was drooling like a Saint Bernard. And what's worse? Max couldn't take his eyes off me—though my exposed cleavage may have had something to do with that.

Poor Grayson pasted on a brave face, nursing his assaulted eye throughout the entire pitch, and Max ... Christ, his gaze was lethal. Like I was facing a firing squad. He tracked my every move, and despite the mortification, despite everything that went *wrong*, I was hyperaware of him in ways that had nothing to do with my embarrassment.

I'm not usually ruffled around men. But Max has me nervous—*me!* This never happens. I need to find a way to ignore my physical attraction to Max and go into this with purely a professional lens, and the reasons are crystal clear ...

First, I'm working on this campaign with him, and mixing business with pleasure only ever ends in tears and HR paperwork.

Second, he's Anna's brother. She'd kill me. Not metaphorically—actually kill me.

And let's not forget the most important part: Max Browne is a bit of a tosser.

Ugh. I can picture his smug, infuriatingly self-assured face right now.

At least Henry was up there with me. Nevertheless, I slapped on my best *I've got my shit together* face and did what I do best. My job. Well, sex—but still, my job.

I yank my phone from my pocket, thumbs attacking the cracked screen as I shoot off a message to Anna.

Me: *WTF?! You failed to mention your brother is the chief development officer working with Grayson-Bloody-Livingstone on the Gray Hotel campaign!*

Her response is instant.

Anna: *Oh, is he? Good for him. I never actually bothered to ask what his role is. Or maybe he told me and I forgot ...*

Me: *Obviously.*

Anna: *... I fail to see the problem.*

Me: *The problem is, I forgot how ridiculously gorgeous he is. And I just made a total arse of myself in front of him.*

Anna: *Well, keep forgetting. I swear to God, Gemma, do NOT hit on my brother.*

I huff in frustration, exiting the chat.

Henry grips my biceps and practically marches me to his office.

I collapse into the armchair opposite his desk while he rocks back and forth in his computer chair like Dr Evil, worrying his bottom lip between his teeth.

The moment I open my mouth to speak, his eyebrow arches, silencing me instantly.

We sit, wordless, for what feels like forever.

"So," Henry says.

"Hmmm."

"What in the fresh hell was that?" He leans forward, hands splayed on his desk.

"Am I fired?"

He expels a heavy breath. "No. You aren't fired."

"Is the CEO going to kill me?"

"No, he isn't going to kill you. But I might."

"How was I supposed to know my button was going to pop out?"

He rubs his temples, frustrated.

"I didn't mean to, Henry. It's not my fault I have improbably large breasts."

"You presented your pitch with your lacy bra showing."

"What choice did I have? Besides, no one else seemed troubled by it. What happened to empowering women in the workforce? I know you're not bothered by a bra. You're a modern man, Henry."

"I'm gay."

"Semantics." I cross my legs. "At least the pitch went well?"

"You're lucky Grayson even bloody saw the projector!"

I wave my hand dismissively. "He'll be fine."

I hope.

"He's a BILLIONAIRE, Gemma!" Henry bellows.

I wince. "He could just buy a new eye?"

"Very funny," he deadpans.

I shrug. "Look, he said he was fine. We got the pitch out of the way. They *seemed* to be impressed. I'm sure they've both forgotten about the whole button incident by now."

He grunts. "Max Browne had to lead him out by the hand. Do you know what that does to a man's ego?"

"I'm sorry, Henry." I don't know what else to say.

He looks at me earnestly. "I know you are."

"Would you like me to go talk to him? See if he's okay?"

"No. That won't be necessary. Go and have a break. I'll talk to Grayson in the meantime and attempt damage control."

I rise, smoothing a hand down my skirt with trembling fingers. The lump in my throat betrays me. Despite my calm exterior, I'm terrified. Our pitch was brilliant—exceptional, even—but I could have blown this entire campaign. I looked a total mess. Who would want to work with someone after *that*?

Henry must see through my bravado because his expression softens as I reach for the door handle.

"Gemma," he says, stopping me.

I peer over my shoulder.

"Despite the button—and your overall state—you did a brilliant job. Well done. I hope you're proud."

Tears prick my eyes, but I blink them back. I swing the door open, about to leave when—

"Oh, and Gemma?"

"Yeah?" I turn to face him.

He points to his cheekbone. "Take care of that, please."

Confused, I touch my cheek before heading to the bathroom. Once inside, I inspect my reflection.

Because this day couldn't possibly get any worse, there's a perfect line of blood across my cheekbone.

"Oh, you're bloody joking."

Chapter Six

Max

The rich, nutty aroma of coffee wafts through the kitchenette as I press the Nespresso machine button.

After a quick dash to Harrods for a new shirt—and dropping Grayson at the optometrist to have his eye checked, the poor bloke—I can finally settle in with the pitch notes Gemma and Henry provided.

Gemma.

Anna's best friend.

I knew I'd seen her before.

I pull up Anna's Instagram, scroll through her following list, and open Gemma's profile when I find it.

I squint when I click on her most recent post, using my thumb and index finger to zoom in. Gone is the silk shirt and mid-length skirt. Instead, she's wearing a tiny leather skirt, come-fuck-me boots, and a lace bodysuit.

Now, *this* look suits her.

There's poise and certainty in the way she carries herself. Like she knows exactly what she's doing—knows the effect she'll have on any poor bastard who looks. The way she smirks at the camera—it's like she's daring anyone to look away, and that glint in her eye has me making my decision: I don't want to.

A smile tugs at my lips as I picture the way she'd burst into the boardroom looking delightfully dishevelled. Her hair was a mess, I swear there was blood smeared on her cheek—I don't even want to know whose—and her coat matched my shirt.

Despite all that, she still looked gorgeous. Sexy.

You'd think Grayson would be irritated about taking a button to the eyeball, but I have a feeling Gemma's impressive cleavage might have softened the blow. And despite the shitshow, her and Henry's pitch was absolutely brilliant.

I sink into a nearby chair, flipping through Gemma's pitch folder. Page after page demonstrate her passion and enthusiasm for the project. There isn't a single detail she's missed. She hasn't created a marketing plan; she's crafted an entire experience.

And it's not just good.

It's exceptional.

Heels click against tiles, the sound drawing closer. I stash my phone and glance up just as Gemma appears.

She falters, surprised when she sees me.

"Hello, Gemma."

"Max," she says, nodding in recognition.

Her soft, velvety voice wraps around me, and all I can focus on are her lips.

She hesitates, her eyes darting to the folder, and she fidgets with her necklace.

I lift the folder. "This is good."

"I know."

She's confident, I have to hand it to her. I like it.

She moves toward the fridge, pulling out the milk as she prepares her coffee. My eyes zero in on the way her hips move, the fabric of her skirt hugging her perfect arse.

"I particularly like the piece you've included around the neighbourhood guide. It makes Mayfair seem exclusive but accessible."

She nods, pivoting to face me as the coffee machine hums, filling her mug. "Guides are one of my favourite things to develop. Mayfair has a reputation for being pompous. It's all private members' clubs and old money, but there's this whole other side to it that I think Gray Hotel can really tap into." She tucks her hair behind her ear, casually leaning against the counter as she continues. "When people think of Mayfair, they think of wealth. But we want them to picture the hottest wine bars, modern fine-dining restaurants, and edgy art galleries. There's so much more we can get guests excited about. We want them to feel like they have the best of both worlds—that sense of exclusivity while staying connected to the latest trends and hotspots."

Well, well, well. She can carry a normal conversation, after all.

I close the folder, lowering it to my lap. "I'm impressed. You've really thought this through."

She crosses her arms. "Obviously—it's my job."

I smirk. Cheeky.

"What? You took one look at me and thought I was nothing but great tits and a perfect arse?" Her green eyes flash behind her glasses. "I worked my way up to this position all on my own."

My jaw clenches.

"Of course not. Your pitch is evidence of that," I say, my voice even.

My gaze catches on the safety pin holding her shirt together and I bite back a laugh. I'd be lying if I said I hadn't noticed her assets—it's impossible not to—but her presentation speaks volumes about her skill set and talent. I'm annoyed she assumed I was surprised by her intellect.

She rolls her eyes, turning to add a splash of milk to her coffee before taking a sip.

"Are you always this defensive?" I cock my head, studying her.

She spins around. "Are you always a dick?"

This time I laugh. The fire in her eyes, the sharp tongue—it's all too familiar.

"What's so funny?" she asks, drumming her fingers against her mug.

"Nothing. Now I understand why you're close with my sister." I stand, moving closer, enjoying how she tenses slightly at my proximity. "You're a little spitfire, aren't you?"

Her eyes narrow. "And you're exactly the kind of arrogant arse she warned me about."

I raise my eyebrows, intrigued. "Oh? She warned you about me, did she?" I lean against the counter.

"Mm-hmm." She takes another sip.

I fold my arms over my chest. "I see. And why, exactly, did she warn you?"

She sighs, setting her mug gently on the counter. "It doesn't matter. I'm just trying to do my job, despite your best efforts to be insufferable."

"Insufferable?" I press a hand to my chest. "Here I thought we were having a pleasant conversation."

"Pleasant?" She arches an eyebrow. "Is that what you call this?"

"What did she warn you about?" I press further, curious now.

Her cheeks tinge pink and she looks away. This is the first crack in her armour I've seen. She opens her mouth to respond just as Grayson strides in, a white patch covering one eye.

I clench my jaw, annoyed at his timing. She almost dropped her wall, and damn if I'm not dying to know what's behind it.

The Suite Secret

I wonder what she was going to say. What did Anna warn her of? And why?

What could my sister possibly be worried about?

Gemma steps toward Grayson cautiously. "Grayson, sir. I am so, *so* sorry about your eye."

He waves a hand dismissively. "Please, it's fine. No harm done. Nothing a few lubricating drops can't fix."

Gemma's face crumples at his words.

"Well, not too much harm, at least," he adds with a chuckle. "It was an honest mistake."

Her shoulders visibly drop with relief as she nods. But Grayson's expression hardens as he turns to me. "Max, I hate to drop this on you, but I just got a call from Cole. I need to handle something urgent in New York."

"Is everything okay?" I ask.

His eyes dart to Gemma before he ushers me around the corner, out of earshot.

"Dad's contesting the will," he says, voice grim.

I freeze. "What? He can't do that."

"The old geezer will do anything to get his hands on the company and Granddad's fortune." Grayson's fingers rake through his hair. "This could drag on for *months*. Dad's lawyers are ruthless."

I understand his fury. Grayson and his brothers were always closer to their grandparents than their father. When their grandfather passed nearly two years ago, he left his entire fortune and three businesses to Grayson, Cole, and Noah. Their father got nothing and he was livid. I guess now he's ready to fight them for it.

"Surely he's bluffing. You have all the money and resources," I remind him, crossing my arms. "You guys have all the power here, not him."

"Screwing over your own sons—could you imagine?" He pinches the bridge of his nose. "Apparently, he's sitting on

35

twenty years' worth of dirt on the company and he's angry enough to use it."

My eyebrows shoot up in surprise. "Shit."

"I'm fucking stressed, Max." His voice drops to barely above a whisper. "He's threatening to go to the press about supposed sketchy business practices in the eighties—whatever the hell that means. It's all bullshit, but the scandal alone could tank our stock prices." He rubs the back of his neck. "Cole's already dealing with nervous investors and trying to calm the board. Emerson's focused on college. This is the last thing we need."

"Jesus," I mutter, running a hand down my face.

"Exactly. He'll do everything he can to destroy our success, which is exactly why we can't let him win." Grayson's fists clench at his sides. "Max, I'm going to need you to take over Gray Hotel for me while this is going on. I can't do both."

"Of course," I assure him. "I'll hold things down here and see the launch through—you take care of things in New York. I can handle this."

He arches an eyebrow. "Even the crazy woman in the kitchen?"

I laugh. "Even her."

He straightens the lapels on his jacket. "I was impressed with their presentation. What do you think?"

"I think we go ahead. I'm happy with everything I've seen."

He nods. "I trust your judgement."

"Thanks. They know what they're doing." I nod. "We could create something exceptional here."

He claps me on the shoulder. "I know I can count on you. Ring me if you need anything, yeah?"

"Of course. Now, piss off," I say. He laughs, turning to leave, but I catch him. "And look after that eye, will you? You're going to need it."

"It feels like someone's taken sandpaper to it." Despite his mood, he smiles. "But worth it for that pitch." He checks his watch. "Shit. I better run before I miss my flight." He starts toward the elevator before spinning back, pointing at me. "If anything feels off—"

"I'll call you immediately. Good luck," I say.

"I'm going to need it." He steps into the elevator car and calls over his shoulder, "See you back in New York in two months!"

I return to the kitchenette, where the spitfire calmly sips her coffee, tapping away at her shattered phone screen.

Yeah, I have a feeling I'm going to need a little of that luck too.

Chapter Seven

Gemma

I arrive at Anna's red-brick terrace house in Putney armed with a bottle of Cabernet. After the day I've had, I'll be snapping off the neck and guzzling the whole lot.

"What happened to your shirt?" The moment I step through Anna's front door, her eyes zero in on the safety pin currently fighting for its life to hold my shirt together.

"That's what I was messaging you about earlier. I'm going to need a very large glass of this before we get into that."

I kick off my heels and follow Anna into her kitchen. She rummages through her cabinets, wine glasses clinking as she plucks three from the top shelf.

My eyes sweep the downstairs area. "Where's Mason?"

Anna sets the glasses on the counter. "Boys' night."

I frown. Her tone catches my attention. I've noticed she and Mason haven't been spending much time together lately, and Mason always seems to vanish whenever Anna hosts us. They've been together since our early twenties and married for eight years, and for the most part, they've had a happy marriage. I'm beginning to wonder if not everything is as it seems. But if something were wrong, she'd tell us ... wouldn't she?

A gust of crisp winter air whooshes through the house as April swings the door open, causing a shiver to snake down my spine.

"Close the bloody door!" I say.

April pushes it shut then shrugs off her coat, tossing it over the sofa before joining us in the kitchen. "Coming from the woman who slams my door into my wall every time she visits. You frighten the daylights out of poor Basil. It makes him stress poop!"

"I'm telling you right now, that cat isn't crapping on the floor due to stress," Anna says.

April rolls her eyes before noticing and pointing at my shirt. "Hey, what happened?"

I turn to Anna. "Pour the wine."

Anna twists the cap, and it releases with a satisfying crack.

I close my eyes and tilt my head to the ceiling. "God, I love that sound."

April chuckles as Anna pours three generous glasses. She drags a stool around the island bench to face April and me.

"Get on with it, then," she says, crossing her legs.

I take a deep breath and recount every horrid detail, from Lance being forced to raise his prices to spilling my coffee on Max, right up to the button incident with Grayson's eye.

April hides her face in her hands.

Anna glares at me in stunned silence momentarily before throwing her head back and releasing a deep belly laugh.

"Why are you laughing? This isn't funny," I say.

"Isn't funny? It's hilarious. You spilled coffee on my brother's Tom Ford suit and nearly blinded one of the world's richest men, while flashing everyone in your meeting!" Anna chokes out.

April raises a hand. "If Grayson needs surgery, I can get him in to see my old boss."

April used to work as a PA to one of London's leading eye surgeons, but she pivoted to her hobby of ceramics a couple of years ago and managed to turn it into a thriving full-time business. She's super talented and makes the most gorgeous pieces. She even made me a penis vase for my birthday last year—I swear I nearly cried, it was so perfect.

I shake my head, taking a long sip. "He left the country, thank God."

"That's almost as good as the time April shat her pants at work," Anna says, wiping the tears from her eyes.

April points a finger in Anna's direction, her voice serious. "That wasn't my fault. How was I supposed to know that taking too much magnesium can cause diarrhoea?"

"Oh, April, you sweet, innocent thing," Anna says.

"My pants were white too ..." April adds, trailing off.

I drop my head into my hands. "Guys, can we please focus? How am I supposed to show my face at work tomorrow?"

Anna tuts. "You're overreacting."

"Overreacting? Grayson could have lost his eye. I nearly blinded a billionaire with a bloody *button*. Plus, the entire executive team saw my bra! Have you *seen* your brother? He's gorgeous, which makes it so much worse."

"Oh no." Anna straightens. "I know that tone. Absolutely not. You are not getting any ideas about Max."

I look up. "I didn't say—"

"You didn't have to, you little minx. I know you too well." She points her glass at me, wine sloshing. "My brother is absolutely off-limits. I mean it, Gem. One of my friends from high school—Nicole—dated Max briefly after we finished our GCSEs. She was head over heels for him, but then he moved to the States to study at NYU. He didn't see the relationship going anywhere, so he broke it off and she was left devastated. She never spoke to me again. It ruined our friendship, and I won't let that happen to us. You mean far too much to me."

Christ, no wonder she's so protective of her brother. That's unfair of Nicole—she sounds like a twat. It's not Anna's fault the relationship didn't work out.

"Oh, I remember that. Nicole was so obsessed with Max at high school. She was completely out of line for letting that affect your friendship," April says.

"It was so upsetting. Besides, I've spent years trying to forget walking in on him with Casey, his ex-wife—" she shivers "—I don't need trauma flashbacks with my best friend."

Ex-wife? The word hits me like a splash of ice water. Anna's mentioned Max here and there over the years, but I never paid much attention to the fact he was once married.

Now, after meeting him, the questions pile up faster than I can suppress them: *How long were Max and Casey together? When was he married? Why did they divorce?*

But I swallow them back, forcing a neutral expression.

"Gross," April says, pretending to gag.

Anna points to April. "See that? *That's* the reaction you need to have toward my brother. I already know far too much about your sex life, and I'd like to keep at least one man in London sacred in my mind."

I wink at her playfully, lightening the mood.

Her eyes narrow. "I saw that look. That's the same look you had before you corrupted my poor yoga instructor last weekend."

I scoff. "It was one date. I hardly think I corrupted the man. *You* told me he was normal." It's my turn to point a finger at her. "He literally asked me to piss in his mouth."

"Please tell me you didn't do that," April says, horror creeping across her face.

"Of course I didn't! I draw the line at certain bodily fluids. I blocked his number after that. Though, I will say, his chakras were certainly aligned by the time I was through with him."

"And there goes my favourite yoga studio," Anna grumbles. "How could I ever do the downward dog again in front of him, now that I know that?"

"If it helps, neither can he. Not since the amethyst crystal-up-the-butt incident."

"We don't want to know," they say in unison.

I groan. "Seriously, though. The CEO is going to have my arse for this." I tap my finger against my glass.

April reaches across and rests her hand over mine. "Everything will be okay. You're good at what you do—you've got this."

It's only now that I notice the massive rock on her ring finger.

My pupils dilate as I grab her hand and yank it up to show Anna.

"What. The hell. Is this?"

April's cheeks turn pink, and a huge smile splits her face. "I wanted to tell you in person."

Anna shoots up from her stool so fast it crashes to the floor behind her. "Oh my God! You're engaged!"

"Jesus Christ, you let me sit here rambling about *work* and sticking crystals up a yoga instructor's sphincter when you just got engaged?! What's wrong with you?" I say.

April has been with her rock star boyfriend, James, for the past year and a half. He plays for one of the hottest new bands in progressive rock, Atlas Veil. Before that, she was engaged to his wet fart of a brother, Lucas—until she found out he was running a faceless Instagram account, luring women in with romantic poems and thirst traps behind her back. Naturally, she kicked him to the curb, and it was his younger brother, James, who stepped in to pick up the pieces.

I'm absolutely thrilled for her.

"What kind of friend are you? Tell us everything!" Anna squeals, racing around the kitchen island to squeeze April in a hug. "When did he propose? How did he do it? What were you wearing?"

"Well, to start, we weren't actually wearing anything," April says, a blush creeping from her cheeks down her neck. She catches my eye, and I waggle my eyebrows suggestively.

"That's my girl," I say, grinning. "Go on."

"It was only two nights ago—"

"Hold up. You waited *two whole days* to tell us?" I interrupt.

"We wanted to enjoy our little bubble for a couple of days before telling anyone," April says, her voice gentle.

"I'm going to assume *little bubble* is code for a two-day shag fest," Anna says.

"Correct." April nods.

I swivel to face Anna. "You have a special way with words, did you know that?"

Anna raises her glass in salute. "Thank you."

I turn to April. "Continue."

"So, we'd just ... *finished*," April continues, "and I was all wrapped up in his arms." She glances between Anna and me with a knowing smile. "You know how much I love his arms."

"He does have a decent set of arms," I say, lifting my glass in agreement.

"So, anyway, he brushed my hair away from my face and gave me this whole speech. Started with '*You're my whole world, April. Ever since you came into my life, everything's been brighter.*'"

She takes another sip of wine. "Funny thing is, I can't remember a single thing he said after that. My heart was racing so fast. As soon as he started talking, my stomach dropped."

Tears prick my eyes, and I take a deep breath to stifle them.

April is undeniably the soft one of our group. She wears her heart on her sleeve, and that's what makes her so beautiful.

She loves love. Her parents passed when she was only twenty-two, and she went through hell with Lucas. To see her finally get her fairy tale, to find someone who cherishes both her and her turd-slinging cat—it makes even my cynical heart swell with emotion.

Anna chuckles. "Same thing happened to me. I remember where Mason and I were. He got down on one knee and everything, but I couldn't tell you anything he said to me." Her voice goes quiet, distant, like she's recalling a different time in her life. She reaches across the bench to top off her glass, avoiding our eyes.

April glances at me with a flicker of worry.

I give a tiny shake of my head—*not now*—before pulling her into a tight hug.

"I'm so happy for you, sweetheart," I whisper, rubbing my hand over her back in a soothing circle.

"Thank you, Gem," she says, her voice choked.

I can't imagine how she must feel. Last time she was engaged, Lucas destroyed her. She was completely broken after that, a shell of the woman she was before. God, I remember holding her while she cried, watching her try to piece herself back together.

Seeing her like this, happy and trusting and completely in love again ... it means everything.

"Right. Well"—Anna perks up, a twinkle in her eye—"I think this calls for something more celebratory than red."

"I wholeheartedly agree," I say.

We settle onto Anna's sofas with our celebration spread—a platter of assorted cheeses, dried fruit, quince paste, and crackers—and sip on bubbly.

"So," April says, fiddling with the stem of her glass, "I know this is mental, but we wanted to get married in two months. James's manager knows someone who works at the botanical gardens, and they managed to get us a spot after a last-minute cancellation. With James touring for the new album next year, it was either now or wait eighteen months."

Anna's eyebrows shoot up. "April getting married in April. Adorable. But that *is* fast. Can you even plan a wedding in two months?"

"Well, with my two bridesmaids by my side, I think we can pull it off."

Anna fake gags.

I set my flute gently on the coffee table, pressing a hand to my heart with exaggerated emotion. "Are we your bridesmaids?"

"Of course we are, you boob. She doesn't have any other female friends," Anna deadpans.

April chokes on her champagne, spraying it all over my lap.

"Hey! My shirt's already ruined. Don't take my skirt down with it."

We burst into laughter.

The rest of the evening is spent mapping out weekends for dress shopping, cake testing, and other tidbits.

"Oh," April says. "Since Max will be around, tell him to come. He was always like a big brother growing up—I'd love to have him there."

April and Anna have been friends since the age of five, so they have a long history together. I became the third musketeer thirteen years ago after meeting April in the romance section of our local bookstore. She introduced me to Anna, and the three of us have been inseparable since.

Anna shrugs. "Sure."

For Christ's sake, I can't escape this man. He's like a venereal disease passing from person to bloody person.

Ping.

My phone chimes with a message. I pull it from my pocket—Henry.

Henry: *The CEO wants a meeting with us tomorrow morning. 9:00 am.*

"Crap," I mutter.

"What's wrong?" Anna says, peering at me over the rim of her glass.

I huff. "Henry and I have to meet with the CEO first thing tomorrow."

"I'm serious, Gem. It'll be fine," April says, offering me a small, reassuring smile.

"Exactly." Anna nods. "And you don't have to worry about Max. He may be an arrogant prick sometimes, but he's fair. He won't let this morning's *incident* affect the project."

I scoff, tossing back the rest of my champagne. "Famous last words."

Chapter Eight

Max

I push open the door to my Knightsbridge penthouse, letting my satchel drop to the floor as I step inside. Loosening my cufflinks, I roll my shoulders back, unbuttoning my shirt en route to the bathroom.

Grayson insisted I stay in the Livingstone Hotel in Mayfair with him, but I was happier staying in my old penthouse—the one I rented out on a month-by-month basis after moving to New York. He decided he'd rather stay at the hotel than room with me, and I respect his decision.

We both have rather active social lives and enjoy our ... extracurricular activities, and now that I'm completely alone for the duration of this trip, weekends included, I fully intend to indulge.

I finish undressing and step under the spray, the hot water pounding against my skin as I scrub.

I'm exhausted and, honestly, wound up. I gave Grayson my word I'd see this launch go off without a hitch, and I plan to deliver. I wasn't lying earlier when I told Gemma her pitch was impressive. It was. On paper, everything looked great, but the way she conducted herself today does have me second-guessing. She's smart, no doubt, but the attitude problem? That's something to be addressed.

Something I wouldn't mind taking care of myself.

My mind wanders back to that Instagram photo—sexy as sin—and a sharp breath hisses through my teeth as I wrap a hand around my hard, aching cock.

I rub the pre-cum over my tip before I start pumping, my grip firm.

I picture her bent over my desk, her skirt hiked up, silencing that smart mouth of hers until all she can do is scream my name as I pound into her. I'd kick her legs wider, my hand sliding down to where we're connected, collecting her wetness and smearing it over that perfect arse. I'd sink my finger knuckle deep in her tight hole while I'm taking her from behind.

Warmth courses through me before I explode, lashing the tiled wall with my cum.

Fuck.

This woman.

After showering and freshening up, I pour myself two fingers of fifty-year-old Macallan—only the best. I swirl the crystal tumbler, letting the rich toffee notes of the amber liquid open before throwing it back.

My phone buzzes on the coffee table; Casey's name flashes across this screen.

Casey and I divorced four years ago, but she still reaches out on the odd occasion—usually when she's had too much to drink, or when reality seems to be slipping away from her entirely.

Perfect timing, as always. Even years after divorce, she still has an uncanny ability to surface exactly when I'm trying to unwind. The calls and texts have become more frequent lately—sometimes three or four in a day. Whether it's rambling voicemails about how much she misses "what we had", or bizarre texts claiming she's seen me in bars and restaurants I've never stepped foot in, I can't seem to escape her, despite being an ocean apart.

When I told her about my move to New York, she was devastated. She begged me not to leave and insisted we could "work it out", but I couldn't stay—there was nothing left to give. I let her down as gently as I could, and she finally seemed to accept it. We weren't together anymore, and we hadn't been in years. So, to my knowledge, things with Casey had ended amicably—or as amicably as things can when you realise the person you promised forever to isn't your forever at all.

But when she started messaging me about her supposed sightings while I was clearly thousands of miles away, I began to worry. She doesn't know I'm back in the country, and I haven't told her deliberately.

I was completing my MBA with Grayson in New York when I met Casey. I had only recently broken up with my ex, Nicole.

Casey was in a few of the same classes as Grayson and me, and it felt like fate that she was from London too.

We had only been together for two years before I proposed, but everything was moving fast. It seemed to happen so naturally.

Looking back, I think we both mistook familiarity for destiny.

It felt like the universe had lined it all up: two Londoners finding each other across an ocean, both dreaming of a future back home.

It was a perfect fairy tale ... until it wasn't.

Casey was beautiful, vivacious, hungry for life ... and I loved that about her. Her passion for living drew people in. That's what first caught my eye—she was electric. She had that spark that made everyone want to be in her orbit. I never realised she'd burn through our life together just as fast.

I think I proposed because it felt like the next box to tick. Everyone around us was settling down, buying houses, planning futures. I followed their direction without looking at where the road led.

Little did I know that shortly after we married, Casey would develop an expensive shopping habit to keep herself busy, and the path I chose would lead to maxed-out credit cards, endless hours slogging away at my desk to pay the bills, and weekends spent searching for Casey while she disappeared on four-day benders.

As time went on, we drifted apart. We barely had sex. We never saw each other. Casey decided she didn't want to work after we got married, and when I was home in the evenings, she was out with friends. When she was home or out shopping during the day, I was working.

I was more than happy to give Casey a life where work wasn't something she had to worry about. In fact, I loved the idea of earning enough to take care of the person I loved—if that was what they wanted. But the late nights, the incessant spending, the not knowing where she was or who she was with ... that chipped away at me. It broke me down, piece by piece. She had no problem spending our money but couldn't show me the basic courtesy of letting me know she was safe, and it killed me.

I assumed Casey would grow out of the partying eventually, but she didn't. And while I take control in my life—in business, in my plans, when I fuck—I don't force other people's decisions.

I shouldn't have to tell my wife how to live. I could share my worries, sure. Express how I felt when she disappeared for days, but ultimately, they were her choices to make. She simply kept making ones that pushed us further apart.

I tried to make it work, but there's only so much you can give of yourself before your pockets are empty. I was running on fumes, pouring everything I had into a marriage that was already dry. I was a shell of the person I used to be.

By the time I hit thirty-five, I'd stopped begging to reignite something that had long since burned out.

She noticed the shift—my distancing, my silence. That's when the desperate talk of starting a family began, but by then, it was too late. I didn't trust her anymore. I felt like I was married to a stranger.

Besides, I wasn't cut out for fatherhood. At least not the kind where my kids would grow up watching their mother spiral while I cleaned up the mess. To be honest, I'm not sure I want children at all. The white picket fence was never desirable for me. I want a life where my partner and I can do whatever we want, whenever we want. Midnight dinners in Paris, last-minute flights to Tokyo—a life built on shared ambition, spontaneity, and mutual respect. Someone who understands that luxury isn't just about spending money—it's about creating something worth sharing with someone.

I won't settle for anything less.

I let the phone ring out.

Though I still have love for Casey, the romantic love I once held dissolved long ago. She's a dance I no longer remember the steps to. I could try and try, but the rhythm will always escape me.

I'll always remember our best times together fondly. For a period of my life, she was everything. I wouldn't be who I am today without her, and for a while, we made each other happy. I can't look back at that with disdain. But it's because I care for her that I can't continue the late-night chats. Her love never faded, and although we remained friends, I can't do it anymore. I figure sometimes healing comes with walking away. I hope she finds the person who can get the steps right.

If I learned anything from the divorce, it's to keep things simple.

Purely physical.

Just two adults wringing out their needs before going their separate ways. I like to set the pace, determine the rules. In the bedroom, that means I take what I want, how I want it. Without the messiness of emotions, no post-coital cuddling, no morning-after awkwardness. Just pure, simple release.

Right now, between my career and the people I care about, my life is exactly how I want it.

Measured.

But I'm unsettled.

My thoughts should be focused on the hotel launch. Not my sister's best friend.

The fact that she's made herself at home in my mind after one day is dangerous.

Because for the first time since Casey, I'm not just craving a body—I'm craving the challenge.

Chapter Nine

Gemma

It's half seven and I'm freezing my tits off.

"Just the usual this morning?" Lance asks.

"Better make it extra strong, thanks."

It's safe to say my mind kept me awake all night.

"Oh dear. Do I want to know?" Lance asks, plucking a to-go cup from the packet sleeve and getting to work on my coffee.

"I sort of screwed up at work yesterday," I start. "The CEO caught wind of it, and he's pissed. I have a meeting with him this morning."

I set my alarm extra early this morning, determined to get into the office with enough time to meet with Henry before we face the music with Chadwick. Our CEO is the type of man who doesn't hesitate to lose his shit at someone for breathing too loudly in a client meeting, and after yesterday's clusterfuck, I'm pretty sure I'm about to get a proper bollocking. I've never been called to his office before. He usually speaks directly with Henry. I've only ever communicated with him in board meetings, and to say he's scary would be an understatement.

This man is ruthless.

He might be a total dinosaur, but when it comes to business, he's sharp as a tack. He's built this place from the ground up, so he doesn't tolerate anyone or anything that might jeopardise Prestige's reputation.

He expects nothing less than perfection. So let's just say yesterday's button and bra setbacks don't bode well.

Now everyone knows Victoria's Secret.

"I'm sure he'll be sympathetic when you explain," Lance says, adding an extra shot to my cup.

"Lance, I'm not sure whether you've met a CEO, but sometimes they have a reputation of being a bit of a twat. Mine lives up to that reputation," I say.

He barks out a laugh. "Aye, lass. I've served plenty of them in my years. But they're not all bad."

"Hmm." I hum sceptically. "Well, this one makes Gordon Ramsay look like a teddy bear."

"What did you do?" he asks.

I explain the situation and Lance's eyes widen before he starts chuckling. "Oh, lass. That's quite the story."

"It's not funny!" I protest, even though I'm fighting my own smile.

"Well, at least you'll be memorable," he says, passing me my latte and Danish. "They can't say you're a bore."

"Thanks for the pep talk," I say dryly, accepting my breakfast. "If you don't see me tomorrow morning, I've been fired." I raise my coffee in a toast. "It's been great knowing you." I turn to walk away.

"Not so fast, you little shite." He nods to his EFTPOS machine. "Thirteen pounds."

I pause, shivering, whipping out my phone to pay. "Ugh, don't say it out loud. I might have an aneurysm."

"You and me both," he says, his eyes sad.

Shit. How could I be so thoughtless? This man is literally fighting to keep his business alive.

We usually have our light-hearted morning banter, but this time, when Lance returns my smile, the usual twinkle in his eyes has dimmed, and it breaks my heart. He's right—I'm once again the only customer at his kiosk this morning. When I first started at Prestige Partners, I'd arrive five minutes early just to get in the queue. The morning rush has completely dried up.

He starts wiping down the already clean counter. "You're a good lass, Gemma. Don't let that fancy CEO tell you otherwise today."

The corner of my mouth tilts up in a small smile.

"Now off with you." He waves a hand. "You have better places to be than chatting with an old fool in the cold."

"Never," I say firmly, and I mean it.

* * *

The elevator doors slide open, and I'm immediately met with the sight of Louise and Theo whispering in the kitchenette. Rolling my eyes, I step toward my office, hoping to slip by unnoticed—tall order considering my figure-hugging skirt suit and stilettos.

Henry emerges from a poky corridor, cutting off my escape.

"Good morning," he says.

"Is it?" I reply.

"Oh, Gemma," Louise calls out, her voice like nails on a chalkboard. "I barely recognised you without blood on your face."

Theo snickers beside her.

Henry arches a brow, but I exhale slowly before acknowledging her.

"If you're here, Louise, then who's running hell?"

She crosses her arm, popping her hip. "Funny, coming from someone who's about to have their arse handed to them by the CEO."

I narrow my eyes. How the hell did she find out?

"You do realise Henry and I still got the job over you, right?" I say, tilting my head.

"For now," she quips, lifting her chin.

I flip her the bird before grabbing Henry by the elbow and hauling him into my office.

Once inside, I slam the door, drop my bag onto the nearest chair, and let out a sharp huff.

"God, she's a bitch. I'm half-tempted to march back out there and shove my stiletto up her arse."

"Ignore her," he shrugs. "She's got nothing better to do than piss you off."

I drag a hand through my hair. "Well, it's bloody working."

"Relax. Focus on the meeting."

He's right. I have no idea what The CEO is going to say, but I need to centre myself.

I keep referring to him as *The CEO* because, honestly, calling someone with enough money to buy a small country *Chadwick Cashman* feels like an insult to my intelligence.

He sounds like a 1970s porn star, but the man couldn't be further from it.

I sigh. "Alright, let's get this over with."

I take a deep breath and feign all the confidence in the world as Henry knocks on The CEO's door.

"Come in."

I steal a glance at Henry, who gives me a brisk nod.

We've got this.

We're settled in the armchairs across from his desk while he leans back in his computer chair, hands resting on his rotund belly. The fluorescent office lights catch the shine of his bald spot.

"Gemma," he says.

I straighten. "Yes, sir."

The Suite Secret

He lunges forward, slamming his palms onto the mahogany desk. The sharp slap echoes around the room, making Henry and me jolt.

"His fucking EYE!" he roars, his face turning an alarming shade of red. "Do you realise how embarrassing this is?"

"Sir, I-I didn't mean to," I stammer, my pulse accelerating. "It was an accident. I was just taking off my coat, and the button—just popped off. I swear, I'm sorry."

His breath whistles through his nose sharp and loud. His nostrils flare, his jaw locked so tight it looks like it might crack.

Henry shifts in his seat, his voice steady. "Sir, if I may," he says, cutting in. "It truly was an accident. No one was seriously hurt, and Grayson himself assured us he was fine. The presentation was a success. In fact, I'd argue it was one of our strongest yet. I'm incredibly proud of the work Gemma delivered yesterday. Max and Grayson clearly were too. I can guarantee it won't happen again."

His words hang in the air.

Henry's always ready to defend me. I realise how lucky I am to have such a wonderful boss.

The CEO's eyes pierce holes through me. "Gemma, I've always been impressed with your work. You're one of our best. But yesterday"—he shakes his head, his lips pressing into a thin line—"yesterday was the first time I've ever felt truly let down. And in such a disastrous way."

A lump forms in my throat as tears prick my eyes. I battle with myself to maintain composure. I *won't* cry in front of him.

He leans forward. "He could have filed a report—drag our name through the mud. Do you understand? You represent Prestige Partners. Your conduct should reflect the standards we uphold. Whether the *button* incident was an accident or not, it simply was not good enough."

He lets the words sink in before continuing. "I also heard you were rather ... flustered when you arrived."

Who on earth told him that?

Then it hits me—Louise.

That mole.

He continues. "I don't know why, and frankly, I don't care. What I *do* care about is professionalism. When you arrive at work, I expect you to bring your A-game. My employees are expected to show composure. We don't bring chaos into the workplace. We are better than that."

I nod. "Yes, sir. I understand. You have my word—it won't happen again."

He gives a small nod in return, satisfied.

Folding his hands together on top of his desk, he leans back in his chair. "Good. Now, this brings me to why I wanted to speak with you."

Crap. There's more. My stomach feels like it's about to fall out of my arsehole.

I brace myself, but what he says next catches me completely off guard.

"I'd like to give Louise and Theo the opportunity to pitch their ideas to Mr Browne. Louise came to see me after yesterday's meeting and provided a full debrief of what transpired. Her enthusiasm to rectify the situation hasn't gone unnoticed."

That slimy little turd.

He drums his fingers on the desk. "Given the circumstances, I think it's prudent to give our client options. Louise and Theo will be presenting their alternative vision for the campaign to Mr Browne this Friday. If their vision resonates more than yours, well ..." He pauses, shrugging. "That's how business works."

My eyes widen in shock.

I've *never* been taken off a project. If this opportunity is stripped away from me, I'll be humiliated. What chances will I have to progress within Prestige in the future?

No. Louise can't take what I've worked so hard to have. I won't let her.

He can't be serious. I realise that yesterday was a colossal shitshow, but we won that project fair and square. I have years of successful launches to prove it.

I'd sooner fuck a scarecrow than let Louise take away what I've earned.

This is utterly humiliating

Henry leans forward, his expression serious but composed. "Sir, with all due respect, I have to challenge you on that. What happened yesterday was a mistake—one that was entirely out of our control. I'd like to be clear: the quality of the pitch was exceptional. Brilliant, even. The work we presented was of the highest standard, as per usual, and that shouldn't be disregarded or overshadowed by a single, accidental mishap."

Henry holds The CEO's gaze as he continues. "I don't believe reprimanding Gemma and myself for something that had no bearing on the work itself is fair. We should be judged on our performance, not on an unfortunate moment that didn't reflect our capabilities."

Bless him. I have to hand it to him—he's ballsy. It's hot.

My eyes dart to The CEO, who rolls his lips thoughtfully. He raises his eyebrows, seeming surprised by Henry's courage.

"I would have to agree with you," he says, his tone firm.

A wave of relief washes over me, and my shoulders relax.

"But," he continues, his eyes focusing on mine, "I expect my employees to maintain composure in every aspect of their work. *Especially* when presenting to high-profile clients. That button flying off was unacceptable. But your *bra?* I don't need to explain why that's a problem. The pitch may have been stellar, but this ... *distraction* was beyond unprofessional."

I feel the heat rise to my cheeks, and I keep my breathing even. Henry remains silent. I cut my gaze to him quickly, but he looks helpless.

He tried.

"If Max still chooses you two to handle the project after Louise and Theo give their pitch, then I'll have no problem with you moving forward. However, if their pitch proves stronger, you'll both be reassigned to another project immediately." He twists his mouth as he searches for the right words. "Something more ... manageable."

So, a demotion, in a sense.

I fight the tremor in my bottom lip, my voice barely above a whisper. "I understand."

"Excellent," he says, his tone final. "Make sure this doesn't happen again."

Over my dead body will I let those two take this project from us. We've worked too damn hard for it.

The determination builds within me.

I need to sway our friend Max.

Chapter Ten

Max

I'm working out my frustrations in the gym.

Chadwick dropped the bomb three days ago that Louise and Theo had prepared their own pitch, which they presented to me this afternoon. He claimed he "wants us to have the full Prestige Partners experience and see everything we have to offer". My money's on him finding out about Gemma's impromptu show and wanting to give us an escape route.

Honestly, I'm pissed that he's making me choose. It's what we're hiring Prestige Partners for, for God's sake. But when I mentioned the competing pitch to Grayson yesterday morning, he was impressed—asked me to hear out the other team and think about it carefully. Of course, I did what he instructed me to. But there's more at stake here than just the launch.

It's not that simple anymore.

To a certain extent, this *is* personal. Gemma's my sister's best friend. I need to keep Gray Hotel's best interests at heart, but I can already imagine Anna's reaction if I don't choose Gemma and Henry. My sister is a ballbreaker at the best of times—she'll rain down on me if I go with the other team.

And then there's the little spitfire in question herself, who I'm sure will have plenty to say if she gets me alone.

The thought shouldn't intrigue me as much as it does.

Not that I'm too worried about that happening—Louise has been circling like a shark ever since she presented, making sure Gemma can't get within ten feet of me.

As much as I hate to admit it, Louise and Theo came up with a solid pitch. Was it exceptional? No—Theo's about as sharp as a butter knife—but Louise had points Gemma and Henry missed, and vice versa.

Louise and Theo have opted for a safer, proven approach, which I can certainly appreciate, whereas Gemma and Henry are willing to take risks with potential for higher reward.

I meant what I said about Gemma's conduct being less than satisfactory, but I can't fault her work. Henry clearly runs a tight ship and knows what he's doing. If they can get their shit together, they could be exactly what we need.

If only I could get the image of her in that lingerie out of my head long enough to think straight.

And that's part of the problem. She's a beautiful distraction.

Sweat gathers at my temples and my muscles burn as I grunt through one final chest press.

All week, Gemma's been parading around the office in heels that make her legs look even longer, low-cut tops and—the thing that kills me the most—tight little skirts that hug every delicious contour and curve. It's driving me mad.

Even her laugh is sexy. And I hear it all. The. Time.

I've even noticed that she has a laugh which she only reserves for Henry, and it makes my blood boil.

I'm not a man who gets jealous. I've never been that guy. But the way she smiles at Henry is enough to change me. To make me want things I have no right to want.

The Suite Secret

I pat my forehead with a towel before stalking to the kitchen. I finish my glass of water in three gulps, chased with a shot of Macallan that drags a path of fire down my throat.

I slap my palms against the stone countertop and drop my head, attempting to ground myself. The workout helped, but it's not enough. Not when every time I close my eyes I'm haunted by blonde hair and those jade eyes.

I need something stronger than endorphins and whisky tonight.

I need to rein in what I feel is slipping—self-restraint.

Ruby Lounge has always been good for that. It's exclusive, discreet, the perfect place to clear my head and relieve my stress.

At Ruby Lounge, anonymity is sacred, and complications don't exist. It's a sanctuary where indulgence is currency and members can unleash their reckless desires.

A place where I can forget about creative directors in tight skirts.

Chapter Eleven

Gemma

I fish out the keys to my Paddington flat and collapse on my sofa the moment I cross the threshold. The week dragged on at a snail's pace, and I only caught glimpses of Max in passing. But every time I tried to approach him, I was always interrupted.

I've watched him swan through the office in his sleek designer suits. The man is so handsome, I swear he could cause a heart attack just from a glance.

The most infuriating part? He knows exactly how good he looks.

On the rare occasion we locked eyes in the corridor or shared kitchenette, he shot me that arrogant smirk, like he knows my career is hanging in the balance and he holds the power.

I bet the bastard gets off on it.

Louise and Theo gave their pitch this afternoon. It was decent—not incredible, but I can't deny that they did a good job, as much as it pains me to admit it. Max hasn't made his decision yet, and ever since, Louise has been circling him like a cat in heat. Honestly, I'm surprised she hasn't rubbed up against him or dropped down on all fours.

I need to find the right moment with Max, away from prying eyes. A chance to make my case without the risk of Louise nearby.

My phone vibrates and I pull it from my pocket to find a ping from KinkApp. Perhaps this is exactly what I need to escape the chaos swirling around me.

A quick shag to relieve the stress.

I swipe to check his profile. Tim. Thirty-eight. He's cute—tall, built, with the right interests ticked. Size king, which is important. Into toys, breath play, foot fetish (not my usual thing, but who am I to yuck someone's yum? I peer at my feet—not bad), and he's open to arse play.

KinkApp is a paid dating app, and most users are working professionals at an executive level. Listing club memberships in profiles is practically a status symbol in London's scene.

Scanning Tim's profile, I spot Ruby Lounge amongst his memberships. I know it well—the exclusive club sits above the Mayfair Lounge, my regular spot with Anna and April. There's a separate entrance behind the Mayfair, which is for members only, and they don't let just anyone through those doors. The vetting process is rigorous—interviews, background checks, the works. It's expensive, but safe play is top priority.

Particularly when it comes to strangers.

If I'm going to mess around, Ruby Lounge is my preferred meeting place. I refuse to invite men into my personal space. It's a safety precaution. I don't like them to know where I live. That's something my mum instilled in me from an early age, with good reason.

The girls only know half of what really goes on at Ruby Lounge. I've divulged *some* details, but it's much more my scene than theirs.

Fortunately for Tim, I'm also a member.

His photos show a body covered in tattoos and muscle, neatly trimmed facial hair, and dark eyes that hold promise. He's cute enough to help me forget my problems for a night.

I accept his ping and moments later, three dots appear, indicating he's typing a message.

Tim: *Hey.*

Groundbreaking chat, Tim. Sometimes being hot really is enough.

Me: *Hey.*

Tim: *Saw your profile and couldn't scroll past without saying hi. You're absolutely stunning. Looks like we're not too far from each other—fancy a drink?*

I check the time. 6:45 pm. I consider his offer. Can I be bothered?

I mull it over.

Screw it.

My thumbs fly across the screen.

Me: *Sure. Time and place?*

Tim: *You a member at Ruby Lounge?*

It's on my profile. He knows I am.

Me: *Yes.*

Tim: *I'll meet you at the bar at nine.*

That gives me plenty of time to relax, eat and get ready. Perfect.

Me: *See you then.*

Tim: *I can't wait.*

I've been using KinkApp for a while now, and while I've encountered some truly horrendous—not to mention downright insane—men, the good times have definitely outweighed the bad.

At work, I'm career-oriented, composed, corporate Gemma. But after hours? That's where I really come out to play.

Nighttime is when I let my teeth show.

The Suite Secret

In bed is where I can truly be myself. Just pure pleasure and power.

I had the whole *long-term relationship* thing with my university boyfriend, Todd, from twenty-two to twenty-nine. After breaking up, I promised myself I'd enjoy every aspect of my life. Particularly sex. We were happy enough, doing the usual couple things that we were raised to believe were the right thing to do.

Ugh.

Don't even get me started on societal "shoulds".

Todd was lovely. He had all the right qualities—a promising future as a partner in his father's law firm in Oxford, which he was groomed to take over. He came from money, had great friends, and an excellent sense of humour. But there was one significant area where he fell short: sex.

He consistently underdelivered in that department.

Communication was never a problem; sex was.

I'm the type who speaks my mind. I'm honest, sometimes to a fault. I'd never fake an orgasm just to please a man or boost his ego—sex is a two-way street. I'm just as entitled to an orgasm as my partner is. It was Todd's unwillingness to explore new experiences, things that might feel good but aren't typically discussed amongst friends, that was the real issue.

He was just so .... beige. Bland. Boring, same old day-in, day-out kind of guy. I couldn't handle it anymore. So, I broke it off. I sat by as our friends got engaged, teasing us that *You're next!* and I'd think to myself, *This can't be my future. I can't do this for the rest of my life.* Todd was devastated. People couldn't understand why sex was so important, but it's not until you're having bad sex that you realise how damaging it is to you—mind, body, and soul.

April and Anna were my rocks throughout that time. They understood. They've always had my back and stood by me through everything, accepting every part of me—no questions asked. While others might raise their eyebrows at my sex life, Anna and April pour more margaritas and ask for details. They love me for exactly who I am, not who they think I should be.

Hot oil spits and sizzles as I lay the eye fillet in the pan, searing each side to perfection. I spoon the steamed broccoli and carrots onto my plate, then settle in to eat before getting ready for Tim.

I swap my glasses for contacts and wipe away the day's make-up, opting to apply a fresh coat. I paint my lips their usual crimson. There's something about red lipstick. The way it transforms a mouth into a weapon.

I tousle my hair then quickly pull some daily tarot cards—a ritual I've come to love, kind of like journalling—before I slip into a slinky moss-green dress, which hugs every curve. The delicate spaghetti straps expose my collarbones, which are dusted with a hint of champagne shimmer. I look sexy and sensual.

Grabbing my black shawl, I step into a pair of pumps, and head out.

I arrive outside Ruby Lounge just past nine.

Stepping through the unmarked black doors, I enter a reception area of gleaming marble floors and polished, blacked-out mirror walls.

The club is made up of four designed sections. The sleek and minimal reception area leads to the main lounge, where sensual music plays throughout.

In the centre of the room is a sunken pit—the crown jewel of the space. An enormous lounge sprawls across it. Women roll their hips while riding cocks. Men sit back, heads reclined and eyes closed as mouths work eagerly in their laps. Nearby, two women are held open, legs pinned by greedy hands while others take their time, feasting on their pussies without shame.

On surrounding sofas, members drink, hands and mouths exploring each other in plain view.

To the left, a towering cross stands. It's where members are bound and blindfolded, their bodies offered up to be devoured, flogged, spanked, or whipped—depending on the kink. But tonight, it is empty.

Past this open playground is a long corridor lined with doors to private rooms, leading to the main bar at the rear of the building—which is where I'm headed.

As I move through the long corridor, I hear muffled screams and moans of pleasure, pain, or both.

Leather-upholstered stools curve around the bar, which is lined with expensive liquor.

I clench my thighs when I spot a woman surrender to pleasure in a booth situated at the far corner of the room. One man is biting and sucking her heavy breasts while another worships between her legs. Her head's thrown back, lost in sensation.

Next to her, a woman straddles another woman, her dress hiked up around her hips while her partner's hand disappears up her skirt. Her grip on the other woman's shoulders is tight as she grinds her hips, moaning.

I take a seat at the bar, ordering a flute of bubbly. The bartender's just tipping champagne into my glass when fabric brushes against my bare arm.

I turn, ready to meet Tim.

But the universe, it seems, has other plans.

Because standing there, in all his arrogant glory, is Max Fucking Browne.

Chapter Twelve

Max

I clocked her the moment she sauntered in—all dark green fabric clinging to every curve, her hair mussed like she had just stepped out of a sex dream.

This is the last place I expected to see her. But she's here, and my plan for an easy, fun distraction was immediately eviscerated.

I was reclined on the leather sofa, murmuring something low against a redhead's lips when I felt a shift in the room's energy. Heads turned. My eyes followed their line of sight only to land right on the very woman I've been trying to avoid.

I pressed my lips into a thin line to hide my smile. I can't say I was disappointed to see her.

Nagging thoughts chipped away at me. *Is she here alone? Does she come here often? Is she meeting someone?*

The thought of her coming here to fuck someone else ignited a savage heat beneath my skin. Normally, I'm not the type to get hung up on who someone might be meeting—hell, I'm here for the same reason—but seeing her here struck an uncomfortable nerve.

The Suite Secret

I plucked my drink from the table. "Excuse me," I murmured to the woman I'd been entertaining. She shrugged and turned to face the man on her other side. Standing and rolling my shoulders, I observed from a distance as Gemma prowled through the main room toward the bar.

Then I moved.

Now I follow her at a distance through a long, shadowed corridor with adjoining doors.

Gemma sweeps her gaze across the room before settling at the bar and ordering a drink.

So, she *is* meeting someone.

I move past writhing bodies, couples tangled up, exploring each other freely.

The bartender pours her champagne and as I approach, it's like she senses my presence. Her body stiffens as I brush her arm, my shirt grazing her naked skin. She swivels in her seat, her eyes meeting mine and widening.

Christ, she's stunning. My dick stirs in my trousers.

"Hello, Gemma," I say, my voice low and cool.

She cranes her neck, peeking over her shoulder.

"Max? What are you doing here?"

She's surprised, but considering the nature of our working relationship, she doesn't seem ashamed or embarrassed. A flicker of admiration sparks through me, catching me off guard.

Her lack of shame speaks volumes, and it's not just confidence. It's unfiltered sexuality she wears like a second skin. And hell, if that doesn't make her ten times more fascinating.

"Judging by the establishment, I figure it's safe to assume we're here for the same reason."

She frowns. "You're meeting Tim?"

I let out a low chuckle, my fingers grazing my chin.

Tim, is it? I catalogue that name for later.

"No, sweetheart. I'm not here to see *Tim*."

Gemma's eyes spark in challenge and she bats her lashes. "Then what, pray tell, are you here for?"

I focus on those plump, cherry lips, and lean in a little closer, catching the scent of jasmine that clings to her skin. My gaze drops, taking in the outline of her taut nipples through the thin fabric of her dress. Jesus Christ, I'm beyond hope of maintaining professional boundaries.

"I'm here because I'm a little ... distracted." My lips graze her ear, and she draws in a breath. "And I don't like distractions, Gemma."

My hand finds the exposed skin between her shoulder blades, and she shivers.

Sod it.

I'm going for broke.

"You see, there's a woman at work. And I can't seem to get her and her tight little skirts off my mind."

"Oh?" she asks, her voice barely above a whisper.

"Mm-hmm."

"And what are you planning to do about it?"

"I intend to find someone to accompany me into one of those rooms." I nod toward the hallway, a smile playing at the edge of my lips.

Her gaze follows mine before it drifts to a man on his knees before a striking brunette, his tongue and fingers working her centre as she moans softly. Gemma swallows, then turns her attention back to me.

"What do you think about that?" I murmur.

Air leaves her nostrils in a sharp huff. She's trying to restrain herself, and I'm glad to see I have the same effect on her that she has on me.

"I don't think much, actually. It's not like I have any interest in sleeping with you."

"No?" I ask, tilting my head.

"No," she says, feigning resignation. She presses her thighs together. She's fooling absolutely no one.

"So, you're saying you wouldn't care if I were to find myself a beautiful woman, put her over my knee, and spank her senseless until she's a wet, writhing mess before fucking her with my fingers?"

She's staring at me, lips parted and eyes swimming with arousal. Her pupils dilate and her breath catches at my brashness. "No."

I lean in. "I don't believe you."

She scoffs. "You're so full of yourself. I don't even find you attractive. And even if I did, I would never sleep with you. I wouldn't give you the satisfaction."

"Satisfaction?" I chuckle darkly. "Oh, sweetheart. You've got it all wrong."

I lean in closer, our noses almost touching. Her breath is soft against my lips, and I can feel the heat of her skin. "The satisfaction would be all yours."

She swallows hard and I watch the movement in her delicate throat.

I drain my glass before placing it down on the bar. I give her a small nod before turning on my heel. "Enjoy the rest of your evening."

I don't wait for her to respond before I leave.

Tonight was meant to be an escape. Instead, I've thrown gasoline on an already stoked fire.

I may have pushed things too far with Gemma, but I saw the hunger in her eyes, caught the way her breath hitched when I moved closer. She was aroused. And seeing her in that environment has awakened something primal in me.

She's managed to make me forget every reason why I shouldn't want her. Why I went to Ruby Lounge in the first place.

I'm not used to wanting something I can't have. It's entitled, I know, but it's the truth.

I've crossed a line with Gemma that can't be uncrossed. There was nothing professional about that exchange.

Have I made things more complicated at work? Absolutely. There are two obvious reasons why I need to move on from this little fixation I have. One, my sister. And second, I need to ensure my focus is on the hotel launch. Two perfectly rational reasons to walk away.

I pride myself on being a rational man, but right now, logic has never felt more irrelevant.

Chapter Thirteen

Gemma

Well, that turned out to be a complete disaster.

Tim arrived, and while he was perfectly pleasant, I couldn't go through with it. I took one look at his underwhelming cock, zipped him back up, and called it a day.

His profile claimed he was a "size king", but that was clearly false advertising. I felt robbed. If I was going to forget my problems for an evening, it'd take a lot more than a mediocre cock and a nice personality to get the job done.

I need a proper seeing to. A penis that's going to pierce through my uterus and tickle my brain. I'm a woman with needs, and tonight they weren't met, no thanks to Max.

Now I'm just horny *and* frustrated.

All that effort—shaving, applying lotion, fluffing about with my hair and make-up—wasted.

Then again, how was poor Tim supposed to compete with the likes of Max Fucking Browne?

After seeing him tonight, of course I wasn't going to be able to focus on another man.

Knowing Max is a member of Ruby Lounge sends a thrill through me. The thought of him shedding his stiff, corporate exterior to seek the same kind of pleasures that I do ...

No.

I need to feel nothing but irritation toward Max. Not this dangerous excitement that makes me wonder what else we have in common.

What he likes. How he likes it.

He's the kind of man I imagine thrives on taking charge. I can see it in how he conducts himself. He's the type who would dominate every inch of a woman's body. I bet he'd take his time, pushing limits, and denying pleasure until all composure is replaced with desperate need.

He'd reduce you to nothing but a writhing, begging mess.

Stop it, Gemma. You can't go there.

God, I could practically smell sex appeal oozing from his pores tonight. All silky voice and dangerous presence. He looked at me like he wanted to eat me. And damn if I didn't want him to. I got wet at the mere sight of him in those perfectly tailored trousers and black shirt that stretched across his strong shoulders.

I was *so* close to buying into his smooth words, but Anna's voice sliced through my lust-filled haze.

Anna is like the sister I never had, and the threat of losing her trust and potentially destroying our friendship absolutely terrifies me.

I need to put mind over vagina.

That, and the chance of derailing my career. If we keep the account, HR will be breathing down my neck after my and Henry's meeting with Chadwick. I can't throw away everything I've worked so hard for because Max Browne looks at me like he wants to ruin me.

Even if part of me wants him to.

The Suite Secret

* * *

Warm sunlight filters through the curtains and I slowly open my eyes. My hand skates over my bedside table until I find my wire-framed glasses. I slide them onto the bridge of my nose and peel myself out of bed.

It's Saturday, and I'm meeting Anna and April to go bridesmaid dress shopping in Mayfair. I'm so excited—trying on dresses, drinking champagne, and enjoying some much-needed girl time. I think this will be the perfect thing to get my mind off the man currently occupying it.

I figure I can use the trip to my advantage—scout out the area to see if anything sparks creative ideas. Something I can add to the Gray Hotel campaign to give the project a fresh edge and me an advantage to stay on the account.

I make myself a coffee, frothing the milk and pouring it into my mug, creating a little foam penis. I smile at my latte art and take unhurried sips while I get ready for the day.

I arrive in Mayfair, spotting Anna outside a fancy boutique April selected on New Bond Street, waving excitedly when she sees me approach.

Anna greets me with a warm hug, and when she pulls away her brows pinch as she assesses me. "I say this with love. You look tired."

I sigh. "I slept like crap. I need another coffee."

Just then, April sneaks up behind us, draping her arms over our shoulders. "Eep! I'm so excited!"

"And I'm freezing my tits off. Let's get inside," Anna says.

We file into the boutique, sifting through the array of expensive dresses.

Anna leans in close, her voice a hushed whisper. "Holy shit, this dress costs a thousand pounds!"

April breezes by, flicking her long, auburn hair dramatically over her shoulder. "These are on me, by the way."

I turn to her, surprised. "What? No. We can't let you pay for our dresses. You're already paying for the wedding! We can find somewhere else to look. There are plenty of great places around."

April fixes me with an exasperated look. "My fiancé is rich. I'm buying the bloody dresses, end of story."

Anna raises an eyebrow. "Who are you, and what have you done with my sweet, modest April?"

April shrugs, biting back a smile.

"Well, in that case." Anna snatches the dress off the rack, slings it over her shoulder, and marches to the dressing room like a woman on a mission.

I step closer to April, lowering my voice. "Hey, I forgot to ask the other night—how did Lucas take the news about your engagement?"

She rolls her eyes. "He hasn't said anything. James has tried calling him a few times, but he's just sending him straight to voicemail."

Classic Lucas. When he and April broke up, he disappeared without a word—blocking her number and wiping her from all social media as if their relationship never happened. Then months later, he popped up out of nowhere, begging her to take him back. So it's no surprise he's handling this like a sulking man-child.

I hold a hand to my chest. "Lucas? Ghosting? How shocking," I joke. "How's James handling it?"

"He's doing alright," she says, shrugging. "It's a bit of an odd situation, though. I honestly don't know if Lucas will even come to the wedding—not that I'm complaining. But James made peace with the reality that they were never going to be close a long time ago. We knew what we were getting into when we chose to be together. Besides, James's parents were over the moon about our engagement, and that's what really matters."

I nod along. "Right. Just because someone's family doesn't mean you have to like them."

"Exactly," she says, shooting me a small smile.

We continue to peruse the beautiful fabrics. Turns out Anna's dress was one of the cheapest in the entire store. My fingers skim over liquid silk, satin, tulle, and chiffon.

My eyes are drawn to an exquisite purple halter dress with a shimmering overlay that catches the light. I smooth my hand over the fabric, hearts in my eyes.

"Try it on," April says.

I look at her. "No, I couldn't. It's too much."

She places her hand on my shoulder affectionately. "Please, try it on. It's beautiful."

When Anna and I emerge from our dressing rooms, April gasps.

"I can't tell if that's good or you're horrified," Anna says.

April's eyes water. "You both look amazing!"

"Oh, this is *lush*. But bloody hell, it's tight," Anna mutters, twisting her arms behind her back, struggling with the zipper. She wobbles on her tiptoes as she attempts to drag the zip down.

She takes a large step forward and the dress surrenders with a horrific ripping sound. We all gasp as the back of the dress splits open and Anna stumbles, trying desperately to hold the fabric together. "Crap! I'm totally naked underneath!"

I reach out to catch her, but she's falling too fast. She topples into a mannequin, which sets off a domino effect. The mannequin crashes into a rack of expensive dresses, which then tumbles into another row of display mannequins positioned in the boutique's front window. We watch, frozen, as each mannequin goes down with a thunderous bang.

"No, no, no!" The shop assistant bolts toward the front of the store, as if she can somehow stop the disaster from unfolding.

Anna rights herself and finally finds her footing, but in her panicked state, she steps on the inner hem of her long skirt. The fabric pulls down, revealing her breasts and vag in all their uncovered glory. She stands, naked as the day she was born, exposed to the street outside, where a growing crowd of onlookers gapes through the window, witnessing the entire mortifying spectacle.

A group of girls erupt into laughter as a mother covers her son's eyes, and I swear I hear someone wolf-whistle.

My hands fly to my mouth.

We stand in silence for what feels like an eternity before Anna closes her eyes in horror and clears her throat. "Ladies. I'm about to bend over to pick up this dress, and I'd really appreciate it if you both averted your eyes."

Crack out, she slowly bends down, snatching up the dress and covering herself with as much dignity as she can muster before shuffling back into the dressing room.

Of course, I say the only thing that springs to mind. "You've got a great set for a good tit-wank."

* * *

Safe to say we didn't buy the dresses.

Aside from Anna being totally humiliated, the shop assistant looked as though she was about to murder us.

We stop for a delicious and much-needed boozy lunch at a seafood bar by the Ritz Carlton. I throw back an oyster and take a long pull of bubbly.

"Why didn't you wear any knickers if you knew we'd be trying on dresses?" April asks Anna.

"I like to let it breathe," Anna says.

I choke. "Sorry. What?"

She shrugs. "Sometimes I forgo underwear to let my fanny breathe."

"Well, at least you weren't trying on trousers," I say.

April scrunches her nose. "Ew."

The Suite Secret

"Don't knock it till you try it," Anna says, raising her champagne in salute.

"Moving on ... Are you guys free in two Saturdays' time? James and I want to host a little engagement dinner at ours," April says. "And before either of you say we're moving too fast, we're just so excited, we don't want to wait another minute."

"Considering my plans only ever involve the two of you, yes, I am free in two Saturdays' time," Anna says.

"Me too," I say.

"Oh Gemma, I've been meaning to ask—what happened at work?" Anna asks.

I launch into the details of my workweek from hell, detailing my disastrous meeting with *The CEO* and how Louise and her little minion Theo are trying to take the account from Henry and me.

"It's turned into a corporate showdown for the account!" I finish.

Anna tilts her head. "So, let me get this straight. *My brother* is the one deciding between Louise and Theo ... and you and Henry?"

"Yup," I say, popping the *P*.

Her eyes narrow. "It might be time to pay my dear old brother a visit."

April laughs, waggling her eyebrows. "Ooh, I've always wanted to say something that dramatic. It's very soap opera. Should we get you a trench coat and dark sunglasses? Maybe a fedora?"

My spine snaps straight. "You don't need to do anything. This is my mess. I'm confident Henry and I have what it takes to keep this account. It's just frustrating, that's all."

I don't need Anna weighing in. Max saw right through my pathetic attempt to play it cool last night, so he knows exactly how much he affects me. I can already picture his smug satisfaction when we're back at work on Monday.

If Anna gets involved for my benefit, it'll only fuel his ego more.

I lean forward. "Promise you won't say anything to him? I don't think he needs another reason to be pissed off with me."

The last part slips out before I can catch it, and my mind scrambles for damage control.

Shit.

"What do you mean 'another reason to be pissed off' with you?" Anna asks, confused.

"After spilling the coffee and the button," I blurt, trying to make it sound obvious.

"Oh, right," she says, sipping her bubbles.

I keep the details of my night at Ruby Lounge to myself. The girls know me far too well—I don't turn down penis on a platter without a damn good reason. They'd immediately become suspicious.

My shoulders sag with relief when Anna and April dive into a conversation about floral arrangements, and I nod along. Meanwhile, a battle rages inside me. I keep recounting the way Max's lips brushed against my ear last night.

I haven't even touched the man and I already feel like I've committed a forbidden sin.

The worst part? *I think I want to.*

* * *

I pass London's new Gallery of Contemporary Art on my way home. I peer through the window, catching a glimpse of canvases hung on stark white walls, splashed with a kaleidoscope of bold colours and abstract shapes. Sculptures, from small to massive and imposing, bring the space to life. The pieces make a statement and command my attention the moment I see them. And just like that, an idea strikes me. One that could take Gray Hotel to an entirely new level.

Chapter Fourteen

Max

I still haven't made my decision. Grayson's been on my arse ever since Friday's pitch.

Do I want to work closely with Gemma? Abso-fucking-lutely.

Do I want to fuck her? Naturally.

Do I feel like having my dick kicked in by my sister? Can't say I do.

It's Sunday evening and I'm dropping into Mum and Dad's flat for dinner. Anna will be there. Despite the Gemma complications, I can't wait to give my baby sister a hug. We've only spoken briefly over the phone these last couple of weeks—I've been so exhausted from work.

If I'm not horizontal on the sofa, I'm pushing myself in the gym until my muscles scream, then giving in and jacking off to the thought of *her*, before distracting myself with whisky and mindless shitty Netflix recommendations. Rinse. Repeat.

The endless cycle of trying to burn her out of my system isn't working.

The more I try to exhaust myself, the more she creeps into the corners of my thoughts.

Mum opens the door, beaming at me. "My favourite son!"

"I'm your only son," I reply.

Her hand whips out and she grabs my forearm, dragging me inside before reaching up on her tiptoes to wrap her arms around my neck. I duck down, encasing her in a tight hug.

I take a deep breath in. "Hey, Ma."

It's not until I catch the scent of rose and talcum powder that a wave of emotion swirls around me and pulls me under. I forgot the way she smells. It's home. It's been two whole years since I've seen her, and guilt crashes over me. I've been avoiding London—avoiding memories of Casey and our miserable marriage. It was easier to bury myself in work, to build on the New York business with Grayson rather than return to the life I used to have here. But being here now, holding my mother, I realise how much I've missed. How much I've let Casey's ghost keep me from the people who matter—the people I should be focusing on. It's only now that I realise how much I take the people I love for granted.

I *miss* her.

She pulls back, gripping my biceps as she drags an assessing gaze over me. "My boy's back."

"I'm forty-two, Mum," I say, a smile tipping the corner of my lips.

"You'll always be my baby boy," she says, her eyes glassy.

I plant a quick kiss to the top of her head before following her through to the main living room.

The flat smells like it always did—old books and wood and leather from well-loved furniture.

Dad relaxes in his usual maroon recliner in the corner of the room, remote in hand, a half-finished crossword laid out on the small table beside him. He's wearing his fraying blue overalls with a white shirt underneath, a comb peeking out of the breast pocket. His leather trainers are laced up as tight as they can be.

The Suite Secret

No matter how far I go, no matter how much of the world I see, I'm grateful that home never changes.

"Old man," I say, making my way toward him.

"Son." He groans as he peels himself off the chair, meeting me halfway for a hug.

"You're shrinking," I say.

"Watch yourself, boy," he says, clapping my shoulder with a light laugh.

The door to the flat flies open, hitting the wall with a loud *bang*.

"Shit, sorry!" Anna calls as she balances a plate of food. She steps inside, kicking the door closed behind her. When she sees me, she screams. Fully screams, and I wince.

"Jesus Christ, Anna," I say, bringing a hand to cover an ear. "You're going to burst my eardrums."

"Oh, piss off," she says, rushing into the kitchen to deposit the plate. She launches into the living area, flinging herself at me. I wrap my arms around her.

"Hi," she says, her voice broken.

"Hey, weasel," I say, pinching her nose. I frown when I notice she's come alone. "No Mason?"

She sucks her bottom lip into her mouth and shakes her head no.

Mum appears behind Anna, shaking her head as if to warn me not to press it.

That's not like Anna. She's loud, mouthy, fun. If anything, she overshares. This can't be good. She and Mason have always been inseparable. If things aren't going well for them now, she certainly hasn't said anything to me about it. We keep in touch via FaceTime, but perhaps we haven't been as open with each other since I moved to New York as I thought. Maybe the distance has made it harder for her to confide in me the way she used to. Now that I think about it, Mason hasn't appeared in our calls for months, and I've been too distracted by paperwork and meetings to notice. I bite back the urge to press her for more information. "I missed you," I tell her instead.

A tear traces a path down her cheek. "I've missed you," she says, pulling me in for another hug. "So, so much."

I peer over her shoulder to find Mum softly weeping as she watches our exchange.

What have I missed?

"Weasel, you okay?" I ask her, my voice soft.

She sniffles, wiping her tears with the sleeve of her jumper. "I'm fine, Max. I'll talk to you about it later," she says, forcing a weak smile.

Mum steps forward, wiping her tears. "Alright, you lot, dinner's ready." She flings a tea towel over her shoulder before ushering us all to the dining room.

As we gather around the table, I catch Mum and Dad up on Gray Hotel and the plans leading up to my return to London as well as the challenges and design concepts. They barrage me with questions about Grayson and how he and his brothers are coping following their grandfather's passing.

Anna chimes in about her work, singing her own praises when she describes her grade three students' latest reading project. She gushes over April and James's wedding plans—I've not met James yet, but I've known April since we moved back to London after a stint in Fiji for Dad's work. She was around so often, she practically became a second sister to me, and I'm honoured to be invited to witness her big day.

When Dad peppers me with more questions related to work, I find myself detailing both pitches—Gemma and Henry's versus Louise and Theo's. I'm careful not to show any preference, even as Anna perks up at Gemma's name.

By the time we finish, Anna's sitting straighter, smiling more, and laughing at Dad's terrible jokes. That sombre look

The Suite Secret

has faded, temporarily replaced by something closer to her usual self.

Anna's always been my weakness. It's always been just me and her against the world, especially with all the moving around for Dad's work. The one constant we had was each other.

She was my rock throughout my divorce—those late-night calls when I was at my lowest, the weekends she turned up unannounced at my flat, practically dragging my sorry arse out the door. She never let me wallow in self-pity, and I'll be damned if she thinks she has to face whatever this is alone. I owe her that much.

I like Mason. Always have. He's a good guy who's always treated Anna well. Or at least, he did. But I swear to God, if he's behind whatever's making my sister cry, I'll end him.

A protective instinct surges through me, the same feeling I've had since we were kids when I'd find her crying over some schoolyard bullshit. I'm grateful to be in London for the next two months. Whatever's going on with her and Mason, I'll make sure she knows she's not alone.

Do Gemma and April know?

This is exactly why I need to get Gemma out of my head. I can't be distracted by fantasies of her while Anna's clearly struggling. Pursuing Gemma would put me in the middle of Anna's personal life in ways I'm not prepared to handle, especially when she's still sensitive about what happened with Nicole. I don't want to be the reason she gets hurt again.

The irony isn't lost on me. I've spent days trying to figure out how to handle the Gemma situation, and now life throws me something that makes the decision painfully clear.

But the question remains—can I fight this attraction to Gemma? I want to say with confidence that I can, but if I'm being honest, I'm not so sure anymore.

But for Anna, I need to try.

I'll keep my distance. For now. Until I figure out whatever's going on and how I can help her.

She might be all grown up now, but some things never change. Anna comes first. Always.

* * *

After dinner, Mum and Dad settle onto the sofas while Anna and I tackle washing up. She dips her hand into the sink before flicking me with soapy water.

"Watch it. This shirt is Boss," I joke.

"Since when did you turn into such a wanker?"

I shrug. "Since I became a millionaire."

"Show-off."

I laugh, shaking my head as I lather up another dish. Seeing that she's in a better mood, I decide to test the waters. "What's going on with you and Mason?"

She pauses, taking a deep breath before scrunching the tea towel up and depositing it on the counter. She turns to me. "I want a baby."

My eyebrows jump. "Hey, that's great, Anna," I say, nudging her with my elbow.

"Hold your horses. Don't get too excited." I frown before she continues. "*He* doesn't."

"Oh, shit."

"Yeah."

I release the dish in the sink, drying my hands with the discarded tea towel, fully facing her.

"I thought Mason wanted kids?" I ask, confused.

She nods. "He did. He always wanted them." She scoffs. "Probably more than I did."

"So, what happened?"

She clears her throat. "I guess he changed his mind."

"Just like that?" I lean back against the counter. "After how many years of marriage?"

"Eight years," she says, her gaze fixed on the tile floor. "Said he'd been thinking about it for a while now. That maybe our life is perfect as it is—just the two of us, happy in our jobs, the freedom to do what we want whenever we want."

"And you?"

"I always thought we'd have them by now. We've been married long enough. We've seen the world. To be honest, I'm over the travelling, especially after our childhood and moving around all the time for Dad's work. I'm happy in my job. I feel settled. But I'm thirty-five this year, Max. My body has its own timeline. And the longer I wait ... I don't think I want to wait around for something that might never come."

"Do April and Gemma know?"

She shakes her head. "I haven't told them anything yet."

"Are you going to?"

"Eventually, maybe. April's just got engaged, and I don't want to bring the mood down with my problems. I don't want them to think differently of Mason. He's their friend too."

"They're *your* friends, weasel."

"I'll tell them when I'm ready." Her voice is final, so I don't bother arguing. Instead, I pull her into a hug, feeling her shoulders shake.

"Have you tried counselling?" I ask into her hair.

"I'm so sick of crying," she says, pulling back and wiping her tears. "He doesn't want to try counselling. He says there's nothing to discuss."

"Nothing to discuss? Look at you. You're bloody upset," I say, growing agitated.

"I'm kind of counting on him changing his mind. We've gone through phases over the years of wanting kids and not wanting them, but we always agreed we'd have them, eventually. I'm hoping this is another phase."

"Is it a deal breaker?" I ask carefully.

"I hope not," she whispers. "I love Mason, and I've wanted to be a mother since I was a little girl. You know that." She exhales. "I just thought I'd have a baby by now. And working as a teacher? I see the way the children run toward their parents who wait for them by the school gate at the end of the day. *I* want that."

"Did he say when he changed his mind?"

"Apparently he's felt this way for a few years."

"And when did he tell you?"

She pauses, hesitating to answer me.

"Weasel," I urge.

"A month ago."

"Christ, Anna. I'm so sorry." I shake my head in disbelief. "That's not good enough."

"That's life."

"Bullshit," I snap. She watches me, wordless, as I try to rein in my emotions.

I clench my jaw, a bitter taste rising in the back of my throat. It wasn't until I was in my mid-thirties that I realised I didn't want to be a father. The difference is, Casey and I had never really spoken about starting a family—at least not in any way that mattered. She was too busy chasing the next party or shopping, and I was too wrapped up in my work and trying to salvage something that was already broken. By the time I pulled away from her, she saw a baby as a quick fix. A way to keep me tied to her. In her eyes, a child was a solution. To me, it was a life sentence. That's when I knew it was over.

But Mason? I'm surprised.

Anna *has* always been honest about wanting kids. This isn't some whim she's suddenly landed on.

I sympathise with Mason for not wanting to be a father— what I can't get my head around is watching someone you love plan and lay out your whole future, knowing you'll never give it to them. He's kept his feelings from her for *years*, and that pisses me off.

"So, what are you going to do?"

She shrugs, attempting a smile. "Question of the century, isn't it?"

"And you," I say, emphasising my point. "How are you?"

"I'm generally doing well. I have my good days and my bad days ... I'm sure we'll get through this. It's all very new. I just need to consider what's more important to me. I'm trying not to let it take over my life at the moment or ruin our marriage."

"It's a big decision, Anna."

"I agree. It is a big decision. Which is why I need some time. We might be able to work on it yet."

"I'm a phone call away. You know that, right? And if you ever need a space to stay ..."

I don't finish my sentence. She knows I'd do anything for her. My home is her home, and I mean it. I'd do anything for Anna.

She shoots me a grateful smile. "I know, thank you." She perks up suddenly. "Oh! Speaking of big decisions ..."

I know exactly where this is going.

"Don't," I warn. She has that look in her eye, that cunning expression she gets when she's up to something. And I can already guess the words that are about to come out of her mouth.

"You need to pick Gemma and Henry for the campaign."

I roll up the damp tea towel and flick it at her thigh. She yelps, dancing out of reach. "Nice way to change the subject."

"You have to do what I say. I'm sad. Pick Gemma and Henry."

"Don't give me the guilt trip."

"Why not?"

I sling the tea towel over my shoulder and place my hands on my hips. "Because that's not how life works."

"But Gemma and Henry's pitch was amazing, right?" she says, her eyes glazing over.

"Yes. It was," I say, my patience thinning.

"Then you know they're the right team for the job. You want the best. Well, *they're* the best." She sticks out her bottom lip in a ridiculous pout. The little shit.

"I'm serious. Stop it, Anna," I say. The corner of my mouth twitches, threatening to blow my cover.

Her eyes go wide and watery. Jesus Christ.

"I'm just so sad," she says, forcing a croak in her voice. "Please make me happy."

She bats her lashes.

"No."

A single tear rolls down her cheek. "*Please*, Max. Gemma means so much to me and it would make me feel so much better."

She throws in a sniffle for good measure.

Oh God. Now she's wailing—loud, hiccupping sobs.

"What's going on in there?" Dad yells from the living room.

"Nothing!" I call out, dragging a hand down my face before glaring at Anna. "You're a menace."

A small, pathetic sound escapes her, one I know for a fact she thinks is going to win this little battle.

"You're not going to stop, are you?"

"No," she says through fake tears.

I stare at her, holding out for a grand total of ten more seconds before I blow a sharp breath through my nose.

"I was going to pick them anyway," I say, resigned. "They had the more innovative pitch."

The tears stop immediately, and she wipes her eyes as a wide grin spreads across her splotchy face. "Of course they did."

I laugh. "You should have been a bloody actress, not a teacher."

She takes a dramatic bow.

Chapter Fifteen

Gemma

My face scrunches in disgust as I open the chat with Tim on KinkApp.

He's sent me a nude.

Again.

"Ugh," I groan. "I didn't like what you had to offer the last time, Tim. Sorry. But it's time to pack your bags. You've been voted off the island," I say, muttering to myself as the lift ascends.

"What are you on about now?" Henry asks, peeking over my shoulder. He catches sight of the photos before I have the chance to hit the block button.

"Well, that's underwhelming," he says. "I've seen more impressive pickles at Tesco."

"Hey, you have a boyfriend. You don't get to look," I say, pulling my phone into my chest to hide the screen.

"I'm a human being, Gemma. I can look if I want to," he says, shrugging his shoulder nonchalantly. "Besides, Nate and I have an understanding—I can window-shop as long as I don't buy anything. And trust me, I wouldn't even think about putting *that* in my cart."

"It's basically a clit," I say.

"What does he expect you to do with it?" Henry asks.

"Hence why I sent him on his merry way on Friday."

"Good choice."

I perk up, hopeful. "Speaking of choices, have you heard anything about Max making a decision yet?"

He shakes his head. "No comms came in over the weekend. I'm assuming we'll find out today."

I blow out a breath, nodding in acceptance. The doors slide open, and Henry follows me to my office. My pulse spikes when we pass Louise in the kitchenette, laughing like a hyena with Chadwick.

"Why is The CEO in the kitchen? He never comes down to these floors."

"Not sure," Henry says.

"Do you think we should be worried?" I ask, glancing at Henry.

"About Louise's hideous laugh or about her and Theo stealing the account?" he asks, closing my office door behind us.

"Both. She's such a kiss arse," I say, dropping my handbag and coat beside my desk.

"It's not up to Chadwick, and Max doesn't strike me as the kind of man who buys into schmoozing." He perches on my desk as I take a seat and log in to my computer.

I have no idea how Max is going to react after running into him on Friday. He essentially propositioned me, and I rejected him.

And now my body is electric with nerves, wondering if I did the right thing. What does Max Browne do when he's rejected? Is he emotionally mature enough to stay professional inside the office? Will he see my rejection as a challenge, or will he use it as a catalyst to get rid of me?

I hate not knowing.

"I'm nervous, Henry." I glance at the door to make sure it's closed and lower my voice. "After what happened on Friday at Ruby Lounge ... I don't know what Max will be thinking," I say, allowing myself to be vulnerable with him.

That's the thing about Henry and me—he knows all the dirty details of my dating life. I called him right after shopping with the girls on Saturday and spilled everything about my Ruby run-in with Max.

What makes our relationship work so well is the unspoken rule: What happens outside these office walls stays there. Yes, he's technically my boss, but he would never hold my personal choices against me. The line between Max and me is already blurred as hell, and Henry knows that, but he knows I'd never let a man—no matter how irritatingly attractive—compromise my work. I never have. I never will. My vagina and my career have an understanding—they operate on entirely different circuits.

Henry folds his arms over his chest. "My guess? He wouldn't let that dictate the job. This account is career-defining for him—more so than it is for us. He's not going to mess it up over running into you at some club." He pauses, considering. "Anna's level-headed, right? I can't imagine her brother making business decisions based on something so ... personal."

I lean forward. "It wasn't just *some club*, Henry. It was a *sex* club."

He shrugs. "So what? You have similar interests."

"I rejected him," I deadpan.

He straightens his spine. "He'll probably respect you more for it. I know I would."

I shoot him a look. "You're just saying that to make me feel better."

His eyes narrow. "When have I ever said anything just to make you feel better?"

He has a point. Henry is brutally honest.

"Fair," I say, straightening a pile of papers that doesn't need straightening. "So, what now? Just wait?"

"Yes. And when Max makes his decision, we'll either celebrate or drink ourselves into oblivion. Either way, there will be alcohol."

I press my palms together in a prayer position. "Amen."

* * *

My pulse kicks into overdrive as Henry and I make our way to the CEO's office. The call came just after lunch—Chadwick wants us to join a meeting with him and Max regarding the campaign.

This is it.

We either keep it, or we lose it.

I swear to God, if Louise steals this project from me because I have voluptuous breasts that two thin pieces of silk couldn't hold together, I'll go apeshit.

The silence between Henry and me is deafening. Neither of us has said a word. We're both too busy clenching our cheeks to avoid shitting ourselves. It feels like we're being marched into a room where we have to choose the red pill or the blue pill.

We step into the lift and Henry rubs a comforting circle over my back, soothing my anxiety.

I shoot Henry a thankful smile and I blow out a deep breath when the lift pings and the doors slide open.

Max is there. Perched on the edge of Molly's desk while she leans forward, batting her lashes and pushing out her tits.

That's *my* move.

Ugh. I hate the wave of annoyance that rushes through me, my skin heating as I watch the exchange.

Am I *jealous*?

Ew.

What is happening to me? I don't get jealous. I like Molly. It's not *her* fault that Max is flirting with her. And

The Suite Secret

to be honest, I can hardly blame the woman. The man is sex on legs.

Molly's only ever been friendly toward me and works her arse off for Henry and the rest of the executive team. She's a wonderful secretary. It infuriates me that Max has somehow unlocked emotions I thought I'd successfully buried years ago. I'm Gemma Clarke, for crying out loud—I make other people jealous. This is uncharted territory, and I don't like it one bit. I've spent years perfecting the art of not giving a shit, and now I'm suddenly possessive over a man I barely know.

It must be stress.

It's the only feasible explanation. Or simply that I haven't had a decent shag in weeks and I have all this pent-up stress that Tim couldn't assist me with.

Yeah, that's it.

I'm just horny.

"You've got this. We'll be totally fine," Henry says, cutting through my mini meltdown.

I tear my eyes away from Max, forcing myself to remember what matters here. My career.

Molly's phone rings, and Max casts his gaze away from her while she answers it in hushed tones.

Max turns his head, immediately locking eyes with me.

"Gemma, good morning," he says, nodding in acknowledgement.

It's like staring into twin oceans, crystal blue whirlpools pulling me under and losing me to infinity. I almost forget to breathe. He's so handsome it's offensive.

The corner of his lips tugs upward as he stands to full height, straightening the lapels of his navy jacket.

His eyes heat as he watches me move toward him, as if he's tracked down fresh prey. Instinct tells me to ignore him because he was just caught flirting with the executive team's secretary, but my body hasn't got the memo.

"Max," I reply, lifting my chin in greeting. "Good morning."

"How was your weekend?" he asks, arching an eyebrow.

My eyes turn to slits. "Great, thanks. How was yours?"

He shrugs, smirking. "Could have been better."

The turd. He's referring to Friday night.

"Good to see you," Henry interrupts, stepping forward to shake his hand.

"You too, mate," Max says, shaking his hand and clapping Henry on the shoulder.

Molly hangs up the phone. "Max, Henry, and Gemma, that was Chadwick. He's ready for you now."

"Thanks, Molly," Max says, shooting her a panty-dropping smile. I clench my jaw.

We follow Max down the corridor, my eyes glued to how good his arse looks in those tailored suit trousers.

As we approach Chadwick's office, his door swings open to reveal a very sullen, very disappointed-looking Louise and Theo. We step aside to let them by, and as Louise passes, she mutters a quiet "Fuck you" under her breath. I roll my lips to avoid smiling. I can taste the victory already, and it's sweet. My shoulders deflate, releasing all the tension I've been holding since stepping foot in the building this morning.

"Henry, Gemma." Chadwick's deep voice booms from where he sits in the centre of the room. "Take a seat."

There are three chairs arranged in front of Chadwick's desk, one isolated on the left and two positioned on the right. Max claims the lone seat while we occupy the others.

"Max, I appreciate you stepping out so I could talk to Louise and Theo." His tone is neutral but obvious. He just delivered bad news.

"I'm sure you both know why you're here," Chadwick says, leaning back in his chair.

Henry and I nod in unison. I cross my legs, fidgeting with my fingers.

"Max, share the exciting news." Chadwick gestures toward us. *Exciting news?* Bleedin' hell. I woke up this morning thinking there was a decent chance we were getting the axe, but now I'm practically vibrating in my seat. Max turns his body to address us, and a wide smile spreads across his gorgeous face. There's something almost predatory in his eyes when they hold mine.

"After careful consideration, I couldn't go past your incredible pitch. Your ideas for the campaign were exceptional—innovative but practical, bold without carrying too much risk." He leans forward slightly. "The way you captured the essence of what we want Gray Hotel to be ..."

He stares directly at me for the next part.

"You are exactly what I am looking for."

Henry turns to me with a *What was that?* expression.

Were those words supposed to have a deeper meaning? My base desires want them to.

Max continues. "You both know London intimately, and more importantly, you understand our target demographic very well. That's ultimately what won you the project. Gray Hotel would be honoured to work with you to bring this vision to life." Max's eyes linger on mine for a beat longer than necessary when he says the next part. "I, personally, am looking forward to our collaboration."

The breath is sucked out of me. The way he says *collaboration* makes my insides tingle in a way that has nothing to do with professional pride and everything to do with my libido.

Henry and Chadwick begin to discuss timelines and other tidbits, but their voices fade into the background as I notice Max watching me. The way we stare at each other feels like the room has emptied, leaving the two of us locked in this moment.

He knows what this means for me. For Henry. For our careers. This isn't just another project; it's validation for everything we've worked hard to achieve.

It tells me that he trusts us.

It's going to be okay. We haven't lost anything.

I try to convey everything I'm feeling without words, without the physical intimacy which I'm used to—gratitude and relief pool in my eyes as tears subtly gather along my lash line. I inhale deeply, keeping the tears at bay. Momentarily, I allow my professional facade to slip just enough to reveal how thankful I am underneath.

I allow him to see my unfiltered appreciation.

Time slows as he holds my focus. His expression shifts slightly. The hardness in his eyes softens and surprise flashes across his face, like he's seeing me—really seeing me—for the first time. He looks at me with what I can only describe as understanding. It's a look that feels intimate. Right now, he isn't arrogant. He isn't whispering sweet temptations in my ear. He isn't Anna's brother. He's just Max, seeing Gemma. The Gemma I allow a very select few to see. Not the creative director. Not Anna's friend, not the woman from Ruby Lounge—just me.

Eventually, Henry clears his throat, and I dart my gaze around the room, seeing he and Chadwick have finished their conversation.

Henry stands at the same time Chadwick does, reaching over to shake his hand. "Well done, you two," Chadwick says.

"Thank you, sir," Henry replies before turning to Max. "We look forward to working with you."

Max frowns slightly, as if he's confused about what just passed between us. "Yeah," he says. "You too."

I stand, smoothing the fabric of my skirt before extending my own hand to shake Chadwick's. When I look back at Max, I can see his mask has slid back into place. But it's too late—I've seen him without it now.

I extend my hand to shake his.

"Thank you," I say, my voice barely above a whisper.

"You earned it, Gemma," he says.

As his hand clasps mine, his thumb brushes deliberately across my knuckles. The touch is subtle. It isn't sleazy but comforting.

I swallow the lump in my throat, release his hold, and nod before following Henry out.

I know there's another side to Max that exists beneath his cool exterior now. And I suspect neither of us will be able to unsee whatever it was we just shared.

Chapter Sixteen

Max

I gave the campaign to Henry and Gemma. Of course I did. Grayson and I want the best, and Henry and Gemma are it.

There. Anna's happy. Everyone's happy.

Things *should* be fine now. Decisions made, time to move forward with the job. But the way Gemma locked eyes with me this afternoon has messed with my head.

I tried to ignore how stunning she looked. Tried to distract myself with the secretary who was practically throwing herself at me. It was working ... somewhat, anyway. But then Gemma pierced me with those pale green eyes and I saw something I haven't seen in her before. It wasn't the fire she usually throws at me. It wasn't irritation. It wasn't even sexual.

She looked at me like she was revisiting a memory she thought was lost forever.

She looked like she was about to cry, and something inside me reoriented.

I was just a man seeing a woman baring herself, her protective layers peeled back to expose raw, unfiltered honesty. And Christ, it hit me harder than any look of desire ever could.

I'm turning soft. I don't know what's happening to me.

I need to get a grip. Leading by emotions never ends well.

Not only is it a terrible idea to sleep with a colleague, but I can't do that to Anna. My sister would absolutely lose her mind if I laid a finger on her best friend, especially after what happened with Nicole.

With everything she's going through with Mason, the last thing she needs is me causing further stress.

Right. Think of Anna.

Good. It's working.

Now that boundaries have been established, we can begin again and forge ahead.

Problem solved.

* * *

"Max." A knock sounds at the door before the handle moves and the door cracks open. "Sorry to interrupt." The melodic voice pulls me from my work, and I lift my head to lock eyes with Gemma.

I lean back in my chair, fighting the urge to let my gaze peruse her stunning figure. "No problem. How can I help?"

She steps forward and my eyes betray me, darting down to where her fitted shirt is snug against her tits, doing absolutely nothing for my concentration.

"There are a couple things I wanted to go over with you. Do you have any spare time this afternoon?" she asks. Her tone is measured and purely business, but I don't miss the way her focus darts to my forearms before returning to my face.

I quickly click through my calendar for the day, already knowing what I'll find. "Sorry, I'm booked solid with back-to-backs until six."

"Right, no worries." She shifts her weight. "I'm happy to send you an email, but I'd much rather we discussed this in person. Face-to-face is always ... easier," she says.

"I'm happy to stay back if it's pressing," I offer, telling myself it's courteous.

Her chest rises as she takes a deep breath, and I force my eyes to remain on her face instead of that silly little shirt. She pulls out her phone, swiping through what I assume is her calendar. "I can do that."

"You sure? I'd hate to keep you back unnecessarily." My words come out rougher than intended.

She lifts her brows. "I'm sure. It's important." She pauses. "The work, I mean. It's important work we need to discuss."

"Of course," I say, my voice taking on a slightly teasing edge, unable to help myself. "I'll see you at six, then."

"Great."

I refocus on my laptop, trying to ignore the way she's still standing there, but my hands hover over the keyboard. Without looking up, I mutter, "You can leave now."

Her eyes narrow. "I was just—"

I regard her without turning my head. "Making sure I understood the meeting time? Yes, Gemma. Message received."

She scoffs. "You're such an arse." She spins on her heel.

"What was that?" I say, finally looking at her, my lips curving into a smug grin.

"Oh, sod off," she tosses over her shoulder before slamming the door behind her.

I stare at the closed door, my pulse racing.

Her attitude doesn't seem to have improved, and I hate that I like it.

This is going to be a long evening.

Chapter Seventeen

Gemma

The clink of the metal spoon as I stir my tea fills the kitchenette.

"Are you ready?" His smoky voice startles me and I drop my spoon, spinning around to see Max standing in the doorway. I press a hand over my thudding heart.

"Bloody hell." I glare daggers at him. "You nearly gave me a heart attack!"

The prick has the audacity to smirk. "Apologies."

I fish the teaspoon out of the mug.

"I've finished up," he says, and I notice he's popped another button on his shirt, exposing a ridiculously defined dent between two painfully obvious pectorals.

Jesus Christ, even with his shirt on, that chest should come with a warning label.

"Obviously," I retort, finally focusing.

He jerks his chin toward the lift. "My office."

Bossy. I school my expression into neutrality. "I'll meet you up there—just have to grab a few things."

He nods in acknowledgement before leaving, and I take a moment to collect myself.

Snatching my mug from the counter, I rush to my office to collect my documents and then head upstairs. The office, now eerily quiet, feels different when it's empty. I've been here after hours plenty of times before, but knowing there's barely anyone left, save me and Max, it feels quieter. Private.

His door closes with a quiet *snick* behind me. He's at his desk, focused on his laptop screen. The muscles in his forearms shift as he clicks the mouse pad, and the sight is almost pornographic.

"Right," he says, glancing up. "What did you want to discuss?"

I set my mug and documents on his desk, smoothing my skirt as I sit across from him. I push my glasses further up my nose and arrange my papers.

His office smells more like him than it did this morning—strong and masculine.

"I wanted to discuss the timeline for the hotel photo shoot. I understand this isn't something I'd usually bring to your attention, but I've been going through the logistics, and I think we need to persuade some contractors to bring things forward if we want to get the best photographs to meet the launch date."

"Show me." He lifts his brows expectantly, but when I stand and bend to arrange the right paperwork, I'm acutely aware that my position gives him an excellent view down my cleavage. From the way his breathing changes, he's noticed. When I glance up, I catch him quickly looking from my chest back to my face.

"Actually, it's probably best if you come around here. It'll be easier to look at the documents together," he suggests, his voice rough.

I swallow a lump in my throat. Coming around to his side of the desk means standing close to him. Very close.

I drag a chair around and take a seat beside him, shifting my papers.

Clearing my throat, I point to the timeline. "Right here. If we can confirm the necessary permits for the rooftop pools by next week instead of two weeks' time, we can move the entire shoot forward. That gives us more time to focus on the penthouse suites. After all, they're the rooms that will attract the clientele we most want—the guests who think nothing of spending six figures on a holiday."

He's studying the documents, and I feel his eyes flick to me. "Makes sense. I'll see if I can sway the planning department to fast-track the permits sooner." His brows crease as he continues reading. "We'll need to have the designers and stylists confirmed sooner too. Can you look into their availability for me, please?"

"Already on it," I say. Our fingers brush as I flip the page and we both freeze, neither of us moving our hands away.

"I've got three backup options if our first choices fall through. One of them worked on the Ritz-Carlton on Piccadilly. I can send their information and portfolios through, if you like?" I'm trying to focus on the words in front of me instead of the warmth of his hand.

I continue pretending to read the timeline.

"Very proactive, and yes, please do." His voice is lower now, and when I glance at him, I find him watching me instead of looking at the papers. "You keep impressing me."

"Don't sound so surprised," I say, but there's no real bite to it. Something in his tone and his gaze has me drawing closer to him.

"I'm not surprised at all." He shifts in his chair and our shoulders brush. "Thank you for running this by me. It's great. You're very good at your job, Gemma."

"Thank you," I say.

We're staring at each other now and the space between us pulses. His eyes dart to my mouth and I lick my lips.

He makes a low sound at the back of his throat. I should create some distance. But I can't seem to move.

His pinkie finger brushes mine. That *had* to be deliberate.

"We should—" I start.

"Should what?" he asks, his eyes darkening.

"Focus," I breathe.

"Right." But he's not looking at my work. He's looking at me.

When I uncross my legs instinctively, a few strands of hair fall in my face. He reaches up and tucks them behind my ear, his hand lingering against my cheek.

All rational thought scatters like marbles.

"Max," I say, unsure if it's a warning or a plea.

"I know," he rasps. I'm unsure exactly *what* he knows, but the thoughts that sift through my mind are *this is a terrible idea*, *we should probably move*, and *kiss me*.

"Anna would kill us," I say.

"For what?" he says, leaning closer.

"You know what." This time, it is a warning.

"We aren't doing anything," he says, the corner of his eyes crinkling as he fights a smirk.

"Max," I warn again.

"Gemma." He says my name like a confession.

I'm drowning in the depth of his eyes, his pupils almost totally dilated. I still can't move away. It's as if some unseen force tugs me closer to him.

His hand slides to the back of my neck as he leans in, close enough to steal my next breath. My eyes fall shut automatically.

He inhales sharply, and then his lips brush mine, barely. So soft, so tentative, it feels too delicate to be real.

Then my phone buzzes loudly on the desk and our trance is broken. We spring apart like the moment singed us. I lean over and grab my phone, seeing Anna's name on the screen.

The Suite Secret

Anna: *Just messaging to let you know that April called. She took too much magnesium and shat her pants again.*

And if that's not a sign, I don't know what is. What on earth was I thinking, staying late with Max? It *was* entirely unnecessary—of course, I could have handled this over an email like any normal person. I don't know why I insisted.

Actually, that's a lie—I know why. When it comes to Max Browne, my vagina tries to stage a coup and takes over all decision making.

Is there such a thing as female pre-nut clarity? Because I could really use some right now.

Max runs a hand through his hair, looking as shaken as I feel.

"I should go," I say, standing abruptly and gathering my things. "I'll work on this and send you an updated timeline tomorrow."

"Gemma," he says evenly, but I'm already at the door.

"Gemma," he repeats more forcefully.

I hesitate and eye him cautiously.

He shakes his head. "I'll see you tomorrow."

I nod, slipping out of his office and practically running to the lift.

Crap.

Chapter Eighteen

Max

I've finished another gruelling workout after a long day, and I'm sitting with a glass of Macallan and my book, *The Art of War* by Sun Tzu. I have a great deal of respect for Sun Tzu's approach to strategy—applied to business, it means that every negotiation is a battlefield where the smartest player wins. Seems rather fitting.

Aside from the almost-kiss with Gemma yesterday, the rest of my week has gone smoothly. I kept my distance today, deciding to work from my apartment as much as possible going forward. I'll only venture into Prestige's office when necessary.

Gemma and I have been corresponding via email all day, and everything she's sent regarding the timeline shift has been outstanding. She even sent through a new idea for Gray Hotel to collaborate with London's newest Gallery of Contemporary Art, and I gave her the green light to investigate it further. I also spoke to the planning department this morning, dropping Grayson's name—you have to use all your resources in this industry—and they fast-tracked our application. I should have approval in my inbox by Monday.

Thankfully, it seems we've both managed to move on from last night.

The Suite Secret

My phone buzzes with a text from Noah, asking where the hell I am. It's Thursday night and I'm meeting my uni mate at our old haunt in SoHo, which happens to be right near Prestige's building. I haven't seen Noah since leaving for New York. I've kept in touch with old friends, but everyone has their own lives now. Things aren't the same as when we were in our twenties and early thirties. Some friendships changed after Casey and I split; others dissolved naturally due to distance and different pathways. Most of the lads have moved on—wives, kids, some even with teenagers now.

Christ.

That makes me feel old.

Priorities change. They have lives that revolve around playdates, barbecues, and football practice, and I'd never hold that against them—it's what they wanted. It's just not what *I* wanted.

There's a strange disconnect sometimes—they talk about private schooling and mortgages, while I talk about the latest art museums I've visited, books I've read, and weekend trips to the Hamptons.

Different worlds, but I stay connected with those who reciprocate the friendship.

I shrug on my coat, comb my fingers through my hair, and roll my shoulders. Maybe a night with Noah is just what I need to get my head straight and stop thinking about Gemma Clarke's plush lips and that lacy, flimsy bra.

I hop into an Uber—I don't do the Tube. Not after my first day at Prestige Partners.

I walk into the bar, which is teeming with people, as per usual on a Thursday. It's comforting returning to a place so familiar after years away and feeling like nothing's changed. I scan the crowd until I spot Noah perched on a stool at the far end of the bar, paying for his lager before turning around. He locates me through the sea of faces.

It's like a punch to the gut.

He looks the same, a few more greys peppered around his ears and lines etched around his eyes. In an instant, I'm transported back to 2006 when we would all stumble in here after work, ties loosened after busting our arses all day in our junior roles.

I love New York, but damn, I've missed this.

"Mate," Noah says, shaking my hand and pulling me in for a hug.

"Good to see you, mate," I say.

"It's been too long," he says.

"It has. How's Elena? How are the kids?" Noah married Elena shortly after Casey and I tied the knot. His wife was best friends with Casey, but when she started partying, they grew apart. Three kids later, I'm so thankful Noah and Elena and I have remained close friends.

Noah fills me in on life and how the lads are. I laugh as we reminisce about old times, the nights we'd get rip-roaring drunk and stumble home at dawn and somehow make it into the office a few hours later. I tell him all about New York, my new role and why I'm currently in London, about Gray Hotel and, I suspect due to the three pints I drink, I tell him about Gemma.

His eyes light up with that old glint. "It's been a while since you've fancied anyone, innit?" he says, nudging me with his elbow.

I shake my head and smile. "I don't fancy her. She's Anna's best friend. A pain in my arse, more like it."

He guffaws. "Oh, bollocks." He points at me with his index finger, the way he always did when calling out my bullshit. "I know that look. It's the same look you had when you first told me about Casey. You like her."

My smile drops at the mention of my ex, but I quickly recover, taking a swig of my beer.

He notices and quickly adds, "All I'm saying is that it wouldn't be the worst thing to explore your attraction to Gemma. Just have a shag and move on with it, yeah? You've been wound tighter than a pair of testicles in skinny jeans since the divorce."

That earns him a laugh. He has no idea how many women I've bedded since moving to New York.

"Anna's going through some shit with her husband," I say, staring into my lager. "I don't think it's the right time to get in her best friend's knickers."

He frowns, turning to fully face me. "You're telling me your sister, who's nearly thirty-five years old, has a problem with two of her favourite people enjoying each other's company?" He shakes his head. "That's just an excuse, mate. You're all adults. You're entitled to make your own decisions. She'll get over it."

"I work with the woman," I say, as if it's obvious that I shouldn't be entertaining the idea of sleeping with her. Because it *is* obvious.

I take another sip and his eyes narrow. "Yeah, but only for this campaign. Once the hotel's opened, you'll fly back to New York and you won't have to worry about seeing her again."

He chuckles before taking a sip of his drink. "You're making this a bigger deal than it is, you realise? It's only sex."

And that's just it. She's the kind of woman who could absolutely ruin me. She's witty, ambitious, and sexy as sin. She's everything I'd ever want in a woman, which is why I can't have her. Because the second I sink into her, I'll be done for.

Getting through six more weeks of working together will be hell when all I can think about is touching her. And once I get a taste? There's no chance it'll be the last.

And, at that moment, as if I manifested the woman herself, I hear a laugh.

Her laugh.

Of all the thousands of bars in London, of course she'd be at this one.

I close my eyes and release a long exhale before turning around. I immediately locate the source of the unmistakable sound.

She's there with her fingers elegantly curled around a glass of white wine, her head thrown back as she giggles at something I can't hear. One leg elegantly crossed over the other, revealing toned calf muscles. The hem of her skirt rides up enough to expose a glimpse of her shapely thigh.

Henry sits opposite her wearing a wide smile I immediately want to punch off his face. He leans in, speaks again, and she guffaws again.

I hate that he makes her laugh like that. It should be mine to draw out, not his.

The intrusive questions invade my thoughts. *Has he fucked her? Is this what they do every week? Meet after work for a drink before he takes her back to his place and bends her over every flat surface? Has he tasted her? Licked that smooth skin? Heard his name while she cried it out?*

My body tenses.

"Jesus, mate. What's gotten into you?" Noah asks, following my gaze until he stops on Gemma. He lifts his eyebrows with understanding. "Ah. Let me guess—"

"Please don't."

"That's her, isn't it?"

I sigh. "Yes."

He whistles lowly. "She's a bit of alright, isn't she?" He pauses to study her with appreciation. "No wonder you're twisted up. She's bloody gorgeous."

My mouth tightens. "She is."

"Who's the bloke?" he asks, jerking his chin toward Henry.

"Henry Matthews. Her boss. He's working on the campaign with us," I deadpan as my eyes narrow, watching their exchange.

"Certainly doesn't look like her boss," he says, his voice laced with amusement.

He's not helping. This sudden possessiveness is totally foreign to me. As much as I'm trying to fight it, seeing her with another man, colleague or no, grates against me.

I try to remind myself how miserable Anna looked at dinner on Sunday. I try to talk myself out of walking over and claiming her best friend.

"Why don't you go over there?" Noah suggests.

"And what? Leave you?"

He chugs the remainder of his beer, placing it down on the bar with a light thud, wiping his mouth with the back of his hand. He checks his watch. "It's getting late, anyway. Elena's going to need a hand after bathing the kids. I like to be there to tuck them into bed."

His youngest is only two. I nod. "Alright, I'll get going too."

"Oh, piss off. Stop worrying about your sister—she'll survive. It has nothing to do with her. Go over there and see to it that gorgeous woman enjoys the rest of her night, yeah?" he says.

I exhale, feeling my last tether of restraint snap clean in two.

He slaps my back. "Good lad."

Fuck it.

I can't resist any longer. I'm going over there.

I'm not a religious man, but I'll take her being here as a sign from the universe.

Noah claps me on the shoulder before pulling me in for another hug as we say our goodbyes.

"Give my love to the family. We'll catch up before I leave," I assure him.

"We'd bloody better. Have fun," he says with a shit-eating grin. He turns and leaves.

I down the last of my beer and walk straight to their table. Henry spots me first, his eyes widening. He leans forward and says something to Gemma a second before he nods toward me in acknowledgement.

Gemma turns in her seat, and when those jade green eyes lock with me, everything else in the bar fades into the background.

I've made my decision.

She's mine.

Chapter Nineteen

Gemma

It's been a productive week, and I'm relieved Max and I didn't ruin it by kissing yesterday. Anna's name flashing on my screen in that moment was like standing barefoot in snow. A damn cold reality check.

After leaving the office with my tail between my legs, I was buzzing to start fresh this morning. By day's end, it seemed Max was impressed with everything I sent through—I even contacted London's newest Gallery of Contemporary Art to see if they would be interested in collaborating with Gray Hotel, which he seemed pleased with. I was so proud of my idea that Henry and I decided to treat ourselves to some well-deserved vino at our usual haunt around the corner from work.

Henry's busy telling me all about his partner Nate's latest work fiasco, which has me howling, when his face suddenly drops. He plants his palms on the tabletop before leaning in.

"Gemma, Max is here."

"What?" Confusion cuts through my wine buzz. He jerks his chin, and I follow his gaze, only to land on the very man who's been haunting my every thought.

My mouth dries instantly.

Crap.

Max looks good. I mean, *really* good.

Damn it.

He's more laid-back and at ease, forgoing his usual tailored suit for simple trousers and a button-down that fit him way too well.

I swear I hear Celine Dion, see wisps of smoke, and watch as doves burst into flight behind him as he makes his way over. The man looks like some kind of Adonis carved specifically to torture me. Honestly, he could have stepped out of *GQ*.

My vagina develops its own heartbeat, thudding harder with every step he takes.

"What's he doing here? He wasn't even in the bloody office today!" I hiss at Henry.

I straighten my posture and take a desperate sip of my chilled Chardonnay, hoping the cool liquid reduces the heat flushing my cheeks. I can *feel* his eyes on me, like cool water lapping the shoreline, and suddenly, I am bare and exposed.

I know what this means. *He* knows what this means. For Christ's sake, even Henry knows what this means, which is precisely why he's pressing his lips together to hide his amusement.

Rejecting Max at Ruby Lounge on Friday took every ounce of willpower I could scrape together from my traitorous body. I don't think I can turn him away a second time. Not when he looks like *this*. Not when this French Chardonnay tastes so good and I've already helped myself to two large glasses.

Shite.

Anna is going to murder me.

I can smell Max's cologne before he says a word.

"Hello, Gemma," he says.

God, that voice. It's like melted chocolate. Dark, rich, and delicious.

"Henry." His voice shifts into something rougher, colder as he addresses Henry.

"Max, great to see you, mate," Henry says, extending his hand for a shake. Max accepts but says nothing. Instead, he throws his coat over an empty stool's back, pulls it out, and settles in. I watch his large hands as he taps his knuckles against the hard wooden tabletop.

"What are you doing here?" he asks, directing his question at me.

Henry shoots me a confused *what the hell* look from across the table before I respond.

I lift my wine glass, saluting Max before I take a long pull. "After-work drinks."

"Is this something you do often, just the two of you?"

His focus remains fixed on me.

"Um. Often enough." My brows pinch together.

Why do I feel like I'm justifying myself? Am I being scolded?

Henry clears his throat. "Can I get you something to drink, Max?" His tone is friendly, and I can tell he's attempting to lighten the mood.

Max's jaw tightens. "No. Thank you."

Henry wets his lips, clearly unsure of what to do next. After a beat, he stands to shrug his coat on, and I immediately sit up straighter.

"What are you doing?" I ask, almost desperately.

Henry offers a small, tired smile. "I think I'm going to call it a night. It's late and I'm exhausted." He turns to Max. "I'll see you tomorrow. Enjoy the rest of your evening."

Max gives a curt nod in acknowledgement, and I track Henry as he leaves. Turning back to Max, I slam my palms down on the table. "What the fuck was that?"

"Excuse me?" Max asks, his lips curling up ever so slightly.

The arrogant prick.

"You might as well have been beating your chest like a bloody gorilla," I snap. "You were *so* rude to him. What the hell is your problem?"

"Me?" he asks, smirking. "I don't have a problem."

Liar.

I shake my head, resigned. "Whatever." I lift my glass to my lips, taking a sip. I watch him over the rim, and it happens again. That relentless riptide, dragging us toward each other.

Sighing, I lower my glass, deciding to take the high road and steer us back to a safer conversation.

"Thank you for choosing Henry and me. We won't let you down." I tap my fingers against the stem of my wine glass. "We both really wanted this, and we'll do whatever it takes to prove that Prestige Partners is the right company for Gray Hotel. We can make this launch extremely successful. I promise, Gray Hotel will be the 'it' destination. It'll be on everyone's Instagram."

He clasps his hands. "I have absolutely no doubts about your capabilities," he says, his voice dropping half an octave. "Anna has told me how clever you are."

I swallow. His eyes track my movements.

"Well, she's not often wrong," I say.

"She's wrong about some things."

"Such as?" I ask.

He leans forward, crossing his arms over the table, his expression turning curious. "You never told me why she warned you against me."

I shoot him an incredulous look. "I'm sure you can put two and two together. You aren't a complete moron."

He chuckles. "I have my theories." His eyes darken. "Tell me, Gemma. Do you always do what my sister tells you to?"

Oh God.

"No. I make my own decisions," I say finally.

"I was hoping you'd say that." His smile is subtle but unmistakable, and I feel my professional mask slipping.

"This is a business relationship, Max. Nothing more." I remind him and myself.

"What if we made it more?" he asks.

I fidget with the stem of my glass, feeling cornered in the most delicious way. This is risky territory—the exact thing I've been trying to avoid, because I know that once I give in, I'll only want more.

"I don't think either of us want to complicate things," I say.

"I think we're both mature enough to ensure things remain uncomplicated."

The way he says it is so matter of fact, like it's that easy.

I shake my head. "It's a bad idea."

He leans in slightly, a slow smile spreading across his face. "I think it's a *very* good idea."

I pause. "And why would you think that?"

He shrugs. "Because we want each other."

"I do *not* want you." I grip my glass tighter.

"You do. And you know what I think?"

I tilt my head. "Enlighten me."

"I think my sister warned you against me because she knew that there would be something between us. And I think we both know she was right. But I also think it's pointless putting off the inevitable."

"The inevitable?" I raise my eyebrows.

"Yes."

"And what exactly is *inevitable*?" I take another sip of wine, my heart already racing.

He scoots his stool closer, gaze locking onto mine. "By the time I board my plane back home to New York, I'll know what you smell like. What you taste like. How you sound when you moan my name as I'm fucking you."

I freeze. His words produce the most intoxicating, provocative image, and fire ignites in my core.

"You're delusional," I snap.

"And you're denying yourself."

"Of what, exactly? You? I hardly think so." My words sound hollow, even to me.

He rests his elbow on the table. "Of the opportunity to come."

A sharp breath catches in my throat. We've overstepped—I know it. My body betrays me once more as my insides liquify at how feral the word *come* sounds leaving his mouth.

"I'm perfectly capable of taking care of that myself," I say, crossing one leg over the other.

"What if you didn't have to," he replies.

"I don't *have to*," I bite back. "I'll have you know, I have no trouble finding a man to satisfy my needs when they arise."

His lips curve slightly. "I can't imagine you would." He studies me with those infuriating blue eyes. "Speaking of, we haven't had a chance to speak privately since last Friday."

I gulp. Last Friday—Ruby Lounge. The mention of that night sends heat rushing through me and my carefully constructed walls begin to crumble. "There wasn't much to discuss."

"No?" He tilts his head. "How was it?"

He's relentless.

"How was what?" I ask, playing dumb.

"Tim." His voice is almost a growl.

I avert my gaze, unable to look at him. Unable to admit that I couldn't go through with *Tim* after Max left me so unbelievably hot and needy for *him*.

"Ah," he says. "Things didn't go to plan, then?"

I force myself to hold his gaze, even though every instinct tells me to look away.

"Things were left ... unfinished," I say, irritated.

His eyes light up.

I release a huff. "Max—"

"Were you thinking about me, Gemma?" he asks, his voice dangerously low.

I'm determined not to let him see how much he affects me. "Don't flatter yourself."

He leans in. "You really are a terrible liar."

"And you're unbearable."

His eyebrows lift. "Unbearable? Is that why you're flushed? Why your chest is red and the pulse in your ..." He reaches to brush a finger against my neck, and my breath hitches. "Right here, is fluttering? Because I'm *unbearable*?"

I swallow hard, fighting the rush his touch sends through me. This close, I can see the flecks of darker blue in his eyes, the slight stubble along his jaw that would be rough against my skin.

"Anna already lost a friend because of you. I have no interest in jeopardising our friendship," I say.

"That was different. Nicole and I were just two twenty-somethings having fun, it was never a serious relationship. I chose to move to the States for further study. Nicole took it badly because I didn't ask her to join me, so she made Anna pay for it. You and I are nothing like that situation, Clarke," he says.

I grind my teeth together, fighting the urge to give in.

"Will it be easier for you to admit that you want me if I tell you I haven't been able to get you out of my mind?"

His admission hangs in the silence. This thing between us defies all logic and sensible boundaries. I've never had a man challenge me the way Max does, and honestly, it's thrilling. But I don't know what to do with it.

"We work together. You're Anna's brother," I whisper, but my words lack conviction.

"Is that why you said no at Ruby Lounge?" He tucks a stray strand of hair behind my ear, softly trailing his fingertips down the side of my throat. "Or is it because you knew if you stayed, we wouldn't have been able to stop?"

His words hit me like a physical blow. I feel defenceless. My body reacts as if it's been waiting for his touch—as if he's a drug I'm already addicted to. Anna's face flashes in my mind, and a cloud of guilt forms over me for entertaining any thoughts of Max.

"This isn't appropriate," I say, glancing around, as if an excuse to leave will materialise, but I'm rooted to the spot.

"Very little about what I want to do to you is appropriate, Gemma."

Christ. The way he says my name—like he's tasting it—tightens my stomach.

I should move away. I should leave. I should do anything except sit here and drown in his eyes, because right now, I'm imagining exactly what those inappropriate things might be.

"When I look at you, I have one thing on my mind. And I can't stop thinking about it. I've tried to control myself when it comes to you, but I can't. And I don't think I can fight it anymore," he says.

I'm not sure I can hold out much longer either.

"So, tell me, Gemma. Have. You. Thought. About. Me?"

I exhale a long breath. "Fine. If it'll make you stop, yes. I have thought about you."

A Cheshire cat smile stretches across his perfect face. He knows he's won.

"I suppose the question now, smart-arse, is what do you propose we do about it?" I ask.

"Come home with me."

Four words. Fourteen letters. That's all it takes for Max *Fucking* Browne to eviscerate my resolve.

Chapter Twenty

Max

We stand in complete silence as I hit the button for the penthouse. The moment the lift doors close, I'm on her. I slam her back against the wall, my hands threading through her hair, tilting her head to mine. She grabs fistfuls of my shirt, her fingers digging into the fabric as she pulls me closer, just as desperate as I am. When our lips finally collide, everything else falls away. Any nagging thoughts of the hotel, of Anna's disapproval, flicker out as Gemma opens her mouth to let me in. The kiss is wild and urgent.

She rolls her hips, rubbing against my painfully hard erection. I groan at the contact, pressing further into her. I've spent two weeks imagining how she would taste, how she would *sound*, and reality is infinitely better than fantasy. I need to be inside her.

A loud *ding* sounds through the lift as the doors slowly open.

I clasp Gemma's hand and lead her toward my penthouse, flicking on the light.

Closing the door, Gemma surveys our surroundings.

"Max," she says, her voice breathy. "This is where you live?"

I come up behind her, kissing her exposed, elegant neck. "You should see the view."

I follow as she pulls away and saunters over to the expanse of windows overlooking Hyde Park's stunning greenery and the historic London architecture lining Brompton Road. The lights of the city cast a golden glow across her dainty features.

"No wonder you work from home most days. I wouldn't want to leave this place either."

"The office has its perks."

"Oh?" she says innocently, fluttering her lashes.

I like this fun, playful side of her. I chuckle and she smiles, turning back to the windows.

"It's beautiful," she whispers.

"You're beautiful," I say, swirling her around and pulling her close. Gemma wastes no time reaching to unbutton my shirt.

"Fuck, I want you," I growl.

Her cherry lipstick is smeared and her hair is wild, her lips kiss-swollen and her eyes sparkling with desire. She's never looked more alluring than she does right now, undone and wanting.

Our lips collide once more and I snake a hand around her, finding the zipper of her skirt, dragging it down. The fabric pools at her feet as she pushes my shirt off my shoulders, letting it drop to the floor.

Once we're both undressed, we stand in nothing but our underwear, Gemma still in her heels. My gaze roams over her, appreciating every curve and dip of her soft, creamy skin, made all the more enticing by the black lace that wraps around her most sacred parts—like a delectable gift.

"I knew you'd be exquisite," I say, my voice rough.

"I know," she says with a confident smirk. I want to devour her.

I huff a laugh as I spin her around, pulling her back against my chest, my arousal digging into her arse. We both groan at the contact.

My hands skim the front of her legs, climbing higher with deliberate speed, and she shivers beneath my touch. When I reach the juncture of her thighs, I trace her lace thong with my fingertips, feeling the damp fabric. She exhales sharply as I bypass her centre, continuing until I reach the softness of her breasts.

"This bra is utterly pointless," I say. It's true—the material barely covers her, the fullness of her breasts spilling over the top.

"I've been wanting to get my hands on these tits since your button popped off during your pitch. This lace has been haunting me, you little tease," I say against her ear.

She hums, and I work her nipple between my thumb and forefinger, pulling and pinching.

Reaching back, she wraps her hand around me, stroking over the fabric of my briefs. I'm impossibly hard.

"Step forward. Hands against the glass and bend over," I command.

She obeys without hesitation, pressing her palms flat against the cool glass. Her back arches, hips swaying with a teasing shimmy that makes my breath hitch.

I drag my hand over the curve of her pale arse. "Open wider, sweetheart."

She steps her feet further apart, granting me access, and the sight of her—bent over, heels still on—is enough to unravel me. Leaning in, I kiss along her spine, my free hand gripping her hip as I slide the lace aside, baring her completely. I run my fingers through her slit, groaning when I feel how ready she is for me.

"Sopping wet, aren't you?"

"Just touch me, Max," she says, her voice husky.

I oblige, teasing her with my fingers, circling them slowly over her clit, just enough to make her shift but not enough to satisfy.

"Look at you," I murmur. "So ready, so fucking desperate."

Her answer is a soft whimper, her hips rocking back and forth, chasing my touch. I give in, slipping two fingers inside her, slow and knuckle deep, while my other hand grips her waist to hold her steady.

She clenches around me, and I groan against her back, already imagining how it will feel when I finally sink my cock into her.

My thumb finds her clit and I start moving my fingers in tandem, dropping kisses against her naked back as she fucks my hand. Her body arches into every touch, greedy for more.

"More, Max," she demands.

"What do you need?" I ask, wanting to hear her say it.

"Another finger."

I slip a third finger in, curling it to hit that perfect spot inside her, and relish the way she rocks over my hand before nearly bouncing up and down, chasing her release.

I can't hold back anymore. The sight of her standing at the window, legs spread, tits out for any onlookers to see, almost has me exploding in my briefs. The thought of being watched, of someone witnessing her pleasure, seeing what I'm doing to her, sends a surge of possessive fire through me.

I drop to my knees between her legs, burying my face in her drenched heat. Her head drops forward, and she releases a soft cry that goes straight to my cock.

"Are you going to come on my fingers and tongue for everyone to see, Gemma?" I growl against her, the vibration making her shudder.

"Oh God, yes. Don't stop," she whimpers, maintaining her hands on the glass.

I indulge, lapping at her slit, drinking up her arousal like a starved man. She tastes better than any whisky I've had—richer, more complex and intoxicating. Her sweet scent and musky flavour coat my tongue, and I'm done for. This is all I want to taste. Forever.

I continue to stroke and pump and lick when—

"Ah! I'm going to—Max, I'm going—"

I don't let up as her inner walls squeeze my fingers. She saturates my hand as she comes apart so magnificently. She cries and moans, and I lap up every drop of her release until her legs begin to tremble.

I release her and stand, but she doesn't move.

Good girl.

"You did so well for me," I say, smoothing a hand over her arse cheek. "Do you want more?"

She peers over her shoulder, hair tousled, skin flushed, eyes glossy as she bites her lower lip, nodding. I reel back and deliver a sharp spank. Her porcelain skin blooms the most beautiful pink under my palm. I continue, alternating between firm slaps and gentle caresses, running my fingers between her cheeks and down to her core, where she's impossibly wet. I stroke her swollen clit, feeling her quiver before withdrawing to land another strike against her reddening skin.

By the time I've reached five spanks, she's whimpering and moaning, crying out beautifully. I'm in awe of her beauty—how she welcomes each strike fervently. How she's submitting to me. It's like she was made specifically for me, crafted to fit every dark desire I've ever had. I need to feel her—bare. No barriers. Nothing between us.

"Do you want my cock?" I ask her, my voice low.

"So badly," she says.

"Then come and get it," I tease.

She spins on her heels, her confidence taking over as she plants her palm firmly against my bare chest. Her shoes click against the wooden floor as she walks me back toward my sofa, each step slow and purposeful, her lips curved into a wry smirk. I watch, enraptured as her hips sway with each step. I drop into the cushions, legs spread wide, as she settles between my thighs. The power between us shifts immediately. She holds all the cards now. I'm completely at her mercy.

On her knees, she reaches for the elastic of my briefs, and I lift myself to help her peel them off, my aching cock springing free and standing proud.

Her eyes widen momentarily, so slightly that I almost miss it.

"Like what you see?" I ask, arching a brow.

She shrugs—the brat. "It's fine."

I huff a laugh as she wraps one hand around my base. Her touch is feather-light at first and it drives me insane. I need it hard and rough.

She looks up at me through her dark lashes.

"Is this what you've been thinking about?" she asks, her breath warm against my skin.

"Amongst other things," I manage, my voice strained as she begins to stroke me slowly. "Christ, Gemma."

She holds my gaze as she leans forward, her tongue darting out to taste the pre-cum on my tip.

The sight of this fierce woman on her knees might be the most erotic thing I've ever seen. When her crimson lips finally wrap around me, taking me into the wet heat of her mouth, I grip the sofa cushions to refrain from instinctively thrusting up.

This is her game now.

Instead, I thread my fingers through her hair, gripping tight as she takes me deeper. Each slide of her lips and swirl of her tongue has my muscles tightening, pressure building in the base of my spine.

"Fuck, just like that," I groan, watching her take me. "Your mouth is perfect."

She hums around me, the vibration sending a jolt of pleasure straight through me, and I know I need to stop this soon or else—

"Where do you want my come? Your mouth, your tits, or your pussy?"

"My mouth," she mumbles around me.

She increases her pace and I'm helpless as she pushes me further toward the edge. My grip in her hair tightens as every muscle in my body tenses.

"Gemma, I'm close," I warn, giving her one last chance to pull away.

Instead, she takes me deeper, looking up with those challenging green eyes, tears falling down her cheeks, and that's what does it. With a guttural groan, I come hard, spilling down her throat as pleasure rips through me. She swallows everything, never letting up until I'm completely empty.

When she finally pulls back, she wipes her lips with the back of her hand, a satisfied glint in her eyes. I pull her up onto my lap, claiming her mouth in a punishing kiss, tasting myself on her tongue.

That was, hands down, the best blow job I've ever received.

"I intend to have you every way possible before the sun rises," I say. I'm only just getting started with her.

She leans back, pats me on the shoulder like I'm a dog, and slips off my lap. "Maybe another time."

My brows furrow as I watch her pick up her clothing to get dressed.

"What are you doing?" I ask, my ego bruising with every step she takes.

"I should go," she says, zipping up her skirt.

"You're leaving?" I ask, standing and making my way over to her.

She—I shit you not—fakes a yawn. "It's late. This has been fun, but I'm exhausted."

"You're serious?" I say, my arms spread wide as she struts to the door. I know I've just blown a load, but I'm ready to go again.

"As a heart attack. See you tomorrow." She turns, shooting me a wink. "Sweet dreams." She swings open the door and slams it closed behind her.

I'm left stark naked, in the middle of the living room, sporting a semi.

Did she seriously just leave?

I chuckle to myself, shaking my head in amusement as I rub my hand over my stubble.

The cheeky little shit.

For the first time in years, a woman has left me wanting more.

And somehow, I'm not even mad about it.

Chapter Twenty-One

Gemma

My heart pounds as I jab the elevator button repeatedly.

I can't believe I did that. The look on his face was priceless.

Max Browne just delivered the best orgasm I've ever received, and he managed to do it with only his tongue and fingers. The smug satisfaction in his eyes afterward told me everything I needed to know—he had me right where he wanted me. I had to get out of there.

This was supposed to be purely physical—a fantasy to indulge in once and get out of my system.

Not only am I extremely attracted to him—I'd have to be dead to not recognise how gorgeous he is—but our chemistry is amazing, the foreplay is off the charts, and I think I'm, God forbid, starting to *like* him. I don't get crushes. Especially not on a man who holds my career in his hands. Not on my best friend's brother. And especially not on someone who could *actually* hurt me.

Because, ultimately, that's the truth I'm running from. I think he could hurt me. I've spent years having emotionless fun. I'm the queen of no-strings attached. But something about the way he touched me, the way he looked at me, felt dangerously close to meaningful.

The elevator finally arrives, and I step inside, leaning against the wall I was pressed against only an hour ago. I close my eyes, trying to steady my breathing.

I flag down a cab as I exit his building, glancing back up at his penthouse windows.

We can't do that again. I can't come back here.

I shake my head as I slide into the black cab. *We were just messing around.* I tell myself. *It was nothing more than incredible, mind-blowing fun.*

Then why does it feel like I've left something behind?

* * *

Stepping off the Tube, I follow the crowd of early-morning commuters like a zombie. I barely slept a wink last night. All I could think about was the way Max's fingertips felt gliding over my skin as he mapped out my body and planted kisses across my back. How delectable he tasted and how luscious he smelled.

The first thing I did after arriving at my flat was make a beeline for my dildo so I could finish what Max and I had started. Only problem was, the toy kept turning into Max's mouth in my mind. His voice whispering in my ear. His hands pinning my wrists.

Even my self-care routine failed me. I tried everything—slapped on a hydrating face mask, pulled tarot cards, burnt some incense, and read my newest monster romance where the heroine gets railed by a kraken.

And nothing I tried removed that man from my thoughts.

He was even in my bloody dreams. He gives me one orgasm and somehow manages to conquer my subconscious.

Maybe I'm coming down with something ... like food poisoning of the brain.

Max poisoning.

I need a pastry.

I pull my stained trench coat tighter as I make my way to Lance's kiosk, the cutting wind nipping at my exposed skin.

On approach, I watch Lance place a row of fresh, glistening pastries in the display case. He positions each one perfectly, as always. The smell of butter and sugar wafts through the air and my stomach growls.

"Morning, Lance!" I call.

He glances up, his face brightening. "If it isn't my favourite troublemaker!" He takes one look at me and lets out a low whistle. "Blimey, lass. You look like you've seen a ghost."

"I feel like I have," I mutter. A very tall, handsome ghost with hands like sin, and a penis that honestly might qualify as a deadly weapon.

"Late night, then?"

I huff. "Not intentionally."

He quirks an eyebrow. "Oh. Was there a date involved?"

I roll my eyes. "Define *date*."

He grins. "Well, whatever it was, I hope he knows he's a lucky bastard."

"Believe me, I shouldn't have gone there," I deadpan.

His expression shifts, brow furrowing. "He didn't hurt you, did he?"

My tone softens. "No, no. God, nothing like that. He's just …" I trail off, unsure how to explain Max without sounding unhinged.

Lance leans forward. "Aye, I see. What's his name?"

I hesitate. "Max."

He nods, as if he's already decided he likes the name. "Max. Max and Gemma. Got a nice ring to it."

I shake my head. "Nope. Abort mission. This is *not* a good thing."

He folds his arms, his voice teasing. "Why?"

"Because he's Anna's brother."

"Your best friend Anna?"

"Ugh, please don't say it out loud. It makes it worse." I bury my head in my gloved hands.

He chuckles. "It's alright, lass. These things happen."

"Not to *me*, they don't! And now I've got to see him every day. At *work*. I mean—what the hell was I thinking?"

Lance rests against the counter, his voice gentling. "Right, I'll say this once."

"Here we go."

He points a finger at me. "Oi. I want you to really hear me for a wee second. I'm serious."

"Fine."

"Life's too bloody short to spend it worrying about what other people think. Even Anna. I know she's your friend, but if something feels good, if it feels *right*—don't run from it. Lean into it." He tips his chin, all knowing and annoyingly wise. "Now, did it feel good?"

I squint at him. "You do realise you're ancient and this conversation is wildly inappropriate, right?"

He waits, unmoved.

I sigh. "Yes."

"Aye. There you are, then."

I shake my head. "It isn't that simple, Lance."

"When you get to my age, believe me—*it is*."

I scrunch my nose. "Yeah, but you're like ... *really* old."

He laughs, shaking his head, and I smirk back. "And still in love with my Everly, forty-five years later. Must've done something right."

I smile despite myself.

"The usual?" he asks, already sliding an apricot Danish into a bag.

I bat my lashes. "You're the best."

The Suite Secret

"I'm not too bad for an old geezer."

"Your words, not mine." I grin, rummaging in my handbag for my wallet.

I lift my gaze to pay and look around, noticing that I'm still the only customer. My brow furrows. "Is business getting any better?"

He sets the coffee in front of me, his eyes misting over. "I hate to tell you this, lass."

"Oh no." I lift a hand to cover my mouth.

He nods. "Aye. I've done my best. I've even gone and remortgaged mine and Everly's flat to cover expenses for a little longer, but it's not looking good."

My stomach drops. Lance must be—what?—sixty-five? It's criminal to think someone who works so hard needs to take out money against their home to cover costs. My heart breaks for him. I know I've been the only customer here every morning this week, but I never thought he'd *actually* be forced into considering closing.

When I started at Prestige, people were queued right up to the edge of the grass, all willing to freeze their tits off because Lance's coffee and pastries were worth enduring frostbite—they still are.

I look forward to our chats each morning. He knows exactly how I like my coffee, he knows I need it stronger on a Monday and a Friday; he can tell when I'm hungover versus when I'm stressed and when I've had a shite date the night before. Lance is my little rock.

My brain scrambles to find a solution. "I can help you. We can figure something out," I say.

His hand covers my own. "You've done enough just by being here every morning, Gemma." He gives me a sad smile, and my throat burns as I swallow the emotion threatening to spill over. I need to be strong for him. "I'm still here for now," he says quietly. "But sometimes we have to accept when things naturally come to an end. That's life, isn't it? Nothing's guaranteed. We've had a good run."

I nod, unable to speak.

"Now, you best be off to work. Don't worry about me. I haven't gone anywhere just yet. I'll be alright." He pats my hand affectionately.

My nostrils flare as I take a deep breath. "So, when?"

"When what, lass?"

"When will you close?"

He exhales sharply. "When it's time."

Chapter Twenty-Two

Gemma

I polish off my Danish while I complete the short walk from Lance's kiosk to the office. My coffee's still warm in my hand, and I roll my shoulders as I step into the elevator, telling myself to get a bloody grip. But by the time I press the button, I'm worried about how Max will behave after last night.

Will he be pissed? Will he get even?

Bloody hell. I can't escape my emotions this morning.

I count slowly as the lift ascends, taking the moment to compose myself. Professionalism. Maturity. Poise.

Right, Gemma. Lance will be okay. He's a big boy—he has Everly. And you can handle Max. You run through men like it's a sport. You've got this. He's just a man. No big deal.

The office is already running at full speed, humming with *thank God it's Friday* energy, and I must admit, I couldn't be more relieved.

People laugh loudly, the scent of coffee wafting through the kitchenette.

And then I spot him. Max is leaning against the kitchenette counter, listening intently to something Louise is saying.

I'm certain Max is simply being polite, because her conversation's about as dry as a nun's vagina.

He's wearing a charcoal suit today—tailored within an inch of its life—and I don't mean to stare, but my eyes drop, anyway. Straight to those veiny, strong, capable hands cradling a mug. My body remembers those hands. The wicked things they did to me last night. The way he touched me like he'd branded me. And damn if my body doesn't want him to.

You've got this, Gemma.
Scratch that—you don't have this at all.

I watch, completely dazed, as he lifts his mug to his lips. His thick throat bobs with the swallow, and then, Christ, his tongue darts out to lick his full bottom lip.

As if he senses me, his gaze slides across the room to meet mine. I freeze mid-step. And while I should turn and march straight down the corridor, my feet have fused to the traffic-worn carpet.

Louise continues babbling, but he pays her no mind. Because his sinful eyes spark like cinders as he regards me, brimming with lust. By the time I take a cautious step forward, his gaze flicks back to Louise, who throws her head back in laughter. I cringe at the sound. Max smiles. A full-on, teeth-baring, panty-destroying smile.

A pang of something almost territorial hits me, which is ridiculous. We didn't even sleep together.

I straighten my spine and force myself to move.

"Morning," I say brightly, slipping out of my coat and tossing it over a free chair next to Henry. I approach Louise and Max, stepping between them. Louise scoffs as she's forced to move back and I reach for the biscuit tin in the top cupboard. I arch my spine slightly as I do, knowing full well Max has a perfect view of my arse. I'm in high-waisted trousers that accentuate every curve, my sheer blouse tucked in, the white lace of my bodysuit peeking out subtly from underneath. I've perfected my corporate attire, maintaining professionalism with just enough sexy to not be overt.

Beside me, Max's sentence trails off. He clears his throat as my arm brushes against his shoulder, the warmth of his gaze following the line of my body. When I turn around, biscuit tin in hand, Max's eyes shift straight to my lips.

"Gemma," he says, my name dripping like honey. "How was your evening?"

Louise's expression morphs from insufferable friendliness to something more hostile. She's pissed she's lost her audience, and I couldn't be more pleased. I pretend she isn't there and refocus on Max.

"Great, thanks. Nothing exciting to report, unfortunately. But I slept like the dead," I lie, popping the biscuit in my mouth and chewing slowly. "You?"

He smirks.

"Can't complain," he replies, shrugging coolly. But his jaw ticks—just for a second—and I catch it. He didn't sleep well, either. Good.

Louise, ever the desperate opportunist, leans in. "Mine was good too."

I blink at her. "I'm thrilled for you."

"Max was just telling me *all* about New York. Weren't you, Max?" Louise bats her lashes at him, and my biscuit threatens to resurface.

"Yes," Max says, his eyes never leaving mine. "Louise was asking about the New York office."

"I bet she was," I mutter.

Louise shifts closer to Max, pressing herself against his arm. "I've always wanted to see New York. The Empire State Building, Central Park ..."

I wrinkle my nose in pure disdain as the beige conversation dribbles on. I knew the woman was awful, but her flirting is akin to watching someone trying to lick their own elbow.

Fine. If giving Louise attention is his way of retaliating for my walking out last night, then I already know I've won.

Does he think flirting with Louise will make me beg for it? Let him try. Two can play this game. If this man thinks he's capable of making me envious, he has another think coming.

This is my game. I *own* this game. Hell, I invented the bloody rules.

Before Max can respond, I saunter toward the long dining table where Henry sits, wholly focused on his phone. I drop into the seat beside him, scooting a little closer and crossing one leg over the other. Max can see us perfectly here.

Henry lifts his gaze from the screen, eyes darting between Max, Louise, and me, and narrowing when he realises I'm dragging him into whatever this is.

Louise has more or less moulded herself to Max's side with one manicured hand resting on his forearm, the other toying with her ebony hair. My stomach clenches when Max's lips curve into a smile at something she says.

"Hi, Henry," I say, my voice sweet and loud enough for everyone in the room to hear. I touch his shoulder briefly. "I've been looking for you *all* morning."

"Ew. What are you doing?" he whispers, recoiling slightly.

"Just go with it," I murmur through my smile, flicking my eyes back to Louise and Max.

Max is watching us now, his interest split between Louise's incessant chattering and whatever I'm saying to Henry. Our gazes collide for a split second and the heat in his glare sears through me like a brand.

He deliberately turns his body toward Louise.

Henry looks in Max's direction before shifting his gaze back to me, horror dawning on his face. "Absolutely not. Don't use me as a pawn in your little game."

I ignore him and place my hand on his arm, letting it linger as I laugh at something he hasn't said. I toss my hair back, making sure to angle my body so Max has a perfect view of my tits and waist.

Over Henry's shoulder, I see Louise lean in closer to Max, whispering something in his ear. My blood boils when his lips move and she barks out another laugh.

I press my breasts into Henry's biceps, his eyebrows shooting up to his hairline. "Wow, you're really going for it, huh?" he asks. "Should I give you the Oscar now or wait until you've finished this riveting performance?"

"Shut up. Do me a solid and make him jealous," I say through gritted teeth.

Louise's hand is on Max's chest now. Is this bitch serious? That has to violate workplace policy. Where is Chadwick Fuck-Face when I need him?

Henry releases a long exhale. "Gemma, I'm your boss. This is beyond petty and unprofessional."

"I'll buy you coffee for a week."

He groans. "Goddammit, you know I'm a slut for Lance's coffee."

"Is that a yes?" I wiggle my eyebrows.

He sighs. "Fine, whatever."

"Thank you," I say, shifting even closer.

Henry's eyes pierce through my soul and his brow twitches, just slightly. He looks like he might actually throw up. I would be offended if it weren't for Max occupying every part of me that cares.

"Sorry, I can't do this," Henry says, trying to pull away. "My body is physically rejecting you."

"Yes, you can!" I whisper-shout, pulling him back in. "Pretend I'm Nate."

"Are you serious? Christ—I am *so* gay."

"Henry! Be a team player," I say, smacking his chest.

He rolls his eyes dramatically before wrapping an arm around my shoulders and leaning in, pretending to whisper in my ear without getting too close.

I risk another glance and lock eyes with Max again, and this time, his smile evaporates.

"Is he looking yet?" Henry mutters quietly.

"Yes."

"Excellent. Now, care to tell me what this is all about? What happened last night after I left the bar?"

"Everything but penetration."

Henry gags. "Please, for the sake of our friendship, don't ever say the word *penetration* again."

Louise laughs way too loudly at something Max says, but I can see it written all over his face—he isn't into her. Not in the slightest. His spine's gone rigid, his chin's tilted. He's on high alert, uncomfortable, awkward. *Good.*

I pump my eyebrows. "It's working, Henry. I think he's going to come over here."

"Finally. Can I get up now?" Henry asks, his tone exasperated.

I quickly assess the situation.

Max places his mug on the countertop and shoots Louise a tight, polite smile before subtly edging away from her touch.

Ugh, his bone structure is impossibly perfect.

He gives Louise a dismissive nod and his entire demeanour shifts into something predatory, and I know exactly who he's hunting. That lazy charm he was pretending to have with her vanishes as his attention on me sharpens.

For a second, time forgets how to move.

"Bingo." I smirk.

"Oh, screw this—I'm out," Henry says, standing and retreating before I can say another word.

Behind Max, Louise scowls at me. It's delightful.

"A word, Gemma," Max says.

"Here?" I ask, my voice innocent.

"In private," he says through gritted teeth.

The Suite Secret

I rise from my chair slowly, feeling Louise's eyes stalk me as I do.

"Now," Max barks, and I roll my lips to hide a wry smile.

"After you," I say, gesturing to the doorway.

His nostrils flare as he runs a hand over his stubble. The very stubble that chafed my most sensitive areas last night, leaving a delicious burn.

Max storms out, and I don't miss the venomous look Louise sends me before I follow him into the elevator.

He aggressively stabs the button to the executive floor until the doors slide shut. The moment they do, his hands grip my waist. He spins me around and presses me against the cool metal. His warm breath fans against my neck, igniting my core when he whispers, "I know what you're doing."

"Oh?" I say, breathless despite my best attempt to maintain control.

"Mm-hmm," he hums, a deep rumble from his broad chest. "And you're not going to get away with it."

My insides turn liquid. He pulls his head back and I stare into his blue eyes. "What are you going to do about it?"

Jesus Christ, Gemma. What are you doing?

I can't help it. I'm poking the bear. He's going to punish me, and I so desperately want to let him. I want him undone. I want him to beg.

He brings a hand up to my breast, running his thumb over the sheer fabric and lace, teasing my nipple into a taut peak. My hands fly up, digging into his shoulders as I steady myself. A needy moan tumbles past my lips before I can stop it.

He pulls back suddenly. The elevator pings, forcing us to separate as the doors open, and I smooth out my trousers and try to slow my racing heart.

Without a word, he continues to his temporary office, me in tow, slamming the door behind us. He pushes his suit jacket off, discarding it on the large sofa pushed against his office wall, running a frustrated hand through his salt-and-pepper hair. He turns to me with a dangerous glint in his eyes.

This is going to be good.

"What is it you wanted to talk about?" I ask.

He doesn't answer right away. He starts working at the cuffs of his crisp white shirt, slipping off his cufflinks and tucking them into his trouser pocket. Then he deftly rolls up his sleeves to reveal those thick, corded forearms, dusted with dark hair. A platinum ring adorning his index finger catches the light.

I can't look away. Even his bloody forearms are hot.

"See something you like?" he asks, backing up to lean against his desk.

He plants his palms on the polished mahogany on either side of him, and the corner of his mouth quirks up in that infuriatingly hot half-smile.

"You didn't answer me," I say, avoiding his question. The arrogant prick knows I like what I see.

My eyes drop to the obvious bulge concealed beneath his trousers and my mouth waters.

"Do you think you can just flirt with *Henry* in front of me and get away with it? After leaving so abruptly last night?" he says, tilting his head.

I lift my eyebrows. "I think we both know that's exactly what you were using Louise for."

"Are you jealous?" he asks.

"Ha! Believe me, the last thing I feel toward Louise is jealousy." I prowl toward him with deliberate steps. He tracks my movements as I eliminate the space between us.

"You're the one who started this game. You know exactly where my office is. You weren't in that kitchen to chat with Louise—or anyone else, for that matter. Execs have their own damn coffee machine. You were there because you wanted to see *me*," I say.

The Suite Secret

He doesn't move a muscle. "I want you to admit you want me. That's why you left last night, isn't it?" He gestures between us. "You want this—more than you ever meant to—and it's *killing* you to admit it."

His voice drops to a low murmur. "You can't stand how much you feel when I'm near you. When my tongue and fingers are *inside* you."

He's right. It is killing me. I can't think, can't breathe, can't gather a single coherent thought.

I'm fully dickmatised. Under the spell of his monster cock.

So, naturally, all I manage is the weakest response.

"You're pretty sure of yourself," I say. He shifts to widen his stance, so I slip between his thighs, closing the distance until we're inches apart.

"I'm sure of you." His eyes drop to my lips.

"You don't even know me," I retort.

"I wouldn't *quite* say that. I know your body," he says with too much confidence.

I push my glasses up my nose to take my mind off the electricity coursing through my vagina, and he catches my wrist.

"I also know you're intelligent and ambitious—you've built an impressive reputation for yourself, and I have a lot of respect for you in that regard. You're proud of the work you do, and you should be. I know your friendships mean everything to you, that you care more than you let on." His focus shifts to my lips, briefly hesitating. "I know your body craves the same things mine does."

"And what's that?" I keep my tone cool.

"Release. Connection without commitment." He regards me. "I know you want to be taken apart and put back together. Last night was incredible. We both know it. I want more."

My entire body burns and bristles at his blunt admission.

He rubs his thumb over my pulse. He must feel how it races.

"And what makes you so sure you're capable of giving me what I need?"

"Let's drop the act, shall we?" he says. The rasp in his voice is rough enough to make my toes curl.

"There is no act," I lie.

"Then what is this? A game?" His free hand lands on the curve of my waist, his fingers pressing into the silk of my sheer shirt. "Because if it is, I think we should establish some rules. Don't you?"

My breath catches. "What kind of rules?" I ask.

"Rule one," he says, pulling me closer. "You don't walk out on me when we're messing around."

I smirk. "Who said last night wasn't only a one-time thing?"

"I did." His hand slides from my waist to the small of my back, splaying his long fingers. "Rule two. No more using people to make each other jealous. No more Henry. No more Louise."

The way he spits Henry's name is pure possession. Territorial. *Oh*—it clicks—he's actually jealous.

That explains the weird behaviour when he saw us together at the bar last night. Does he think ... does he think I'm *sleeping* with Henry?

I lick my bottom lip, filing that information away for later.

Who knows? It might come in handy. And it's not exactly my place to go broadcasting Henry's sexual orientation, now, is it?

I lift my chin. "You started it."

"And I'm ending it." His tone is final.

"And rule three?" I ask, my breathing grows ragged and my stomach spins.

"Rule three. While I'm fucking you, no one else is."

Chapter Twenty-Three

Max

That last rule slipped out. As soon it leaves my mouth, her eyes widen. I hadn't planned to be so direct. But I want her again. Every delicious inch of her until she's breathless and begging.

These rules aren't just for her—they're for me too.

The more time I spend with her, the further I slip. It's infuriating and intoxicating. Her innocent glasses, her wavy blonde hair, the confident way she carries herself through the office clouds my judgement and makes my fingers itch to touch her. I haven't even been inside her yet, but the thought of her with another man infuriates me.

I understand Anna's feelings are at stake here, but I don't think either Gemma or I can deny whatever this thing is. My sister would have my head if she knew I was constantly thinking about sleeping with her best friend. If she knew what I've *already done* with her best friend. But every time I'm in Gemma's presence, resistance is futile.

Noah had a point yesterday—I'm only here for two months. Then it's back to New York and my usual life. But while I'm here, the idea of something casual but consistent sounds pretty bloody appealing.

No strings, no promises, no disappointments. And because we're working together, it makes sense that we don't sleep with other people.

I haven't been exclusive with anyone since my marriage fell apart. Seeing Gemma with Henry this morning, watching her smile at something he said, stirred green-eyed fury within me. It's not rational, but the moment I saw her step out of the elevator in those high-waisted trousers and that sheer excuse for a shirt, I turned feral.

I need to take back some control after she walked out last night. After she left me so hard I could've shattered glass. Don't get me wrong—I *like* that she left me wanting. I like that she has the power to affect me this way. Ever since my divorce, the women I've bedded have been so agreeable, so eager to please they'd take whatever I gave them without question.

Gemma makes me work for it, and I love the chase.

After last night and knowing we have no option but to work closely together, I know neither of us will be able to resist the urge again. So, if we agree to continue messing around under the guise of something fleeting but exclusive, we can have our fun and nail this hotel launch without the worries of a relationship. When I return to New York, that'll be it. We both walk away unscathed

At least, that's what I tell myself as I look into her sage-green eyes swimming with questions.

"I don't do exclusive. Sorry," she says.

"Neither do I," I say. "But seeing as I'm only here for a short while and we're going to be in proximity, I think it's best to avoid any possible conflict. This way we can be available to each other whenever we need to be. If we're doing this, it's exclusive. There won't be anyone else. Not while you're in my bed." The words come out rough.

"Not even Tim?" she asks, a smile playing at the corner of her lips.

Hellcat.

I laugh. "Especially not fucking Tim. There will be no visit to Ruby Lounge unless we go together."

"I have some conditions."

"Oh?" I ask, lowering the hand splayed across her back, pulling her into my groin where she can feel exactly what she does to me. I groan at the same time she gasps. "And what would they be?"

Her hands come up to rest on my chest. "If I agree to this arrangement, then we need to establish clear limits around work. No displays of affection. No lingering stares. I work too damn hard to put my job on the line."

"Done. What else?"

"You're here for two months, right?"

"Right."

"I want a clean break when you go back to New York. No texts, no calls, no attachments."

I nod. "I can do that."

"And Anna?" she prompts, a flicker of guilt crossing her features.

I exhale slowly. This is the trickiest part. What we're doing doesn't just blur the lines, it distinctly crosses them. Our relationships with Anna run deep, and this would feel like betrayal if she ever found out—especially after the shitstorm with Nicole.

"Anna complicates things," I admit. "But if this is to remain casual and not go further than the time I'm here, then I don't think there's much harm in keeping it from her."

Her eyes close momentarily, and for the first time I see a flicker of vulnerability. "I hate lying to my best friend ... but ..." Her voice trails off.

I take her hand in mine, rubbing my thumb over her knuckles in a soothing circle. "I understand. I don't either. But I think, for now, it's what's best for everyone."

She looks down where our hands join, deep in thought, her brow furrowed. The touch is intimate, but she isn't pulling away.

"Are you alright?" I ask, capturing her eyes with my own.

She nods. "Yes. Maybe one more thing."

"And what's that?" I ask.

She takes a measured breath before speaking. "Don't fall in love with me, Max."

I almost laugh.

"That won't be an issue," I say.

"I mean it." She pulls her hand from mine. "I'm not the kind of woman who will fawn over you and cater to your every whim. I won't be sitting up at night waiting for your call or text—I have my own life, one I'm perfectly content with, and I plan to keep it that way. I don't *do* feelings—I fuck." She adjusts her stance. "If we do this, that's all it will be."

Her bluntness shouldn't catch me off guard, but it almost does. The corner of my mouth twitches upward.

"Thank you for elaborating," I say.

"Don't mock me."

"I'm not." I pull her closer. "Believe me, you continue to impress me. Most people dance around what they want. Your directness is ..." I search for the right word. "Refreshing."

"I'm not most people."

"I'm discovering that." I run a hand over my jaw, studying her. "For what it's worth, I don't do feelings either. This is merely a convenient, consensual arrangement."

"Good. So, we're clear then?"

"We are," I agree.

"Excellent. When do we start?"

"Tonight," I say without hesitation. "My apartment. Nine o'clock. Don't be late."

She runs a red painted fingernail down the front of my shirt at a torturous pace, watching my reaction through those deceivingly innocent glasses. When she reaches my belt, she keeps going. Her palm cups my hard cock over my trousers and my breath hitches.

"I have work to do," she says with a ghost of a grin, snatching her hand back abruptly. She spins on her heels and marches toward the door.

"Gemma. See you tonight," I call after her. "Don't leave me waiting. You won't like the consequences."

She pauses in the doorway to glance over her shoulder.

"You might want to do something about that," she says, nodding toward the obvious tent in my pants.

And then she's gone, leaving me impossibly hard, frustrated, and already counting down the hours until I can make her scream my name.

There's a chance this could blow up in our faces. But as I watch Gemma's hips sway out of my office, I squash that internal voice of reason.

I can't wait to have my wicked way with her.

Again.

Chapter Twenty-Four

Gemma

What on earth have I just signed up for?

Agreeing to an exclusive arrangement? What am I *doing*? I swore black and blue that I wouldn't commit to a man again after Todd, and here I am, champing at the bit as soon as Max dangles his monstrosity of a cock in front of me. It's like waving a red flag at a bull. I can't resist.

If I'm completely honest with myself, I've been attracted to Max since the moment I laid eyes on him. That attraction might have been concealed by sarcasm and irritation, but it's always been there. But I can absolutely enjoy this attraction without turning it into something more.

Truth be told, I like the way he tests me. I like the way he pushes me past my comfort zone. There aren't a lot of men brave enough to do that.

His arrogance paired with how incredible he looks in an Italian suit has me counting down the hours until nine o'clock.

A loud buzz sounds through my office as my phone vibrates, lighting up with a message from April. We'd planned earlier in the week to meet at the new Contemporary Art Gallery in Knightsbridge during our lunch break. Since her

The Suite Secret

work is only ten minutes away, and she has an excellent eye for art, it's perfect timing.

The gallery's manager graciously carved out time for us to peruse pieces recently donated from private collections. We're hoping to find something perfect for a potential collaboration with Gray Hotel. I'm hopeful if we find suitable pieces, we'll be able to bring prestige for both the gallery and our hotel opening.

I jump off the underground, adjusting my scarf against the frigid wind.

April stands just inside the doorway to the gallery, throwing her arms around me in a tight hug when I arrive.

"I'm so happy to see you! I've been looking forward to visiting this gallery for the longest time. Apparently, they have an incredible ceramic collection by an up-and-coming Spanish sculptor!" she says.

"Me too. God, I hope I can find something suitable. I feel like I need to prove myself to Chad-dick and Max," I say as I adjust my bag on my shoulder.

Her brows tug together. "Why? You're brilliant. You don't need to prove anything to anyone."

Bless her, the angel. I need to tell her about Max and me. I know we agreed to keep our arrangement from Anna, but if I only have Henry to talk to about this, I'll go insane.

I shoot her a small smile as we approach the reception desk.

"Good afternoon, ladies. How can I help you today?" says a cheerful woman.

"Hi!" April says. "We made an appointment to view the private collections today. I'm April and this"—she gestures to me—"is Gemma."

The woman's face brightens. "Ah, yes. Of course, I spoke with you earlier. Absolutely. My name is Camille and I'll be showing you around the gallery. Just let me fetch our receptionist and I'll take you through."

We link arms as Camille begins our tour. We walk from room to room, ooh-ing and aah-ing at the gorgeous works.

"We've curated several pieces we believe would complement Gray Hotel's aesthetic and vision," she explains, gesturing to a brightly coloured installation. She then walks us through a room of abstract paintings and sculptures. They're edgy and sophisticated, exactly what I'm looking for.

"Oh, these are fabulous," I say. April beams as she studies the canvases.

Each acrylic painting captures the London cityscape in an abstract style, contrasting various seasons and times of day. Not only has the artist captured the city in a physical sense but also its emotion through moody colours, brush strokes, and lighting.

"Oh my God," April whispers, stepping closer to study the paintings. "These are stunning."

I nod, completely enraptured. "They're perfect."

"These aren't on public display yet, so you've picked a great time to view them. This is the most extensive collection we've had in the gallery to date," Camille says.

We share an impressed glance before continuing through to another room.

April dances a little jig and squeezes my arm excitedly as we approach a glass cabinet showcasing all sorts of ceramic sculptures.

"Oooh! Imagine these scattered across various counters throughout the hotel. They're so edgy and modern. They would be perfect," she says.

I nod along as she points out her favourites, admiring the colours, shapes, and mediums used to create them.

"Excellent. I'm thrilled the pieces resonate with you!" Camille claps her hands. "I'll give you ladies space to peruse and discuss privately. If you have any questions or need additional information, just wave me over," she says before disappearing around a corner. I still hear her footsteps, so I know she hasn't gone far. Just far enough to eavesdrop.

When April's done ogling the ceramics and sculptures, I drag her through to the initial viewing room with the paintings we loved so much. She scans the room before popping her hip and crossing her arms. "Now that we're alone, explain why you feel the need to prove yourself to Max."

I release a long sigh.

Her facial features twist into concern. "Don't tell me he's giving you a hard time—he's lovely, Gemma. Honestly. I've known him a long time. He's just a serious guy at work. Outside of the office, he's really fun. He used to tease Anna and me all the time."

Her history with Max growing up only makes this more awkward. April and Anna met when they were five—Anna had just moved back to London from Fiji—so Max has been like a brother to April, in a way.

I glance around, double-checking that Camille isn't within earshot.

"No, it isn't quite that ... You see ... Max and I ..." I trail off, unsure how much to disclose.

She cocks a brow, lowering her voice. "Max and you ... what?"

"I know you might tell James, but I'd rather you didn't. Please."

"Okay. If you don't want me to, then, of course, I won't," she says, crossing her heart.

April is one of the most loyal friends I've ever had. She means every word she says.

I press my lips into a thin line, studying the ceiling as if it can provide perfect words to phrase this.

She gasps. "You slept with him, didn't you? Gemma!"

"No, no. Not that," I assure her quickly. *Not yet, at least.*

Her shoulders visibly relax. "Okay, then what?"

"Max fingered me."

I'll admit, that came out much louder than I intended, the words echoing through the space. An elderly lady examining a painting nearby scowls at me while April's eyes widen.

A clattering sound comes from behind, and we both spin to find Camille fishing her pen from the floor, opening and closing her mouth like a fish when she looks up at us. I didn't even hear her approach.

"Sorry, I—I was just passing back through to reception," she says, her face beet red. "Don't mind me."

We watch Camille scurry away, her heels clacking in haste. The elderly woman huffs and moves to another room—probably for the best.

April turns to me and stands stock still, staring into my soul. Her expression is so unreadable, I'm worried she might be having a stroke.

My brows knit as I step closer, pressing the back of my hand to her forehead. "Can you feel your face? Are you numb anywhere?"

She blinks and I sigh in relief, lowering my hand.

"Say something!" I plead, flapping my hands.

"Sorry, I'm just ... processing," she says, stunned. "I mean, I thought you might be attracted to him, but—"

"There isn't much to process. Anna's older brother stuck his hand in me and used me as his own personal finger puppet."

She drags me back into the sculpture room. "When? Where?" she whispers, eyes darting around.

I run her through all the dirty details of last night. By the time I'm finished, her jaw is tight and she throws me a worried look.

"Please tell me Anna doesn't know."

"Of course she doesn't. I hardly think ringing her immediately after sucking her brother like a lollipop is appropriate," I answer.

"Is this just going to be a one-time thing?" she asks, ignoring my sarcasm.

"Does the pope shit in his hat?"

"I have no idea whether the answer to that is yes or no."

"Me neither. Probably no." I check the time on my phone. "He's invited me over tonight."

She drags a hand down her face. "Gemma, I don't really know what to say. This is—"

"Complicated. I know." I nod.

"Is this really a good idea if you're working together?" she asks, her voice gentle but concerned.

"We're adults. We've set rules and will remain professional. And we agreed that once he returns to New York, it'll be a clean break. No emotions, no attachments, no one gets hurt."

She gives me a sceptical look. "Anna is your best friend, Gem. I'm worried about what it will do to your friendship if she finds out. She told you what happened with Nicole."

April's words slice through me. It's nothing I haven't already considered. And usually, I'd never go there with anyone if April or Anna told me not to. But Max isn't just *anyone*. If I thought neither of us could hack the arrangement, I wouldn't have agreed to it. Max views sex the same way I do—as something that doesn't require commitment and can be just that—a physical release.

If we both follow the rules and conditions of our arrangement, then no one will get hurt in the process. He'll go back home to his fancy office in New York, and I'll stay here. It's not like I need to worry about running into him at the local bookstore.

"We should be allowed to follow our desires. So long as no one else is affected, which they won't be, then it's something we can both walk away from unscathed."

After a moment, April sighs and puts a hand on my shoulder. "I should be the last person lecturing you about who you should and shouldn't be with. I slept with my ex-fiancé's brother, for Pete's sake." She gives me a determined look. "If it feels good, enjoy it. As long as you both know what you're doing. I won't say anything to Anna, because I trust you. If you say this is nothing more, then I believe you. Just ... if this goes wrong, then it could blow up spectacularly. Just be careful, okay? Please?"

"I appreciate it. Thanks, hon." I pull her in for a tight squeeze.

"And be careful with your heart," she murmurs into my hair. "I'd hate for you to get hurt."

I scoff as we separate. "Me? I don't think I'm the one you need to worry about."

"You do know that Max doesn't do relationships, right? Not since his divorce, anyway."

"No one's getting down on one knee. This is sex, April. A fuck-buddy arrangement with a two-month expiration date."

She shudders. "This is a little disturbing. You're both like family to me."

"We love a taboo romance trope," I say, nudging her playfully with my elbow.

A ghost of a smile paints her lips.

"Now, let's go find Camille and pretend she didn't just hear about the chief development officer of Gray Hotel fingering me."

April snorts. "Charming."

We locate Camille, who does an excellent job of keeping her shit together despite my confession. Her cheeks are still tinted pink when she leads us to a small office with a portfolio containing details about the paintings we loved.

Apparently, they belong to a young Lord Harrington's private collection. He temporarily donated them to the gallery following his father's death three months ago. His snotty father never approved of contemporary art, favouring Renaissance pieces with lots of naked cherubs and people looking constipated in frills. So, his son specifically wanted these paintings displayed somewhere they could be appreciated by the public, without his father having a bitch-fit from beyond the grave.

I thumb through the portfolio with April. I always thought lords would be stiff and boring, but this man has *good* taste. I think we could definitely set up an exclusive collaboration with Gray Hotel.

I can already envision the marketing campaign. Social media ads, Instagram and TikTok posts, involving popular British lifestyle influencers, appealing to lavish women who want to spend a day at the spa surrounded by gorgeous products and paintings while they indulge in the luxury of Gray Hotel.

The idea of bringing these works to an audience who might not visit art galleries makes my corporate heart thrum. Not only do the artists benefit from exposure, but Lord Harrington can peacock the shit out of his impressive art repertoire with a similar demographic.

After Camille hands over a brochure including the pieces we've seen today, she scribbles his contact details on the back of a gallery business card. I set a reminder to arrange a meeting to view more of his private collection with Henry and Max.

As April and I say goodbye outside, a sheepish look crosses her face. She surveys our surroundings to make sure we're alone before leaning in. "So ... was it good at least? With Max?"

A slow, satisfied grin spreads across my face. "Mind-blowing. Let's just say the man has a reason to be as confident as he is. His cock is enormous."

"Oh God, I knew you'd give me too much detail. I shouldn't have asked!" She groans, covering her ears. "I need to be able to look him in the eye at our dinner next weekend!"

Shit. I totally forgot that Max was attending that.

"You okay? You didn't forget about the dinner, did you?" April asks.

"No! Of course not," I say, a half lie. "I just remembered I needed to finish something for Henry."

"Oh, sure. Well, have fun. Give Henry my best. I'll see you soon!" She waves.

"Love you!"

I head back to the office where I flip through Lord Harrington's brochure with Henry. Thankfully, he loves the artwork. He tells me he'll eventually have a chat to Max about visiting the Harrington Estate to view the collection in person, and excitement fizzes through me.

* * *

By five-thirty, I'm out the door and racing home to prepare for tonight.

As I get ready, I conclude that if he's expecting sex tonight, he's in for a disappointment.

Why? Because I'm not about to hand over exactly what he wants on a silver platter. If Max Browne wants exclusivity, then he can wait a little longer. As much as I'm dying to feel him stretch me open with that gorgeous cock, I'm not letting him call all the shots. He's not the only one steering the ship.

I swap out my glasses for a pair of daily wear contacts, which I wear as an insurance policy, so I don't end up staying the night. Because I *never* stay the night. It screams attachment, and there will be none of that.

By the time eight forty-five rolls around, I'm fluffing my hair and slipping on my shoes.

Game time.

Chapter Twenty-Five

Gemma

I arrive at exactly nine. Max buzzes me up and by the time I reach his apartment, I find him leaning against his doorframe. Gone is his expensive suit and in its place, he's wearing low-slung grey joggers—help me, God—and a tight black t-shirt.

His hair is damp and pushed back, his skin glowing.

He's so effortlessly handsome it's annoying.

"Gemma," he coos.

I prowl toward him, my heels clicking. "Max."

"Let me take your coat." He extends his hand, and I peel off my jacket.

He inhales sharply when he sees what I'm wearing—a pleated navy mini skirt and a matching navy lace bodysuit. London's weather doesn't dictate my clothing choices. He accepts the coat, hangs it up, and leads me inside.

Like last time, I drift toward the wide stretch of windows and take in the cityscape. It's breathtaking. Clouds roll like smoke and city lights twinkle through the dark. The outlines of distant buildings blur into the inky sky.

"Would you like some wine?" he offers, heading for the kitchen.

I turn to him. "Please."

He nods, fetching two long-stemmed glasses and a bottle of red, serving an indulgent pour.

"Cheers," he says, lifting his glass to mine, and we clink them together.

"Cheers," I say, taking a small sip.

We study each other, as if we're both waiting for the other to make the first move. He smirks.

"So, how long have you had the apartment?" I ask, looking around.

"Four years. I bought it after the divorce."

Something cold settles in my chest at the mention of his past marriage, catching me completely off guard.

The way he presents himself—so calm, cool, and collected—screams fierce independence. It's difficult to imagine him surrendering that autonomy to someone, caring enough about them to promise forever.

I'm not quite sure how the thought of Max loving someone that deeply makes me feel. Surprised, sure. But also ... *thrown*. It challenges everything I thought I knew about him and makes me want to dig deeper.

"Has it been left empty all this time?" I ask. It looks like *his* furniture. Sleek, modern, leather, and stone. Soft-focus lighting. This place suits him—well, what I know to be him.

He takes a sip. "I rented it out on a month-to-month basis."

"So, you kicked them out to come back for two months?" I ask, narrowing my eyes.

He shakes his head. "Don't look at me like that. I'm not a total prick. They moved out a couple months ago. I knew I was coming back, so I didn't bother finding another tenant."

"Oh," I say.

"I'll relist it when I go back home."

Home. Right. To New York. That brings me right back to reality.

He assesses me quietly.

"What?" I ask, the question coming out harsher than intended.

"What are you thinking?" he asks.

"That you're in a better mood than you were this morning," I say.

He chuckles, lowering his wine. "I am. I like having you here."

"Is that so?" I ask, taking a sip to hide my widening smile.

His lips press together to hide his own. "It is."

"And what exactly do you plan on doing with me?" I ask, batting my lashes like I'm innocent, as if I'm not already soaked with anticipation.

"Tease," he murmurs, smiling like a devil.

I arch a brow and wait for more, keeping my expression cool.

He sets his glass on the marble with a quiet clink, then braces both palms against the counter, leaning in. My gaze darts to his muscles that flex at the movement.

"What I plan to do, Gemma," he says, his voice lethal, "is tear off that pathetic little excuse for an outfit"—he then jerks his chin toward the massive sofa across the room—"spread you open on that sofa, and make you come so hard on my tongue you forget your own name."

My pulse accelerates like a drumbeat. I set my glass down.

"Then," he continues, slowly rounding the island bench and walking me backward. "I'm going to lie down on that same sofa, flat on my back, and you're going to crawl up and straddle my face—*reverse*." He emphasises the word. "Arse in the air, that pretty little pussy on my face, and you're going to suck my cock."

My throat dries.

"I'm going to tongue-fuck you until you're dripping down my chin and you'll suck me like the good girl I know you can be, and swallow everything I give you." A devilish smile splits his face as my knees hit the back of the sofa, and I fall into the cushions. "I wonder how many times I can make you scream my name."

God help me, I want to find out.

Max leans in close, his face inches from mine. "You like control, don't you, Gemma?" His breath is warm against the shell of my ear. "But you're going to give it up for me. Do you want to know why?"

"Why?" I breathe, focusing on the giant tent in his trousers.

"Because you know I eat pussy better than anyone ever has."

Lust claws at me. I part my legs for him to step between my thighs, which are already trembling like jelly at his filthy words.

Damn, he's good at this.

"So far, Max," I purr, "you're all talk."

He laughs. "You know I'm not."

"Then get on your knees and prove it," I demand.

His stare doesn't waver as he lowers himself to his knees and runs his hands up my thighs at a punishing pace. When he reaches my skirt, he finds the zipper at the side, and drags it down, the fabric loosening around my hips. He peels the skirt down my legs and tosses it over his shoulder.

My bodysuit has two buttons that clip together at the crotch, and he pops them open, rucking the lace up over my stomach.

I'm fully exposed, and the cool air kisses my slick skin, alerting me to just how wet and ready I am.

"Fuck, Gemma," he growls, hooking his hands under my knees and dragging me forward until my arse nearly hangs off the sofa. "You're glistening."

I tilt my pelvis slightly and bite my lip to keep from begging.

He doesn't waste time, burying his face between my legs with a guttural groan. His mouth latches onto me like he's starved, tongue licking a long strip before plunging deep inside my pussy.

"God, yes," I cry, my head tipping back, my spine arching off the cushions.

His hands pin my thighs apart.

"Hold your legs up for me," he commands.

I obey, replacing his hands with my own. I'm completely spread, shaking and uncaring that he can see all of me.

He pulls away, lips shining, eyes blazing. Then, he delivers a sharp slap right to my pussy, making me jolt.

I cry out, the sting shooting straight through my core.

"You like that," he says, his voice thick like treacle. Before I can answer, he does it again—another smack right against my clit.

The pain is there, but it's perfect. My breath shudders and I swear I grow wetter.

His smile is dangerous as he leans in again, lapping firm circles around my clit as two fingers push deep inside. When he bends them just right and rubs the spot that makes my vision blur, I unravel. Moaning, I babble a string of incoherent praise as he does exactly what he promised—eats my pussy better than anyone ever has.

His fingers don't stop, alternating between scissoring and stroking that perfect pressure point, dragging every last drop of pleasure from me.

My fingers itch to pull at his hair and bury his head even deeper, but I'm helpless as I hold myself wide, utterly at his mercy.

Heat builds in my core, and I know I won't last much longer. It feels too good. "Max," I whimper.

He hums, and the vibration finally sets me off. My orgasm slams through me. I convulse around his fingers, mouth open in a soundless gasp. And still, he doesn't stop. His tongue drags through every ripple of my release, drinking me up.

Finally, his fingers slow. My chest rises and falls like I've run a marathon. I gasp for breath.

"Jesus Christ," I whisper.

He pulls back, wiping his mouth with the back of his hand like he's just finished his favourite meal.

I release my legs and wince at the discomfort of being in that position for so long—not that I'm complaining.

He places a kiss on my inner thigh, and the tenderness rattles me.

"Still all talk?" he asks, his tone smug.

And the tenderness is gone.

I scoff. "Just take off your pants, already."

He stands, shoving his joggers down his legs and yanking his shirt over his head.

I'm already moving, shifting down and pushing him back until his shoulders hit the sofa cushions. I climb over him slowly, facing away, and lower myself until my knees are on either side of his head.

His hands grip my arse cheeks, dragging me down to his mouth like he's hungry all over again.

His cock is long, hard, thick and twitching against his stomach, waiting for me.

At the sight of its glory, I don't make him wait long.

I wrap a hand around the base and drag my tongue up his length, tasting him. Salt and musk. He jerks beneath me, latching onto my pussy. We moan at the same time, finding relief in each other.

I take him into my mouth, my tongue curling around the tip before sucking with purpose. He grunts, loudly, his mouth working between my thighs. My hips rock against his face, each flick of his tongue making it harder to focus. I push myself to take more, relaxing my throat to choke down another inch.

The sounds we make are unrestrained and wild, totally primitive.

The Suite Secret

He laps at my clit. I moan around his cock.

His hips buck. I swallow him deeper.

We lose ourselves in each other, locking in a sweaty, filthy, perfect rhythm.

He begins to swell in my grip, and I know he's getting close. He twitches in my mouth, so I stroke him with fever—sucking, licking, and swirling him into a frenzy.

"Fuck, Gemma," he growls into me. The vibrations he makes against my most sensitive parts spark my next orgasm. "You're gonna make me come."

His finger teases my arsehole and my back arches, my moan strangled around his cock. And just like that, I fall apart with a sob. My body locks up, every muscle clenching as I whimper around his length.

The feel of me coming on his face must tip him over, because seconds later, a primal sound tears from his throat and his cock jerks against my tongue.

Hot, thick liquid fills my mouth, and I swallow around him, sucking him through it while he keeps lapping at my pussy.

We're both panting.

He unlatches his mouth. "Fuck. I think I blacked out."

I lick my lips and smile. "Well done, Browne," I say breathlessly, adjusting myself so I face him. "Not bad."

He huffs a laugh.

I stand, gather my scraps of clothing, and pad over to my coat.

He sits up in the same spot I left him last night.

"You're leaving again?" His voice is dangerously low.

Shrugging on my coat, I swing open his front door. "Yep. Same time next week?"

His answering growl is all I hear before I slam it shut.

I'll take that as a yes.

Chapter Twenty-Six

Gemma

It's Saturday night and April and Anna are coming to mine for wine, nibbles, and proper girl time.

While I'm business Gemma during the day, I've done my best to create a cosy environment that's just for me outside the office. It's nothing fancy, but it's all mine—a place where the people I love most know they're always welcome.

It's a space where Anna and April can kick off their shoes, muddle up a margarita strong enough to strip paint, and belt out our favourite songs.

I grew up with a single mum who made sure my friends always knew they were welcome. My mum is kooky—of course she is, she created me—but her heart is pure gold wrapped in tie-dye fabrics and essential oils. I wanted to carry that love through to my own home.

I spent most of my morning wandering through Borough Market, collecting the good stuff—cold cuts, wedges of cheese, fancy nuts, and dried fruit. I can absolutely nail a charcuterie board.

Since the Gray Hotel campaign launched, my friends and I haven't had as much time together as usual, especially with April and James trying to pull off a last-minute wedding—

which is mental even for a rock star, but somehow, they're making it work.

I haven't complained about being busy because it's given me the perfect excuse to avoid any chance of letting my and Max's secret slip. Every time Anna's around, I'm shitting myself about accidentally spilling the beans. The woman knows me better than I know myself, and I'm usually terrible at keeping secrets. But I need to get my act together, because this secret is different. It's not just about me.

* * *

"What does it say?" April leans over so far, her wine sloshes dangerously close to the rim.

"Shit! Watch the sofa!" I warn.

"Oops." She giggles, carefully placing her wine beside the tarot spread Anna's got laid out on my coffee table. Naturally, the tarot cards came out the moment we opened the first bottle.

We're now on our second.

Anna picks up a card, squinting as she flips through *The Tarot Bible* to decode its meaning.

"Right," she announces. "It says you're a massive cunt."

We lose it, falling into fits of laughter.

"But seriously, what does it say?" April asks, wheezing as she catches her breath.

Anna's eyebrow kicks up. "You know this is all a load of shite, right?" She gives April a pointed look.

"It is not!" I defend. "Just read the damn meaning."

Anna rolls her eyes light-heartedly. "The Empress basically says that you're about to become a domestic goddess or ... get pregnant ... Or both."

I pump my eyebrows at April. "Is there something you're not telling us?"

Out of the corner of my eye, I see Anna's face fall slightly before she quickly recovers, forcing her expression back into a smile.

April blushes, reaching to take a healthy sip. "Clearly not," she says, raising her glass. "But I will just say that we aren't *not* trying."

"Oh my God!" I exclaim. "You're trying for a baby!?"

April shrugs nonchalantly. "I guess. If it happens, it happens. If it doesn't, it doesn't."

"That's so exciting!" I scoot forward, wrapping April in a firm hug. "You and James are going to make the most beautiful babies," I say.

Pulling back, I see Anna's strained expression. Her smile doesn't quite reach her eyes, but I can tell she's trying.

"Anna?" I venture quietly. "You alright?"

She shakes from her daze as soon as the words leave my mouth, straightening her spine and perking up. "Oh, sorry, I was in a daydream. I'm fine!"

"Is it the red wine? Sometimes it makes me gassy," April says.

I scoff. "Doubt it. Considering the number of times she's dropped her guts in an Uber when we've been drinking tequila."

"Oh, piss off! You're the one who farts!" Anna retorts.

"Me?" I say, hand over heart. "You wound me."

"Yeah, well, so does your lethal arsehole," Anna mutters.

"I've never had *any* complaints about my arsehole, thank you very much," I say, turning my nose up mockingly.

Anna finally laughs, waving me off before pointing to my near-empty glass. "Need a top-up?"

"Sure, thanks." I hand her my drink, and she takes it into the kitchen.

I turn to April. "Is she okay?" I ask.

"I don't know ... She went a little quiet as soon as I mentioned that we're trying. I'm sure she's just distracted," April says.

"I know she wants children, but she's never mentioned anything about her and Mason trying," I say.

"Maybe they are and it's not going well?" April suggests, picking at the corner of a cushion. "I hate to think she might be struggling with something and not telling us."

"You know Anna—if she had something important to tell us, she would've brought it up already," I say.

April's voice drops. "God, I feel terrible now."

"Hey, don't do that to yourself." I reach over and squeeze her hand. "You're allowed to be excited about your future."

April sighs. "I just want everyone to be happy, you know?"

"I know you do, hon," I say.

Guilt floods my chest. Here we are, worrying about Anna keeping secrets from us, when I'm sitting here harbouring a big fat one of my own.

If Anna *is* struggling with personal issues and I'm ... well, shagging her brother behind her back, am I the worst friend in existence?

Jesus. What kind of person does that make me?

But no matter how guilty I feel, I can't bring myself to say anything. Certainly not without talking to Max about it first. Then again, we both agreed there's no point in telling Anna because he'll be gone soon enough.

"We could be wrong. I think it's rude to ask outright. I hate it when people ask James and me if we're having kids—it's no one's bloody business," April says, her tone slightly more hopeful. "I think you're right. I'm sure she'll tell us when she's ready."

I'm not sure if April could see the cogs turning and put two and two together about my guilt over Max, but her words soothe me, nonetheless.

Upon hearing Anna's footsteps, we quickly shift our attention back to the tarot cards.

"Now, where were we?" Anna asks brightly as she rejoins us, placing three full wine glasses on the table.

"I was just about to tell April that I know all about her second magnesium mishap at work," I blurt.

"What the hell, Anna! I told you that in confidence!" April squeaks, attempting to hide her grin as she admonishes Anna.

"What?" Anna says innocently, dropping to the floor and crossing her legs. "You can't tell me something as brilliant as you shitting your pants *again* and expect me *not* to tell Gemma," Anna says.

I swivel to face April with faux outrage. "Honestly, I think the only person with the right to be shocked here is *me*. After everything we've been through together, you kept this absolute gem a secret?" I drop my voice to a theatrical whisper, pretending to tear up. "I told you about that vibrator getting stuck up that bloke's arse and everything."

"Speaking of," Anna interrupts, "Gemma, I haven't heard any juicy dating stories lately—what's going on?"

Shit. *Shit, shit, shit. Quick—think of something!*

"Work. Yeah, work's been super busy. Henry and I have been pulling heaps of late nights to bring the project timeline forward, so I haven't put much effort into meeting anyone lately," I say.

She lifts her brow in surprise. "Huh. Makes sense. Max has been really busy too."

My stomach drops as I rush to think of an excuse. "Yeah. Calls to New York and stuff."

"Oh, of course, I forget about the time difference," she concludes, nodding to herself.

"But I did try to meet this guy from KinkApp the other week. Unfortunately, his equipment couldn't handle the job, so I sent him on his way," I divulge, hoping that will appease her.

The Suite Secret

"That's more like it. Atta girl," she says, raising her glass in a toast.

April slyly nudges me with her elbow, shooting me a small, knowing smile.

I owe her one for not saying anything to Anna. As long as I keep my promise and ensure this deal remains a simple arrangement, we should be fine.

Before I can dig myself a hole, April launches into wedding mode, pulling out her phone to show us venue photos.

Thank God, because I was about thirty seconds away from having a faecal accident myself.

Chapter Twenty-Seven

Max

I haven't touched Gemma in a week and I'm twitchy as hell.

I'm lounging on the sofa, answering emails when my phone cuts through the silence. I look down and see Casey's name flash on the screen, and my chest tightens.

She doesn't know that I'm back in London.

I set my laptop aside, staring at her name. It's the third time she's called this month. I ignored the previous two.

I thought we were getting better—thought *she* was getting better. That after I screened her last two calls, she'd finally understood I can't be her emotional crutch anymore.

I clench my jaw, running a hand over my stubble. It's not her fault that this has been happening for years, not entirely. I've entertained her calls because this is a woman with whom I shared my bed, my last name, my *life* for seven years. Seven whole years. I've watched her break and tried to put her back together again countless times. Even now, years after the divorce settlement, an inflated sense of responsibility has me hovering my finger over the accept button because, to be honest, I've been scared of what might happen if I don't answer.

But I can't keep doing this. It isn't fair—to either of us. I don't love her. I haven't loved her for a long time. I've tried to be there for her, lending an ear when she needed to talk through her issues, offering advice when she asked or talking her through tears at 2 am because there hasn't been anyone else.

She misses me. She misses us. I still care for her. How could I not? But it's over and was long before we put ink to paper. She's reaching for something that no longer exists.

I gave Casey more than I've ever given any other woman, and it led me to heartbreak and disarray.

I let the call go to voicemail and block her number before I can change my mind. I can't move forward if I'm constantly revisiting the past.

I'm about to spend the night with another woman, for Christ's sake. With Gemma.

Someone who wants exactly what I can give—nothing more, nothing less. No history, no promises. Just fun.

I've been waiting patiently for our designated evening together ever since she sauntered out of my apartment last Friday, and I won't let anything spoil the mood.

* * *

After a punishing workout, I shower, steam billowing around me as I towel off. My phone sounds from my bedroom and I accept Grayson's call, switching to speaker as I dress. While he updates me on everything back in New York, my mind keeps drifting to the impending nine o'clock appointment.

My cock reacts and I try to maintain control while talking to my best friend. Even talking to a man can't turn me off depraved thoughts of what I want to do to Gemma Clarke.

I roll my shoulders as Grayson barks down the line. "Violet Ashwood will be the death of me," he complains. "She's putting me through the wringer with these depositions. Six hours yesterday, another four today. The woman doesn't stop."

Violet Ashwood has been hired as Grayson's attorney, and by the sounds of it, is keeping Grayson in line. His father is waging a brutal battle over the brothers' inheritance of the Livingstone empire.

I pull on a pair of grey joggers and a simple white t-shirt.

"She's just doing her job," I respond, knowing how high the stakes are. "Your father's lawyers won't hesitate to exploit any weakness. Violet's preparing you for that."

"I know, I know." Grayson sighs. "But she talks to me as if I'm entirely unprepared. I'm the CEO of a multibillion-dollar company!"

"Just remember, Violet's on your side. She's the expert. I know this is personal, but you need to approach it like any other legal case," I say.

I hear him take a deep breath on the other end.

"View Violet as your best asset and your father as any other competitor trying to take what belongs to you," I continue—I know how Grayson works. "You've dealt with worse corporate takeover attempts and gotten through them. You'll win this too. Do exactly what Violet asks of you and let her do her job. You and your brothers inherited everything fair and square."

He grunts, which I've come to recognise as Grayson's way of begrudgingly agreeing. Grumpy arsehole.

"Do you need anything from my end?" I ask, checking my watch. 8:30 pm.

"No. I don't mean to drag you into this. It's just driving me insane. Dad's being a total prick, Cole has a very obvious hard-on for his secretary, Noah has decided he wants to join the NHL instead of the family business, and Violet, while irritating, is proving to be the most difficult woman I've ever had to resist."

"Ah. That explains why she's a pain in your arse. Are you telling me someone has finally caught the interest of Grayson Livingstone?" I ask, my tone mocking.

The Suite Secret

"Piss off," he shoots back, his voice light. "Speaking of women—how's everything going with Prestige Partners and the firecracker who clocked me in the eye with her button? What was her name again?" The sound of him snapping his fingers comes through the phone. "Ah, Gemma. How's it all going with her and Henry? Everything progressing as planned?"

"On schedule," I reply coolly, not mentioning that Gemma will be coming all over my tongue within the hour.

"Excellent. I knew Gray Hotel was in good hands with you at the helm," he says, and I hear a rustle of fabric. "What time is it there?"

"Half eight."

"I'll leave you to your night, I'm sure there's a bottle of aged whisky somewhere waiting to be poured. If you need anything, just give me a call. Otherwise, I'll be buried balls deep in legal paperwork."

"And your attorney, by the sounds of it," I say.

"Not if I can damn well help it," he says.

I laugh. "Good luck, mate."

* * *

I knock back the last of my whisky as the buzzer sounds, the amber liquid warming my throat. With a quick glance at the oven, I confirm what I already know.

Nine o'clock. Right on time. Good girl.

A satisfied smirk plays at my lips as I buzz her in.

I move around the kitchen unhurriedly, selecting two long-stemmed wine glasses from the cabinet. I swirl the decanter filled with pinot noir, which I left to breathe earlier, as footsteps sound from the hallway.

As I run a hand through my hair, she knocks twice on the door.

I smirk and anticipation coils in my gut.

Showtime.

Chapter Twenty-Eight

Gemma

The door swings open to reveal—holy shit—Max. And he looks *good*. Similar to last week, he's in a pair of grey joggers but this time wears a fitted white t-shirt that moulds perfectly to his washboard abs and muscular biceps. He isn't wearing shoes or socks.

"Hello, Gemma," his velvety voice purrs.

The scent of his cologne settles over me, making him even more alluring.

"Hi," I reply, my advanced education shining through with my complex response.

His wolfish glare threatens to set my panties aflame. He steps aside for me to enter. I've seen his apartment before, obviously, but the view will never get old. I cross through the living area to the wall of windows.

"I wouldn't leave this spot if this were my view. It's breathtaking," I say.

"It is," he says, his hungry eyes boring into mine. "Would you like a glass of wine?"

"Please," I respond.

The Suite Secret

I follow him to the kitchen where he carefully pours two healthy glasses of red. I accept the glass, clinking against his in a silent cheers before taking a sip.

"This is delicious. Thank you." I lick a drop from my lower lip.

He tracks the movement. "You're welcome."

I perch on a bar-stool, putting the island between us. He leans against the counter opposite, casually crossing one leg over the other. I watch the way his joggers hang low on his hips.

Seeing him like this—relaxed, at ease, a glass of wine in hand—is positively intoxicating.

"So, it's been a few weeks—how have you enjoyed being back in London?" I ask, forcing myself to make conversation. We'll be in each other's company at April's engagement dinner tomorrow night, after all.

Usually, I approach my dates with the simple agenda of sussing them out over a glass of wine, unzipping, getting off, and grabbing an Uber home. I *never* bring them back to my flat—that's my sacred space. But between work and our arrangement, Max and I see each other regularly now, and what can I say? I'm curious about the man behind the giant cock.

He lifts a brow, as if my question surprises him. "It's good to be back. Though I'll admit, seeing my family again hit me harder than anticipated. I feel like I'm missing out on time with them. Especially Anna."

His vulnerability catches me off guard.

"I get that," I say, nodding. "I know Anna has missed you. She's really happy you're back. Maybe you can visit more once the hotel is open."

The corner of his lips twitch. "Maybe." He shifts his stance, eyes studying me in a way that feels far too intimate. "How is the campaign going?"

"I'm looking into the private collections at the new Contemporary Art Gallery. I think I've found one with lots of beautiful paintings that would work perfectly with the hotel's aesthetic. The collection belongs to a young Lord Harrington."

"I've heard of him," he says.

I roll my eyes. "Of course you have. You rich people flock together. Is there some sort of secret society that us plebs don't know about where you all sit around in a circle, jerking each other off and comparing offshore accounts?"

He laughs, the sound rich and sexy. "Not that I'm aware of. I've heard about him through Grayson."

"Ah, the billionaire. That makes sense," I say, taking another sip.

"The Harringtons come from old money, so it doesn't surprise me that they have private collections. Most do."

"The gallery manager gave me his contact details," I say.

"Excellent. We can go see him together."

"With Henry. He mentioned he was going to talk to you about it soon," I add.

"No. Just us," he says, his voice dropping. His tone leaves no room for argument.

Okay, then.

He sets his wine down and steps around the kitchen island into my personal space, planting a palm on the counter next to me. "I must admit, I'm finding it very difficult to focus on art right now."

I wet my bottom lip, tipping my head back to watch him. "Really? Then what is it you're focusing on right now?"

"I think you know exactly what has my attention, Gemma."

His eyes dip to the hollow of my throat. Mine dip to his very obvious erection.

"Let me take your coat," he offers.

"Thank you," I say, standing to turn my back to his chest. I slowly shrug it off my shoulders, revealing my emerald lingerie underneath. A smile flits across my lips upon his low growl behind me.

"Christ, Gemma. If I'd known you were wearing that, I wouldn't have bothered with the wine."

"Good boys wait," I reply.

"I can assure you, I'm not a good boy." He tosses my coat over the back of the bar-stool.

His fingertips skate across my collarbone and down my arm in a lazy exploration, leaving goose bumps in their wake. The simple touch melts my insides. All my senses are heightened. Suddenly, he drops his hand and steps back.

"Turn around. Slowly," he instructs.

Watching Max's perfect composure crack at the sight of my body makes me feel invincible. His stare is ravenous, eating up every inch of me. I may be the one standing bare while he's still dressed, but I've never felt more in command.

Women will always hold all the power.

I turn around slowly, giving him a full 360-degree view of my body. When my gaze finally lands on his stormy eyes, the flimsy material between my legs dampens. This man looks like he's struggling to restrain his urgency for me.

"Look at you," he says, his voice a low rumble. "Tempting little thing."

"Who, me?" I ask, my voice innocent.

"You're a troublemaker," he says, stepping closer. "Do you know what happens to troublemakers?"

"I'm hoping you'll show me."

"Mmm ..." He hums in appreciation, tracing the delicate strap of my bra with his thumb and forefinger. His knuckles follow a path from my shoulder down to my breast, sending shivers across my skin. My nipple stiffens as he leans in, peppering soft kisses along my jawline. I close my eyes, my head falling back as a sound of contentment escapes my lips.

"Tell me," he murmurs against my skin, his fingers travelling down my stomach. "If I touch you, will I find you wet?"

"Yeah," I breathe. "Your doorman is just really hot. I can't help it. Sorry."

He laughs against my neck as his fingers toy with the elastic of my thong.

"Take this off," he whispers.

I oblige, carefully stepping out of the lacy thong and dropping it to the floor.

He continues dotting kisses along my throat, alternating between soft and gentle, then a scrape of teeth, as his hand dips lower. I hold my breath, my body tensing as his fingers finally run over my wet centre.

When he makes contact with my slit, the groan that escapes him is nothing short of wild.

"Fuck," he says, collecting my juices on his fingers. I watch with hooded eyes as he lifts his hand to suck my liquid off. His nostrils flare and my pussy throbs at the sight.

"All I've been able to think about since last week is how *good* you taste," he says.

I bite my bottom lip. He dips his hand back to my core, circling my needy clit before collecting more wetness. This time when he lifts his hand, it's my mouth he's offering a taste to. Silently, I lean forward and wrap my lips around his fingers. I begin circling my tongue, taking him deeper into the back of my throat.

I clench my thighs when his breath becomes laboured, his eyes darkening as he watches me.

When I finally release his fingers with a soft pop, his chest rises and falls rapidly.

A small bead of pre-cum wets the crotch of his joggers. I reach for his cock, but he shakes his head.

"Not yet," he says, staring down at me and gripping my jaw. "Understand?"

The Suite Secret

Even in my heels, he towers over me. I lift my brow, considering whether to defy him for a split second. I'll play along. For now.

"Yes."

"Good girl," he says, cradling my head and crashing his lips against mine. I moan as his tongue runs along the seam of my mouth, and I open for him. His touch is gentle, but his kiss is savage. He tastes like expensive wine and whisky. Every sweep of his tongue and press of fingers against my skin threatens to unravel me. His touch scorches me with need.

He reaches around me to unclasp my bra, and it falls to the floor. Weighing my heavy breasts in his palms, he begins to knead.

I place one leg between his thick thighs. He slightly bends his knee, an invitation I accept, rubbing my core against his leg. I fuck his thigh shamelessly. He grunts and groans as my arousal soaks the fabric of his joggers.

I circle my hips and grind, feeling the cotton rub against my delicate skin in the most delicious way. But it's not enough. I need more. His hand slides down to cup my arse, fingers digging into my flesh as he moves me faster over his leg, building up the friction. He breaks the kiss.

"Are you going to come on my leg, Gemma?" he asks, his voice gravelly and rough. His eyes are locked on mine, watching my face as pleasure builds.

"Yes," I gasp. His answering smile is wolfish as he increases the pressure, his strong thigh flexing beneath me.

"I'm going to watch you fall apart. And then I'm going to take you to my bedroom and make you come again. And again."

Fuck, if I wasn't about to explode from rubbing myself on him, the absolute certainty in his voice sends me over the edge. My head falls back as my release crests, my body shuddering against him as I ride out the wave.

When I finally catch my breath, he lifts me effortlessly, cradling me against his chest. I let out a surprised yelp as he carries me down the hallway to his bedroom, placing me gently onto the mattress.

He stands before me, his face painted with desire. I prop myself up on my elbows. When he removes his shirt, I take a moment to appreciate the view. His toned stomach tenses as he approaches the bed.

"Not bad, Browne," I say, wiggling my brows.

A smirk tips his lips, and he pulls his trousers down. The sharp V between his hip bones points to his hard, beefy cock, standing proud between his powerful legs. The man looks like he's been carved from marble, and he bloody well knows it.

He fists his length, stroking himself slowly as he watches me watching him. He swallows hard, his eyes never leaving mine.

I've seen men touch themselves countless times and it's never fazed me, but the way Max looks as he works himself over is an entirely new experience. It's pornographic.

"Come here," he says, and I scoot to the edge of the bed, spreading my legs slightly so he can see my glistening pussy.

"Do you want this?" he asks, glancing at his cock, his tone serious.

"Obviously," I reply.

"Then suck it."

My hand replaces his as I take him deep into my mouth. I continue to pump him; then, using my other hand, I fondle his balls.

"Gemma ..." He groans his approval as I tap his cock at the back of my throat. I relax my mouth and breathe through my nose like the champion I am.

His hands thread through my hair and he really lets me have it. He pistons his hips, fucking my mouth. I push myself to my limits, determined not to back down, even as I gag and my eyes water. Watching Max come undone sends a rush of adrenaline through me.

"Fuck, you're too good at that," he grunts.

"I know," I murmur around him.

His jaw tenses. "The only place I'm coming tonight is inside you."

Holy. Shit.

He gently pulls me off him and I wipe my mouth, unable to stop the smug smile that spreads across my face.

"On your back," he says.

I make a show of shimmying up the bed, spreading my legs for him once I'm in place.

The mattress dips beneath his weight as he joins me, dropping a soft kiss to the inside of my knee. Then the other. Softly. Slowly. He scatters kisses along my inner thighs, lavishing attention on my skin. He takes his time, building my need until I'm brimming with anticipation.

"You don't get to do what you just did and think I'm not going to return the favour," he murmurs against me. "I intend to worship you properly."

I suck in a breath at both his words and the first contact of his mouth on my centre. My hips rise, seeking more pressure. His strong hands grip my thighs, holding me still as he begins to feast. He starts off with long, firm languid licks from my entrance to my clit, stopping and circling my swollen nub.

Max knows what he's doing. Too well.

He groans against me, as if I'm the only thing that'll ever satisfy him again. I gasp, white-knuckling the sheets as he alternates between open-mouthed kisses and sharper, methodical flicks of his tongue that make my thighs quiver.

"Max," I moan, threading my fingers through his hair to hold him in place. I cling to him, certain that if I let go, I'll float away.

He slips a hand from my thigh to grasp my waist, anchoring me. His tongue flattens and runs over my clit before sucking, gently at first, then rougher.

My back arches as a strangled whimper rips from my throat.

The ceiling above me blurs as my eyes lose focus, stars dotting my vision.

"That's it, sweetheart," he murmurs against me. "I want to hear you."

Releasing my waist, he teases my entrance with two fingers, adding to the sensation. Slowly, he sinks inside me until he's knuckle deep, his hand working in tandem with his tongue—licking, nipping, sucking, and rubbing.

I feel pressure building, like a coil tightening, signalling I'm getting close.

"Ah. Yes. More," I moan.

My legs tremble uncontrollably and my breath saws in and out of me as I finally give up the fight.

His fingers stretch me while he teases my clit. His stubble rubs against me as he works, and I silently pray that he leaves a mark.

A gush of wetness spills out of my pussy, slicking his hand as I clench around his thick fingers, my body shuddering through the aftershocks.

Max doesn't pull away. If anything, he works me through it, continuing his ministrations. His fingers stroke though my folds, drive into me and curl deep, rubbing my G-spot. Finally, he lifts his head. His thumb replaces his tongue. The intensity in his eyes is pure, filthy pride as watches me unspool, his gaze latched on mine like he never wants to forget the way I look when I fall apart for him.

"That's it," he says, his voice low and hoarse. "Look at you. So beautiful when you come."

He leans in, pressing a kiss just below my navel while his

fingers still move inside me, pumping over and over. He licks a long line up my stomach.

"You're dripping for me, Gem. Can feel you pulsing around my fingers. Can't wait to feel you do that on my cock."

His words spur me on, prolonging the euphoric sensation. Part of me wants to hold back and not give him the satisfaction of making me orgasm so quickly. But another part—namely, my vagina—couldn't stop if my life depended on it. Somewhere in the back of my mind, I register that I'm shouting his name over and over, like he's my salvation.

My body finally stills. My legs are jelly, a sheen of sweat coating both of us.

What the hell was that? Last time was incredible, but this ... this was another level.

His hand slides out of me, and he watches me closely as he sucks his glistening fingers clean.

"That's one," he says. "I'm not finished with you yet."

Thank. Fuck.

Usually this is the part where I gather my belongings and my pride, make a swift exit, and pull some tarot cards once I'm home.

Leave before they want cuddles, cleanse myself of their energy, move on to the next.

But tonight is new. The raw desire in his eyes is gravitational. Against every morsel of my being, I find myself wanting him, *needing* him again.

Regardless of how hesitant I was to agree to our little arrangement, I'm forced to admit that Max Browne isn't someone I can get out of my system with a few sexual encounters.

And—shit—it's starting to feel like Anna might not be the only thing I need to worry about.

It doesn't feel like Max is simply spreading my legs anymore. Instead, he's thawing out the part of me that's been frozen for a long time. The part of me I locked up tight, sealed off by years of keeping men at arm's length.

I might have set the condition that Max doesn't fall in love with me—but I didn't say anything about what happens if *I* feel something for him.

And I definitely didn't account for the idea that this arrangement could screw *me* over.

Max kisses his way up my body, dragging that perfect mouth along my stomach, over my breasts, until he's hovering above me. He rubs his cock through my sensitive folds as his forearms cage my head. I rock my hips, his cock sliding through the mess between my legs like it was made to fit there. He groans, moving in sync with me. I watch the way his abs tense and flex. My eyes dip lower to where his cock lies thick and heavy, coated with my arousal.

"Are you good?" He breathes, brushing a knuckle over my jaw.

"Great," I whimper.

His lips curl in a satisfied smirk.

"Just so you know, we aren't cuddling," I say, my voice barely above a whisper.

He laughs, a deep rumble. "We haven't even started yet."

My stomach flips and swells. Before he can say another word, I push him onto his back, swinging my leg over his hips in one fluid motion. His eyes darken to midnight as I settle atop his cock, his hard length pressed against me. I plant my palms on his muscular chest, feeling his heartbeat thundering beneath my hands as I continue to grind against him.

"My turn?" I ask, my voice husky.

He reaches around to squeeze my arse, making me gasp. "I want you so badly."

"Condoms?" My body screams to feel him inside me.

He strokes his hands up and down my thighs. "I will if

you want me to. But I want you to know—I'm clean. I get tested every month."

"That's very responsible of you," I say. "But unfortunately, I'm not on birth control."

His lips curve into something dangerously smug. "I've had a vasectomy."

My brain short-circuits.

Oh. My. God.

His beautiful words suck the air out of my lungs. I'm hit with such an enormous wave of happiness, I think I might cry. Those words aren't just music to my ears; they're the whole damn symphony.

"That might be the sexiest sentence ever spoken," I say.

His gaze is as penetrating as it is torturous. His next command severs the thin tether I was clinging on to.

"Ride me."

Chapter Twenty-Nine

Max

I help guide her until she's hovering just above my cock, the angry head notched perfectly against her entrance. I'm so desperate to feel her—all of her—that I'm fighting the fiery urge to slam her down onto me and fuck her senseless.

We groan in unison as she finally starts to sink, inch by inch, her tight heat swallowing me whole.

"Fuck, Gemma," I grind out. "You were *made* for me."

Her palms flatten against my chest, then she hooks her toes under my shins for leverage and begins to move. She starts with slow, deliberate circles. Every downward grind has me sinking deeper, stretching her.

I can't wait to come inside her, claim her like she's *my* property.

She moves as if she knows exactly what she's doing to me. And I bet she bloody does. Those needy little cries, the way her perfect tits bounce each time she sinks down onto me, the way her soft belly moves with her, the way her head tips back, chanting my name as if I'm her very own sacred vow.

"Jesus Christ," I mutter, my hands gripping her hips.

She smirks, her cheeks stained the most glorious pink.

Her hands slide further up my chest to land on my shoulders as she picks up her pace.

"You feel so, so good," she moans, her eyes hooded.

I can feel every ridge, every curve, every inch of her perfect little pussy as it grips me like a vice.

Grasping her hips, I pound into her, meeting her stroke for stroke. The sound of skin slapping together fills the large room, echoing off the walls as I thrust into her.

"Ah! Max! I think you're touching my cervix."

"I am, baby, I can feel you," I grit out.

"Do you like watching me ride you?" she asks, breathless.

"I would frame this moment if I could," I say. "You're so gorgeous like this."

I don't just like it. I'm obsessed. The image of her riding me has scored itself into my memory. Now I've had her, I know I'll never get enough.

She feels as perfect as I imagined. All those nights I spent jerking myself off to the image of her, doing exactly this, taking her pleasure from me. Falling apart for *me*.

I keep my pace, releasing a hand to reach for her perfect breast. She gasps as I knead and squeeze, pinching and pulling her taut, rosy nipple.

"I love your cock," she breathes.

"Show me," I say raggedly. "Show me how much you love coming all over my cock."

I swap out her nipple for her ripe clit, sucking my thumb and pressing it against her hot little bud. She's absolutely saturated.

"I don't need any lube, do I? You're soaked, you greedy girl." I rub her while she grinds herself all over me. Her fingernails dig into my skin, sure to leave a mark, but I don't care. I want them all.

"Ah!" she cries, tipping her head back. My eyes trace the delicate curve of her swan-like neck, imagining pressing my hand there to feel her pulse flutter. Gripping until she sees stars before releasing the pressure for her to come for me.

"You make me so wet," she says, her voice coming out in breathy moans.

She lifts herself up, just enough for the tip of my cock to almost fall out, before dropping back down with a wet slap.

"Yeah. Just like that," I hiss, my hands burrowing into her soft flesh as she continues building her rhythm. Her tits sway and her breath catches as her movements slow from exertion, but she doesn't let up. I can tell that the fire in my eyes sparks something inside her, spurring her on. The sounds we're making are obscene. Debauched. I'm completely at her mercy.

She releases my shoulders, scratching a line down my stomach before cupping her breasts, pinching herself. She breathes and pants as she tugs and rubs her tits, pressing them together, her eyes closed in ecstasy as she bounces up and down.

I can't take it anymore. I need to pound into that sweet little pussy and fill her with my cum.

I sit up in a rush so we're chest to chest and catch her whimper in my mouth. One hand grips the nape of her neck, the other slips to her lower back, pulling her to me as I drive up hard.

"Max," she pants.

"I'm going to fuck you so deep you'll still feel me tomorrow," I growl, my forehead pressed to hers.

"I'm gonna come!" she shouts, her body trembling. She clings to me as her pussy throbs around my dick, squeezing and milking me like she needs it as much as I do.

"Yeah?" I whisper, biting her bottom lip. "You gonna come all over my cock?"

She nods frantically as I hammer into her.

"I'm coming," she whispers. Her mouth parts in a silent cry as she jacks me off with her throbbing pussy.

My jaw tightens as pressure builds at the base of my spine, and I know I'm about to come with her. My hips falter as every muscle inside me tightens.

"Gemma," I grunt into her neck. "I'm going to come like this."

"Give it to me," she begs. "Don't hold back. I want every drop."

Christ. That mouth of hers is as foul as mine.

Her eyes are fierce and penetrating as she focuses on me, like a plea. She almost looks surprised as I hold her close while she surrenders to the storm inside her.

Unable to hold back any longer, I let go. Thick spurts of cum paint her insides as she moans, grinding and shuddering as she milks me.

I claim her mouth with mine, tongues tangling as I fuck her through it. We kiss and crash and come untethered together, like waves breaking against the shore.

It feels so natural, so human, so *right*.

"I've got you, baby," I assure her, my voice low.

The air shifts, turning thick. The vulnerability of what we just did catches me off guard. It's tender and fragile. Nothing has ever been more perfect than this woman coming apart in my arms. With me inside her.

Seeing her like this ... it's the most honest she's been with me.

"So," she says. "That was ..."

"Intense," I finish for her.

"I was going to say *adequate*, but whatever works."

I laugh. "Is lying a perpetual thing with you? Should I be concerned?"

"Someone needs to stop your head from disappearing right up your own bum. Soon you'll have more ego than sense."

I laugh, dropping a kiss on the tip of her nose. Just as quickly as the tenderness settles over us, I feel her adjust in my lap. She pulls back ever so slightly, turning her head away.

"This doesn't change anything," she murmurs. Her voice carries an undercurrent of doubt, and I'm right there with her.

I crook a smile. "Are you falling for me, Clarke?"

She scoffs. "Yeah, right. The only thing falling around here are my standards."

I hold my hand over my heart. "Really? You're going to say that after everything we've shared? You wound me."

"You'll get over it," she replies, her lips curling.

She shifts to get off me.

I reach for her wrist, feeling her delicate pulse beneath my thumb.

"Can I offer you a glass of water? More wine?"

For purely selfish reasons, I don't want her to leave. Not like last time. Something about her walking out that door feels wrong tonight. I never ask women to stay after we fuck. But knowing I'll see her in the office on Monday—and at April's engagement dinner tomorrow—makes me feel like we could benefit by forming a friendship. She's my sister's best friend. I know this is a superficial arrangement, but I don't want her to feel like I'm using her, like I don't value her or what she's given me.

She exhales. "Sure. Wine would be nice. Thanks."

I follow her into the hallway, naked, watching as she collects her trench, wrapping it around herself.

"I have clothes," I say, rounding the island and twisting open a new wine bottle. "What do you need? Joggers? A jumper?"

She cocks a brow. "You want me to wear your clothes?"

I shrug. "They'd look good on you."

"I have clothes," she says.

"Gemma, you came here wearing the equivalent of dental floss."

"You didn't seem to mind my *dental floss* an hour ago."

"Believe me, I *love* your dental floss. But throw something comfortable on, something warm. I promise, you can put your floss back on later."

She rolls her eyes dramatically. "Fine. But not because I want to. I'm only accepting your offer because I don't feel like having lace wedged up my crack right now."

"Are you always so alluring?" I ask, pouring another two glasses of wine.

She flashes a smile and winks. "Only for you."

I hand her the wine and lead her to my bedroom, pulling open a drawer. "Take your pick."

She rummages through my jumpers, eventually selecting a well-worn NYU jumper. "NYU? How predictably elite of you."

"I got restless and wanted to get out of London," I say, my voice casual.

I hold her wine and watch her sultry hips sway as she disappears into the bathroom. "Really? Why? London isn't that bad," she calls from behind the closed door.

I lean, one hand braced against the top of the doorframe. "Our upbringing, I suppose. I got so used to moving from city to city for Dad's work when I was a kid, well before Anna came along. It felt constricting staying in one place for so long. I got itchy feet."

I hear the toilet flush followed by the pitter-patter of footsteps against tiles, then she swings the door open, freezing.

"Oh, for God's sake, Max. Yes, you've got a body that belongs on the cover of *Men's Health* and a dick that deserves its own Instagram, but could you please put some trousers on?"

I'm rooted on the spot. Her half compliment goes way over my head, because there's something about the way she looks in my clothes that sets off an inherent need to claim her all over again.

It's primal.

The long sleeves fall past her dainty fingertips, the hem reaching just above her knees. Her hair is mussed, make-up slightly smudged, and she smells like sex.

She looks more breathtaking now than when she arrived in that emerald number.

"What?" she asks, suddenly self-conscious as I regard her.

"Nothing," I say, stepping back to put some much-needed distance between us. I finally reach for my joggers, pulling them on. "Better? Or should I find a turtleneck too?"

"Hilarious." She snatches her wine glass and makes her way back out to the sofa. "So." She settles into the cushions, crossing her legs. She looks small. Fragile. The total opposite of who she presents outside the comfort of an apartment.

I throw an arm over the back, cradling the wine glass on my knee. I don't say anything. I don't want to. I'm curious to see what she wants to talk about, what version of Gemma emerges when she's stripped bare. I can tell this isn't her usual routine—staying after sex. Maybe if I let her settle in without any pressure on conversation, she'll open up more. Finally let her guard down to show me something real.

"What was it like, moving around so much for your father's work?" she asks, taking a sip.

I consider my response carefully. "It had its moments. The constant change became normal. New cities, new languages, new homes. That carried excitement." I lean forward. "There's a freedom to it. If you're experiencing new places, nothing is too precious to leave behind. It's the people you're surrounded by that matter." I take a drink. "But my early schooling years were ... difficult. Unlike Anna, who had those formative earlier years in London, I was enrolled in new schools, new curriculums, every year. My parents created stability wherever they could, but friendships ..."

I pause, surprised at how willing I am to share this part of my life with her. "Those were always temporary. I learned not to invest too deeply because I knew I'd be leaving."

Her brows crease slightly. "I'm sorry. That must've been difficult. You were just a kid. Friendships are everything."

"I know it was a privileged upbringing—I saw more of the world before ten than most see in a lifetime. But I've come to learn that privilege doesn't necessarily equate to connection." I meet her eyes. "Children need stability. Constancy." I shrug. "I had adventure instead."

"So why did you move to New York?"

I point to my jumper she's wearing with my glass. "I did my MBA at NYU, which is where I met Grayson." I smile. "He's my best mate. His life was always going to be in New York ..." I pause briefly before continuing. "I met Casey. She was from London. It felt like fate, if there is such a thing. I guess we found each other, fell in love, and she always planned on returning to London. So, I decided to follow her and plant roots ... try something more permanent."

She nods. "You got married."

My jaw ticks. Her tone has a finality to it. I hate talking about Casey. Not because I'm ashamed, and not because I have regrets—but because the failure sits with me still. Like a reminder of my inability to sustain the one thing I'd tried to make permanent.

"I did." The wine tastes bitter on my tongue. "It didn't work."

"I'm sorry. I shouldn't have brought it up. We don't have to talk about it if you don't want to," she says.

Her face is sincere. I don't usually reveal too much of myself to people. Perhaps it's a defence mechanism ingrained from my childhood. I've only ever allowed myself to open up to a handful of people in my life—my family, Grayson, Noah ... and Casey. But something about Gemma, maybe that she expects nothing from me beyond our arrangement, makes talking to her much easier than I'd predicted.

"Don't be sorry," I say, keeping my voice steady. "It's part of my life. Regardless of how it turned out, it played a part in shaping who I am today, and I like where I am."

She frowns slightly. I can't decide whether it's out of sympathy, curiosity, or something else entirely.

"To answer your question," I continue, shifting back to a safer conversation. "I moved to New York because Grayson needed help when he took over his grandparents' company with his brothers. After everything with Casey ended, leaving London behind was ... convenient. Staying here wasn't good for either of us."

She takes another sip, and I can tell she's resisting the urge to press me for more details, but she doesn't. Which I appreciate.

For a second, I wonder if she can relate to the appeal of leaving something behind and reinventing yourself, your life.

"I was excited for a fresh start in New York with my best mate," I finish.

"Do you miss it? London?"

I think of my parents. I think of Anna and what she's going through with Mason. I think of Noah and how quickly his kids are growing up.

"Yeah ... I do," I admit. That's the first time I've voiced it out loud since being back.

I track the movement of her delicate throat as she swallows.

"And what about Nicole?" she presses.

"There really isn't anything to tell. We were young, it was short-lived. We weren't right for each other. I hope she can see that now we're older. It's a shame her reaction ruined things with Anna, but that was her choice."

She seems to accept that answer, nodding.

"And what about you? What's your story?" I ask.

She considers me over the lip of her wine glass. "Ha. Believe me. It's not very interesting."

"I doubt that," I counter. "Someone like you doesn't develop that sharp edge without a reason."

She raises an eyebrow. "Someone like me?"

"Brilliant. Ambitious. Independent." As I rattle off all her amazing qualities, I realise she meets the criteria I promised myself I'd look for if I were ever to date again. I swore to myself, the next woman I would commit to would have to have these qualities ... and Gemma does.

She yawns. "You forgot to mention ridiculously good-looking."

I smile. "I was getting to that."

"Sure you were," she says, stretching. My jumper rides up slightly, revealing the smooth, creamy skin of her thighs.

"You're deflecting," I say.

Her jaw tenses before she releases a heavy breath. "Fine. I suppose it's only fair since you shared." She places her near-empty glass on the side table, hugging both legs to her chest and resting her chin on her knees. "His name was Todd."

I frown, becoming irrationally jealous of a total stranger. "What happened?"

"The usual. We fell madly in love as teenagers, dated through uni, moved in together, had the rest of our lives planned." She pauses, sucking her lower lip in while she contemplates her next words. I don't rush her; instead, I study the curve of her button nose, the perfect arch of her eyebrows, the full lines of her lips.

"I just couldn't do it anymore," she says finally, her voice quieter than usual.

"Couldn't do what?" I ask, my tone soft.

"The sex."

Not what I was expecting. "It wasn't good?"

She shakes her head. "It was always the same. Monotonous. Like we were just going through the motions till it was over. We lost our spark. I never got excited to see him. I never felt the urge to tear off his clothes ... when our friends started getting engaged and married, I realised I couldn't do the boring marriage with the boring sex." She shrugs. "It was never going to be my life."

I get it. Sex plays a huge part in a romantic relationship. Sometimes, in life's emptiest moments, passion is the only thing we have left to get us through.

"So, you left," I finish for her.

She nods, her fingers tracing patterns on her knee. "So, I left."

"And now?"

She looks at me, her gaze unwavering. "I don't do relationships. I can't endure years of boring sex again."

"I don't think being in a relationship means you'll exclusively have boring sex," I say, surprised by my own words. For some reason, the thought that this young, beautiful woman has closed herself off to love doesn't sit well with me. "Some couples manage a happy relationship with great sex."

"I don't see you jumping at the opportunity to fall in love."

"Fair point," I concede, smirking. "No, I'm not jumping at the opportunity to fall in love."

"But you fuck," she says bluntly.

I meet her eyes. "Yes, Gemma. I fuck."

The corner of her mouth quirks up. "Then we understand each other perfectly."

I laugh, shaking my head. We lapse into a comfortable silence as I finish off my wine. Gemma stifles another yawn, trying to hide it behind her hand.

"Tired?" I ask.

"No," she says too quickly, yawning again.

"Liar."

She closes her eyes. "I'm just resting my eyes."

"Of course," I say, watching as she settles deeper into the sofa.

When her breathing deepens and her body relaxes, I stand. For a moment, I debate waking her, calling her a cab or an Uber, but I don't know where she lives. And I can't message Anna without giving us away. The Max Browne of mere weeks ago wouldn't have hesitated. But something stops me as I take in the sight of her.

Instead, I gather her in my arms, surprised by how much I love the scent of her shampoo and how perfectly she fits against my chest. She stirs slightly, murmuring something unintelligible, and I freeze, holding my breath. The last thing I want is for her to wake and accuse me of overstepping. I realise we didn't agree on overnight stays, but it's nearly midnight and the thought of putting her in a cab, half asleep and vulnerable, doesn't sit right. This isn't for my own benefit; it's for hers. At least here, I know she's safe.

When she settles again, I continue to my bedroom and lay her down gently on the bed, pulling the duvet over her.

Her hair fans across my pillow and her long lashes kiss the top of her cheekbones. She looks so unguarded.

I'm half-tempted to slip in beside her. But having already pushed her further than she's comfortable with this evening, I grab a thick blanket from the end of the bed and make my way back to the sofa.

There's a strange comfort in knowing she's here, sleeping in my bed, even if I'm not beside her.

And it's when I realise: I think I care for Gemma more than I'm willing to admit.

Chapter Thirty

Gemma

My heart thuds erratically against my ribcage as panic sets in. I attempt to peel my eyes open, aware that it's morning, but I can't. I can't see anything.

I reach up and rub my eyes. A crumbly feeling against my fingers confirms one of my worst fears—my eyes are sealed shut with a thick layer of crusty gunk.

"Oh my God!" I shout, fully awake now. "I fell asleep! No!"

I buck and thrash around in a mad panic, the sheets rustling around me. That's when I inhale a distinct scent that stops me cold.

Max.

It smells like Max.

Oh shit. I'm in Max's bed. Because I fell asleep. With my bloody daily contact lenses in.

"I'm blind!" I cry. My stomach swirls and swells with anxiety. "I can't see anything. Shit!"

"What's wrong?" His alarmed, gravelly voice comes from somewhere nearby. "Gemma? What's wrong?"

"My contacts," I moan, rubbing frantically at my eyes. "I fell asleep wearing my contacts. I can't open my eyes!"

The Suite Secret

Firm fingers wrap around my wrists. "Stop rubbing," he says, voice calm, gently pulling my hands away from my face. "You'll make it worse."

"This is why I never stay over. It's why I put the bloody contacts in! I wasn't meant to stay here!"

"Just hold still," Max instructs, his voice firm. I feel the bed dip and his weight shifts. He must be standing. Footsteps retreat from the bed and my heart plummets. "No, no, please don't leave me! Where the hell are you going?"

He laughs. The sick bastard. "Don't go anywhere. I'll be right back."

"Not like I can go very far like this, can I?" I say.

I hear the twist of a tap and the sound of water from his en suite. A moment later, he returns.

"I'm going to help you. Just stay calm," he says.

"I am being bloody calm!" I hiss.

Something warm and damp touches my eyelid—a washcloth. He gently wipes away the crusty buildup with tender movements. I cling to his wrist like a monkey to a tree as I attempt to settle my nerves. I inhale deeply and count to four before exhaling to the same count. A trick my therapist taught me that I always thought was bullshit until this very moment. He moves from one eye to the other, his touch careful and reassuring.

"Can you open them now?" he asks.

I attempt to blink, my eyelids unsticking painfully. Rich sunshine filters through. "Sort of," I croak, squinting through hazy, irritated eyes. Max's face gradually swims into handsome focus above me, his expression painted with genuine concern.

"This is karma for Grayson's eye, isn't it?" I ask.

He chuckles. "No, I'm sure it's not."

His brows are furrowed, and his hair is adorably dishevelled. He's wearing those sexy grey joggers, but he's lost the t-shirt from last night. Even with my shitty eyesight, I can make out his perfectly cut muscles.

Of course he looks perfect first thing in the morning. No puffy eyes, no bad breath, no drool stains.

He leans in, placing a gentle kiss under one eye, then the other. "Better?" he asks, his tone gentle.

His softness catches me unaware.

"Uh ... Somewhat. They sting. I need to get these contacts out before they permanently fuse to my corneas."

He stands, offering me his hand, which I hesitantly accept. The moment I try to stand, my foot catches in the tangled sheet dangling off the edge of the bed. I lurch forward, blindly grabbing for anything as I go down. My hands instinctively find the waistband of his joggers and I cling on for dear life, dragging them down to his ankles as I fall.

I land on my knees with a loud thud, coming face-to-face with Max's most impressive asset.

"Jesus!" I shout, falling back on my arse.

"Are you okay?" Max asks, his voice laced with concern.

"I can't see shit!"

He bends to help me up at the same time I ungracefully push myself off the floor, his exposed manhood slapping me across the cheek.

We both freeze.

"Did you just—did your penis just slap me in the face?" I ask, horrified.

"I think technically you pulled my pants down and positioned yourself there," he says, hauling his joggers back into place.

"Why is it hard?!"

"It's the morning," he says, like it's obvious.

"Please just help me up."

Hooking his hands under my armpits, he pulls me to stand and walks me through to his bathroom, guiding me to the basin. I lather with soap and rinse before attempting the contact lens extraction. I pull down my lower eyelid and try to fish out the dried-up lens.

My eyes feel like they've been scrubbed raw. I squint against the bathroom lights. Tears well and I blink rapidly to keep them at bay. Each flutter of my eyelid feels like fire.

"Here, let me help you," he offers, stepping forward.

"No, please don't. It will only make me more anxious," I say.

He watches helplessly as I poke and prod. "Ah, ouch!" I wince, dropping my hands with frustration. "It hurts. I don't think I can get them," I say, wringing my hands in front of me. "You see, *this* is why I don't do exclusive. It's a sign."

"It's not a sign. You're being dramatic."

I pivot to face him, trying my best to pin him with my most intimidating look. "Tell me I'm being dramatic one more time and, I swear to God, I'll tittie-twist your nipples so hard, they'll pop off."

"If you wanted to touch my nipples, sweetheart, all you had to do was ask," he deadpans.

Sweetheart. My stomach somersaults at the endearment and rasp in his voice.

I swivel back to the sink for another attempt, carefully extracting my contacts on the second try. I toss the little plastic discs on the bathroom counter and rub my eyes in a bid to alleviate the sting.

"Ugh," I groan. "They hurt."

"Hey," he says, his hands resting on my shoulders. "Don't panic. It's okay. I can take you to an optometrist."

"Max, I don't know if you realise," I say, gesturing to myself. "But the only clothes I have with me are my *dental floss* lingerie, or your jumper. Not exactly appropriate."

"Let's try getting you home for clothes and your glasses," he offers.

I sigh. "Fine."

***

My flat is my sanctuary, filled with my favourite things—tarot cards, crystals, dead indoor plants I keep meaning to replace, smutty books, and, of course, my colourful collection of dildos.

Max Browne being in my flat is a *big* deal.

He stands in my living room, hands in his pockets, head tilted while he reads through my book titles.

"*Front Loader?*" he says.

"It's about a sentient washing machine," I say.

He looks at me as if the idea is preposterous, a crease forming between his eyebrows.

"How does that work?" he asks, puzzled.

"Easy. The drawer where you load the washing liquid turns into a dick."

His forehead wrinkles in confusion before he begins flipping through the pages.

While he busies himself with my books, I change. I snatch my glasses off the bedside table and almost cry from relief when I put them on. My eyes are still sore and a little fuzzy, but at least I don't have to worry about falling face-first into anyone's crotch for the time being.

I pull on the nearest outfit draped over the armchair—the chair that became my unofficial clothes-horse as soon as I moved in—then turn to the full-length mirror hanging on the back of my door.

My eyes widen in horror as I take in my appearance. My hair looks like it could host a family of birds, my complexion resembles a patchwork blanket with half-rubbed-off make-up clinging to dry areas of skin, and my eyes are red and puffy.

David Attenborough could document this. I look like a newly discovered species.

If Max declares he never wants to sleep with me again, I'd understand.

Deciding I don't have time to fuss about my presentation, I quickly toss my hair into a topknot. I brush my teeth and, erasing evidence of last night, gently run a washcloth over my skin, taking extra care around my eyes, which protest at even the lightest touch.

Max is sat on my sofa reading—oh God—*Fifty Shades of Gravy*, a smutty book about a woman and her Sunday roast.

This is why I hate men in my flat. They poke around when I'd rather them just poke me and be done with it.

"I must admit, this has me intrigued," he says as I approach, not lifting his gaze from the book. His lips quirk up. "Particularly chapter three where she uses the basting brush."

"Wait until you get to the part where he uses the thermometer. That'll really blow your mind," I say, slinging my handbag over my shoulder. "You ready?"

Ignoring me, he points to a row of crystals lined up beneath my windowsill.

"I must admit, I didn't take you for the spiritual type. What are they for?"

My gaze is immediately drawn to the amethyst crystal, and I cringe internally at the memory of depositing it up Anna's yoga instructor's butt.

"I use them to keep all the men out," I say, stone-faced.

He smirks, dropping the book to the coffee table and walking toward me. My heart beats in Morse code with each step.

"Your place is cosy. It suits you," he says.

I scan the room, and of course Max sticks out like a sore, ridiculously well-groomed thumb against my clutter. He looks so out of place here. His penthouse is all glass and stainless steel. My flat? It's tiny, colourful, and dotted with mismatched knick-knacks I'm certain he quietly loathes.

"What you mean is it's small, the view's shit, and it lacks a stone countertop," I say. "We can't all have penthouse views and German appliances."

"That's not at all what I meant," he says, perplexed.

"You were just being polite," I say.

Reaching up, he brushes a loose hair behind my ear, trailing his thumb across my cheekbone and tipping my head back slightly.

"I'm not bullshitting you. I like it. This place has personality. It feels lived in." He shrugs. "It feels like a home."

I search his face for signs he's taking the piss, finding none.

The morning light illuminates his handsome features, the light catching the hazel flecks dotted across his crystal blue irises.

The image of him as we came together flashes through my mind without permission—his strong jaw clenched, his eyes half-lidded.

Up close, and now with my glasses on, I can see the shadow of his stubble and the slight creasing around his eyes as he regards me with an intensity I'm beginning to know well. His touch is tender and anything but platonic.

"How are your eyes feeling?" he asks, worried.

"Sore," I say, my voice low.

My body thrums with the same adrenaline that had me climbing him like a tree last night. For a moment, I think he might kiss me.

"We should go," I whisper.

He drops his hand as if my skin scalds and steps back, clearing his throat.

"Good idea." He gestures to the front door. "After you."

As I lock up behind us and we head to the optometrist, I think about tonight and how on earth I'm going to explain my irritated, bloodshot eyes to Anna.

Chapter Thirty-One

Gemma

The redness and irritation have somewhat subsided by the time I'm getting ready for April and James's engagement dinner.

Fortunately, after a few scans, the optometrist determined there wasn't any damage to my corneas and sent me home with medicated eye drops and strict instructions to avoid contact lenses for a week. Apparently, the crusty gunk around my eyes was an increase of mucus due to the contacts as a protective response to the irritation. Hot. Nothing says *sexy* quite like excessive corneal discharge and a penis face-slapping the night after a decent shag.

I'm sure Max was very aroused.

To his credit, he stayed with me throughout the entire appointment, helping me fill out paperwork and asking questions when necessary. He even insisted on taking the same Uber home as me, stopping by my flat first to ensure I got home safely. He might be a cocky prick, but he's a gentleman when he wants to be.

And, oddly enough, I enjoyed his company. Not just the naked, sweaty parts of his company that I already knew were worth my time, but the fully clothed, conversational bits as well.

The whole way to the appointment he kept chatting, asking about my studies and first job in marketing. I knew it was a distraction, and it worked. His barrage drew me out of my discomfort almost completely, so much so, I found myself laughing with him.

His overconfident swagger and wicked hands, I can deal with. Sex, I can compartmentalise and file away as nothingness. But his kindness and attentiveness? I don't quite know what to make of it.

I turn off the curling iron and ruffle my hair to bring volume to the roots before swiping crimson across my lips.

Stepping back, I assess myself in the mirror. Thankfully, the glasses and bold lip draw attention away from the faint redness lingering in my eyes.

I've paired black pumps with a soft, high-waisted skirt that finishes just above my knees and a cropped halter neck, which leaves my back bare.

This is as good as it'll get.

Now, I just need to avoid direct eye contact with Max.

* * *

"Jesus Christ, did someone fuck your eye sockets?" Will bellows as April pops the cork on a champagne bottle.

"Ever the gentleman, Will. It's a pleasure to be in your company again," I say, my expression stoic as I take a seat at the kitchen bench.

Will is the lead guitarist in Atlas Veil, and has been close friends with James for years. Unfortunately, he has the IQ of a goldfish and hasn't stopped hitting on me since we met.

"You still look hot," he says.

"It's never going to happen." I fix him with a stern look.

He shrugs. "Worth a try."

"Will!" April admonishes.

The Suite Secret

James casually reaches over and claps Will over the back of his head.

"Oi, what was that for?" Will asks James.

"You're a dickhead," James deadpans.

Tom, the lead singer in Atlas Veil and longtime friend of James, snickers throughout the entire exchange. Will and Tom are trouble when they're together.

I've been here precisely seven minutes, and in that time, Basil—April's cat—has taken a shit on the utility room floor, Tom's spilt his drink all over the good rug, and Lucas has stormed outside in a huff over something James said.

Caroline, James's mum, sweeps into the kitchen to attempt damage control, shooing April away from the charcuterie board, taking the champagne bottle from her and seamlessly assuming hosting duties.

"Will, what have I told you about internal thoughts?" Caroline asks, pouring me a bubbly.

Will's sheepish gaze drops to the floor like a toddler in trouble. "That they don't always need to be voiced."

"Very good," she says with a patient smile. "Now you can have a beer."

"Yes!" He pumps his arm in excitement. He and Tom grab a couple of beers and head out to the courtyard.

My eyes scan the room, noticing we're a band member short. "Where's Oliver?"

Oliver is James's closest friend and the drummer for Atlas Veil. Unlike Will and Tom, who share approximately one functioning brain cell between them, Oliver is genuinely great company. He's the kind of man who remembers your birthday and doesn't ask inappropriate questions about your sex life within thirty seconds of saying hello. Not that I never do that—I do—but I have my limits for *who* those questions extend to, i.e., April and Anna. Oh, and sometimes Henry.

"Speak of the devil," James says, popping a piece of salami into his mouth.

Our heads swivel as Oliver joins us in the kitchen with a gleeful smile.

"Team," he says, nodding to us in greeting. We chorus our hellos as he pulls April in for a hug, congratulating the soon-to-be-wedded couple.

James snags a second piece of salami, throws me a cheeky wink, and grabs two beers—one for himself and one for Oliver—before heading out to join the testosterone convention in the garden. Caroline and Peter, James's father, follow them.

"So," April says, bumping me with her hip the moment they're out of earshot. "What *did* happen to your eyes?"

I do a quick once-over like a detective to ensure Anna and Max haven't quietly arrived.

"I left my contacts in overnight," I confess in a hushed tone.

This requires no further explanation. Both Anna and April know my foolproof escape plan—that I strategically wear my daily wear contact lenses to hookups specifically to avoid sleepovers.

Her eyes widen comically.

"You slept at Max's?" she whisper-shouts.

"It was an accident," I insist. "I fell asleep. It wasn't intentional."

"Gemma." She gapes at me, stunned. "This is a big deal."

"It is not a big deal," I say, waving her off.

James sneaks in, sauntering by at the worst moment, grabbing yet another beer from the fridge. How many are these guys putting away? We haven't started eating yet.

"What's not a big deal?" James asks.

"Gemma stayed at a guy's house last night," April blurts.

I release a tiresome exhale. I'm really pleased she hasn't disclosed my and Max's little arrangement to James.

Then again, I'm not surprised. She's one of the most loyal people I know, but my pulse races as if I'm standing under a spotlight.

"Gemma," James echoes, equally stunned. "That is a big deal."

"It is *not* a big deal," I hiss through gritted teeth.

"What's not a big deal?" Anna's voice cuts through our little huddle, causing all three of us to jump in surprise.

April freezes and glares at me. She doesn't deal well under pressure and can't think on the spot to save her life. She's too innocent—too pure. Her eyes scream *What do we do?* while mine plead *Act normal, for the love of God.*

The three of us turn to see Anna, Mason, and Max stroll in together.

My mouth instantly dries. Anna looks beautiful—she always does—but *Max*. Devastatingly handsome.

He's wearing a crisp white button-down with the sleeves rolled to his elbows, revealing the perfect forearms that had me pinned to his mattress last night. Dark tailored slacks fit him perfectly, and his loafers probably cost more than my entire monthly salary.

The bastard looks like he just stepped off a runway while I look like I have a bad case of pink eye.

He casually slips his hands into his trouser pockets, and his eyes latch onto mine from across the room. Fire licks at my skin and I feel a faint blush creep up my neck.

Anna gasps in surprise and her eyes narrow on me. "What the fuck happened to your eyes?"

"I slept in my contacts," I say.

"Oh, hon." She leans in closer to inspect my face. "Your eyes are as red as the devil's dick!"

"Gemma stayed at a guy's house last night," James announces with the subtlety of a foghorn.

I choke on my champagne, banging my fist against my chest to clear my throat.

Anna is wide-eyed. "Shit. That *is* a big deal," she says, reaching across the island to cut herself a piece of cheese. "Who's the lucky guy?" she asks around the mouthful. My blood pressure drops to zero because *the guy* happens to be standing three feet away from us both.

I quickly turn my head to look at Max, who is doing a fabulous job at schooling his expression. I'm glad one of us is keeping their cool, because inside, I'm absolutely shitting myself.

"You don't know him," April rushes, jumping in to rescue me.

Anna's brows pull together. "And you do?" she asks April, suspicion creeping into her tone.

April's eyes bounce around the room like a ping-pong ball. Good Lord, this is hopeless. She's the worst liar on the planet.

"N-No," she stammers. Her voice isn't convincing *at all*.

"Help yourself to some champagne," I deflect, gesturing to the open bottle with my glass.

"Ooo!" Anna claps before pouring a flute of champagne.

My insides clench like I'm preparing for a punch as I divert my gaze, attempting to look anywhere but at Max. I suddenly find the side of April's head fascinating. But my attempt at avoidance is squandered as Max invades my space, the scent of his smoky cologne wrapping around me. He leans down, his warm breath dusting against my ear as he whispers roughly, "You look beautiful."

Three words spoken low enough that only I can hear them. I'm acutely aware that there are four other people in this kitchen, including his sister.

I take a large gulp of champagne, desperate to extinguish the wildfire spreading through me.

The Suite Secret

I look up, locking onto his aquamarine gaze.

"Hi, Max," I manage, keeping my voice as even as possible.

A small smile tips the corner of his lips. "Hi."

"Max, it's so great to see you!" April exclaims, shattering our bubble. She rounds the island and reaches up on tiptoes to wrap her arms around his neck. Her enthusiasm is entirely innocent, but a hideous feeling—something uninvited—threatens to blanket me. I remind myself they've known each other for years and April is marrying James.

"I'm so happy you're here! I have to introduce you to James," she says, grabbing his hand and pulling him behind her.

Max is all charm and charisma as he introduces himself to the rock star, the two instantly hitting it off and discussing travel and work.

What the hell is wrong with you, Gemma? You don't do jealousy. Especially with men you're casually sleeping with.

Suddenly, the remaining six weeks look like an eternity.

"Mason!" I say, scooting off the bar-stool and pulling him in for a hug. "It's so nice to see you. It's been ages!"

Mason's smile doesn't reach his eyes, not like it usually does, as he greets us. "Hey, Gem. It's good to see you."

He moves on to greet April, who shares a brief worried glance with me before continuing our small talk, discussing how we all are, what we've all been up to, and how work's going.

Throughout the entire conversation, I notice that Mason doesn't touch Anna once—not like he used to. The conversation is stiff and forced. They've never shied away when it comes to public displays of affection.

Max's jaw ticks as Mason catches us up on his latest news. It's been a long time since either April or I have seen Mason, and I can't help but wonder if Max knows something we don't. Something about Anna and Mason's relationship that he's keeping close to his chest.

I'm pulled from my thoughts as everyone from outside files in. Lucas enters wearing a scorned look that suggests he's miserable, and I revel in it.

I'll never forgive him for hurting April the way he did, even if she's happier than she's ever been.

Will and Tom nurse two large trays piled high with different cuts of succulent barbecued meats and colourful salads. The aroma hits me, and my mouth waters.

As Anna, April, James, and Caroline fuss about gathering cutlery, plates, and glasses, Will drops the tray to the kitchen counter with the delicacy of an elephant. His eyes lock onto mine with disconcerting intensity.

"Ew, what?" I ask, shifting and feeling mildly uncomfortable under his scrutiny.

A wolfish smile spreads across his face, and I scrunch my nose in repulsion.

"I'm sitting next to you."

Anna chokes on her champagne, stifling her laugh.

This day just keeps getting better and better.

Chapter Thirty-Two

Max

I clock the stupid one as Will, lead guitarist of Atlas Veil. The way he obviously ogles Gemma opens a pit in my stomach, and a wave of possessiveness laps at my skin like an incoming tide.

He wants her. And he isn't subtle about it.

Gemma's eyes shift to me, a brief panicked glance, and I watch her with indifference painted across my face. Not doing anything is foreign to me. I'm used to taking what I want, and what I want is Gemma. But with my sister sitting across from Gemma and me as we're seated at the table, I'm unable to show Will that she's mine.

The word *mine* echoes in my head.

She isn't mine—not really. *But God, I think I want her to be.*

It was hard enough to peel away from her after the optometrist. After ensuring her eyes were okay, I saw her home safely and proceeded to my apartment, pumped iron until my muscles screamed, then fucked my hand in the shower.

Gemma is sitting in the middle of the long dining table that's dotted with various trays, plates, and bowls of meats, salads, and roasted vegetables. The spread is impressive, but I'm finding it difficult to focus on the food when all I can think about is the curve of Gemma's neck as she deliberately avoids looking at me.

April and James give each other loving looks from the far end of the table. Meanwhile, Gemma sits between Will and me. Anna is opposite us, next to Oliver with Mason on her other side, the tension evident as she maintains just enough distance from him to make it obvious she's avoiding his touch. Something you'd only notice if you were really paying attention.

I've seen him attempt to slip his hand into hers or wrap his arm around her waist, but each time she's sent him a small smile and pulled away.

"Do you like my sausage?" Will's voice cuts in, and I see him lean into Gemma with a sly smirk that makes me want to introduce his face to the table.

"You're in my burger," Gemma says, her voice low and dry.

Will pumps his eyebrows suggestively. "Oh, really?"

"No. I mean, your sleeve is *actually* in my burger. Move it." She shoves his arm away.

Will looks down at his sleeve and huffs in frustration when he sees sauce on his cuff. Gemma and Anna roll their lips to stop from laughing, their eyes dancing with amusement.

"So, Max," Oliver says across the table as he cuts into his steak, "April tells me you're in from New York."

I appreciate the guy making an effort. He seems like a nice bloke, and I can tell he's the most similar to James out of the group.

If I'm honest, it's an honour being invited to this dinner. Anna and April have been best friends for the better part of thirty years, so I've known April a long time, seen her through some of the most horrific events as she leaned on Anna and my family for support. Growing up, she was like another little sister to annoy and pick on, so I carry a lot of affection for her.

"I am, yes. I've only been there for two years, but it's become home." The words feel true as I say them, but there's a twinge of unease when I see Anna's eyes drop to the table and Gemma's fleeting glance.

"What brings you back?" he asks.

"Work, mainly. And seeing family, of course." I gesture to Anna, who gives me a warm smile. "I work with Grayson Livingstone—"

"Shit," he says with light laughter. "He's a big deal. What do you do for him?"

"I'm his chief development officer."

"Ah, that's right," he says, nodding. "You're opening that swanky new hotel."

"That's right, Gray Hotel."

"His company hired mine," Gemma inserts before looking at me with a quick smile. "So we're working together too."

"You are?" Will says, looking around Gemma to regard us both. His jaw tightens as worry creases his face. He's jealous that I'm working with Gemma. I know the guy is harmless and certainly no competition, but I revel in his obvious discomfort. The fact that I've seen Gemma naked—that *I* know the exact sound she makes when she comes all over my cock—while he's sat making immature sausage jokes, is a silent but assured victory.

I meet Oliver's gaze coolly.

"Yes. Gemma's agency is handling the marketing for the hotel launch, so we'll be working closely over the next six weeks." I look at Gemma as I say the next part. "She's proven herself to be one of the most capable people I've worked with."

The compliment comes easy because it's entirely true.

Under the table, Gemma's knee briefly presses against my thigh. I'm not sure whether it was deliberate or accidental, but it sends a jolt up my leg and straight to my dick.

"Wow. Impressive," Oliver says, lifting his brows appreciatively. Just as I'm about to elaborate, James's mother cuts in, taking over the conversation. I notice Gemma place her napkin over her lap before she scoots her chair in closer to the table.

The dinner proceeds around us—April describing wedding plans, James's brother, Lucas, sulking in the corner while he taps away madly at his phone, and Will entertaining the other end of the table with band stories.

Stealthily, I slide my hand under the table and play with the hem of Gemma's skirt. I feel her tense beside me as she nods along to something Anna is saying, but she doesn't shift or stop me, so I take it as permission to continue.

I gather the fabric in my hand, bunching it up as slowly as possible before dragging my fingertips along her soft skin. Her breath hitches as I reach the delicate skin of her inner thigh. She widens her legs ever so slightly, granting me better access while maintaining composure. Everyone seems to be occupied with their conversations, completely oblivious. Gemma takes a sip of her wine with her left hand.

When I reach the juncture of her thighs, my fingers glide over wet fabric as it clings to her pussy, creating a perfect mould of her intimate parts. I almost groan at the contact.

She half-coughs, half-gasps as soon as I graze my knuckles against her.

Anna lifts her eyes to Gemma's.

"Are you alright?"

"Yes," Gemma squeaks, lifting her glass. "Just went down the wrong pipe."

"Maybe you should slow down," Anna says with a laugh.

I realise this is totally messed up. I'm playing with my sister's best friend right in front of her, but I can't stop.

Gemma tilts her pelvis ever so slightly, just enough to press against my fingers. I move my hand back down her thigh and begin to draw slow, tight circles over her skin.

Her spine straightens and she sucks in a deep breath when I hover back over her entrance, running my fingers over her wetness before withdrawing my hand completely. My cock thickens beneath my zipper.

"Are you sure you're alright?" Anna says, concern etched on her face.

"Mm-hmm," Gemma responds, snaking her hands underneath the table and gripping my wrist.

Anna drops her fork and leans in closer to whisper-shout. "Are you holding in a fart?"

"No!" Gemma says, looking thoroughly mortified.

April appears behind Anna to refill her glass. "What are we talking about?"

"Nothing," Gemma grinds out, tightening her hold on my wrist. I'm still able to move my fingers, so I do, sawing the tips of my fingers back and forth over her slit as subtly as possible.

"Gemma just has a little gas trapped, that's all," Anna says.

"Oh no," April says. "Do you think it's the food? Have you had too much dairy? I told James we overdid it with the cheese."

"It's not the bloody dairy," Gemma grinds out.

I hide my smile by lifting my wine glass with my free hand and taking a long pull, finding her discomfort far more entertaining than I should.

"Is this like that time you douched too hard, and all the air got trapped in your bum?" Anna continues.

The wine almost escapes from my nostrils as I hold in the liquid, forcing myself to swallow rather than spray it across the table.

"Anna!" Gemma hisses, shooting a panicked glance around the table to see if anyone else heard. "Can we not?"

"I'm just looking out for you." Anna shrugs, completely unbothered. "You couldn't fart properly for three days."

"Oh, yes!" April says, snapping her fingers as she recalls the memory. "That was awful, remember? You were in so much pain. I have a container with all sorts of medications in the utility room. Help yourself if you need to."

April walks away, refilling empty glasses as she goes before taking her seat.

"Anna, not everyone wants to hear about Gemma's hygiene issues over dinner," Mason cuts in.

"Excuse me," Gemma says. "I do *not* have hygiene issues."

Anna waves a hand at Gemma. "Exactly. Because you don't douche anymore."

Gemma looks at me sheepishly. I agree entirely with Mason. The topic isn't exactly dinner party material, but right now I'm too caught up in the way Gemma's squirming under my touch.

Her pupils are blown wide, chest rising with a shaky inhale as I keep a steady rhythm—fingertips dragging back and forth across her skin, teasing her pussy with feather-light strokes before pulling away again. Then her thighs clamp shut around my hand, trapping it.

If it weren't for company around us, I'd sink three fingers knuckle deep inside her.

"I think I need some air," Mason mutters, tossing his napkin on the table before making a quick exit.

"That's it—I can't let you suffer in silence any longer, Gem. I'm going to find some Wind-Eze," Anna announces, already standing and heading off in search of meds.

"Screw. You," Gemma grits out between clenched teeth.

I lean in, close enough that only she can hear. "I'm dying to sink my fingers and cock into this sopping-wet pussy."

She fiddles with the cutlery as she tries to distract herself from my touch. Before it goes too far, I pull out my hand and wipe my fingers over my own napkin before taking another sip of my wine.

When I sit back, April's eyes are already on us. Her expression is tight with worry, her lips parted like she just witnessed something she can't quite make sense of.

"Everything alright?" James asks April, noticing her sudden silence.

"Perfect," April chirps, her voice overly bright. "I'll go check on Anna and Mason."

Gemma shifts in her seat, reaching for her water as I discreetly readjust my napkin to conceal my obvious erection.

She tips her head toward me, keeping her voice low enough that only I can hear. "You're going to pay for that."

I lick my lower lip. "Yeah? How wet are you, Gemma?"

I swear I hear her whimper. "*So* wet."

I survey the room to see what everyone's up to. No one pays us any attention, all preoccupied drinking, chatting, or cleaning up.

Through the French doors connecting the open living area to the courtyard, I spot Mason seated alone. He looks deep in thought. Anna flits around the kitchen, opening and closing cabinets until she pulls out a plastic tub filled with small boxes—medication, I'm assuming, for Gemma's supposed wind.

"Gem," she calls across the room, waving a box labelled *Wind-Eze* around like a flag. "I'll leave it on the bench here for you."

Every head in the room turns toward Gemma, who attempts to hide behind the rim of her glass.

"Fuck my life," she mutters, and I stifle a smirk.

Anna joins Mason outside, balancing a drink in each hand as she approaches him.

With everyone now distracted, I make a quick decision.

If I want Gemma's tight little pussy—and I do, with an intensity that's beginning to burn—I need to act now.

Chapter Thirty-Three

Gemma

My thong is soaked through.

I'm sitting in a pool of my own arousal. I'm desperate to do something about the throb between my legs, but truth be told, I'm hesitant to stand for fear of having a wet patch on the back of my skirt.

The fact that everyone thinks I'm either constipated or unable to fart isn't helping my situation. Will and Tom have been tossing me quizzical glances since Anna announced to the entire party that my butt's apparently on strike.

My core throbs and heat lashes my skin. I need to get myself off. It's like trying to scratch an itch you can't reach—except the one person who could help is sitting right beside you.

"I want you."

His voice is like gravel. Rough and raspy. I close my eyes, taking a deep breath to steady myself, his words sending another pulse through me.

His fingers connect with my thigh again under the table, but this time he stays on top of the fabric.

"I can't," I breathe, while every cell in my body screams the opposite.

I cast a look around, observing what everyone else is doing. They're all a few drinks deep and nicely buzzed. They look busy. Thankfully, Tom, Will, and Oliver have relocated to the couch, chatting about their upcoming US tour. April and James are helping Caroline in the kitchen, all of them smiling and laughing about something I can't hear.

"Anna's right there," I say, punctuating my words as I tip my head toward the courtyard where my best friend is in the middle of what looks to be an intense conversation.

"No one will notice. They're all focused elsewhere," he says.

I chew the inside of my cheek, mulling over my options. I could say no, knowing he'll only continue to tempt me with those masterful fingers. I could excuse myself and dash to the bathroom to take care of my itch and clean myself up. Or ... I could give in to the reckless impulse coursing through me.

The part of my brain that isn't drowning in hormones knows this isn't a wise idea. But rationality seems to evacuate whenever Max Browne is around.

"Follow me in thirty seconds. Down the hallway next to the stairs. Second door on the left," I instruct.

His eyes darken.

No one watches as I stand without another word and make my way to the guest bedroom.

Chapter Thirty-Four

Max

My cock twitches as I count down each second from thirty. The sound of conversation and clinking utensils fades as I navigate the hallway. I reach the second door on the left and turn the knob.

Gemma stands in the middle of the modest bedroom, her chest rising and falling in shallow breaths. Her legs are pressed together, shifting as if she's desperate for relief.

Yeah, she wants me. It's written all over her gorgeous face. Her eyes are wild—pupils wide with desire. The blush that stained her cheeks earlier now trails down her neck and disappears beneath her blouse.

She looks desperate. And completely perfect.

"This is a bad idea," she says. Her words land, but her body tells a different story.

I take measured steps toward her, eliminating the air between us.

"Then tell me to stop," I challenge, dropping my voice. "Tell me this isn't what you've needed since I touched you under the table."

Her eyes flash. "I hate you so much."

The lie makes me smile. "Show me how much you hate me."

Her back meets the dresser, leaving her nowhere to go. I cage her in with my hands firmly planted on either side of her hips. Her pulse flutters at the base of her throat. I haven't even touched her yet, but my heart races with the thoughts of what I want to do with her.

When we have time, I tell myself. Right now, we don't. Every second counts, and I don't plan to waste them.

"Someone might come looking for us," she whispers, making no move to push me away. Her hands find my chest, her fingers splaying as she toys with the expensive fabric.

"Then we'd better make this quick," I murmur, closing the last inch of space.

Our lips meet with matched hunger. The kiss is desperate, messy, and hot. A groan rumbles low in my chest as she drags me closer. I open for her, and our tongues slide together. She tastes so damn sweet.

My hands move to her arse, squeezing the soft flesh as I grind my cock against her. She whimpers, rocking and rubbing her hips, chasing friction.

I break the kiss to drag my mouth down her neck. One hand slides into her hair, twisting it through my fist and giving it a firm tug, baring her neck to me. I lay a trail of wet kisses along her throat, nipping and sucking as her warm breath stutters against my cheek.

Time falls away, silencing the rest of the world until there's nothing left but the sensation of her skin against mine.

"Take me out," I say.

Her hands fall to my belt, dragging my zipper down and exposing my hard cock. Her thumb sweeps over my crown, rubbing the pre-cum over the head. I bite into her neck and soothe the mark with my tongue.

Her delicate hand wraps around my shaft with just the right amount of pressure, pumping me from tip to base. My balls grow heavy as desire coils around me like smoke. I release my hold on her hair to hike her skirt up to her waist. She widens her stance ever so slightly, and I accept her unspoken invitation, pushing her pathetic excuse for panties to the side and sliding my fingers through her slit.

I tsk. "I've barely touched you and you're already a mess."

"I need you *now*, Max," she grits out.

I squeeze her left arse cheek with my free hand and pull my fingers out.

"Put me in," I say, my voice rough.

Her gaze drops as I wrap my hand around hers, guiding both our grips down my cock as we drag it through her weeping seam.

"Eyes on me when I'm filling you."

Her eyes snap to mine as I breach her entrance. Shifting my hold, I hook my hands beneath her knees, lifting her. Her arse hovers just off the dresser as I bury myself deep inside her hot channel.

She tilts her hips, pushing out her tits as I rut into her—deep and relentless.

"You feel so fucking good," I pant.

"Faster, Max. Please," she begs.

This isn't like last night. Last night we took our time, savouring and indulging in each other. This is rough and dirty. Greedy. We're both taking. This isn't simply a want—it's a *need*.

I snap my hips and the slick sound of our bodies clapping together echoes through the small space.

My grip tightens as I pick up the pace, drawing back before slamming to the hilt, over and over.

"You f-feel *so* good," she moans, her voice a string of

breathy whimpers that rise into a sweet siren song, drowning out the blood pounding in my ears.

As if compelled, I thrust harder, muscles straining as I fuck her senseless. My eyes are locked on the bounce of her tits and the way her mouth falls open in perfect bliss. My balls tighten, becoming heavy, and my cock swells. I'm desperate to come.

I wring every drop of pleasure from us. Nothing else exists—all the reasons why this is a terrible idea—they all evaporate into nothing. None of it matters. Because what could possibly justify starving ourselves of this? Of something this good? This consuming?

Her body takes every urgent thrust, giving in to me completely. My hands keep her steady and spread wide open as I drive myself into her, hard flesh meeting tender in perfect, reckless rhythm.

A fine sheen of sweat clings to my brow, but I don't care. I burn for this. For *her*.

"No one touches you but me, do they?" I ask.

"No one," she gasps.

"Fuck. You feel incredible, sweetheart."

We're both lost in each other's bodies and I'm finding it difficult to hold back my release.

"I want you to come for me," I say. "Look at us."

She joins me, dropping her gaze to where our bodies join—my cock disappearing inside her.

"You're perfect," I tell her. "You take me so well."

Her arm curls around my neck, pulling me in and gripping me tight. Her lips seek mine and I happily oblige. Our tongues tangle as we both edge closer.

She heaves a shallow breath against my mouth. "I'm going to—I'm—"

"Me too, baby," I groan.

"I want all of it," she begs.

Her words are the end of me. I dive off the cliff, grinding my molars at the same time she climaxes. Her walls convulse around my rigid shaft, milking me. I bear down, gripping her tight as I expel thick, hot ropes of cum, filling her up.

Every shudder and quiver rushes through me like molten lava as we come down from our high. My thrusts turn lazy, pumping languidly to ensure she gets every last drop.

I press my lips to her forehead as we catch our breaths.

I kneel before her, holding her skirt up and watching in awe as our combined liquid trickles down her inner thigh.

Leaning in, I kiss one knee, then the other, lowering her skirt back into place.

"Feel good?" I ask. My voice comes out rougher than I intended.

"It'll do for now," she says, smirking down at me.

Brat.

Reality slowly creeps back, pulling me from our haze. My thoughts race to the other guests. How long have we been gone? Has anyone noticed our absence?

"We should get back out there," I say, reluctantly pulling away to stand.

Gemma nods, smoothing over her rumpled skirt. "Right. Yes." She turns to fix her smudged lipstick in the hanging mirror while I straighten my shirt, refolding the sleeves.

"You go first. I'll wait a minute or two, then follow," I suggest.

Her jade eyes find mine in the mirror, and something vulnerable flashes across her features.

"As hot as that was, we should probably be more mindful next time," she says.

Guilt spears through me. And it's deserved. I did this to her. This was *my* doing, *my* impulsivity. Not hers. If someone—especially Anna—caught us, she would be devastated.

This wasn't the time, and this wasn't the place.

"Agreed," I say. This was rash and careless. It felt right, but the aftermath could have ended terribly for both of us.

Gemma steps toward the door and I reach out and clasp her wrist, stopping her. Her gaze drops to where my fingers encircle her and a frown creases her brow.

"I'm so sorry for putting you at risk like that," I say, my tone earnest. "We shouldn't have done this at all."

Hurt flickers across her face. She pulls away and I see her rebuilding her defences, brick by brick. The moment her guard rises, she tears her hand from my grasp.

"Let's not get ahead of ourselves, Browne," she says, her voice cold and cutting. "It was nothing. *This*"—she gestures between us—"is nothing, remember?"

The words land like a bucket of ice water, and I mentally kick myself for screwing up so spectacularly.

"Gemma, wait," I say, stepping forward.

"No. Don't bother. I'll see you on Monday," she says.

I watch as she swings the door open and walks through it without sparing me a second glance.

Fuck.

Chapter Thirty-Five

Max

I don't know what's gotten into me, but every minute since Saturday night feels as though it's stretched into an eternity.

I slept like total shit the past two nights. Partly because I've replayed my thoughtless words to Gemma and her cold dismissal more times than I care to admit. And partly because her scent is everywhere—lingering on my sheets, my pillow, in my bathroom. Even if I wanted to, I can't escape her. I've jerked off twice trying to purge her from my system. It didn't work.

Her cutting words—*this is nothing*—flood me like a current, washing away any lingering afterglow. I didn't even have time to hold her before I opened my mouth and ruined everything.

The shower pounds my skin like a gavel, but it fails to wash away the thought that's been circling my mind since she walked out: I wanted more time with her. I wanted to hold her.

Like Gemma, I never cuddle after sex. That's why Ruby Lounge worked so well for me, along with similar clubs in New York. It's transactional. I don't obsess over women, replay conversations, and I certainly never second-guess my actions.

We simply enjoy each other, then we part ways. Rinse. Repeat. No morning-after awkwardness. No regrets.

I don't have any second thoughts about what we did in that bedroom Saturday night; that's a memory I'll enjoy carrying with me forever. But I *do* regret my shitty apology that made her think I considered it a mistake.

My only real concern was coming between Anna and Gemma's friendship. I'd hate either of them to get hurt in the fallout. I can handle my sister, but Gemma? I don't want to be the reason they argue. Which is why we need to be more careful.

I slam the water off and grab a towel, rubbing it vigorously against my skin before roughly running my hands through my hair.

I dress in my usual—navy suit pants, a white shirt, and black shoes.

I need to focus. My mind needs to be on today. Work. The reason I'm here in the first place.

This whole arrangement was my idea, so I need to see that it continues without a hitch, just as we planned.

I make myself an espresso. The rich, nutty aroma of fresh coffee fills my kitchen, and I already feel more alert. I sip on the bitter brew, but my thoughts return to worrying about Gemma.

I've checked my phone a dozen times, half-expecting, half-hoping to see her name appear. Each time a new notification sounds, I'm hit with a jolt of unease, and each time it isn't her, the disappointment hits harder than it should. How pathetic. I'm acting like a lovesick teenager.

I toss my phone onto the counter face-down, determined not to check it again. But as I reach for my jacket, the familiar vibration hums against the marble. I pause, then flip it over, screen up.

Remorse swells inside me as Anna's name flashes on the screen. For a split second, panic sparks. What if she knows what Gemma and I were doing in the guest bedroom? But logic overrides the instinct. That's unlikely. I swipe to answer.

"Hey, weasel," I say.

"Hey, are you at work?" she asks.

I glance at my watch. "Not yet. It's only half seven. Why?" I take another sip of coffee.

There's a pause. "Casey's been messaging me on Instagram."

My stomach drops. I set the espresso cup down. "What?"

"She's sent me three DMs in the last twelve hours."

I sigh, already knowing where this is going. I begin pacing the length of my kitchen. "What's she saying?"

I hear rustling on the other end of the phone as she pulls up their conversation. "The last one says, 'Hi, Anna, has your brother blocked me?'"

I exhale sharply, running my free hand through my still-damp hair. "Yes. I have."

"She's sent another message asking what's going on."

"She won't stop calling and I just ... I can't keep doing this," I say, keeping my voice even. I stop by the large windows, staring out at the London skyline without really seeing it.

There's another pause. "What do you want me to say?"

I pinch the bridge of my nose, irritated that Casey's involved my sister. I force my shoulders to relax. "Just tell her you're not getting in the middle of this. Or that I'm busy. That I'm not available—whatever you want."

Anna hesitates. "That seems ... harsh, don't you think? You were married to her."

I nod, even though she can't see it. This is the last thing I need to be focusing on. "It is cold, I know. And I hate that. But I need it to be. She's using you to get to me because I've finally drawn a line. She doesn't know I'm back in London, and I'd like to keep it that way."

Another brief pause.

"She's replying," Anna says, her voice tight. "I already messaged her before I called you."

My jaw clenches as I check my watch again, walking back toward the kitchen. "You did?"

"Yeah," she says, casually. "I didn't say much. Just that I'd ask you what was going on. She says she wants to talk."

I press my palm flat against the cool counter, grounding myself. "I've been talking to her, Anna. For the last *four years*. I stayed in touch longer than I probably should have—because I didn't want to be the arsehole who cut her off completely."

"She still loves you, Max," Anna says, her voice quiet.

"That's the problem." I move to pick up my suit jacket, slipping it on with the phone tucked between my ear and shoulder. "She hasn't let go. And I did—a long time ago. It's not fair to keep having the same conversations when they lead nowhere. She needs to move on. I've tried to be kind about it, but kindness turned into false hope. And that's not fair either."

"I get it," she says finally. "I just don't like seeing people hurt. Even Casey."

"I don't either," I reply. "But I can't be the one to help her through it anymore. That's not my place—it hasn't been for years."

"She's not going to take it well," Anna warns.

"I know." I run a hand down my face, feeling the slight stubble I've neglected to shave. "But that's not my responsibility anymore."

"Are you okay?" Anna asks.

We've always been open and honest with each other. Anna's stoic; she always has been. It's how she presents to the world. But underneath it all is a gentle softness. She's kind. She cares about people, even when it isn't her place. My sister has a big heart, and I love her for it.

"Yeah," I say, pressing my thumb and forefinger to my eyes, trying to chase off the exhaustion. "Just tired."

"Okay. I won't say anything else to her. I promise."

"I appreciate that. How are you?" I ask, changing the subject. "I saw things were a little tense between you and Mason on Saturday."

"I'm fine. Nothing's changed." Her tone has a finality to it.

I frown. "You know I'm always here, right?"

"I know. And I love you for it ... I'd better let you go. I've got parent meetings to prepare for this afternoon."

"Have a good day," I say, tapping my hand against the counter. "And weasel? Thanks."

"Don't call me that."

I smile faintly. "You love it."

"Not even a little bit." She hangs up.

Smirking, I slide the phone into my jacket pocket and head toward the door.

Another quick glance at my watch tells me it's not yet 8 am, and I wonder what other fresh hell Monday can bring.

And how can I make up with Gemma.

Chapter Thirty-Six

Max

I hate the Tube. Especially on Monday mornings when the weekend's filth hasn't been cleaned away. It's even more crowded than usual, which is saying something. The stench is a nauseating cocktail of dried piss, stale vomit, and brake dust.

I'd forgotten how much I loathe this morning ritual. After two years with Grayson Livingstone's private car service in New York, I've grown accustomed to a certain standard. One that, unfortunately, the London Tube can't hold a candle to.

I'm also lucky enough to be standing next to someone's sweaty armpit, trying my best to avoid touching the poles that thousands of unwashed hands have held. On top of that, wafts of sickeningly sweet floral perfume occasionally infiltrate my senses.

The only reason I'm subjecting myself to this circle of hell is Gemma. The first day we met is seared into my memory—and stained on my shirt—and I figure if I can follow the course of her usual morning routine and grab her favourite coffee and pastry, I might have a shot at breaking through the ice wall she's likely reconstructed. A peace offering of sorts.

Is it pathetic that I've memorised her coffee order? Probably. But at this point, I might as well surrender to the desperation that's overcome my body.

I just hope it fucking works.

* * *

"Hullo, son. What can I get for you?" the old man asks. His accent is strong—northern Scottish, I think.

"A large latte and ..." I scan the pastry selection, trying to recall which she favours. My eyes land on the apricot Danish. Bingo. "An apricot Danish."

The old man narrows his eyes at me suspiciously before shuffling off to make the coffee and bag the Danish.

I stand back, shoving my hands in my pockets. The paint is peeling off the kiosk like a sunburn and there's not a single customer in sight, despite the busy gardens. It's not exactly the establishment I'd choose for my coffee, but this isn't about me.

He places the items on the counter. The stamp on the to-go coffee cup catches my eye. It's the same small green faded logo on the cup Gemma spilled on me the day we met, and I know I've got the right one.

"Anything for yourself?" he asks, eyes knowing.

I knit my brows together. "How did you know this isn't for me?"

He smirks. "Lucky guess, lad."

"Good guess," I say, impressed. I slip my wallet from my pocket. "What do I owe you?"

"Thirteen pounds." He bares his crooked teeth in what I assume is meant to be a smile.

I blink, certain I misheard. "Pardon?"

"Thirteen pounds," he repeats.

For coffee and a pastry? No wonder he doesn't have customers.

My expression must mirror my thoughts because he barks a laugh. "Aye, I know. I'm as outraged as you are. Running costs have skyrocketed and I can't keep up. I'd love to charge you less, but I'm almost at the point of closing. Sorry, lad."

I shoot him a polite grin and pay for the items.

Thirteen bloody pounds. Ridiculous.

It had better not taste like it was filtered through a dirty sock.

Chapter Thirty-Seven

Gemma

I'm so sorry for putting you at risk like that. We shouldn't have done this at all.

The words have been replaying in an endless loop in my mind since Saturday night.

The prick.

First, he convinces me to have sex with him—*only him*, no less—then he has the balls to turn around and tell me it was a mistake.

I realise the word *mistake* didn't exactly leave his mouth, but it didn't have to. I could see it in his stupid, gorgeous baby blues.

I'm punching the buttons on my keyboard far too forcefully, but I'm pissed.

At least my eyes are somewhat back to normal—small mercies.

"Christ, who twisted your knickers?" Henry asks, strolling into my office and falling into the seat opposite my desk.

Ignoring his question, I shoot him a warning glance, lifting my eyes to meet his briefly before proceeding to harass my keyboard.

"Great. Excellent. Well, whatever's happened had better not affect our work," he says, voice dry.

I lift my gaze to his again. "It won't affect our work. I told you it wouldn't. Nothing happened."

"Bollocks," he says, a cheeky smirk lifting his lips.

I roll my eyes. "I have work to do, so if there's a reason for your visit, I'd appreciate it if you'd cut to the chase."

His eyebrows reach his hairline. "Don't forget I'm *your* boss, you little bitch."

I roll my lips to stop myself from cracking a smile.

"Let's try again. What happened?" he says, talking to me like a child.

I release a harsh exhale. "So ... we slept together."

Henry rolls his eyes. "Obviously. We're talking about *you*—that's implied. What went wrong? Was it bad?"

I stop typing. "Firstly," I say, putting one finger up, "I feel like that was an insult. Secondly"—I raise a second finger—"no. It wasn't bad. It was anything *but* bad, and that's the issue."

He scrunches his nose. "Why is that an issue? Last time I checked, a good shag is nothing to sneeze about."

I glare at him.

"*Oh*. You like him, don't you?" His voice has a taunting lilt. He adjusts in his seat, making himself comfortable like he owns the place.

"Of course I don't like him." I pause to consider my next words. "I like his penis."

"You like everyone's penis."

Dammit. He's right. Well, excluding Tim's.

"Excuse me. Rude. I don't like your penis."

"You've never seen my penis," he deadpans.

"Is that an invitation?" I ask, teasing. When he glares at me, I pump my eyebrows suggestively to get a rise out of him. It's working. He's chewing his cheek to stop himself from laughing.

A knock against the wooden doorframe causes Henry and me to jump.

Hand to my chest, I catch my breath as I lock eyes with the man who's been haunting my every thought.

He stands tall in the doorway, looking like a god. He leans on his shoulder, one leg crossed in front of the other, to-go coffee in hand, jawline chiselled. He's wearing my favourite suit—navy blue. It makes the crystalline in his ocean eyes pop.

He doesn't spare Henry a glance as his gaze penetrates mine, and a swarm of butterflies erupts in my stomach.

Detecting the shift in energy, Henry clears his throat.

"Max, good morning. I hope you had a great weekend," Henry says, his face bright.

Max arches a thick brow. "Henry," he says, nodding in acknowledgement before his eyes bore into mine again. "Gemma."

Henry swivels back around to face me, fixing me with a *what the hell* look. I tap my polished nail lightly over the mahogany surface in front of me.

"Good morning, Max." I keep my tone cool while inside, my body doesn't know whether to scream or cream. It's quite the quandary.

"Well," Henry says, clapping his hands, "I'll leave you to it." He turns to Max. "I was wondering if you're free this afternoon to discuss the artwork Gemma's found that might be suitable for the hotel."

Max gives a firm nod. "Sure." He shakes his wrist, checking the time. "How's two o'clock sound?"

"Perfect," Henry replies, standing.

This time I fix *him* with a *don't leave me* look, which he responds with a *screw this* expression.

To be honest, I can't blame him. If I could flee the scene, I would. The tension is so thick, even a blind man could grope it.

I watch as Henry makes his escape, my focus returning to Max.

"Well. If that's all ..." I say.

He steps forward, my heart beating in time with each one.

Wordless, he places the coffee and pastry bag in front of me and steps back.

I take in the green stamp and my eyes widen. "How do you know about Lance?"

"Who is Lance?" he asks, his face turning stormy.

"My barista."

His eyes shift to the coffee and his expression relaxes. Jesus, this man is broody. "His prices are extortionate."

"He's having some financial trouble," I say, leaning back in my chair and folding my arms across my chest. It's defensive, but I feel better having a barrier between us. "How did you know where I get my coffee from? Are you following me?"

His face is unreadable now. "Lucky guess."

"Should I be flattered or concerned?" I ask, cocking an eyebrow.

"That depends," he says, taking the seat Henry just vacated. "Are you still pissed at me?"

I take a sip. "I'm not pissed."

I am pissed.

"Bullshit," he says.

I wait a beat before responding. "Fine. I'm pissed."

A smirk plays at the edge of his mouth. "I figured as much."

I lean forward, lowering my voice. "What did you expect? One minute we're ... you know ..."

"Having sex," he finishes for me. The way he says it makes me remember exactly how it felt when he whispered filthy things in my ear on Saturday night.

"Right. And the next you're apologising like it was some terrible mistake. Let's not forget—this whole thing was *your* idea. If it doesn't work for you anymore, then maybe we need to be honest about that and rethink the arrangement."

There. I've said my piece, and strangely, I feel lighter for it. Because the truth is, we both walked into this with open eyes—or in my case, legs. We knew what it was. But this— this is exactly why I stopped dating. It never stays simple. It always finds a way to twist and before you know it, something good turns to shit.

I have other things I can do besides worry about Max Fucking Browne.

Like reiki.

"That's not—"

"You literally said, and I quote, 'I'm so sorry for putting you at risk like that. We shouldn't have done this at all.'" I mimic his deeper voice, badly.

His expression shifts—surprised, perhaps, that I remember his exact words. Of course I do. They're responsible for the bags under my eyes.

"I didn't mean the sex was a mistake. If you had just let me explain," he says, dropping to a baritone that melts my insides. "I meant the location. The timing. Not ... us."

Us. The word hangs between us like a loaded gun.

The relief that cocoons me after his admission is strangely foreign. The worry that's been festering in my chest since Saturday night finally dissipates. I hadn't realised how much I needed to hear that he doesn't regret what we did.

I sit with his words for a moment, churning them over in my mind. He's right. I know he's right. Our timing was reckless, and our location was impulsive. The night was about celebrating April and James and their deserved happiness, but we made it about us instead. I practically ran out of their dinner after the guest room incident. We put ourselves in a position to hurt Anna—someone we both care for tremendously.

His concern wasn't rejection; it was consideration. For Anna. For us.

The Suite Secret

"I was going to call you," he says.

"I wouldn't have answered," I reply, suddenly finding my cuticles interesting.

"Look at me, please," he commands.

I lift my eyes.

"Right," I say, keeping my tone easy. "Well, thank you for the clarification. And the coffee." I gesture to my computer screen. "But I really do have work to finish before the meeting."

"Gemma, I can see that you're playing Minecraft in the reflection of your glasses."

Shit.

I quickly close the Minecraft window, only for it to minimise and reveal the jewelled butt plug I was looking at on a sex toy website.

I slam my laptop closed, feeling heat burn up my neck.

The corner of his mouth twitches. He definitely saw that.

"Was there something else you needed?" I ask, attempting to salvage any remaining dignity.

He lifts his chin. "Have dinner with me."

"That didn't sound like a question," I retort.

"It wasn't."

My heart does a ridiculous flutter in my chest. "I don't think that's a good idea," I say.

"Why not?" His eyes never leave mine, intense and searching.

Because you're my best friend's brother. Because you're only in London temporarily. Because I can still feel your hands on my skin and your lips on my mouth, and it's driving me insane. Because "nothing" is starting to feel like "something", and that is terrifying.

These thoughts pick at me, pulling a loose thread begging to be unwound. But instead, I repress them and say, "Dinner was never part of the deal."

"The deal's changed."

"You can't just go changing the rules. You're the one who enforced them in the first place." I take another sip.

"And I'm the one changing them."

I cross my legs. "That doesn't seem fair."

"Give me one dinner to make it up to you."

"What do I get out of it?"

His gaze grows heavy. "Whatever you want."

Well, this just got more interesting. I purse my lips and consider his offer. "That's it? That's your grand offer? I get one thing?"

"One dinner, one thing in exchange." His smile turns confident. The cocky bastard knows he's got me.

"Fine. You can have *one* dinner. But not tonight. Thursday."

"Done. I'll have a car pick you up at seven."

I must admit, the coffee paired with a dinner date and private driver is far more appealing than anything any other man has offered me. "Great."

His smile turns sinister. He rises to leave but pauses in the doorway, turning to look at me over his shoulder. "And Gemma?"

"Yes?" I ask, lifting my gaze from my laptop.

"Buy the butt plug."

Chapter Thirty-Eight

Gemma

I twist the cap of my nail polish, inspecting my handiwork on my at-home pedicure. I picked New York Apple. Red always makes me feel confident and put together.

Blowing on the polish to help it dry, I readjust my toe separators and waddle across my flat, trying not to smudge my masterpiece. I've just reached my bookshelf when a loud buzzing noise reverberates. April's here.

I desperately need some girl time. My head has been a mess since Saturday night—since Max and his dumb perfect mouth and his even dumber apology coffee.

When I told him that dinner was a bad idea, I wasn't lying. The words felt hollow when I said them, like an empty promise I knew I couldn't keep.

I never agreed to date the man, and I'm afraid that's exactly what this is turning into. We're both shitting all over the rules.

I should end it. I know we *should* end it. But I can't bring myself to do it. Shit. This is the first time I've allowed myself to think these thoughts properly. To dissect them and articulate what this means—how I feel.

I've fooled around more with Max in a week than I have with any dates over the last few *years*. And now the idea of a dinner date sends cold trickles down my spine—the kind that make me wonder whether I should take it as a warning sign because, against my better judgement, the feeling is suspiciously close to anticipation.

I press the intercom button. "Come up. Door's unlocked."

A moment later, the door swings open and I greet April with a warm hug.

"Thanks so much for coming," I say.

She rummages through her tote bag before pulling out a bottle of champagne. "I brought bubbles. Figured we might need them."

"You know me too well." I take the bottle, pop the cork, and pour us each a flute. Our glasses chime lightly as we toast.

Settling into the sofa, April turns to me, a serious look on her face. "Where did you and Max disappear to Saturday night?"

Shit. She noticed. I wince slightly.

"Was it obvious?" I ask.

She shrugs. "Only because I know what's happening between you two. I don't think anyone realised you were both missing at the same time."

April's eyes dart to my laptop screen. She does a double take and squints. "Are you looking up butt plugs?"

"Yes," I say.

When I don't elaborate, she blinks before taking another long sip. "Do I even want to know?"

I shrug. "I was browsing online at work. Max saw and asked me to buy it."

She closes her eyes slowly. "I shouldn't have asked."

I place my flute gently on the coffee table next to my open laptop, releasing a breath before turning to April. "I'm so sorry I ran out on your special night."

She waves a hand dismissively. "It's fine. You don't need to apologise. Everyone was there for the duration of dinner and that's what matters. The guys were a little tipsy by the time they finished their meals, anyway. Anna, Mason, and Max went home shortly after you did."

She pulls her long auburn hair over one shoulder. "Speaking of—did you notice what was going on between Anna and Mason?"

I nod thoughtfully. "There was definitely tension between them at the dinner table."

"They aren't affectionate with each other anymore." April's eyes turn sad and she worries her lip. "Mason never used to be able to keep his hands off her."

"Have you spoken to Anna?" I ask.

She shakes her head. "No. I didn't want to pry. But next time, let's bring it up."

I nod. "Absolutely."

"So, why did you call me over? Obviously, I'm always happy to see you, but you sounded worried. What happened?"

"Ugh," I say, rolling my eyes. "After we fucked in your guest bedroom—"

"Ewww." She scrunches her nose.

"As I was saying ..." I tell her about what Max said afterward, how I took it as rejection and stormed out. I tell her about the apology coffee from Lance's coffee cart and demand for a dinner date. By the time I finish, she's wearing an expression I can't quite translate.

"What do you think?" I ask.

"I think this is turning into something more than a simple fling a lot faster than I'd guessed it would."

"No, it's not," I lie. "It's still casual, I swear. We're still getting to know each other."

Her look says she's not buying it. "Casual is when you met that guy at Ruby Lounge and he took you back to his to play with wax and it turned out it wasn't sex wax."

"Oh yeah, Moby. I remember him well. Ironically, he was a real dick," I say, reminiscing. "It was an actual candle. I poured the scorching wax directly onto his balls."

"You had to ice his nutsack while he sobbed for forty-five minutes and you never saw him again—*that's* casual."

"So?" I ask, hoping she gets to the point soon.

"Gemma, Max tracked down your favourite coffee shop. He's taking you to dinner. He's asking you to buy ..." She whispers the next part. "A butt plug."

"Jesus Christ, April—this isn't a nunnery. You can say *butt plug*."

"All I'm saying is, this isn't casual."

I top up our champagne, avoiding her eyes. "It's not serious either."

"Then what is it?"

"It's ..." I trail off, unable to finish my sentence, let alone understand my own thoughts and emotions.

"I'm not saying what's happening between you and Max is bad. I actually think it's lovely. I saw the way he looked at you on Saturday when he thought no one else was watching. But I think you both need to admit to yourselves that this isn't throwaway sex. Gemma ..." She places her hand on my knee. "You're allowed to like someone."

"I don't like Max." My words feel thin and brittle.

She tilts her head. "Why are you so against dating and having feelings for someone?"

"I'm not against it," I say defensively.

"You are." Her eyes soften. "You haven't let yourself get into a relationship or entertained the possibility of another relationship since Todd. Why?"

"Because I like sex. I love my job. I like the freedom. I like ..."

I'm scrambling for explanations. It's true that I enjoy having emotionless sex. It's true that I'm proud of how independent I am. But when it comes to Max? Even I've started to feel my excuses fall flat.

"You realise you can still have all of that, right? A relationship isn't a life sentence," she says, shooting me a sympathetic smile.

"You and James can barely go two hours without texting each other," I say.

April laughs. "Fair point. But James and I still have separate lives. I still go out with you girls. I have my own business, which keeps me busy. He still plays online games and tours with the guys. We just ... choose to come home to each other."

I lift my glass again and swirl the champagne. "It isn't that simple with Max."

"No. It isn't, I agree. But avoiding your feelings altogether isn't the answer. You can't repress everything, Gemma."

"He's leaving. He's going back to New York at the end of this." My voice cracks. "What if I let him in and it's too much? What if what I need is ... too much?"

She arches an eyebrow. "What you *need*? Judging by your quickie in my house and the butt plug, I highly doubt you're too much for Max Browne."

I shrug, and a lump forms in my throat.

"Gem, what happened with Todd," April starts.

"I don't want to talk about Todd."

"I know, honey." She brushes my hair back. "But maybe you need to."

She sits, waiting patiently.

I think about how in love I was with Todd. And I was—embarrassingly so. We were happy, or at least I thought we were. But intimacy was never just about ticking a box for me. It was about connection and communication, about feeling seen in the most vulnerable way possible.

When he refused to even try to change his approach to sex, when he made it clear my pleasure was an afterthought, a part of me withered. I watched all our friends walk down the aisles toward suburban nightmares, toward lives where passion was sacrificed at the altar for stability and normality, and I panicked. The thought of coming home every night to someone who saw my desires as sick or "not normal", who treated sex as if only his satisfaction mattered ... I couldn't stomach it.

So, I closed myself off. I built my walls and I ended it. His refusal to give me what I needed—to even see why it mattered—didn't just hurt me. It broke me. It damaged the way I trust and the way I allowed myself to hope. It made me question whether anyone would ever think my needs were worth the effort.

Then I discovered Ruby Lounge and KinkApp. They became havens for me. Somewhere I could shed my exterior and be myself around people who understood me. People who saw sex the way I did: as healing, as fun, not a chore.

The best thing Ruby Lounge and KinkApp provided me was clarity. No one owed me anything, and I owed them nothing in return. We could take from each other, give to each other, and enjoy each other in a safe environment without the messy tangle of expectations. And when it was over, I could come home to my own space. Just me, my dead plants, and my collection of moonlight-charged crystals that Anna swears do nothing.

It's been perfect.

Until Max walked into my life three weeks ago and started making me desire the very things I'd protected myself from.

"Why won't you let him in?" April whispers.

I blink back tears, finally voicing something I've never shared with anyone before. "Because when you accept affection from someone and give it in return, that's when someone can hurt you."

"Oh, hon. You love in a way most people don't. Bravely. With so much depth and tenderness, even if you don't realise it. Do you know that? Todd just wasn't capable of meeting you there. But that doesn't mean no one else will."

A tear slips down my cheek and I brush it away with my jumper sleeve.

"You don't have to carry the weight of how he refused to show up for you. The kind of love you give? Someone else will meet you there. Someone will prioritise your needs as well as their own." She rubs a soothing hand over my leg. "You can meet someone who is just as ambitious. Just as independent. Just as spontaneous."

I drop my gaze to my lap.

"Are you afraid because you think you might have met that person?" she asks carefully.

I nod slowly.

"Are you afraid because that person might be Max?"

A sob escapes me. She moves in closer, twining her arms around me. "I can't. Anna—"

Her palm draws circles over my back. "Anna will understand. I won't push you. I won't say anything to her either. Just promise me you'll tell her if, or when, the time comes that you need to."

I pull back, sniffling. "I promise."

She squeezes my biceps. "Good. Now ..." She wiggles in her seat, leaning over to pluck my laptop off the table. "Let's have a look at these butt plugs."

Chapter Thirty-Nine

Gemma

"I met a young lad yesterday. It's funny, he ordered a large latte and an apricot Danish," Lance says, a wry grin stretching wide over his face. "He wouldn't happen to be your bloke, would he?"

He plucks my Danish out of the display cabinet with tongs, popping it into a paper bag and rolling the bag closed before handing it to me.

I scoff. "He's not young, and he's not my bloke," I say, taking a long sip of coffee. I hum as the warm liquid slides down my throat, thawing my chilled bones.

"If he's younger than fifty, that's a young lad in my books," he laughs. "You're blushing, lass."

"You know what? You're getting cheekier by the day, and I don't know how I feel about it," I tease, tapping my phone against the machine to pay.

"The closer I get to death, the less I care about manners," he says, winking. "He's a handsome young man, that one." He folds his arms over his chest.

"Great. Why don't you date him then?" I retort. "You could rob him blind with your outrageous prices and retire to the Scottish Highlands."

"He's a wee bit young for me." He shrugs. "But he's definitely had an effect on you, judging by the way you're strangling that paper bag."

I look down to find that I'm white-knuckling my breakfast. "I'm just hungry," I mutter.

"Aye, for Mister Tall Dark and Handsome?" Lance wiggles his bushy eyebrows suggestively.

"Oh, piss off. I'm finding a new coffee place," I announce, turning to leave.

"No, you won't," Lance calls after me. "No one else will put up with your bullshite!"

I flip him off over my shoulder without looking back, but we both know he's right.

And we both know I'll be back first thing tomorrow morning.

* * *

When I arrive at the office, I zero in on the kitchenette in search of a biscuit. As usual, I polished off my Danish at a record pace.

My conversation with April replays in my head and I attempt to drown it out with thoughts of shortbread and Hobnobs.

April and Anna have always known about my relationship with Todd and why we broke up, but I've never opened up to April the same way she bravely laid herself bare after breaking up with Lucas and falling for James. It's a conversation I've always sidestepped like a puddle, because I know what I'm avoiding. I just never wanted to admit it to myself.

It's always been easier to bury my demons rather than tackle them head-on, especially when the man who's caused my feelings to surface isn't here long term. The next few weeks is all we have. So, as relieved as I am to lighten the burden and have April validate my feelings without judgement, I'm still hesitant to let Max in. Because at the end of the day, he goes back to his ritzy, glamorous life, and I'll rarely get the chance to see him again.

The last thing I ever expected was to feel anything other than arousal for Max. And it's time I admit that I do.

I know we're a crash waiting to happen, but it feels so damn good, I want to take that risk.

Only question is, will those few weeks of cracking open my heart be worth the inevitable fall when he leaves?

I pluck three biscuits from the tin, stuffing one in my mouth whole.

"Stress-eating again, Gemma?"

I cringe at Louise's condescending tone, turning around to face her. I pop my hip, and instead of responding verbally, I chew with my mouth open—loudly—right in front of her. When I swallow it, I flash her a saccharine smile.

Her perfectly made-up face contorts in disgust.

"That's revolting," she says.

"Did Satan send you up for a lunch break?" I ask.

"It isn't even lunchtime," she says, narrowing her eyes to frosty slits.

"Oh, you're right. You must be on your regularly scheduled bitching hour, then. My mistake." I toss another biscuit in my mouth, refusing to break eye contact.

She crosses her arms. "Ugh. Do you know how many calories are in those things?"

I hold my arms out wide. "Oh no! Looks like I'm fresh out of fucks to give."

"Whatever," she says, her smile razor thin as she flicks her glossy ponytail. "Sugar ages your skin and goes straight to your thighs. If I were you, I'd be more mindful."

I cock my head to the side. "Are you acting like this because you're shitty you didn't get my job?"

"You don't deserve it. That role should be *mine*," she seethes.

"Tell me, does your back hurt from lugging that horrible personality around?"

Her nostrils flare. "Does your heart hurt getting clogged by all that butter?" Her gaze darts to the last biscuit in my hand.

I bark a laugh, genuine amusement slicing through my irritation. "Sweetheart, part of me is getting clogged on the regular, and I can tell you right now—it's not from butter."

She rolls her eyes and swivels on her heels, only to come face-to-face with Henry, who's just entered the kitchenette. His eyes bounce between Louise and me, his expression morphing into something resembling suspicion.

"What are you looking at?" she spits at him, darting around his broad frame to make her escape.

"Wait!" I call out as she retreats down the hallway. "You forgot your pitchfork!"

She grumbles something unintelligible as she rounds the corner, the click of her heels fading as she disappears.

Henry stands stock still, a perplexed look on his face. "What was that all about?"

I brush it off with a wave. "Nothing. She just has sand in her vagina." I notice the two cups of coffee in his hand. "Oh, thank you, but I already had a coffee."

He scrunches his brows, his expression darkening. "This isn't for you."

"Who's it for?" I ask, though an inkling in my gut already tells me the answer.

His smile is so wide it worries me.

"Max," he says.

I frown, confused. "Why are you buying Max coffee?"

"Because you and Max are taking a little day trip out to visit Lord Harrington's estate to view his private collection."

"Why aren't you coming?" The question comes out more desperate than intended.

"I have things to get through here," Henry says, looking far too pleased with himself, like a cat who's found a bowl of cream. The turd.

"The design campaign timeline needs adjusting after that feedback we received. Social media assets are ready to go out, so I'm meeting with the marketing team in thirty minutes, and the guest guide is almost finalised. I just need to send them off to the event planners, travel agencies, and that new concierge staff that Livingstone Hotels have just hired," he says, ticking off his laundry list with smug satisfaction.

"How convenient," I deadpan.

I see a flash of navy behind Henry before Max enters the room.

All the air is sucked from my lungs as I take him in. The way his muscles strain against his suit is indecent. He looks like his suit owes *him* money.

Have his muscles gotten even bigger since he's been here? Or am I just hyperaware of exactly what's hidden underneath that expensive tailoring?

"Gemma," Max says, his voice low and gruff. His eyes flick to appraise Henry, who gives him a curt nod.

"Morning, Max," Henry says, extending him a coffee. "I've just told Gemma about today's visit to the Harrington Estate and thought I'd get you a coffee to go."

Suck up.

"Thank you," Max mutters, accepting the drink. His gaze shifts back to me, his face totally unreadable. "Let's go."

Max's long legs eat up the distance between the hallway and the lift.

My focus darts to Henry, waiting to see whether he's serious.

"I'm going to assume whatever awkwardness I'm sensing between you two will resolve itself before you meet Lord Harrington," he says. When his expression doesn't change,

The Suite Secret

I huff in annoyance, throwing the last biscuit in my mouth and following Max out.

The lift makes its descent toward ground level. Except, we don't stop there. I pivot to find B for basement illuminated.

"Whose car are we taking?"

Max pulls keys from his trouser pocket, spinning the key ring around his index finger once. "Mine."

The doors slide open, and I have to hurry to keep up with his long strides. Clicking the button on the car keys, a Mercedes' taillights blink twice, indicating it's unlocked.

"Since when do you have a car?"

He opens the driver's side with a soft click. "It's mine. I left it here when I went to New York. It's been stored in a private garage."

"Right," I say, sliding into the passenger seat, running a hand over the cool, buttery leather interior. The car smells like him.

The car dips slightly as he gets in. "I usually call a driver for longer trips."

"But not today?" I ask.

His eyes meet mine briefly before he reverses out of the parking garage. "Not today."

As we turn into traffic, we're both silent. The air feels weighted, like the moment before a storm breaks.

"How long is this drive?" I ask.

"About an hour and a half," he replies, staring straight ahead.

I don't respond. I can't speak. All I can think about is my admission to April last night.

An entire day with Max made up of a three-hour road trip, viewing a posh art collection, then dinner tomorrow night.

Just the two of us.

My libido won't be able to handle it.

This is going to be a long day.

Chapter Forty

Max

I organised this trip yesterday after my meeting with Henry about the art collection. He handed me the catalogue Gemma acquired from the gallery, and I must admit, the pieces are exquisite.

The hum of the car's engine fills the cabin as we glide through London's early-morning traffic. The silence is awkward. She's been suspiciously quiet since we left the office, which concerns me. Any other day, she has no issue letting her loose tongue run rampant, but ever since we buckled our seat belts, Gemma's only been providing me with one-word answers. I can't figure out why.

Unable to take the silence, I hook up my iPhone to Apple Play and a gentle track from my playlist drifts faintly through the car.

"You're very quiet," I say.

"I'm tired," she says.

"Hmm."

I catch her rolling her eyes in my peripheral vision.

"*Hmm* what?" she snaps. I feel her gaze boring into the side of my face.

"Usually, I can't get you to shut up."

She turns in her seat, angling toward me. "Why isn't Henry coming with us, Max?"

My jaw tightens, and I wait a beat before answering. "I told him not to."

"What? Why?" Her hand moves to grip her seat belt.

"I told him to stay behind. His expertise is better utilised at the office finalising the campaign materials." There's an edge to my voice. "We're more than capable of assessing Harrington's collection without a third party. I'm not paying you both to take the day off. Henry can stay back and work. This was your proposal, if I recall correctly."

The truth, which I keep to myself, is more selfish. I wanted more time with Gemma alone, away from prying eyes.

The excuse I came up with about Henry's workload is convenient, but it's secondary to my real motivation.

She hums in annoyance. "I suppose that makes sense," she concedes, dropping her hand and sinking back into the seat. The movement releases a wave of coconut scent from her shampoo.

My gaze drops briefly to where her hands now rest in her lap, running her thumb over her polished fingernails.

She's fidgeting. Gemma doesn't fidget. My brows knit together. Is she ... nervous?

"What made you pick this particular collection?" I ask.

I've heard of Alexander—Lord Harrington—before. His father, Alistair Harrington, came from generations of prominent politicians, famous for his conservative approach. He served as a cabinet minister throughout the 1980s and 1990s but was more widely known for his very public affairs that humiliated his wife, Henrietta. Grayson's parents moved in the same circles as the Harringtons, as billionaires do. I've heard, by all accounts, that Alexander is nothing like his father, who Grayson reports to be a pretentious, philandering narcissist with a stick lodged firmly up his arse.

Gemma crosses her ankles. "I liked it."

It's like drawing blood from a stone. Whatever's bothering her, she's determined to keep it locked behind ironclad defences.

My eyes dart to the time displayed on the dash. We're only approaching the outskirts of London now, and we have another forty-five minutes until we reach the estate. I inhale, releasing the breath slowly.

A notification banner pops up on the dash screen. I don't recognise the number, but a preview displays underneath.

Max, this is Casey. Please talk to me. I miss you so much—

Gemma looks down before turning her head away to stare out the window. The temperature in the car seems to drop by ten degrees.

I reach over and dismiss the notification, my jaw clenching. Of all the rotten timing. I know I don't owe Gemma an explanation, but I feel like I need to defend myself, which is ridiculous. As attracted as I am to her, we both know this ends soon.

I'm lost for words. Irritation flares inside me. What can't Casey wrap her bloody mind around? I blocked her for a reason. I don't want to talk to her. And now she's gone to lengths to not only contact my sister, but obtain a random sodding phone number so she can message me?

Gemma remains silent, still facing the window, but I can see the slight purse of her lips in her reflection.

"She's been sending Anna messages," I say, unable to help myself.

She shifts to face me. "Anna? Why?"

"Because she can't get through to me." Gemma just blinks and I squeeze the steering wheel. "I shouldn't have to keep explaining to her why we're not fucking together." The words come out harsher than I intended. "Sorry. It's not you I'm angry with."

The Suite Secret

"You don't need to explain yourself, Max," she says. Her voice has softened and her face has relaxed.

I hold my anger deeply, annoyed that Casey's managed to get to me and we haven't even spoken.

"I respect honesty, Gemma," I say, my voice low. "I don't want to talk about Casey. Ever. But with you ..." I release a deep breath. "I want us to be honest. That's how this works," I say.

She moistens her lip with a quick swipe of her tongue. "Okay."

"I don't want to talk to her," I say. I suddenly need her to understand—like it matters more than anything that she knows.

She meets my eyes. "It's fine. I believe you, Max."

The sincerity in her voice loosens something wound tight in my chest. We lapse into silence, but it feels different now—comfortable.

The countryside rolls by, shifting from the endless grey of London's reach to lush green fields, cottages, and manor houses. Before long, I'm pulling into the driveway of Harrington Estate, announcing myself at the large wrought iron gates. They creak as they open.

I pull up to the estate and turn to Gemma, whose mouth has dropped open.

"Not what you expected?" I ask, allowing myself a small smile at her reaction.

The estate before us is impressive—even by my standards. Limestone walls covered in crawling ivy, tall windows, and a large entrance framed by two stone lions. There's something about old British wealth that not even New York money can replicate.

She blinks. "Holy shit. This place is off its tits!"

Well then. I guess everything really *is* fine.

Chapter Forty-One

Gemma

I don't know what I did to piss off someone in a past life, because the wealth before me is cruel. How can someone actually live in this thing? I'd be shit scared of ghosts. I could burn incense for a week and living in this place would still give me the creeps.

"Ready?" Max asks, switching off the engine.

No. Not even close.

I don't know what came over me in the car. But when he told me why he instructed Henry to stay behind—wanting to be alone with me—I felt nervous. Edgy. Fidgety. I don't get nervous, so my body did what it always does when emotions become inconvenient: it shut down.

And then Casey's message appeared on the dash and my insides hit a panic button and bolted south. I was one text message away from prolapsing.

It's not that the message itself was even dramatic. But the ex who can't let go means *baggage*.

I understand Max is a divorced man. I've done divorced men before. Many times. Usually, it's simpler—they just want to sow their wild oats. But this? Her persistence? Knowing she's using different methods to reach him, all while we're sleeping together? It bothers me. And I hate to admit that.

I can't help but wonder if what they had was so special, so significant, that despite his protests, some connection there—some piece of her—still remains. Why else would she try so desperately to reach him? And why would it bother him so much?

Focus on the task at hand, Gemma.

I smooth my skirt and keep my tone neutral. "Ready."

The front door swings open and out steps a tall—taller than Max—ridiculously good-looking, thirty-something-year-old walking wet dream.

Hello, Christmas.

I plaster on my professional smile, the one I use to impress clients and snobs. I shove all thoughts of Max and Casey to the recesses of my mind.

"Ms Clarke," he says, his tone charming. "Mr Browne."

I extend my hand to shake but he surprises me by bringing the back of my hand to his mouth, placing a small kiss on my knuckles. When his soft lips brush against my skin, I see Max out the corner of my eye clenching his jaw so tightly, I swear he might crack his teeth.

"A pleasure, Lord Harrington," I say.

"Please, call me Alexander. I insist." He shoots me a dazzling white smile. He is otherworldly gorgeous.

"Alexander," I repeat, and he smirks, turning to Max.

"Harrington," Max says, accepting his handshake, and I notice his knuckles whiten. Alexander grimaces.

"Come in," he says, waving us inside. We follow him through the grand entrance, and it takes everything I have not to baulk—the interior is even grander than the outside. Polished marble covers the floor and walls. A grand staircase curves from the far right to the far left of the entrance, leaving a large open walkway through to what I assume is a living area. I crane my neck, inspecting the impressive space as we walk through—to a drawing room? I don't know. I'm not fancy enough for this shit.

Max's penthouse is impressive, but this is spectacular.

"Can I interest either of you in a drink? A tea or coffee, perhaps?" Alexander offers, looking directly at me as he speaks.

"I'd love a tea, thank you."

He nods, fixing his attention on Max.

"I'm fine, thank you," Max says, his voice clipped.

Lord Harrington pivots to face a staff member I didn't even see was there. Has she been following us through the house the entire time?

"Right away, sir," she says, dipping in a short curtsy before scuttling off.

He gestures to what appears to be a sitting room, and as we follow him, I feel the warmth of Max's hand resting on my back, guiding me forward. His touch is light, but visible enough for Alexander to notice.

We each take a seat.

"So, Gemma," Alexander starts, "Camille from the gallery told me you're quite the art enthusiast."

"Oh, no. Not me. That's my friend, April. I appreciate beautiful art, but I couldn't distinguish a Monet from a Manet," I say, chuckling. "I just liked your collection. I guess I'm more into modern contemporary than I realised."

The barest hint of a smile plays on his lips, his eyes never leaving mine. "I appreciate your refreshing honesty. It's rare in my circles." He leans closer. "Well, I'm certainly pleased you stumbled across some of my collection so we could meet." His eyes darken and his voice drops. "After viewing some of my pieces this afternoon, I'd be happy to give you a private tour of some of my more exclusive paintings. The ones I like to keep to myself."

He's flirting with me.

I side-eye Max shifting in his seat beside me, the leather creaking underneath him. It takes everything in me not to laugh at Max's discomfort.

"That won't be necessary," Max says sharply.

Alex and Max have a stare-off, and before any dicks start swinging, I interrupt to attempt damage control.

"What I've already seen is beautiful, thank you. I'd be happy to see more of those. Maybe another time," I say, deliberately fluttering my lashes. "What made you decide to start a collection of your own?"

Max presses his thigh against mine.

"My father began acquiring pieces from the 1300s to 1600s," Alexander says. "But I've taken the collection in a more contemporary direction since his passing. The old man was incredibly conservative. He believed art should be 'respectable' and 'established'. He called all modern art 'graffiti' and an abomination." His eyes meet mine. "I suppose it's my way of rebelling." He chuckles to himself. "Rather juvenile, isn't it?"

I return a soft smile.

"There's something satisfying about attaching the Harrington name to art that challenges convention ... and doing something I know wouldn't please my father." He gestures around the room, adorned with centuries-old paintings and old portraits of stiff-faced ancestors who stare down from fancy frames. It's actually creepy.

As I study the portraits, their lifeless, judging eyes seem to follow my movements. I wrinkle my nose without realising and Max gives me a small nudge. Quickly, I smooth my expression while Alexander continues.

"This house is suffocated by tradition. I want to breathe fresh life into these walls, which is precisely why I began donating pieces from my collection to public institutions.

Art shouldn't be hoarded for selfish enjoyment. Art should be shared, appreciated, even debated," he says.

I must admit, for a prude, it's refreshing to see someone with so much privilege and entitlement appreciate art that would make the older generation clutch their pearls.

Alexander's expression softens. "I find great joy in supporting emerging artists—those voices who might otherwise be silenced by the establishment if it weren't for those with the ability to help them speak. It's liberating."

The staff member returns with a silver tea service that I assume costs more than my car, setting it down before us on an antique table. I thank her, lifting the floral teacup to my mouth and taking a long sip.

Alexander watches as my lips hug the rim of the cup. The way he watches me is so intense it feels like a physical touch.

I chance a quick peek at Max. He's glaring at our host.

"Sir," the staff member says. "Lady Harrington is on the phone and wishes to speak with you."

"Please tell her I'm busy," Alexander says.

"Sir," she insists, nervously fidgeting with her hands as her gaze bounces between the three of us. "It's regarding Ms Freya Larsen."

The shift in the air is immediate. The young lord's nostrils flare as he inhales a deep breath, his face painted with irritation. There's a story there. Who's Freya Larsen?

He gives us a curt nod, standing abruptly. "Please excuse me. Natalie here can show you where my collection is, select as many as you wish—I have plenty more. Stay as long as you like. I'll meet up with you later."

And with that, he leaves the room.

Once the door closes behind him, I turn to Max with a raised eyebrow. "Well, that was interesting," I say.

"He wants you," he says bluntly.

"He's only human."

"He's engaged to be married."

My eyebrows shoot to my hairline. "What? To who? How do you know?"

"Grayson told me."

"Is that who the woman is?"

"Freya Larsen, yes. She's a Dutch heiress." Max's voice drops lower. "It's an arranged marriage."

"An arranged marriage? Why?"

He adjusts his cufflinks, leaning in closer and lowering his voice. "From what Grayson gathered, financial necessity."

My eyes widen. "What do you mean? The Harringtons *clearly* have enough money."

Max nods. "All this? It's expensive to maintain. The estate, the staff, the collections—it costs a fortune to keep up appearances. And word has it Alexander's father had quite the gambling habit."

"Gambling?" I gasp, leaning in. "The plot thickens."

"Yes. But that's not the only reason the marriage would be beneficial. The Larsen family has something more valuable than old money," Max says.

I roll my eyes. "I'm hardly into guessing games—just spit it out already."

"A renewable energy empire. Wind farms, solar technology, green shipping fleets—they're all worth billions and are positioned perfectly for the future economy," he says, his gaze flicking toward the door Alexander disappeared through. "The Harringtons have the land, the social network, and political influence. The Larsens have the cash and the cutting-edge technology."

I scrunch my nose. "So, what? They're selling off their children like cattle for a bunch of windmills and butlers? That's pretty bloody bleak."

Max chuckles. "The Larsens will establish massive wind farms across England—they need someone with the land holdings and government connections to make it happen. And in return, they're essentially funding the Harrington lifestyle and modernising their entire operation."

"And poor Freya gets sacrificed for the cause? I feel like she pulled the short end of the stick in this arrangement," I say, disgusted. Another thought hits me. "Then again, maybe Alexander has a giant penis."

"He certainly seems more interested in flirting with other women than honouring his arrangement," Max grinds out.

"Can't say I blame him," I defend. "God, I couldn't imagine not having a say in who sticks their dick in me for the rest of my life."

"Ms Clarke, Mr Browne," Natalie interrupts gently, "if you'll kindly follow me this way, I'll show you to the viewing gallery."

Max's hand rests against the curve of my lower back once again as we step behind Natalie. We're alone in the corridor, so there isn't any need for him to be touching me.

I think about what April said last night, that I can't carry the responsibility and repercussions of Todd refusing to show up for me. That I can and should let someone in. That I deserve to feel something, to allow myself to experience connection without assuming it will end in disappointment and hurt.

I'm not sure April understands what it's like to open yourself completely to someone, to show them your darkest and most vulnerable parts, only to have them look at you with disgust. To have the person you love tell you your desires are abnormal and refuse to meet you. To have that person make you feel like there's something fundamentally wrong with you for wanting what you want and not being able to help it. But she's right—I should give Max a chance. I deserve it, even if it is short-lived.

Todd made me feel broken when all I wanted was to be seen. Isn't that what any woman wants? I think Max sees me.

Instead of dismissing him, I lean into Max's touch, allowing myself to enjoy it. Whatever might be chasing Max from his past, right now his attention is fixed firmly on me. Maybe this is exactly where I want it to be.

Chapter Forty-Two

Max

It took everything in me not to tell the Harrington twat to keep his eyes off Gemma. His blatant flirting was unsavoury and unprofessional. I understand Grayson is rather fond of him, but I have no connection to the wanker, so as far as I'm concerned, he can piss right off.

I saw red the moment his lips grazed Gemma's skin.

I've been friends with Grayson long enough to see how men like him operate, using their position, their wealth, their lineage to stake claims on whatever they want.

The reckless side of me wanted to press her against one of Harrington's ostentatious walls and make it abundantly clear that she's *mine*.

Natalie leads us through a labyrinth of corridors, each wall decorated and lined with impressive artwork. I bet some of these pieces are worth millions.

I press my hand gently against Gemma's lower back. She leans into it, not moving away, which is a relief. I'm glad she isn't angry about Casey's text, because I'm carrying enough fury for us both.

The moment her name appeared on the dash, a rush of agitation ignited in my chest. I don't know what else I'm supposed to do. I don't want to have to change my bloody number because my ex won't leave me alone. I have too many work connections to do that. She'd better not make this a habit.

I blocked the number as soon as I stepped out of the car. I saw the shift in Gemma's body language. The tension in the air was suffocating, but I'm relieved she believed me.

"The viewing gallery is through here," Natalie says, gesturing toward a set of double doors. "Lord Harrington had everything arranged this morning when he heard you were coming."

Of course he did.

Natalie pushes open the doors to a wide, well-lit space with paintings aligned on tall, pitched walls and propped on easels.

"He thought these might be best suited for Gray Hotel," she says.

"Thank you." Gemma smiles appreciatively.

Natalie dips her chin. "I'll leave you to it. If you need anything, I'll be in the sitting room."

Natalie exits silently and Gemma releases a low whistle, spinning slowly. "Wow, these are amazing."

"They're okay," I say, shrugging.

Gemma stalks toward me slowly, and my gaze drops to the way her hips sway with each step. "Oh, come on, even *you* have to admit this is impressive."

When she's within reach, I loop my arm around her waist and pull her in. She collides with my chest with a light gasp.

Her eyes widen slightly. "What are you doing?" she asks, not pulling away.

I drop my head to her neck, inhaling her sweet scent. I lick a path up the column of her throat, and she shivers against me. My cock stirs in my trousers.

"I don't like how he was looking at you," I grind out, the words barely making it past my clenched teeth.

She drives me mad with need.

"And how was that?" she breathes, her hands clenching my shirt.

I brush my lips against the shell of her ear, letting my voice drop to a growl. "Like he wanted to fuck you."

She trembles in my arms. "And what are you going to do about it?"

I press my cock against her stomach, fusing our hips together and grinding just enough for her to feel how badly I want to be inside her. I bend at the knees, lifting her with one arm and slam her back against one of the walls, rattling the nearby frames.

"Max," she warns. "There are cameras."

I follow her gaze to two cameras hidden in the corner of the ceiling. A slow, wide smile stretches across my face when I see the two blinking lights. Watching. Recording.

Perfect.

"Even better," I murmur. "Let him watch."

Her breath catches. "You can't be serious."

"Then stop me," I challenge, lifting a brow.

Her chest rises and falls, but she doesn't move to stop me. I manoeuvre her weight to keep her steady with one arm while the other slowly begins to trail up the inside of her thigh. She responds immediately, crashing her lips into mine, her spine curving into me as we kiss messily.

Her legs lock around my waist as our tongues slide against each other. I shove her thong to the side to spread her wetness around her slick heat, preparing her.

"So wet," I groan. "Is this all for me?"

"It's for Alexander," she teases with a devilish glint in her eye.

I pause, pulse hammering, then drop my hand from her pussy. She whimpers at the loss of contact, rocking her hips against me for friction—and I slap her pussy, hard and sharp. She gasps, her head tipping back.

"Don't ever say another man's name while I'm playing with your cunt."

"Max," she moans.

I find the thin strip of fabric between her legs and rip it clean off. Her drenched, ruined thong drops to the hardwood floor just as my fingers stroke through her folds, three times, before pushing inside her. I milk my fingers in and out as she rides my hand, bearing down greedily.

"Look at you. So greedy to fuck my hand. Can't even wait for my cock," I tut.

My mouth latches onto the soft skin at her neck, sucking hard enough to ensure I leave a mark. She whimpers and releases breathy pants as I pump my fingers in and out. She's dripping for me, coating my hand in her juice. Slippery and hot and perfect.

Her nails dig into my shoulders for support as I work my belt open with one hand, shoving my trousers down enough to free my cock.

"Does this pussy want my cock?" I ask against her throat, licking and sucking the spot I've just marked.

"Yes." She draws in a ragged breath.

I line myself up, the tip of my cock teasing her entrance, and I drag it through her slick folds.

"*Please*," she begs.

"Please, what?" I ask.

"I need you inside me."

I glance at the cameras, then back at her.

"Do you want everyone to see what a hungry little slut you are for my cock?"

She nods. Her pupils are blown out, her cheeks flushed the prettiest red, and my heart hammers in my chest at the sight of her, desperate for me.

I slam into her in one deep thrust, burying myself to the hilt. She cries out, clutching onto me.

"That's it," I groan. "Take every fucking inch."

Her pussy clenches around me as I stretch her open and I swear I see stars.

Just like Saturday night, I don't take my time. Her chants drip from her lips like thick nectar as I pump my cock inside her. My balls grow heavy, desperate to come as I watch the camera, hoping Harrington can see me taking what's mine. The hand holding her steady against me grips and kneads her soft flesh. I snake my hand between us, seeking out her hot swollen clit, strumming my thumb over it. Her moans kick up in volume and I lose myself to oblivion as I piston my hips, rutting into her shamelessly.

"Ah!" she gasps. "S-so good."

"Feel that?" I groan, and she nods frantically. "That's the only cock this tight little pussy is going to get. Understand me?"

"Y-yes," she whimpers. "Only yours."

My thumb kicks up in speed as her pussy walls begin to flutter, and I can tell she's getting close.

I use my knees to pin her open as wide as possible. She's loving it, arching her back and shifting her hips to take more of me, begging me to go harder and faster. I meet her, thrust for thrust. I look down at where our bodies join and I know I'm about to lose the battle. Knowing we're being watched spurs me on even more.

Her mouth drops open on a low, keening moan. "I'm co— I'm—"

She doesn't finish her sentence, breaking off as her inner walls ripple around my cock, making her impossibly tight. The dam breaks and I lose it, swelling and spilling and exploding into her as I come.

"That's it," I grunt, my voice raw. "Take my cum, sweetheart."

The Suite Secret

My lips find hers and I suck her tongue into my mouth. Releasing my hand from her clit, my hand finds her throat, holding her in place as I continue to spill inside her.

Her breathing is ragged against my neck, and she remains still, clinging onto my shoulders, as if she'd float away if she let go.

I don't move.

I don't pull out.

I can't.

The idea of putting distance between us feels inherently wrong. Like if I move, even an inch, we'll both fall apart.

Gemma blinks up at me, catching her breath. Her eyes are glassy behind her frames, her pupils still eating up the colour of her irises. Her glossy lips are parted, and her hair is strewn around her shoulders. There's no teasing mischief left in her eyes, not anymore.

She's so breathtaking it hurts.

I drop my forehead to hers, our breaths tangling, like we're breathing each other in and out.

I don't want to let you go.

I'm still holding her legs wide and they tremble slightly where they're wound around my waist.

She glances at the cameras before dipping her face to my neck, nuzzling into me. "Someone saw all of that. It's still blinking red."

"I'm assuming so, yes," I say, keeping my voice even.

Her teeth sink into her bottom lip.

"Do you like the idea of someone watching us?" I ask.

She doesn't hesitate. "Yes."

She shifts underneath me, and I gently pull out, feeling our cum trickle out of her.

I set her down gently on the floor, supporting her elbow to ensure she's stable. She straightens her dress, and I watch in awe as tiny, wet droplets fall to the floor. An animalistic possessiveness claws its way up my spine when I see both of us mixed together, dripping out of her.

Good, now Harrington will know exactly who she belongs to.

The double doors burst open and Natalie rushes through.

"Ms Clarke, Mr Browne," she says, her cheeks flushed. "Did you find any pieces you might like to display? I can start the paperwork."

Her eyes flick around the room before locking on the slightly crooked frame on the wall behind Gemma—askew from what we just did. She freezes; her mouth opens. Closes. Opens again. Like she wants to speak but can't quite form the words.

I smirk to myself. I wonder if *she* was watching.

I slip my hands into my trouser pockets, in a far better mood than I was when we first arrived. "We'll take all of them."

Chapter Forty-Three

Gemma

Max: *The design team loves the collection. Well done, Clarke.*

I smile as I reread the message, a surge of pride blooming in my chest. Of course they love it. The art was a bloody good idea.

We completed the paperwork for Alexander's collection before leaving his estate.

At least Max seemed to have worked out some of his caveman frustration by the time Alexander finally rejoined us, thank God. I'm glad he humped his frustration out, because I thought he was going to cock his leg and pee on me if Alexander flirted one more time. I didn't take Max to be the jealous type; I'd guessed he'd be the opposite. Turns out he's quite the territorial alpha male, and I don't mind it one bit. He just gets dirtier and dirtier.

My fingers dance across the screen as I type my reply.

Me: *Do I get a reward?*

Three dots appear.

Max: *Only if you're a good girl tomorrow night.*

Tomorrow night. Dinner.

A tickle develops low in my gut, and I catch myself smiling at his text. Is that excitement? Or am I just horny? I can't tell.

The sound of my doorbell buzzer causes me to jump. "Every single time," I mutter, clutching my chest.

I pad over to my window, peering out at the street below where the postman has already hurried off, leaving a small, innocuous-looking parcel by the building entrance.

Speaking of being horny, that must be my butt plug.

Taking the stairs two at a time, I snatch the parcel and head back inside, tearing into the wrapping as soon as my arse hits the seat.

The product packaging is sleek and black, wrapped in a pretty pink bow. I unravel the ribbon and flick the lid off the box, revealing the glistening jewelled butt plug tucked into its soft, purple silk box.

"Well, hello there," I murmur, lifting the plug from its cushioning.

It's slightly heavier than I expected, stainless steel with a jewelled end that catches the light, casting colourful prisms across the opposite wall.

"This is far too pretty to stick up my arse," I say to myself.

It's so pretty I want to carry it around with me. I tuck the box away safely in my tote bag.

I return to the sofa, flicking on the TV. My eyes bounce back and forth between the screen and my phone. I mindlessly open my text thread with Max, rereading our messages.

I freeze, realising what I'm doing, and toss my phone onto the sofa beside me.

When we parted ways with a professional "Good afternoon" and nothing more, I missed his presence immediately. I longed for it in a way that's utterly embarrassing.

I instinctively reach for my phone again, contemplating whether to cancel dinner, to pull back so it makes detaching easier. But my fingers pause over the screen, unwilling to type the words.

It's pathetic and clichéd. It's exactly what I've been avoiding for years—that ridiculous, adolescent yearning. The kind that makes you check your phone every thirty seconds hoping they've messaged.

I've developed feelings for Max Browne. Actual, proper, grown-up, disgusting feelings that go well beyond appreciating his body.

The worst part isn't admitting that the feelings are there; it's the knowledge that in five weeks' time, Gray Hotel will be open, and he'll be on a plane back to New York.

My gaze fixes on my giant tentacle dildo, which serves exceptionally well as a doorstop for my kitchen door. The deep purple silicone stares back at me.

"You'd better get the job done once he's gone," I say aloud, then immediately cringe at myself. "Oh, God." I slap my forehead with a loud smack. "I'm talking to my dildo."

Chapter Forty-Four

Gemma

"I had a dream last night that I turned up to the hotel launch party topless."

Henry eyes me over the lip of his coffee mug.

"What?" I ask, suddenly feeling self-conscious.

A crease forms between his thick brows. "You literally turned up to Nate's fortieth birthday party topless."

I gawk at him. "In my defence, I wasn't wearing my glasses when I received the invitation."

"Even with your abhorrent eyesight, I still don't understand how you confused 'Champagne and Canapés' for 'Champagne and Cha-Chas'."

"The email was very pixelated!" I retort, straightening in my chair. "I thought it was one of those trendy new concepts—you know, like those naked restaurants in New York."

"It was at his aunt's private member club in SoHo," Henry deadpans.

I sigh, dipping my shortbread in my coffee. "At least the bartenders appreciated it."

Henry shakes his head, setting his mug down on my desk. "The marketing team sent out invitations to influencers last night and put some money behind Instagram and TikTok ads."

The Suite Secret

Excitement fizzles through me like sherbet. "That's so exciting! Have we seen any engagement metrics yet?"

Henry nods, a small smile softening his features. "Thousands of saves, reposts, and comments so far. The Reel concept you came up with is performing extremely well."

"Excellent," I say, crossing one leg over the other. "I've finalised the spa narrative with the manager for the press kit, and I had a call with the copywriters yesterday about the room descriptions for the website."

"I reviewed the copy deck. Good work. Looked flash without sounding pretentious." He shifts in his seat, checking his watch. "I've organised for us to visit the hotel with Max this afternoon for a final walkthrough. Can you review the signature cocktail menu with the bar manager while we're there? I want to make sure the presentation and names align with the brand," he says.

"Of course." I slip my professional mask firmly back in place, ignoring how my stomach almost bottoms out at the mention of spending another afternoon with Max.

"It's interesting, actually."

"What is?" I ask, my eyes snapping up to meet Henry's, which gleam playfully. He smooths a hand down his tie.

"Just that since last week, Max has developed quite the enthusiasm for our client meetings." Henry's eyes gleam. "Especially those with your name on the invite. He was rather insistent on only having you join him for the Harrington Estate visit." He pauses briefly. "And he confirmed today's site visit two minutes after I sent the email."

I tilt my head. "Alright, smart-arse. If you've got something to say, just say it."

A slow, cocky smirk unfurls across his lips. "I don't think I need to say anything at all, do I?"

"I don't know what you're talking about." I bite into my shortbread.

He taps his fingers on the mahogany desk, narrowing his eyes at me.

"What now?" I ask.

He crosses his arms. "Admit it."

"Admit what?"

"This isn't just a little crush anymore. You like Max Browne."

I scoff, sliding my mug across the desk as I open my email.

"And I think he has feelings for you."

"I'm not talking about this with you," I say, tapping away at my keyboard.

"Gem." Henry's voice takes on a soft, serious tone that he rarely uses, and I pause, reluctantly meeting his gaze. "It's okay to like someone. To let someone in."

I roll my eyes. "*Christ*—you sound exactly like April."

"Well, maybe April's right."

I raise an eyebrow. "If you don't drop this right now, I swear I'll take off my top and recreate the Cha-Cha incident right here in my office."

His face contorts with disgust. "God, please don't."

"Then get out." I jerk my chin toward the door. "And take your relationship advice with you."

"Don't forget, Gemma—you report to *me*," he says, standing and leaning over my desk. "And you can repress your emotions all you like. Have at it. But whatever happens, *don't* mess up this launch. Be ready at 1 pm for the site visit."

"Can't wait," I say, waving him off.

* * *

The smell of fresh paint, wood varnish, and fabric treatments cloaks us as we stride through the hotel foyer. My stilettos tap a steady cadence against the burnished stone.

The Suite Secret

I crane my neck, inspecting every nook and cranny in awe. Despite workers still milling about with ladders and tools, I can already envision how spectacular this hotel is going to look in five weeks when it opens to the public.

Elegant guests will glide through and be greeted by two doormen, valet services available. Concierge to the right of the entryway, ready to direct guests to the best the city has to offer. Beyond them, bellmen in crisp charcoal uniforms will run errands, assist with luggage, and escort guests to their rooms.

The property is gorgeous, and the Gray Hotel vision come to life is a true masterpiece.

I note the available space opposite the concierge desk and mentally file it away. A barista station would be perfect there. Guests arriving after transatlantic flights and facing hour-long waits before check-in would kill for a proper coffee. I must remember to tell Max at dinner tonight.

My body throbs at the memory of his hands on me yesterday.

We follow Max through to the hotel cocktail bar, which is the real showpiece of the ground floor. I force my gaze upward from his perfect arse to enjoy the big reveal.

Pendant lights drip from the ceiling, casting a warm, amber glow. Everything is wrapped in smoky blues, plush velvet, and sleek burnished copper.

I step forward, running my fingers along the bar's surface.

"Wow. Max ... this is incredible." I turn to him, standing behind me in a two-piece navy suit, looking like an Adonis. "It's beautiful."

Henry nods approvingly beside me, and I know he's thinking the same thing—this is exactly the sort of space we imagined for the launch party.

"You're thinking what I'm thinking, right?" I say to Henry.

"This is where the content happens," Henry replies, scratching his jaw as he surveys the room.

I gasp dramatically. "You mean you finally agree with me?"

"There's a first time for everything," he says, tipping his head to look down at me, and I roll my eyes.

This will be the heart of our campaign. Cocktails, immaculately dressed guests and modern fusion dining that everyone who's anyone will be posting, tagging, and raving about on socials.

"So," I say, turning my attention to Max. "How do you see guests interacting in this space? I want to make sure it's communicated in the marketing."

Max smirks. "I think it will be a versatile space—businesspeople sipping on cappuccinos in the morning before transitioning into an ambient space in the evening."

"Perfect," I reply, mentally ticking off all the features to pass on to the PR, events, and design teams.

This is why I love my job. As a creative director, I live for these moments when everything aligns—finally seeing the space through the same lens that everyone else will view it once our campaign launches.

Max points to a booth near the far end of the bar. "We're also adding discreet power outlets under the tables, for guests working remotely or holding meetings during off-peak hours."

I feel his enthusiasm. It's infectious, and it makes me grin.

"This hotel is really special, Max. You've done a wonderful job," I say, my eyes softening as they meet his.

"Thank you, but I can't take all the credit. The Livingstone team coordinated all this. They've done an exceptional job," he says gently, pulling his phone from his pocket and checking the time. "The bar staff will be joining us in about fifty minutes to go over the signature cocktails for the launch party, but I'd love to show you the rest of the property first."

"Lead the way," Henry says.

"I can't wait to see the spa," I whisper, leaning into Henry.

Max's expression shifts when his eyes flick to Henry, as if he doesn't like him being too close. I should tell him Henry's gay, but what would be the fun in that?

Without a word, Max nods once and gestures for us to follow.

* * *

The guest floors are finished and just as impressive as the rest of the venue.

As we approach the penthouse suite, Henry's phone buzzes incessantly in his pocket.

"You gonna take that?" I ask, eyeing him sideways.

Henry glances at the screen and sighs, stopping mid-step. "It's Chadwick. I need to take this."

"Do you want us to wait?" I ask. I try to keep my tone friendly but I'm boring holes through him, silently begging him to say no.

"No, you two go ahead. I've seen the other suites—I'm happy with that. I'll see you back at the office."

"You're leaving?" I ask, trying not to sound too hopeful.

"This won't be a short call." Henry reaches out to shake Max's hand. "Thanks for showing us around, and congratulations—it's all looking brilliant."

I hide the victory party being thrown in my head.

Max shakes his hand, his voice cool and even. "My pleasure. Appreciate it."

With that, Henry disappears, his voice echoing down the corridor.

Max's eyes meet mine and the air between us crackles. Need scales my body, and lust coils up my spine like a serpent.

He tilts his head toward the large double doors at the end of the short corridor.

"I want you to see the view."

We both know exactly what's going to happen the moment we step inside that suite.

Naturally, I follow.

Chapter Forty-Five

Gemma

He swipes the key card across the reader and the door unlocks. I take in the suite, trying to focus on the details rather than how badly I want him to touch me.

I follow Max through a dimly lit hallway, peering into various rooms. Not a single cent has been spared on details—the best finishes, the finest furnishings and décor. Max watches me, gauging my reaction with a sexy lopsided grin. His woody scent clings to the air, and I breathe it in hungrily.

My breath stalls in my throat when he leads me to the massive windows taking up the entire back wall of the penthouse, much like his own. I'm again taken aback by the beautiful view.

Holy shit. Opposite is a large terrace dotted with pot plants and—is that an in-ground pool? He leads me down a set of stairs I hadn't even noticed, which opens to a theatre room. The left wall is a viewing window to the pool, an underground terrace pool. In London. Unheard of.

"Oh, how the other half lives," I say wistfully.

"Do you like it?" he asks, his voice low. He follows me back up the steps.

"Like it? I don't think I've ever been in such a gorgeous suite. This view is stunning."

"It is," he says. I pivot to find his aquamarine eyes locked on me, not the skyline, and I turn so he can't see the heat climbing my cheeks.

"How much is this per night?" I ask, trying to distract myself from the warmth pooling low in my belly.

"Twenty-five thousand pounds," he provides. My eyes widen.

Stepping forward, he reaches a hand up to caress my jaw, feathering his thumb back and forth over my cheek as if I'm something precious.

"Max," I whisper, my eyes drifting shut.

His touch is different, as if he's memorising every inch of me.

When I open my eyes, his pupils are wide, his brows cinched together. He looks at me as if he's just placed a missing puzzle piece and now the image makes sense. As if he can predict my thoughts.

"What?" I ask, feeling more exposed than I have before.

He shakes his head.

"You don't even realise, do you? You're extraordinary." His thumb traces my bottom lip.

"You don't have to say that." I cast my gaze downward.

He bristles. "I'm being serious."

"So am I," I say, my voice quieter. "I'm not the kind of woman men write sonnets about. No one's ever scribbled verses about me in the margins of their notebook."

"You're selling yourself short," he says.

"I'm being realistic. I know what and who I am. You don't need to make me feel special to get what you want. We both agreed to the terms. I'm already here."

He looks taken aback. "Is that really all you think this is?"

"Isn't it?" I challenge, though my voice wavers slightly.

"No. Not anymore," he says.

"What changed?" I ask, knowing full well what changed, because I've felt it too.

"I got to know you, Gemma." His eyes burn with intensity.

"Maybe you just like that I don't expect anything from you."

"Bullshit," he fires back. "There isn't a world where you're in someone's life and don't become the centre of it."

I turn my head, but he captures my chin between his thumb and forefinger, forcing me to look into his eyes.

"Don't do that. Don't push me away. Don't hide—not from me." He pauses briefly. "Let me *see* you, Gemma."

"What if you don't like what you see?" I whisper.

He releases a breath. "That's not possible."

"I'm not good at this part," I confess, feeling my heart crack open as I allow myself to say the words.

"You don't have to be," he says quietly. "You don't have to perform, or prove, or pretend with me." His fingers move to thread through my hair. "I just want to see you—messy, scared, brilliant you." He pauses. "I want all of it."

How does he know? How can he *see*?

My face crinkles with confusion. "What if you can't give me what I need?"

"I know I can."

"How do you know?"

Delicately, he brushes a loose lock behind my ear. "Because I think you want to see me too."

My body wants to revert back to what it knows is safe and comfortable—what I can control. "This isn't what we agreed to."

A brisk laugh leaves him. "I don't care anymore."

"It's just sex." The lie barely holds together as it slips from my mouth.

"It's not. It's not, and you know it."

Of course I know it. Lava explodes in my veins, sending my heartbeat soaring. My mind tries to weave together all the reasons this is wrong. All the reasons it can't work. All the reasons we shouldn't.

"But Anna—" I press.

He drops his forehead to mine. "We'll figure it out. She'll hate this, at the beginning. But I can't pretend I don't want you."

My shoulders slump in defeat. "It won't—"

My words are cut off when he slams his mouth against mine, capturing my gasp. My tote bag slides off my shoulder, dropping to the floor with a thud. All excuses fade to smoke the moment his mouth seals over mine. My body recognises him as its master before my mind can catch up and I melt against him. The kiss is frantic and full of need, and I find myself surrendering to the heady rush.

"Gemma," he groans against my mouth, and my knees threaten to buckle.

I whimper as his strong hands twist in my hair, tugging my head back with a slight sting so he can deepen the kiss.

Our tongues dance and his breath becomes mine as I pull him closer by his perfectly pressed suit.

He walks me backward until I feel the cool surface of the island against my skirt. He lifts me like I weigh nothing and sets me on the edge, reaching beneath my skirt and dragging my wet knickers down my legs.

"You're already wet," he groans, dragging his fingers through the mess he's made of me. "Fucking dripping. All for me."

"I need you," I beg, practically shaking.

And I do. I need him. He's the only man who's been able to meet me halfway, offering everything my body craves. He touches me in a way other men are afraid to, in a way that sends liquid fire skittering through me.

His eyes darken at my confession. "Say it again," he commands.

"I need you," I whisper, shocked at my own desperation. I've never needed someone the way I need him now, as if there's a void inside me that only he can fill.

A growl of satisfaction rumbles deep from his chest and his hands pull away from my pussy and bracket my face, my wetness smearing across my cheek. Tilting my head, he exposes my throat. Gooseflesh pebbles my skin as he nips, grazes, and teases me with his tongue and teeth.

My fingers find the fabric of his jacket, peeling it down his shoulders before they get to work unclasping his belt to tug his zipper down.

Releasing my neck, he grips my shirt, ripping it open in one rough tug. I gasp as buttons scatter across the sparkling tiles.

"That was pure silk!"

"I'll buy you another one."

I push his trousers down, exposing his hard cock, and I bite my lip.

"Look at what you do to me," he says.

My fingers wrap around the thick, hot shaft and he groans as I pump him from base to tip, swirling the pre-cum back and forth through his slit.

His eyes are feral and the sounds he's making are animalistic, savage, shooting straight between my legs.

"Jesus, Gemma," he hisses through clenched teeth. "You're going to ruin me."

Good, I think to myself. I want to ruin him the way he's ruined me. I want to wreck every woman who came before the way he's done to me.

"You don't even know," he rasps. "You touch me like that, and I forget my name. Forget what I'm doing. Forget I'm supposed to have any damn control."

"Then don't," I say, my grip tightening as I stroke him harder. "I want to see you lose control."

The words flick a switch inside him, and his hands are suddenly between my legs, pushing my knees wide. I release his cock as he pushes up my skirt, the loose material gathering at my waist. He hooks his forearms under my knees, pulling me forward, my arse hanging off the edge of the smooth bench. I slap my palms against the counter to steady myself.

His eyes drink me in with a fervent hunger—like he's discovered something holy between my thighs.

"Fucking hell," he pants, eyes roaming over my core. "I'll never get enough of seeing you."

He presses himself flush against me, rubbing his erection through my slick centre. My juices coat his velvet skin, and I tip my head back, a moan catching in my throat. My hips tip back and forth, guiding him through me and seeking more.

"Max," I whimper.

"Tell me you're mine," he chokes out. "Say it, Gemma. Say it or I'll stop."

"You're insane," I gasp, circling my hips. A muscle feathers in his jaw, and I fight the urge to roll my eyes, half-tempted to see what the gesture will earn me.

"Say it," he demands.

"I'm yours."

That's all it takes. He drives into me in one brutal thrust. My back arches and a cry rips from my throat as he fills me.

I've just admitted that I'm his. I should feel panic. I should run before I willingly let myself fall. But I can't.

He leans in and kisses me, wet and hot and deep, full of passion and promise. An overwhelming foreign sensation bubbles inside me and my eyes glaze over, wetness clinging to my lashes as I try to decipher its meaning.

"Baby," he says against my lips, and my ribcage splinters. Not because I don't like the endearment, but because I *do*.

The Suite Secret

Time suspends as our eyes remain fastened on each other, and recognition passes between us—like tectonic plates, something between us fundamentally shifts. Realigning into something irreversible.

A lone tear traces a path down my cheek, and he kisses it away.

"I know," he says, his voice low. I can't speak, and as if he can read my mind, he starts to move. Slow at first, pacing himself. I clasp my legs around his waist, locking my ankles together. Needing more, I press my front against his and he drags himself in and out of me, winding my arms around his neck. Without asking, he gives me everything he knows I need.

His hands grip my arse, anchoring us together, and without pulling out, he lifts me. Buried inside me, he carries me to the bedroom, gently sitting at the edge of the bed. My knees sink into the mattress as I straddle him. His cock twitches inside me and I brace my hands on his strong shoulders and begin to move, lifting, sinking again, slower, then faster.

His eyes fix on me as his hands cling to my hips, guiding me up and down.

"You're even more beautiful like this," he groans. "Fucked out and mine."

I roll my hips faster, picking up the pace. He's so much deeper in this position.

"I can feel you everywhere," I breathe.

His muscles flex as he guides me up and down, the sharp sound of flesh meeting flesh cracking through the room as he meets me thrust for thrust.

He lifts his hand, and I watch—panting—as he spits into his palm, curling his fingers to rub them against the saliva. A low, desperate moan escapes me as he slides his thick fingers down, pressing them against my arse.

I curve my spine, anticipating the delicious stretch I crave so badly—I want him to fill me. *Everywhere.*

A finger circles my hole, teasing me, pressing lightly against my back entrance. I gasp, revelling in the sensation.

"Do you want me to take you here?" His breath is hot against my neck, and I nod frantically.

He slaps my arse. "All fours."

Lifting off him, I do as he commands, falling to all fours on the bed, my fingers digging into the expensive cotton sheets.

He drops to his knees behind me—I blush at the way he shamelessly inspects my pussy and arse. It's deeply personal, and I love it.

I wiggle my hips, silently begging.

His mouth latches onto my pussy, dragging a firm, deliberate line from my front to my back. I buck my hips, growing impossibly wet.

I've had rim jobs before, but this is something else entirely.

His tongue draws circles around my tight hole, and I release a low, keening moan.

"I'm going to work you open, sweetheart," he says, thrusting two fingers inside me and curling them. My entire body bows as pleasure rolls through me in waves. I whimper, pressing back against his hand, greedy for more.

"That's it," he coos, spreading my juices up my crack and around my hole. I look back, and gently, ever so slowly, he presses one finger inside my arse.

"I can take you," I pant.

"I know you can. Such a good girl," he growls.

My vision swims as he continues to fuck me deep with both hands, teasing, coaxing and building me up until I'm nothing but raw, exposed nerves.

He carefully slips a second finger in my back hole; this time, I take it easily. My breath hitches, but not from discomfort—from *need*. He patiently works me open, my body turning into a live wire.

"You're nearly ready." His voice is strained.

The Suite Secret

"Plug," I pant, barely able to speak. "In my bag."

He pauses. "You brought the plug?"

I nod, my cheeks pressing into the sheets.

"Fuck," he groans, pressing a kiss to my spine, then stands. "I'm going to get it, okay, baby?"

"O-Okay," I breathe.

The moment he slips from me, the emptiness feels unbearable. I'm so worked up. I close my eyes and listen to his footsteps, the rustle as he rummages through my bag, then he's back.

A click pulls me from my lull. "You keep lube in your handbag?"

"It's me," I murmur, barely lifting my head, and he responds with a light chuckle.

The mattress dips behind me and I jolt as something cold and slick lands between my cheeks.

I gasp, lurching forward. "Jesus."

He strokes a hand down my back. "Ready?"

Chapter Forty-Six

Max

"Yes," she breathes.

I press the plug against her entrance, watching as her tight hole yields, stretching around the cool steel as it sinks into her.

She sucks in a deep breath, and I immediately begin to rub a soothing hand up and down her spine.

"That's it," I murmur. "You're taking it so well."

She whimpers, her hips pressing into the plug, willing it to slide deeper.

"It's in, sweetheart. How's the size?" I ask.

"It's good. I can feel everything."

A sound rumbles from my chest—somewhere between a groan and a curse. I'm seconds away from losing my mind. From gripping her hips and taking her pussy until she's completely stuffed. But I bide my time, forcing myself to steady my breathing.

"Are you ready for more?" I ask.

"Fuck me, Max," she says, her fists curling in the sheets.

Thank God.

Bracing myself behind her, I line up my cock with her pussy. Instinctively, she starts to rock back, feeding my cock

The Suite Secret

into her hot channel inch by inch. Her greedy little slit swallows me deeper with every pass.

The feeling of being inside her while she's wearing the plug is obscene, heightening every sensation.

"I'm so full," she pants.

"Jesus, Gemma. You're so damn tight."

And when I bottom out—when I'm sheathed so deep inside her I forget where she starts and I end—I lose control.

We both release a strangled sound as I hammer into her, desperate to chase our release. I jerk my hips, fucking her relentlessly. She's dripping, painting the inside of her thighs with her arousal.

My cock is so hard and so heavy I can barely breathe. When she peers at me over her shoulder, hair tousled, lips kiss-swollen, eyes lust-filled, I power into her. Sweat clings to our skin and sex fills the air as I pound her brutally.

Pressing my chest to her back, I wind her blond locks around my wrist, giving them a sharp tug. Her spine bows, her mouth drops, and she writhes against me, trying to pull me deeper.

"Max!" she screams. "Make me come!"

That's all the encouragement I need. My thrusts go from brutal to frenzied. The sound of our bodies colliding is thunderous.

"You want to come, baby?" I snarl. "Then take it."

I release her hair and reach between her thighs, my fingers seeking out her swollen clit, rubbing tight circles.

Her muscles tighten, her pussy strangling my cock as her body seizes. She cries out, coming *hard*. The combined feel of her snatched pussy clutching me and the plug snug against my cock, I shatter with her, roaring her name.

She wrings me out, sucking me in as I spill into her, loading her up with my seed. I don't stop until she's chanting my name and I'm empty. Until she's full.

Pulling out, I collapse beside her and gather her into me.

"Damn," I say, catching my breath.

Planting her hand over my heart, she smiles up at me. It almost sucks all the air out of my lungs.

"I love butt plugs," she whispers.

"Yeah?" I smirk, tickling her sides and she bursts out laughing, the sound a sweet melody I want to bottle and keep.

She throws a leg over my waist, still leaking on me, and I smile to myself, holding her flush against my body. Like she might slip through my fingers if I let go. And this time, she stays, tracing her fingertips idly over my skin.

No excuses. No running away. Just *being*.

I know what I've asked of her isn't small. Trust doesn't come easy for her, that much is obvious. As I lie beside her, running my fingers through her silky hair, kissing her forehead, her temple, every soft, sacred place I can reach, I remind myself to crack open too. To let her see all of Max Browne. To offer her the same vulnerability I've asked for.

I just hope like hell that it's enough to make her stay.

Chapter Forty-Seven

Max

"Max, hurry up. I'm about to die of boredom," Anna calls from the other side of the dressing room door.

After dropping Gemma at the office, I asked Anna to meet me at Harrods to help me select a suit for the hotel launch party. Prying myself away from Gemma was physically painful, but I'm seeing her tonight, and that thought's the only thing keeping me sane.

I feel as though I've neglected Anna lately, and I know she's going through a tough time. She deserves my attention.

The irony isn't lost on me—my selfishness about Gemma is likely going to hurt my sister far more than any absence ever has. But the truth? I don't have it in me to stop.

I'm beginning to really care about her best friend, far more than I ever intended to.

We're treating something amazing as if it's forbidden—shameful. But it's real. It's right. And I'm sick of fighting it.

Everything shifted today.

Gemma showed me a part of herself I suspect few have ever witnessed. When those eyes that typically guard everything finally allowed me entry, I was lost entirely.

My wanting Gemma began as pure instinct. It was innate and immediate from the first moment I saw her. But it's evolved into something far deeper than I ever expected or prepared for.

I hate that when we're in the office, we're forced to ignore our desires. The tension between us is so overwhelming, I don't know if we're about to fight or fuck—and I want both.

When I told her I wanted to see her—*truly* see her—I meant it. Throughout my career, I've made it my business to read people, to understand and fulfil their needs before they can articulate them. But with Gemma? She's a language all her own—and I want fluency.

I shrug on the suit jacket, swing open the door, and step up to the wall of floor-to-ceiling mirrors.

"You said you were happy to meet me," I say, adjusting the lapels.

Anna rolls her eyes dramatically. "I am. I love shopping. I just prefer when it's *me* you're spending money on."

"Hmm."

Anna stands, striding toward me and pulling at the tag hanging from the jacket sleeve.

"Bloody hell!" she shouts, her eyebrows shooting to her hairline. "Max, this suit is nine hundred pounds!"

"That's just the jacket," I reply, rolling my shoulders to get a feel for the fit.

Just then, the shop assistant reappears, brandishing her tape measure. "Well? What do we think?" Her hopeful gaze darts between Anna and me. "I think that cut looks fabulous on you."

"I'll take it," I state decisively, stepping back from the mirrors.

"Excellent. The tailoring really is exquisite. I'll just be over by the counter when you're ready," she says, pivoting and marching out.

"I love my job, but sometimes I wonder if I'd have been better off getting into accounting," Anna mutters.

I chuckle. "You couldn't differentiate between a debit and credit when you went to uni."

"Alright, smart-arse."

"Your job is fulfilling, and that's what matters," I reply, meaning it. Anna's passion for teaching has always been something I've respected.

"Fulfilling doesn't afford Tom Ford suits," she says, crossing her arms.

"How are things with you and Mason?" I ask.

Her shoulders tense. "Fine."

"Ah," I say. "The word that means that you're anything *but* fine."

She attempts a smile that doesn't reach her eyes. "It's just the same. I'm okay."

"Anna," I say her name, hoping she'll divulge more information.

"I don't want to talk about it, Max." There's an edge to her voice that stops me from pressing any further. "I still want a baby. He still doesn't. It's that simple."

I give her a sympathetic smile. "I'm sorry, weasel." I soften my approach. "You know my door's always open, right? You have a key to the penthouse—use it anytime. I mean it. Even if it's three in the morning."

She nods in acknowledgement. "I know. Thank you." Her gaze drops to her feet. "April and James are trying for a baby."

I drop my hands to my sides, stepping toward her. "That must be difficult to hear. How does that make you feel?"

"It is." Her voice cracks slightly. "I'm happy for them, I really am. But watching your best friend get everything you desperately want while your husband won't even discuss it anymore ..." She trails off momentarily. "Mason won't try therapy. I asked. He told me last week that if having children is so important to me, then maybe I should reconsider our marriage."

I grind my teeth. "He said that to you?"

"Yeah. I love him. I love our life together. But I can't help but feel that something fundamental is missing. Does that make me selfish?"

"No," I say instantly, pulling her into a hug. "It doesn't make you selfish at all. Wanting children isn't something you can just turn off."

She melts into my embrace, her shoulders shaking slightly. "I thought he might change his mind. I honestly thought—" She cuts herself off. "What if I wake up in ten years and it's too late?"

"Anna, you can't live your life waiting for someone to change their mind."

She pulls back, watching me intently. "What do you think, Max? Be honest."

I know all too well what it's like waiting for someone to change. You can hope, you can beg, you can scream until your ears bleed—but you can't make someone choose what *you* want. You need to let them make their own decisions. And if you have to force the person you love into something to find your own happiness, is that really love? Isn't that just living in bad faith?

"I think you deserve to be with someone who wants the same future you do. Whether it's Mason or someone else." I pause, considering my next words carefully. "Ultimately, you're the only one who can decide what you're willing to sacrifice."

"I know you're right," she says, letting go of a deep breath.

I squeeze her shoulder. "You deserve a life that feels complete. You'll work it out, Anna. Just promise me that you'll live your truth, not someone else's."

She shoots me a sad smile. "I promise." She sniffles. "Thank you for listening."

The Suite Secret

"Always." I wink. "That's what big brothers are for."

"Can we talk about something else?" she asks. "I just ... I need a break from thinking about it."

"Of course. Whatever you want." I nod.

Anna's holding my phone for me when it starts vibrating in her hand.

"Who is it?" I ask, narrowing my eyes to read the screen.

Her gaze darts to mine. "Unknown number."

I grit my teeth hard. I've been receiving these calls more frequently, always from an unlisted number. I think I know who it is, and it's beginning to unsettle me.

"Just ignore it," I instruct, slipping inside the dressing room to change.

When I emerge, Anna's complexion has paled.

"What's wrong?" I ask, though I already know.

She holds my phone out to me. "It's Casey."

I take the phone. The message glows on the screen.

My stomach drops as soon as I read the message.

I know you're back in London.

"How the hell did she find out?" I growl.

Anna shakes her head, her expression troubled. "I'm not sure. I haven't posted anything on social media." Her mouth twists as she thinks. "Could she have read something about the Gray Hotel opening?"

I lift my brows, considering. "I doubt it. Grayson is the face of the hotel—my involvement wouldn't have been mentioned. I'm nobody to the public. Any press coverage would feature his name, not mine." I pinch the bridge of my nose. "I don't have the energy for this."

I close my eyes and take a deep breath. "How about we get a drink from the champagne bar downstairs?"

She stares at me, her face unreadable.

"My treat," I add.

Her eyes light up instantly. "Deal."

Chapter Forty-Eight

Gemma

Since arriving home after catching up with Henry back at the office, I've been counting down the hours until I get to see Max.

My phone beeps from the living room as I swap my glasses out for contacts. I'm determined to actually stick to my rule tonight—I'm coming home to my own flat afterward. As amazing as this afternoon was, it was also extremely confronting. Emotionally, I'm drained.

I couldn't push him away. Not when he was staring into my soul with those baby blues, like he saw every broken, jagged piece of me and wanted to help glue me back together.

The honesty in his eyes and the tone of his voice made me feel *safe*, a nervous response so foreign I almost forgot it existed. I think that's the most dangerous part about all this—not the sex, not that we work together, not even Anna.

I'm beginning to *trust* Max to hold my heart.

I've built my entire life around being the one who needs nothing and no one. Yet, in the space of just over a week, I told Max I was his. And the terrifying part? I meant it.

I pad into my kitchen, make myself a latte with some penis foam art, and grab my phone from the sofa.

Max: *Don't wear any panties.*

I smile, my mind already racing with the wicked possibilities.

Me: *Is that an order?*

His response is immediate.

Max: *Yes.*

Another message follows shortly after.

Max: *I'm looking forward to seeing you.*

My cheeks flush and my heart hammers against my ribs. I tap out my response.

Me: *You're only human.*

I bite my lip, anticipating his response.

Max: *Brat.*

I smile and toss my phone aside, sipping my latte while I continue to get ready.

Max never mentioned where he was taking me tonight, but I'm assuming since he's sending a car, it will be somewhere fancy. Pulling open my wardrobe, I eye the row of lace, silk, and leather, smirking to myself when I spot the perfect dress.

Tight, black, slit up the thigh. Eat your heart out, Max Browne.

* * *

My phone rings at seven o'clock on the dot.

I slide my thumb across the screen to answer. "Hello?"

"I'm downstairs."

My heart does a stupid flutter. "Okay. Coming."

I will myself to breathe in, hold for four seconds, and release for six before heading out.

When I reach the bottom of the building staircase, I spot Max through the glass door and my carefully controlled breathing turns to shit.

He stands beside a sleek grey SUV with tinted windows. He's wearing a simple black suit that does everything to showcase his incredible frame. Tall, dark, and commanding.

I step out into the frigid air and make my way over to him.

"Hi," I say, keeping my voice light and even.

He gives a lopsided grin. "Hi."

As I move closer, his eyes scan me from head to toe, and he shakes his head. "You're devastating," he says.

He offers his hand, which I accept, feeling the warmth of his fingers close around mine as he helps me into the car, sliding in after me.

I cross one leg over the other. The slit in my dress runs all the way up my thigh, revealing just enough freshly shaven skin without risk of exposing my vag.

His eyes track the movement, lingering just where I want them to.

"You look beautiful, Gemma," he says. His voice has a slight roughness to it.

I smile softly. "So do you."

The hum of the engine kicks up as the car starts moving, the privacy partition already raised.

"How was your afternoon?" he asks.

"It was good. Everything for the launch party has been finalised and the marketing all rolls out next week. We're almost set." I shift slightly in my seat, causing the silk to fall further across my skin and reveal another inch of thigh.

His expression remains cool. "I don't want to discuss work tonight." He takes my hand in his, resting it in his lap. His cock is already hard beneath my palm. His other hand moves until his fingertips touch the bare skin of my thigh.

My mouth goes dry as I try to control my breathing.

He drags his fingers higher, taking full advantage of the slit in my dress. My legs part instinctively.

When he reaches the apex of my thighs, my lips separate and my body hums.

"I can't get enough of you," he says, his voice dripping with lust.

I whimper when he slides a finger through my folds, finding me soaked and aching.

"Christ," he groans. "Always so wet for me."

He pulls his fingers away and brings them to his mouth, sucking them clean while he watches me.

My eyes hood.

"Keep looking at me like that, sweetheart, and I'll bend you over the nearest surface," he says.

Holy. Crap.

The car pulls to a stop at the curb before I can get a word out. The driver opens the door and I climb out after Max, who takes my hand tightly in his and leads me inside.

The restaurant is almost as extravagant as the hotel.

"Booking for Browne," Max says as we approach the host.

"Right this way, sir," the waiter says, leading us to a dimly lit corner enclosed with sheer dark curtains. Lanterns dot the room, creating a moody and expensive atmosphere. It's romantic.

"Can I get you something to drink?" the waiter asks after we're seated.

I scan the wine menu, somewhat overwhelmed and blown away by the prices. Jesus Christ, I thought Lance's coffee was overpriced—this wine list is obscene. Eight hundred pounds for an Australian red? What's it made of?

Max watches me patiently over the top of his menu as I carefully make my selection, deciding on the most expensive by-the-glass Grenache—sod it, I might as well make the most of it. He orders a Shiraz.

"I'll be back to take your orders," the waiter says before gliding away, leaving us alone in our little alcove.

I uncross my legs and my dress whispers over my skin. Max's eyes flicker to the sound and I roll my lips to suppress a smile.

"So. What do you want to know?" I ask.

He stares at me for a beat. "Everything."

I clear my throat. "How's Grayson's eye?" I ask, ignoring the way my insides twist.

Max laughs, and it's so boyish and relaxed compared to how I've previously seen him.

"Much better," he says.

He goes on to tell me about New York—not just the glossy parts that everyone hears about, but the gritty details. His time at NYU, moving to a new country in his twenties, and how he came to work for Grayson.

When the waiter returns with our wine, we order entrees and mains without breaking conversation. I'm surprised by how thoroughly I'm enjoying myself. It isn't awkward, it isn't difficult, there aren't any pauses or silences. Just interest. I haven't felt this comfortable on a date in a long time. In fact, I haven't *been* on a proper date like this in years.

This is nicer. And I'm fully prepared to admit that it's because of the company. For someone who lives such a flashy lifestyle—the penthouse, the luxury hotels, the expensive wine, and hired drivers—Max is surprisingly down to earth.

Most surprising of all? He listens when I speak. And I know that it's not because he only wants to get in my knickers. He nods and chimes in at all the right moments; we smile and we laugh.

When I tell him about growing up with a single mother, how she worked her arse off to put me through school and uni, his focus is unwavering. He digs deeper into my internship years and when I explain how I met Anna and April, he asks thoughtful questions.

"What's your favourite thing about working at Prestige?" he asks.

I lift a brow. "I thought we weren't talking about work tonight."

"I'm not asking about the job," he says. "I'm asking what you like."

I roll my eyes. It's a technicality and we both know it. "Lance."

His brow furrows. "Your barista?"

I nod. "Yeah. He's there every morning without fail. Always smiling. No matter how early it is or how dead I look. On the days when I'm stuck at my desk watching the clock, or Louise is being her usual cunty self—" He laughs. "I think of Lance. He reminds me that it's not all meant to be this serious. Life's about the little things."

He hums in agreement. "It's a fine quality."

"He told me once that he makes his coffee with love," I say, a small smile tugging at my lips. "Said it was the secret ingredient."

But my smile fades as quickly as it came.

"He's always come across as so happy, so optimistic," I murmur. "But the council hiked his rent. That's why his prices have gone up. I know he's struggling to keep up with the expenses, and I'm terrified I'll walk past one morning and his kiosk will be boarded up. I feel like it's only a matter of time ..."

There's a pause. Max's hand finds mine across the table.

"I'm sure he loves seeing your smile as much as you love seeing his," he says gently.

I take a sip of my wine.

"And how did you get into crystals and tarot?" he asks, swirling his wine, his eyes amused.

"Doom-scrolling on TikTok," I deadpan. "One of my neighbours was so loud I could hear her from across the hall. I was desperate for quiet, I tried a freezer spell."

He blinks. "What the fuck is a freezer spell?"

"You write their name on a piece of paper, stick it in water, and freeze it to shut them up. But whether it was a coincidence or not, I never heard a peep from her again." My gaze drifts as I think. "Shit. Come to think of it, she was pretty old." My eyes widen. "I hope she didn't die."

His eyes light up as he laughs.

"Oh, piss off," I say, joining him. "You haven't told me what you do for fun," I press, leaning in. My dress shifts with the movement and I'm reminded of what I'm not wearing underneath. "You know I like to read. I told you about my tarot cards and crystals. You have to give me *something*." I take another measured sip, enjoying the earthy flavours as the wine coats my mouth.

He shrugs. "I like to work out."

I gag. "Oh God. That's positively horrendous."

"What? It's good for you."

"People always say that," I huff.

"Because it's true."

"So is a pap smear, but you don't see me jumping to book my next appointment."

He raises his glass to his lips, grinning. "Don't be so quick to dismiss it, you might enjoy it."

"What? Pap smears?"

He laughs. "Exercise."

I shoot him an incredulous look before taking another sip. "I'll take your word for it."

"Travel," he says, placing his wine back down.

"What?" I ask, lowering my glass.

"I like to travel. Not for work, but for me. There's something about getting on a plane and leaving everything behind—the pressure, the expectations. I like that you can land in a new place where no one knows you. No one needs anything from you ... and for a moment, you just exist."

I watch him quietly.

"My whole life is structured. I'm constantly in and out of boardrooms, my weeks planned out months in advance. But travel? I don't need to know what's going to happen next. I can wake up one day and have the freedom to do anything. I can breathe."

I tilt my head. "I get that. I can't imagine the sort of pressure your role entails."

"I love my job," he says, and I believe him. "I love working with Grayson. But I crave spontaneity."

"That's surprising," I admit. "I thought you'd have everything planned down to the minute."

His lips quirk. "Only in business."

I nod, another question tugging at the edge of my mind. Before I can stop myself, I ask it. "Is that why you haven't had a relationship since Casey?"

His jaw tenses, just briefly, and I worry I might have pushed too far. But he doesn't shut me down.

He taps the base of his wine glass. "I told myself if I ever got serious again, it would have to be with someone who gets it. The pace. The ambition. The way I live."

His eyes lift to mine. "My equal."

And I swear—I forget how to breathe. My mind replays his words from this afternoon.

Because I think you want to see me too.

And I do.

I *see* him.

The verbal foreplay has been so intense, the more he talks, the more attractive he is.

By the time we finish our meal and the waiter slides the bill onto the table, I'm thrumming with need. Every time I adjust my legs, the cool air brushes between my thighs. I press my legs together, seeking friction—anything—to take the edge off.

Max catches my eye as he returns his credit card to his wallet, and his knowing look nearly undoes me. He knows. Of *course* he knows. He's been watching me wiggle in my seat all evening. And judging by the way his gaze darkens as he stands and helps me from my chair, he's every bit as desperate as I am.

"Come back to mine," he commands.

"I'm wearing my contacts."

His lips curve and he threads his fingers through mine like he's already decided.

"Fine. Yours it is."

Chapter Forty-Nine

Max

The drive back to her place passes in a blur. I count down the minutes until she's falling apart beneath me.

The whole evening was perfect—Gemma, the wine, the food, the soul-nourishing conversation—everything.

I told Gemma she could have something in return for dinner, and at this rate, I'll give her whatever the hell she wants.

When we finally arrive at her flat, she flings her clutch across the room and kicks off her heels, groaning as she stretches her toes.

My eyes are drawn to a large purple object on the floor.

"Is that a tentacle dildo?" I ask.

She follows my eyes. "Yes."

She doesn't bother to elaborate.

"Come, sit. I want to do your cards," she says, patting the spot on the sofa next to her.

"I don't know if I want to risk it after what might have happened to your neighbour." I smirk, enjoying the way her eyes narrow.

"Just sit, will you?"

I join her and watch as she shuffles the cards, cutting the deck in half and shuffling them again. Pulling three cards, she places them on the coffee table face up.

The first one reads Death.

"What does that mean?" I ask, sceptical. I'm not a superstitious man, but she seems to be enjoying herself.

"It's not as ominous as it sounds," she replies calmly. "It doesn't have to mean literal death in tarot. It's about transformation, endings that make way for new beginnings—letting go of what no longer serves you."

Okay. I guess that resonates.

"Do you do this a lot?" I ask.

She hums. "Every day. I find it's just another form of reflection. I think you can find meaning in any of the cards." She shrugs. "Sometimes when I feel a little stuck, they help me look at things from another perspective."

She points to the middle card. "The Lovers. This doesn't only represent love, but a decision. Usually between heart and head. It asks you to be honest about what you want."

I lean closer, breathing in her jasmine perfume. "And the last card?"

Gemma's knee brushes mine. Her eyes flick up and hold my gaze as she says, "The Tower."

I press my lips to her neck as she explains, feeling her pulse accelerate beneath my mouth. Her breathing becomes laboured.

"It represents ..." She tilts her head to give me better access. "Sudden upheaval. It's about"—she inhales sharply when my teeth graze her silky skin—"truths that can't be ignored."

I hum, running my hand up the inside of her leg, cupping her bare pussy.

"I want this," I growl.

She parts her knees without hesitation, allowing me better access. "You got your dinner. Now give me what I want," she says.

I don't waste a second. Lunging forward, I shove the coffee table away and settle between her legs, flipping up the fabric of her dress.

I hold her pussy open and my mouth waters.

"Fuck, Gemma ..." I drag my thumb through her wet seam, circling her clit. Her hips arch. "I've been wanting to taste this all night. Tell me who this pussy belongs to."

"You," she breathes.

I dive in.

My tongue flattens as I lick a firm stripe up her centre, gathering her taste on my tongue. Sweet and musky and addictive. Her legs clamp together, locking me in place, and I moan against her, devouring her.

She cries out, reaching forward to tug on my hair, pushing her perfect pussy into my face.

I worship her, licking and stroking and sucking until she's a whimpering mess underneath me.

Sliding two digits inside her, I curl them just right, rubbing her sweet spot as I circle my tongue around her clit.

"Yes! Just like that!" she cries.

I obey, rubbing and pumping in and out of her sopping core until she's bucking. Pulling out, I drag her juices lower—down between her cheeks, spreading them over her tight little hole until she's glistening for me there too.

"Fuck, baby," I rasp, smearing her arousal over her arse, getting it nice and ready.

"More," she begs, rocking her hips.

I press a finger against her arse, slowly easing it in. She gasps as I latch my mouth onto her pussy, jamming my tongue into her, fucking her with it while I loosen her arsehole.

She's losing her mind. Crying out and clenching around me like she's unable to stop. And then she explodes, my name tearing from her throat like it's the only word she remembers.

I don't stop—I *can't*. I tongue her deeper, revelling in the feel of every flutter and squeeze of her hot channel as she falls apart around me. We're both making the filthiest, sweetest sounds I've ever heard.

Her voice cracks as she rides out her release before her body tremors and jolts, overwhelmed with sensation. I pull back just enough to see her beautiful face—cheeks flushed, eyes glossy, lips swollen, as if she's been biting them.

I've never seen anything more beautiful in my life. And when she slides down my body and gives it back to me with just as much hunger, I'm done for.

Speechless.

After the delicious worshipping of each other's bodies and the raw honesty we've shared today, I can't imagine surrendering to another's touch again. I don't want to.

"Have breakfast with me tomorrow," I say, knowing that just having her tonight isn't going to be enough. I surprise myself with how much I need her to say yes.

"Breakfast? That would require you to sleep over. We have work tomorrow," she says, and I can hear the caution in her voice.

"I know. I'll work from home. No one will know." Her skin pebbles as I stroke her back, keeping my touch light.

"You know how I feel about sleepovers," she whispers, her wariness now gone.

"Would you change your mind if I told you we didn't need to sleep?" I ask, pressing a kiss to her shoulder.

"And what exactly would you suggest we do instead?"

I smile against her skin, rolling her onto her back and kissing my way down her body. "I have a few ideas."

She lifts her arm, pretending to check an imaginary watch. "Hmm. I've got someone else coming over in ten minutes. You should probably go." Her mouth curves into a beaming smile.

I tickle her sides until she bursts out laughing, squirming beneath me. "Take that back."

"Never!" she squeals between giggles.

When I finally release her, we both go still, studying each other. Our laughter fades.

"Fine," she whispers.

I arch an eyebrow in question.

"You can stay."

When she parts her legs for me, I show her just how grateful I am.

Hours later, I lie there watching the steady rise and fall of her chest, the way her lashes rest gently against her cheeks as she drifts off. A blond curtain of hair spills across my chest, and her leg is slung over my hip.

This woman has marked me in ways I can't explain. And as I listen to her soft breathing in the darkness, I know that I only ever want to be hers.

Chapter Fifty

Gemma

Max slept over. And I let him. On purpose. I've gone soft.

Though I'll admit, we didn't get much sleep, which is why I'm making a coffee strong enough to power a small aircraft.

Walking over to Max, who's sitting in my dining nook—shirtless, might I add—I set down the mug I made him.

"What's this?" he asks, staring at the foam art, his eyes dancing with amusement.

"It's a penis," I state.

"Christ, I hope this isn't supposed to be mine," he says, a grin curling through his words.

It's not my best work, I'll admit. The balls are totally disproportionate to the shaft. The whole thing looks a bit wonky.

"Ha. I wouldn't give up hope just yet," I tease, and he reaches out to smack my arse as I turn away to froth my own milk.

"By the way, the eggs and bacon are in the fridge," I toss over my shoulder. "You wanted to stay for breakfast? Coffee's about as far as my hosting skills extend. If you want actual food, have at it—I like my yolks runny."

This is the first time I've had a man sleep over since Todd. When Max first suggested he stay, my immediate reaction was to create distance. To order the Uber *for* him. But I'm glad he stayed.

I don't hate having him in my calm pocket of the world.

"Lucky for you, I make an excellent British fry-up," Max says, standing to rummage through my fridge.

"Of course you do," I mutter.

So far, he seems good at bloody everything.

"Where are your plates and pans?" he asks.

I point to the cabinets and show him where my utensils are, sipping on my coffee while he gets to work frying up bacon, grilling sourdough, and—impressively—making perfect poached eggs.

"This is really good," I say around a mouthful, ogling the way his abs shift as he scoots his chair in.

"I'm glad you like it," he says, his face content as he watches me chew. "Take today off. Spend it with me."

I look up from my meal. "I can't."

"Why not?" he asks, shrugging. "It's Friday. Everything is on schedule with the hotel, and the launch party is all sorted for next week. You deserve to take a day."

"I'm not taking the day off. I agreed to dinner with you last night. The sleepover wasn't part of the deal—"

"But aren't you glad I stayed?" He winks cheekily.

It's like he can read my bloody mind.

I point my knife at him. "You've had more than enough."

"Sweetheart, I've barely even started with you," he rasps, his morning voice gravel thick.

We watch each other with darkened gazes, and my body reacts before I can stop it—it's become Pavlovian. My thighs clench upon the thought of Max's hands, his mouth, his everything.

"Fine. A half day," I concede.

"Sorry?"

"You can have half a day with me. Then I'm going into the office."

His smile is mischievous. "Deal."

He stands, rounding the small table, and stalks toward me with heat in his eyes.

"What are you doing?" I ask, leaning back in my chair.

He doesn't answer. Instead, he slides his arms beneath me and lifts me.

I squeal, smacking his chest. "Max! Where are you taking me?"

He keeps walking us down the hallway, totally unbothered. When he turns the corner toward my bedroom, I release a breathy laugh. "I'm not sleeping with you again. I'm too sore, my vagina will fall off."

"Just relax," he says. "I'm not trying to fuck you."

I arch a disbelieving brow. "Then where are we going?"

"To shower," he replies, pushing the bathroom door open with his foot and setting me on the floor.

Pulling the shower curtain open, he turns the tap, holding his hand under the spray to test the temperature.

"Max," I warn, crossing my arms. "We both know the moment we're naked in the same room, it's game over."

"I'll keep my hands to myself," he says, turning to me. He unties my bathrobe slowly, pushing it off my shoulders and letting it drop to the floor. I'm not sure I'll ever get over the way he's seen my body so many times now, yet his breath *still* hitches when he takes in my naked form.

He makes me feel beautiful.

True to his word, he doesn't try anything. We just silently wash each other.

There's no groping. No grinding or wandering hands. No cocky grin or filthy words. Just us and our soft, careful movements. He lathers shampoo between his palms and massages my scalp, gently working through any tangles in my hair. When he's done, I return the gesture, running my fingers through his dark strands.

When we rinse each other clean, he holds my waist, and we kiss. Over and over again. It's unhurried and patient, without desperation. We simply take our time, relishing in the feel of each other.

It's only when the water turns cold that I realise I'm not waiting for the morning to end.

Not this time.

I'm wishing it went longer.

Chapter Fifty-One

Max

It's Monday morning and I step toward Lance's kiosk. Gemma will have already swung past for her breakfast, so I know I'm not at risk of bumping into her here.

What I'm about to do has been brewing since our dinner last Thursday. The launch party is this Friday, so I'm aware my time to secure this opportunity is running out.

Lance crosses his arms, nodding at me. "I've already sold a latte and an apricot Danish this morning, son."

I smirk. "Then make mine double strength."

"Aye, anything else?" he asks, already reaching for a cup.

"Yes, actually," I say, leaning in. "Have you ever considered moving your business to a new location?"

His eyes narrow to slits, his voice suspicious. "What do you want?"

"You have something my new hotel could use."

His eyebrows sneak up to his hairline. "And what's that?"

"I need a café space—something authentic, not another soulless corporate chain. I want guests walking into the lobby and feeling like they've found a local gem." I pause. "What if I offered you a prime spot in a new luxury Mayfair hotel? Full fit-out, guaranteed foot traffic, and year-round customers?"

The Suite Secret

Lance sets the cup down. "What's the catch?"

"There isn't one. Just good business. You'd maintain full autonomy—vendors, menu, branding. All of it is yours. I have no interest in changing what you do. What you've built here is exactly what we're missing."

His expression softens, shifting to curiosity, so I continue.

"I need authenticity. You need visibility."

"Aye."

"I think we can help each other."

He leans his elbows on the counter. "Tell me more."

Chapter Fifty-Two

Gemma

Who the fuck am I?

Seven weeks ago, Max Browne wasn't even a blip on my radar, and now? I'm thinking about him when I'm brushing my teeth. When I'm scrolling through my phone. When I'm reading my monster smut.

I think about the way he presses his lips together to stop himself from laughing during meetings. How he smells after a long day at work—like rich, decadent whisky.

I never liked the smell of whisky before him.

There's something about being the person who gets to see him when the suit comes off. When he's casually preparing dinner. When he's freshly showered after the gym, looking boyish and gorgeous.

I've spent my late twenties and the majority of my thirties keeping men at vagina's length, and he's closing the distance without even trying.

Everything with him is easy. I *like* having someone to share my evenings with. Someone who listens when I talk about my day. Someone who makes my toast exactly the way I like it—burnt around the edges with peanut butter spread right to the corners. Who brings me coffee before I've even realised I need it.

Last weekend, he bought a barista machine so I could make coffee for us in the morning. Not for himself. For *us*. Because he knows how much I love making it.

He knows how I take pride in getting the penis in my foam art just right. So, when I walked into his penthouse on Saturday night and saw the sparkling new De'Longhi gleaming on his kitchen island, I almost cried. Because he noticed. Because he cared enough to include a small part of my world in his. Because he *wanted* to.

We're learning each other.

I'm realising that letting him in isn't the scariest part. It's realising that I don't want him to leave.

"How's that?" the hairstylist asks, fluffing my hair.

I blink, yanked from my thoughts of Max.

"Perfect." I smile, turning my head to check out the stylist's work. The loose, bouncy waves fall elegantly over my shoulders. The look is sexy and simple—exactly what I wanted for tonight. My dress, however, is slightly more risqué.

The launch party has come around so quickly. Every influencer, journalist, and tastemaker will be there. Now we just have to cross our fingers and hope that after tonight, Gray Hotel becomes *the* place to stay in London, and it'll be job done. Just like that. One minute I was flaps deep in preparing my pitch, and the next—bam—seven weeks of intense preparation, last-minute adjustments, and late nights ending in mind-blowing orgasms have flown by.

Despite everything behind the scenes with Max, we've managed to fool everyone at work, and I don't think anyone—except Henry, of course—knows. Thank God.

I pay the stylist, gather my things, and head home to do my make-up.

The moment I walk into my flat, nerves explode through my body. I've worked my arse off to get here—to be in the room, to show off all the amazing things Henry, the team, and I have planned and accomplished to ensure the Gray Hotel launch goes off without a hitch. This is a major project to add to my CV and I'm proud of it.

I pause in front of tonight's dress hung carefully on the frame of my wardrobe, right next to my bridesmaid's dress. April and James's wedding is next week, and thank God the shop assistant didn't recognise me when I returned to the New Bond Street boutique to purchase the beautiful purple dress I tried on weeks ago.

Turning on music, I head into the bathroom to start my make-up routine. I usually avoid doing my eyeshadow too heavy, but tonight? Screw that. Henry and I made this project our bitch and I'm ready to let every person in that room know it.

I slip into my deep emerald dress; the fabric clings to every curve like liquid. The front plunges all the way to my belly button, drawing attention to my cleavage without being too revealing. Two delicate straps trail over my shoulders and down a completely backless V that stops just below the dimples of my spine. I've paired the dress with nude strappy heels.

It's bold, simple and barely decent. It's perfect.

Chin high, tits out, shoulders back. I'm ready.

Max Browne is going to cream his jeans.

An Uber notification flashes across my phone, letting me know my car is here. I give myself one last look in the mirror, inhale deeply, and head out.

* * *

I step through the foyer, which looks even more lush and opulent under the dimmed chandeliers. I'm immediately struck by how effortlessly Lord Harrington's pieces complement and elevate the space.

Two towering statues flank the grand entrance, and women flash their cameras, snapping the best Instagram-worthy photos to share. Behind the long reception desk that stretches across the entire back wall hangs a single, breathtaking painting. Oranges, yellows, reds, and blues swirl together like fire and water.

The lobby teems with immaculately dressed guests who have their names checked off a list at the entrance to the bar. Once I've been accounted for, I saunter in.

A waiter appears with a silver tray of champagne flutes, and I don't hesitate, plucking one off the tray and taking a large gulp.

My gaze sweeps across the room, trying to find a friendly face.

Henry spots me from afar and weaves through the crowd with a glass of amber liquid.

I do a little jig on the spot and reach up on my tiptoes to wrap an arm around his neck.

"We did it! How great does this look?"

He smiles. "The marketing team nailed this party." He tilts his chin toward the far wall lined with more paintings. "And you were right about the art—it's completely transformed the hotel."

"Obviously I was right," I say, swatting his chest.

Henry steps back, giving me an appreciative look.

"You look lovely," he says, taking a sip of his drink.

"I know. I'm gagging for a fingering tonight." Henry chokes on his drink, smacking his chest. I eye him up and down. "You don't scrub up too bad yourself."

We mingle with guests and colleagues as we wander through the party. Around us are bursts of laughter, flashes of cameras, clinking glasses, and *lots* of designer labels—exactly what Gray Hotel was hoping for. Young, rich, and ready to spend.

After polishing off my champagne, I try one of the signature cocktails designed to pair with the artwork. It's pink, topped with fairy floss. I have no idea what's in it, but it tastes good. Henry's cocktail is served in a copper mug—a twist on a Moscow Mule—and we polish them off in record time.

I'm wondering where the hell Max is when Henry's expression shifts.

"Oh shit. Don't look now. El Diablo at two o'clock," Henry mutters.

Which, of course, guarantees I'm *absolutely* going to look.

I pivot on the spot, eyes searching until they land on Louise and Theo standing with Max.

As if he's drawn to me, his eyes lift and lock onto mine. My heart stutters in my chest when I take him in.

He's in a black suit and crisp white shirt, no tie, the top button undone with black dress shoes. His hair isn't tousled in that unstyled hot way but rather slicked back, showcasing his perfect bone structure.

"*Holy shit*," I whisper, leaning into Henry. "He looks like James Bond."

"That," Henry says with a dramatic head tilt, "is why I'm gay."

I nod, eyes still on Max. "Right? I'm so straight it's insane. Could you imagine having *two* of Max? Ugh. All I've ever wanted is a boyfriend that has a boyfriend."

I pause, realisation crashing down on me. "Not that Max is my boyfriend."

Henry presses his lips together. "Sure."

My gaze flicks back just in time to see Louise rest her hand on Max's forearm and laugh at something he's said.

"Looks like Louise is cutting your lunch," Henry says.

"More like cutting the cheese. Let's get another drink," I say, turning.

As we approach the bar, Chadwick is already standing with another suit I'm not familiar with.

"Gemma, Henry," he says, beckoning us over. "I'd like you to meet Cole Livingstone. COO of Livingstone Hotels."

I've heard of him before. The middle brother.

"A pleasure to meet you," he says, extending a hand. His voice is honey and gravel, rough but smooth at the same time.

What are they putting in the water in the Livingstone household? I thought Grayson was handsome—Cole's a whole different breed.

He's built leaner than Grayson but stands at a similar height, with sandy blond hair slicked back much like Max's. His hazel eyes catch flecks of amber and green under the lights, and his olive skin looks airbrushed to perfection.

"Grayson sends his regards," Cole says. "He's dealing with an urgent work matter back home."

Ah. The lawsuit—Max told me about it.

I accept his hand and paste on my best smile, eager to make a strong impression. "Cole, it's so lovely to meet you."

Henry and Cole make a quick introduction.

"Gemma and Henry worked closely with Max on the launch campaign," Chadwick chimes in. "Henry is our chief creative officer, and Gemma's our creative director."

"You've done a spectacular job," Cole says, his tone warm and friendly. "Congratulations. We're all extremely impressed with what you've accomplished. It's clear how much care and creativity went into ensuring this launch was a success—and from what I've seen tonight, it absolutely is."

Before I can reply, I feel it—that familiar pull, as if he's tugging on a string tethering us together. I know it's Max before he even speaks.

"Cole."

That voice. Low. Commanding. It slides down my spine like molasses. I turn my head slightly, heart pattering in my chest. He looks like every fantasy I never meant to have.

"Max," Cole says, clapping a hand on his shoulder. "It's good to see you."

"You too, mate." Max turns his focus to Henry and me. "I see you've met the brains of the operation." His eyes land on me and linger.

"I have," Cole says, smiling. "Very impressive."

Someone taps Cole on the shoulder, drawing his attention.

"You'll have to excuse me," he says, nodding politely to Henry and me. "It was lovely meeting you both."

He shakes Max's hand. "I'm in London all week for work, so I'll catch up with you later."

With one last charming smile, he disappears into the crowd with Chadwick, leaving just the three of us.

"Well," Henry says, clapping his hands together. "I think I see someone calling me."

"No one's calling you," I deadpan.

"See you later." He slinks off, and I draw my lips into a thin line.

The turd.

"Do you think he did that on purpose?" Max asks with an amused grin.

"Definitely."

"You look absolutely stunning," he says in a low voice as he leans in so only I can hear.

"I know," I manage, trying to keep my voice steady.

He chuckles softly. "Brat."

Out the corner of my eye, I spot Louise standing with Theo, eyeing us over the rim of her cocktail like the nosy bitch she is.

"We have an audience," I murmur, turning back toward the bar.

Max's hand skims along my exposed arm. "Check your messages," he says, brushing past me. And then he's gone.

Reaching into my purse, I check my phone. One unread message.

Max: *Meet me outside in fifteen minutes.*

The smile comes before I can stop it. Fifteen minutes. Just enough time to throw back a spicy margarita.

Around me, everyone seems preoccupied and blissfully unaware.

I shoot off a quick text to Henry, letting him know I'm bailing. I lock my phone, slip it into my clutch, and flag down the bartender like a woman on a mission. One margarita later, I make my way to the entrance.

Stepping outside, it starts to sprinkle just as a familiar grey SUV pulls up to the curb.

The door opens to reveal Max sitting inside like sin incarnate. His jacket is gone, his sleeves are rolled up, one arm flung across the back seat.

An arrogant smile curves his lips.

"Get in, sweetheart."

Chapter Fifty-Three

Max

My eyes shamelessly run over her as we stand side by side, waiting for the lift doors to open. I'm convinced this emerald-green gown was created specifically to torture me.

I saw the way she turned heads tonight, the interest in Cole's eyes when I clocked them talking from across the room.

I was excited for the launch tonight—this opening is the very reason I'm in London, but nothing could compare to the thrill of seeing Gemma. All the surrounding noise in the room fell away the moment I spotted her.

These last four weeks wrapped up in each other have been perfect. Not just physically—Christ, that's been perfect too—but in all the small ways. Waking up to her every morning, her golden hair fanned across my pillows like she's always belonged there. Showering together and learning every inch of her body. Every place she's most ticklish. The way her laughter changes depending on her mood—the little one when she's tired and the full belly one when I catch her off guard.

She's the most beautiful woman I've ever laid eyes on. She's become the best part of my day, the one I want to tell everything to. I love getting to know her—every version of her.

The Suite Secret

Fuck.

I love her.

I've fallen for this clever, loud, brilliant woman and I'm so tired of hiding. I'm the lucky bastard taking her home, and I hate that I can't tell anyone.

I hate that I'm leaving after the wedding.

We need more time.

The moment the elevator doors slide open, I take her hand and lead her inside.

The apartment is bathed in moonlight.

As soon as the door closes behind us with a soft click, I've got her pressed up against the wall, my mouth on hers. I kiss her with everything I have, desperate to show her exactly what she does to me. My cock is so damn hard and angry, straining against my zipper. I know the minute I bury myself inside her sweet little channel, I'll erupt.

My fingers find the delicate strap of her dress, teasing it slowly.

"These tiny little straps," I murmur, dragging my knuckles over her collarbone, down to the swell of her breast. "So flimsy. Like you *want* me to tear them off."

My hand trails lower. Over her ribs, across her stomach, until I reach the dip of her belly button. She inhales sharply, arching into my touch.

My voice is low as I palm her hip. "You wore this for me, didn't you?"

Her lips curve in a knowing smile. "Yes."

She reaches for my shirt buttons, and I drop my gaze, watching her pop them open one by one. I could rip off my suit faster, but I let her take her time. By the time she reaches the last button, my shirt is hanging open. She pauses.

"You planning to finish what you started?" I murmur.

Her eyes flick up to meet mine and she smiles—bloody *smiles*. Planting her palms on my chest, she starts walking me backward. She backs me up until my legs hit the sofa, and I sink down, heart thundering in my chest.

Shoulder strap slipping down her arm, eyes glassy with want, she tugs the skirt of her dress at her knees as she sinks to the floor between my legs.

I groan before she even releases my cock because the sight of her on her knees is enough to undo me.

"I need to taste you," she says.

"Then get your pretty mouth around me before I lose my mind."

She yanks my zipper down and grabs my cock. It's thick and hard in her hand, pulsing as I watch her lean forward. She licks a firm line up my shaft, swirling around the top before pumping her hand, her mouth following, sucking me down. Hot. Wet. Heaven.

I drop my head back, my hand flying to her hair.

She moans as I guide her head up and down, the vibrations from all the filthy sounds she's making as she sucks and licks around me.

"Jesus—fuck, Gemma," I groan.

Her eyes flick up to me and I can see she's watching for my reaction.

"You like sucking my dick, baby?" I growl, my grip in her hair tightening, and she works me over like it's what she was born to do. She whimpers around my stiffness, her eyes fluttering shut. My cock taps and curves down the back of her throat as her muscles relax with every pass, opening more for me.

She gags, her eyes watering so prettily. Her free hand lifts to play with my balls, tugging, kneading, and teasing. My breathing turns ragged as she steers me toward the finish line.

"Does this get you wet, sweetheart? Sucking my cock like this?" She nods without breaking rhythm and picks up the pace, bobbing up and down, and my hips jerk up to meet her, matching her movement.

The Suite Secret

A tingle sparks to life at the base of my spine. I'm teetering.

"Christ, Gemma," I gasp. "I'm gonna come. Don't you dare stop."

And then I lose it.

I come hard. Stars dance in my vision and my whole body seizes. I pulse deep in her throat.

"That's it. Swallow all of it," I say, feeling her throat tighten as she drinks me down.

Once I'm empty, she pulls back and smirks. Like she's proud.

I shrug off my open shirt, tossing it aside. I gather her into my arms and tuck her head underneath my chin. She lets out a breathy laugh, sliding her arms around my neck as I lift her with ease. I carry her through the apartment, heading straight for the massive guest bathroom.

I leave the door open and step through, placing her gently on her feet. I kneel and turn the tap on the bath, testing the water temperature with my hand until it's just right.

"What are you doing?" she asks, watching me as I unscrew the cap of a bottle and tip its contents into the bath. Bubbles expand and multiply across the surface.

Standing, I step forward and gently spin her until her back is flush against my chest. I lower my mouth to her neck and the hollow behind her ear, placing soft kisses over the curve of her shoulder and across the bare skin of her upper back.

My fingers find the thin straps of her dress again, sliding them down one at a time.

"We're taking a bath," I say.

The silk slips down her body, pooling at her feet, leaving her in nothing but her heels.

She's mesmerising.

I take her hand and gently turn her to face me once more. Dropping to my haunches, I lift one of her feet and unbuckle her heel, kissing her ankle and easing her foot out of it. Then the other.

She stands before me, naked and so radiant.

"You take my breath away, Gemma," I say, barely able to hold myself together.

"So do you," she whispers.

She helps me undress, tugging my trousers down my legs. I step out of them and lead her to the tub, climbing in behind her and pulling her against my chest. She sighs into me.

Her head drops back to rest on my shoulder, and I wrap my arms around her, winding them tight. My cock presses against her arse, hard and eager for more, but I ignore it as best I can. Not because I don't want her, but because this—holding her, having her—is more than enough.

"Thank you," she says, barely above a whisper.

I nuzzle her neck. "For what, baby?"

"For being patient with me."

My brows pull together. She has no idea. I would give this woman anything. I squeeze her gently. "Thank you for trusting me."

She wiggles slightly, craning to look up at me. It's then I notice her eyes, brimming with unshed tears.

I run my thumb against her cheek, bubbles clinging to her skin. "Sweetheart, what's wrong?"

Her throat bobs with a swallow. "I love you."

The world tilts on its axis.

Her touch seeps through me. Into my marrow and everything that I am.

"I love you too," I say, my voice clogged with emotion.

One tear escapes, sliding down her cheek, and I lean in, kissing it away.

"Baby, why are you crying?" I whisper. "That's a good thing."

The Suite Secret

She shakes her head, her voice cracked and so small. "Because you're leaving."

And just like that, my heart splinters.

"I'm still here. I haven't gone anywhere. We can figure something out," I say.

She opens her mouth to speak when someone calls my name.

"Max!" We both instantly freeze, gazes darting to the open door.

"Was that ..." Gemma breathes, dread written all over her face.

"I think so," I whisper, my throat suddenly dry.

Loud footsteps fall down the hall. With every approaching step, my heartbeat thunders in my ears. We both jolt upright. My arm tightens around Gemma protectively.

Gemma stills in my hold as Anna strides past the doorway. She takes three steps before she falters. She steps back and does a double take when she surveys the scene before her.

Gemma and me, naked in the bath together, my arms around her.

"I tried to call," Anna says. Then she says nothing. She just glares through both of us, betrayal etched in her eyes, the colour drained from her face.

The silence is worse than any shouting could be.

"Anna," Gemma says, her voice breaking.

"Fuck this," Anna finally says, turning and stomping toward the front door.

A sob tears from Gemma's throat.

"Anna, wait!" I say, quickly standing and reaching for a towel.

I don't even bother to dry myself, bubbles cascading down my body and dripping onto the floor.

My sole focus is on stopping her so I have the chance to explain. Explain what Gemma means to me—that I *love* Gemma.

I chase after Anna, feet slapping against the hardwood. Water sloshes behind me as, I assume, Gemma gets out of the bath.

"Anna!" I call again, catching her just before she reaches the foyer. "Please. Don't go! Just let me explain."

I run a hand through my damp hair, pushing it out of my eyes.

Anna whirls around, her expression stony. Hurt. Eyes red, her cheeks tear-streaked.

She looks fucking devastated.

It feels like I've torn stitches. My little sister—who I've protected her whole life—is staring at me like I've committed the worst betrayal.

"Explain *what*?" she spits. "That you're screwing my *best friend*!? AGAIN!"

"Anna, please," Gemma says, rushing after us. My dressing gown is cinched at her small waist and damp patches seep through the woollen fabric.

"This isn't—" she starts, then stops herself. "We didn't mean for you to find out like this." She reaches toward Anna.

"Don't even think about touching me," Anna says.

Gemma's hand falls limply to her side. Her lip trembles as she pulls in a shuddering breath.

Anna's eyes bounce between us. "How long?"

We stand, frozen.

"HOW LONG?" Her voice ricochets through the room like a slingshot. Gemma startles.

"Five weeks," I say, keeping my voice as steady as possible.

Anna turns to Gemma. "Five weeks," she whispers. "How *could* you?"

Then she spins toward the door.

"No! Anna. Please," Gemma cries. "Don't go. Please—don't go." She repeats it like a chant.

Don't go. Don't go. Don't go.

A muscle feathers in Anna's jaw. "I told you what happened with Nicole. I asked you not to touch him. I told you to do *one fucking thing*, Gemma!"

Gemma takes a cautious step forward. "I didn't—"

"—mean to?" Anna scoffs. "I would *never* do this to you, Gemma. I would never betray your trust and go behind your back if you asked me not to do something."

Gemma flinches as if the words land a physical blow.

Anna diverts her gaze back to me. "I told you *everything* I've been going through with Mason, Max! And you still—" Her voice cracks. "You still did this."

"What do you mean, Anna?" Gemma asks through tears.

Anna swipes angrily at the wetness staining her cheeks, her lip wobbling as she tries—and fails—to hold it together.

"Is that why you're here? Because of Mason?" I ask, taking a step closer. "Anna—what happened?" My voice drops.

"Please don't," she whispers, shaking her head as she presses a trembling hand over her mouth. Then, a loud sob rips out of her. So thunderous and raw that it cracks my heart in half.

"What happened?" I say, growing more concerned.

"Anna ..." Gemma says quietly.

And then I see it in Anna's eyes.

She isn't just angry.

She's grieving.

"Weasel," I whisper.

Anna steps up to me and collapses in my arms. "I needed you!" she cries, beating her fists against my chest. "I needed you"—she chokes on her next breath—"and you hurt me too! I *needed* you!"

I wrap my arms around her, holding her as tight as I can. My chest is heavy and my vision blurs. "I'm so sorry," I whisper, burying my face in her hair as she wails. "I didn't know, Anna. I'm so sorry."

When I lift my eyes, Gemma's still there, arms folded across her middle as if she's trying to keep herself together. Her eyes swim with guilt and ... *fear*.

I meet her gaze and beg her with a look that screams everything I can't say out loud. *Please don't leave*.

She reads it. But I see it in the way her chin lifts. In the subtle shake of her head.

She isn't staying.

"I'm so sorry, Anna. This should never have happened," she pleads.

"No," I say to Gemma, my voice low.

She tenses her jaw.

"No, Gemma, please."

Gemma's watery gaze stays fixed on the scene in front of her. On the wreckage that we've made.

"What did we do?" she whispers, her voice splintering. "Anna ... I'm so sorry."

She snatches her phone off the side table and bolts for the door.

"NO!" I shout, torn between my sister, breaking down in my arms, and chasing after the woman running away with my heart.

Gemma pauses long enough to look over her shoulder when she reaches the door.

A tear releases itself from my lashes and falls down my cheek.

"Please, Gemma."

"Anna needs you," she says softly.

And then she leaves.

Chapter Fifty-Four

Gemma

My limbs are numb. The only feeling left is my heart, splitting open and bleeding out. I make it to the sidewalk on unsteady legs, throwing my arm up to hail a cab.

Lightning splits the sky, illuminating the darkness in a flash of white, and rain pours down in punishing sheets.

I'm soaked to the bone.

Everything inside me is screaming.

Screaming to go back.

Screaming to run.

Screaming to hold Anna, to tell her that no matter what's happened, I'm here and she'll be okay. That I'll never cut her out like Nicole did.

Screaming to tell her I love her. To tell her I love Max.

But it's too much.

I can't do it.

I *broke* her. My best friend.

A cab pulls up and I fling open the door, slide inside, and somehow manage to rattle off my address. I don't even recognise my own voice.

I sink into the seat, ready to close the door when I hear him.

"WAIT! NO! STOP!"

Max's voice booms through the night just as he bursts out of his apartment building.

I can't look back.

I slam the cab door shut with shaky hands. The driver accelerates, and in the rearview mirror, I watch Max's silhouette shrink, leaving my heart behind too.

Chapter Fifty-Five

Max

I pump my arms and legs, pushing them to the limit, willing them to move faster as I bolt down the sidewalk.

I have to get to her.

I left Anna inside. She'll be okay for now—I *hope* she'll be okay. I told her to stay, to wait. That I'll explain everything once I'm back.

I grabbed the first clothes I could find, shoved my feet into the nearest pair of trainers, and ran.

I stood there and watched the woman I love walk out of my life without trying to stop her.

I can't lose her. Not like this.

I won't.

Wet fabric clings to my skin as I run, blood pounding in my ears, breathing rough as I try, *try* to catch up to her.

My eyes scan the road. There are cars bloody everywhere. She could be in any one of them.

"TAXI!" I shout, flinging my hand in the air. "TAXI!"

Nothing.

Horns blare around me.

It's useless.

I can't stop.

My body screams, every joint protesting as I sprint, weaving through clusters of people. Strangers call out to me, point, laugh, wolf-whistle—but I don't stop.

I'm chasing one of the few things that's ever truly mattered.

She needs you. Gemma's words replay in my head, her voice like a shot of adrenaline, fuelling me.

I'm exhausted. Shaking. Tired. I'm fucking *crying* and not even trying to hide it.

But all I can see is my beautiful girl's face. That haunted look in her eyes. How gutted she was.

And I'd give anything to erase it.

I'll run all damn night if I have to.

Chapter Fifty-Six

Gemma

By the time I make it upstairs, I'm soaked, and every part of me feels like I've been in a car crash. I shut the door behind me, lean against it, and drop to the floor, my heart pounding.

Anna's face—God, Anna's face. I've known her for over a decade and I've *never* seen her look at anyone the way she looked at me tonight.

Like I was some wicked disease that needed to be cut out before it can spread.

I went behind her back and sabotaged our friendship.

I've been so bloody selfish.

Burying my face in my hands, I release everything I've been holding in the past thirty minutes. The past six weeks. Phlegm catches in my throat and my nose runs as I sob uncontrollably into my empty flat.

Wrapping my arms around myself, I rock back and forth, burying my head in Max's robe as tears spill relentlessly, hot and heavy. The damp fabric smells of him and I ache.

I don't know how long I sit there, but I'm barely standing when the buzzer goes off.

I screw my eyes shut, knowing exactly who it will be.

Max.

The buzzer sounds again, longer this time, like he's holding it down. I stare at the intercom, my heart in my throat, desperately wanting to see him but terrified it'll destroy Anna even further.

My legs feel barely attached as I rise and walk to the window. Peering out through sheets of rain, I see Max. Soaked to the bone, standing at the front steps.

He looks up and we lock eyes.

"GEMMA!" he calls. "GEMMA!"

I want to go to him. I want to run down the stairs, throw open the door, and fall into his arms like every stupid romance movie. I want *so badly* to believe that love is enough.

But how can it be when it hurts the people you care about the most?

How can something so pure and so beautiful be so breakable?

It feels like my heart is tethered to his, and wherever he goes, I'll follow.

But I need to cut the cord. I need to let him go. I can't ruin my friendship with Anna. She asked me to stay away from her brother, and I didn't. I lied to her. Snuck around behind her back like a teenager. I broke her trust.

If I have to choose between them, then I choose Anna.

And all I can do is cry. Because I love Max. I do, with everything I have. But I *can't*.

"GEMMA!" His voice carries through the downpour.

The buzzer goes silent, and for a devastating second, I think he's given up.

Then the pounding starts. His fist slams against the building front door loud enough to wake the whole bloody street.

"I know you're in there. Open the door!"

A cry leaves my body before I can stop it.

"I'm not leaving until you open this door! I'll stay here all night if I have to!"

Of course he will, the stubborn bastard.

Be strong, Gemma.

Before I can talk myself out of it, my feet carry me across the room and down the stairs.

He stands there, drenched and beautiful, rainwater dripping from his hair and down his face. The hallway light catches each droplet. His clothes cling to his broad shoulders.

His eyes are bloodshot and his cheeks are flushed, chest heaving as if he's run miles to reach me.

"Did you run here?" I ask, looking past him to the storm raging outside.

"I love you," he says simply.

"Max," I whisper, closing my eyes. I can't witness the raw honesty in his gaze. I can't bear the weight of it.

He crosses the threshold, and his hands find my biceps with urgency.

"I love you," he repeats, his voice dropping lower.

The words impale me as my breath scrapes in and out of my lungs.

"I love you," he says it again.

"Please stop," I beg, refusing to open my eyes.

I can't look at him. I can't stare into his ocean eyes while he begs me to be his, knowing I have to refuse him.

His icy palms hold my face with such care it almost breaks me.

"I love you." His voice is final, as if he's made the decision for the both of us. I wish I could reach out and help him understand that it isn't that simple.

He lifts my chin with his index finger.

Then, the pads of his thumbs sweep over my cheekbones, catching the tears as they fall. Leaning in, I feel the press of his lips against one cheek, then the other.

I encircle his wrists. I want to push against him, but my body refuses, holding me suspended between what I want and what I *know* I need to do.

"Look at me," he whispers.

I shake my head no.

"Look at me." It's not a request this time but a demand.

I peel my lids open slowly, taking him in. Wet hair is plastered to his forehead. His eyes are red, searching for mine, like if he looked hard enough, he'd find the words I can't bring myself to say.

I want you, too.

Stay. Don't go.

But all I can see is Anna. How, like a coward, I ran away. How I wasn't there for her when I've known deep down, for *weeks*, that she wasn't okay—that I've neglected her. Lied to her. Hurt her. She needed her brother, and I *took* him.

"What did we do?" I pant. "We broke her." I hiccup.

"Gemma—" His voice cracks on my name.

"She needs you, Max. Why are you here?" My words tumble out. "She *needs* you!"

I can tell he's struggling to compose himself, his jaw working. "Please, don't do this. I—"

"I can't hear it," I cry, finally finding the strength to push against his chest. "I can't hear you say it because I don't deserve it."

"You do, Gemma," he tries, but fails. I keep my palms against his chest, but he won't budge.

So I do the only thing I know how.

I push him away.

"Leave," I say, pounding my fists against his chest.

"Gemma," he pleads.

"Go! I don't *want* you here!"

He stumbles back. "You don't mean that."

My lip trembles. "Didn't you see how much we hurt Anna? This can't work. We'll both lose her. And for what? This was just a fling."

"A *fling*?" he says, stepping forward, crowding me.

"That's all this ever was." I sniffle. "It's all we agreed to."

"Don't give me that shit, Gemma. Can you hear yourself?" He points to his ears. "Do you believe your own bullshit?"

"Go!" I shout, fighting back tears.

"Why are you doing this?" he demands. "After what you told me in the bath, you're standing here telling me it meant *nothing*?"

"I'm doing what I should have done from the beginning. Chosen Anna," I say, mustering as much strength as I can. "There's nothing to fight for."

He shakes his head, his arms dropping. "Nothing?"

"Don't you see? You leave next week. What exactly are we fighting for? Long distance? When am I going to see you again? I can't just drop my life here and fly over to New York whenever it suits you."

"I'm not asking you to. You haven't even given us a chance," he says, drawing his brows together. "Is that what this is about? You don't think I'd figure out a way to make this work?"

My shoulders deflate. "What's the point?"

He steps forward again. "You're the point, Gemma! This"—he waves a hand between us—"*us*!"

"No." I wipe angrily at my tears. "Not with your life in New York and mine here—"

"Then I'll stay here," he says.

I scoff. "Don't be ridiculous, Max."

"I mean it."

"And what? Throw away everything you've worked for?"

"No. It doesn't need to be like that. I'll handle it."

My lips thin.

"You're just scared," he says, his voice barely carrying.

He's right. I'm terrified.

He looks so unlike the Max I know. Younger. Smaller. As if all the fight has left his body. And maybe that's what I need. I need him to give in. I need him to leave.

"Go, Max," I bite back.

He blinks, staring in front of me. Muscles loose, eyes glistening with moisture.

"You don't mean that," he whispers.

Sucking in air, I straighten my spine. "Go, Max!"

The words hang in the air between us, and I see the moment they hit home.

I stay silent as he waits for a denial that will never come. When I stand my ground, his eyes harden.

"Fine," he says, moving toward the door. Every part of me screams to stop him, but I stay silent.

"You know, I never thought you were a coward, Gemma," he says quietly. "I guess that was my mistake."

The door closes behind him, and with that, I gather what's left of me and take my broken pieces upstairs.

The sobs I held back crash through me all at once, wracking my body until I can't breathe, until I'm nothing but flayed skin and exposed nerves.

Sleep doesn't find me quickly, but when it finally comes, I'm haunted by crystal blue eyes and the three words that died in my throat before he left.

The three words that could have changed everything.

I love you. I love you. I love you.

Chapter Fifty-Seven

Max

My mind is a jumbled, incoherent mess, and that never happens.

I fucking lost her.

By the time I've walked back to my apartment, I can't feel my fingers, I can't feel my toes. Everything is frozen and all that's left is a hollow throb, like everything inside me has gone quiet.

Anna's in the bathroom when I return, so I go straight to my en suite, turn the water to scorching, and step under the spray. The heat pricks my skin like a million tiny bee stings, waking up nerves I didn't realise had gone numb.

By the time I step out, dry off, and change into warm clothes, I feel like dead weight.

But the night isn't over yet.

I pad into the kitchen and flick on the kettle. Tea for Anna. A hot toddy for me.

I scrub my hand down my face, bone-deep exhausted, when a small voice chimes in from behind me.

"Hi," Anna says softly.

I turn, hand her a mug, and walk us both to the sofa, placing my glass on the coffee table.

For a long time, we sit in silence. Neither of us utters a word.

"What happened?" I ask, resting my elbows on my thighs.

Her lower lip wobbles. "We had a fight. I mentioned that April and James are trying for a baby, and he lost it. Said I keep bringing up the same conversation over and over, and that he's already told me where he stands and nothing's going to change his mind." She swipes her cheek with the back of her hand. "So, I gave him an ultimatum. I told him I couldn't keep waiting around to see whether he would change his mind—he said he wouldn't."

I wait, seeing she hasn't finished.

"He said ..." Her words falter. "He said maybe it was time we stopped torturing ourselves and just accepted that we want different things. That staying together would only make it harder for both of us."

"Jesus, Anna." I rub the back of my neck.

"I really wish he'd changed his mind ... our life was so amazing otherwise," she whispers.

"I'm so sorry."

She reaches for the tissue box on the coffee table, and I hang my head, totally defeated.

She manages a watery smile. "It's for the best."

I lift my chin. "Don't do that. Don't try to be strong. You don't have to pretend, Anna."

Her fingers fiddle with the handle of the mug. "It hurts, Max," she says, her eyes glistening. "It really hurts."

I scoot over to her, encasing her in my arms. I rock her back and forth as she cries, and I let her. I let her wail. Let her scream. I let her push against me, but I don't let go.

We sit like that for what feels like hours until her sobs finally subside.

"You know," I break the silence, "when Casey and I split, I thought I'd never recover from it. I knew I couldn't stay in something that wasn't working, but I also knew that holding on to what was already dead would only hurt us both more. It would have been dishonest to keep pretending."

She looks at me, her eyes red-rimmed.

"The thing is, Anna, sometimes walking away is the bravest thing you can do. And I know this feels like the end of everything right now, but the world will open up for you in ways you can't even imagine yet."

I take her hand and squeeze it. "Everything that's meant to be will find its way to you. And when the time is right—with the right person, or even on your own—you're going to be the most incredible mother. I know it."

She lets out a shaky breath, and I continue. "You and Mason had something beautiful for a long time. You're allowed to grieve that—and you will. But don't let yourself grieve a future you've not had the chance to live. You've got to take this life and turn it into something worth living. Something that brings you meaning and happiness and everything you've dreamt of."

She wipes her nose with the tissue. "What if I'm too old? I'm mid-thirties, Max. What if it's too late?"

"Fuck societal expectations, Anna, they've never stopped you before. It's not too late. And if you don't happen to meet someone, then I know you can do it on your own. You're so much stronger than you give yourself credit for." My voice is firm. "You *have* time. Take it. Live well," I say.

She gives me a small, sad smile. "He's moving out. He won't be home when I return tomorrow morning. He's going to stay with his family until we finalise things," she says.

I rub a soothing circle over her back. "What do you need? Is there anything I can do to help?"

She shakes her head. "Not right now." Her gaze darts to the windows. "I didn't mean to walk in on you two," she says. "I didn't even knock. I just ... I used my key."

I nod slowly. "You don't have to apologise."

She swallows and her eyes drop to the mug in front of her. "I needed you."

"And we're here, weasel. That doesn't change a thing," I tell her.

She sits back, putting some distance between us. "Why didn't you tell me?"

"Would timing have made a difference?"

She tenses. "No."

"And now?" I force the question as my whole body locks up, prepared for her answer.

"I'm pissed at you, Max. Both of you." Her voice hardens.

"So that's it? Your own marriage falls apart so I can't be happy? Your best friend can't be happy?"

Anna watches me carefully. "That's not fair. You lied to me."

"And we're sorry. What more do you want from us?"

"*Us?*" she asks incredulously. "*US?* So, what? You're a couple now?"

I grind my teeth. "I'm in love with her, Anna. I love Gemma."

She freezes. Whatever retort she was preparing dies on her lips. For several beats, she just stares at me.

"You what?" she finally whispers.

"I fucking love her," I say, pushing my hair off my forehead.

She shakes her head dismissively. "You've been back for eight weeks, Max. You don't love her. Sometimes lust just *feels* a lot like love."

Her condescension strikes a match and ignites something fierce in me.

I adore my sister, but who the hell is she to tell me how I feel?

"Don't sit here and minimise what she means to me."

The Suite Secret

"Gemma doesn't love," she says flatly.

"Is it really that hard for you to believe?" I lean forward. "That we aren't capable or deserving of each other's love? Because you selfishly want it all for yourself?"

"That's not—" she starts, affronted.

"It is, Anna. It damn well is." I cut her off. "She let me in." I smack my chest hard enough to hurt. "ME! Finally! She finally fucking let me in!"

Her eyes well up all over again, but I can't stop.

"For the last eight weeks, I've seen everything that amazing woman has to offer," I continue. "Every wall she's built, every fear she hides, every brilliant, maddening part of her. And I'm not going to let anyone—not even you—tell me that I can't love her, because she deserves it, Anna."

I take in a ragged breath. "And I know it's fast, and I know you might not believe me, but I don't care." I press my hand to my heart. "I'm sorry that you're going through a hard time. Truly, I am. But I love her, and I'm *going* to love her, with or without your approval."

"Of course she deserves love. That's not what I'm—"

"Just as long as it's not with me, right?"

Anna recoils like I've slapped her. Her eyes flash. "That's not what I meant," she snaps. "But she's my best friend, Max. I was totally blindsided."

"And you think what I have with Gemma only blindsided *you*?" I fire back. "You think we didn't try to fight it?"

"Maybe you should have tried harder," she whispers.

I push up from the sofa, pacing. "Jesus, Anna. You're acting like we did this to hurt you. Neither of us expected this to happen. But it's real."

She shoots up from the couch. "Okay! Fine! I get it!"

"I know you're hurt." I step closer, putting a hand on her shoulder. "I understand—I do. I've *been* there. Your life is imploding. You needed your people. I'm sorry we didn't tell you the truth from the beginning. But that doesn't mean you get to punish us for finding something good in the middle of all this carnage."

Her face crumples. "When I saw you two ... it felt like I wasn't just losing Mason, but everything ..." She trails off, sniffing. "After what happened with Nicole—"

"I get that. Nicole hurt you all those years ago. But Gemma *isn't* Nicole." I approach her, gripping her shoulders. "You haven't lost us."

She exhales, her hands trembling. "I know I'm not being fair ... I just don't want to lose either of you."

I bend so I'm eye level with her. "Then stop pushing us away. You don't have to lose us, Anna. Not me. Not Gemma. But you *will* if you hold this over our heads."

She closes her eyes.

"I'll always be your brother." I rub her arm. "Nothing changes that." I pause, swallowing the thickness in my throat. "And do you know what Gemma said to me tonight when I went to her?"

She sniffles, tilting her head.

"She didn't choose me, Anna. She chose you." My voice catches on the admission. "She said it wouldn't work between us. That you needed me more than she does. And then she told me to leave."

Anna's chin trembles.

"She's a real friend," I say gently.

Anna closes her eyes. She doesn't speak.

"I fell in love with someone I never expected to," I continue. "Someone who wasn't supposed to be mine. And I'm leaving London next weekend, possibly forever. I don't want to spend the rest of my life wondering what might have been because I let her walk away to protect someone who couldn't find it in herself to meet us halfway." My words come out broken. "And now I've lost her. Not because she doesn't love me, but because she thinks we've destroyed everything that matters to you. Because she doesn't think you'll ever forgive her ... so if you really love her—if she's really the best friend you claim she is—then tell her. Remind her she hasn't lost you. Because I know Gemma. She wants to be here for you, but she won't come back to me as long as she believes she'll lose you."

A tear escapes despite my efforts, and I swipe it away with my sleeve. "I can't lose her, Anna." I whisper, too exhausted to hold myself together anymore. "If I have to love her across an ocean, I will. But I can't bear knowing I lost her because we were both too afraid to fight for love."

Anna exhales a shaky breath. "I just need some time."

"I'm not asking for permission, Anna," I say without hesitation.

"Then what are you asking for?"

"Humility."

Chapter Fifty-Eight

Gemma

Anna won't talk to me. I can barely bring myself to eat. She hasn't answered my calls in five days. Not a text, not an email, not even a "piss off".

Total radio silence. And I don't know what's worse. We've never gone this long without speaking before.

Not that I can blame her. I can barely look at myself. But the part that keeps me up at night—the part that guts me—is knowing that something happened. Something's broken her spirit and I'm not there. I'm not at my best friend's side. I'm not helping her through it. And I'm the reason why. Because I was too wrapped up in my own self-centred distractions.

And Max ... although he hasn't been back in the office since last Friday, he's tried calling me every day. Once, twice, sometimes three times. I've watched his name appear on the screen, desperate to answer and tell him that I didn't mean it. That I want him to stay. But instead, I let them ring out.

He's left nine voice messages on my phone—*nine*—and I can't bring myself to listen to a single one. The thought of hearing his voice makes my chest constrict.

He's leaving Sunday morning after April's wedding.

Three days.

The moment I hear his voice, I'll crumble. I have to stay strong and walk away before any more damage can be done. To him, to Anna, and me.

Opening our text thread, I reread over his messages for what must be the fiftieth time. I'm torturing myself at this point.

Max: *Answer your phone.*

Max: *Please let me know you're okay.*

Max: *You can't just end things like this. We need to talk.*

Max: *I don't want our last interaction to be the last time I see you. I need to see that beautiful face, sweetheart.*

Max: *I know you told me to go. But I'm still here.*

Every time I read his words, a new hole pierces my lungs.

My thumb hovers over the keyboard, tempted to type out a response, but I catch myself, chewing my nail instead. I've almost bitten them down to the bloody quick.

To make matters worse, I've fallen down the deep, dark rabbit hole of TikTok tarot readers. My page has been inundated with videos of women telling me that "a divine masculine energy is coming toward me" and that "Spirit wants you to know that you've been separated from your love in order to grow and heal your inner child."

Sod right off.

I drop my phone as if it's on fire and bury my head in my hands. I've officially hit rock bottom.

I manage to shower, pull on clothes, and pretend I'm a functioning adult. My hair is still damp, dark circles below my eyes, and my chest feels like it's collapsing, but I put one foot in front of the other, dragging myself to work.

First things first: coffee.

I walk the same route I take every morning after hopping off the Tube, rounding the corner to SoHo Gardens, reaching into my pocket for my phone to pay.

And then I stop in my tracks.

"No," I breathe. "No, no, no—"

Lance's kiosk is boarded up. Closed.

It's never closed.

I hurry toward it, my eyes burning as I squint to read the small handwritten sign propped against the shutter.

Closed until further notice.

"Lance," I whisper, a tear spilling. "I didn't even get to say goodbye."

I didn't even get to smell his fresh Danishes one last time.

"What's your favourite thing about your job?"

And now he's gone too.

* * *

"Ah!" Louise jumps and Theo yelps as they round the corner of the kitchenette, almost running into me.

I roll my eyes. We side-step each other awkwardly, like some sort of Irish Riverdance.

I'm in no mood for her bullshit this morning.

"You ..." Louise's eyes narrow to thin slits.

She gives me a once-over, scoffing when she takes in my appearance. "Wow. You look *great*," she says. "Up all night boozing?"

Theo snorts, knocking his elbow against hers. "Good one, Louise."

"Do you practise being awful in the mirror each morning, or does being a massive twat just come naturally?" I snap.

She crosses her arms. "Whatever, Gemma. At least I actually *checked* the mirror when I left home this morning."

"Oh, fuck off, Louise, you miserable cow."

"GEMMA!" Henry's voice booms across the office. I flit my gaze to him.

Louise and Theo snicker.

He lifts his brows. "My office. Now."

Shit.

"What was that about?" Henry asks, sitting across from me.

"I'm in a bad mood," I say, waving him off.

"You've been in a foul mood all week. The launch went well, the hotel is open, and people are loving it. So, what's the problem?" he presses.

I swallow thickly.

He leans back in his chair. "Damn it, Gemma." He points a finger at me. "I warned you about this."

"I know you did," I shoot back.

He sighs. "So, what happened?"

Reluctantly, I recount everything. From the launch party to Anna discovering us together, to me fleeing and Max running after me in the rain. I tell him about my decision to push him away, and—finally—I tell him about Lance.

By the time I'm finished, I'm emotionally spent.

"And that's why I told Louise to fuck off," I conclude.

Henry doesn't react. He watches me with an expression I can't decipher.

"What?" I finally ask, feeling uncomfortable under his scrutiny.

"You told Max you love him?" he asks, visibly startled.

"Is *that* all you took from everything I just said?"

"No, I heard you ... let me get this straight." He rubs his temples. "Max told you he loves you."

I nod.

He shifts in his chair. "Then Anna finds you two together and your response was to run away—literally—then he chased after you *in the rain* and poured his heart out to you a second time."

I nibble on my lower lip, flinching, because it does sound pretty bad. "Yeah."

"And your strategic decision was to push him away. Do I have that right?" he asks.

I hum in approval.

He throws out his arms. "You bloody clown!"

"Hey!" I warn him.

"No! Come on, Gemma," he says, astonished. "The man *loves* you. Are you seriously *that* emotionally stunted?"

My spine snaps straight as my defence kicks in. "Anna's my *best friend*, Henry. You should have seen how hurt she was. She asked me not to touch her brother, she's been through this with a friend before, and I—"

"Stop. Just stop." He holds up a hand to silence me. "Have you put *yourself* first in any of this?"

"Henry—" I plant my palms on his desk, leaning in. "All I've done these past few weeks is think of myself. I thought of myself when I should have been thinking about Anna!"

"Anna is a big girl. She'll live. And then what?" He shrugs. "Max goes back to New York, and you stay here, both completely miserable? A true friend doesn't do that to the people they love."

I fall silent.

He sighs. "You think it's always been smooth sailing with me and Nate? We've been through hell and back to be together. But it was all worth it. It was never going to be easy, Gemma. But real love never is. It's seeing someone for everything they are and accepting all of it—fighting for it. It's knowing that no matter how hard things get, that person is worth every battle, every uncomfortable conversation. Every sacrifice. It's messy and it's inconvenient and it rarely comes when we're ready for it."

His voice softens. "I've known you a long time now. And in all those years, I've never seen you light up the way you do when Max walks into the room. And from what *I've* seen during his time here, I'm willing to bet he feels the same. You've hit a roadblock with Anna. Fine. Work through it like adults. Talk to her, send a carrier pigeon—I don't give a damn what you do. But don't use her as an excuse to run away from something that scares you just because it's real."

He fixes me with a stern look. "You've gotten this far in your career because you've never been afraid to take risks. So why is your personal life any different?"

"It's not that simple," I protest weakly.

"Who *are* you? Because this isn't the Gemma I know. The Gemma *I* know isn't afraid to fight for what she wants. The Gemma *I* know doesn't give up. Of course it's not simple. Emotions rarely are. But are you really going to let him go without even trying? Without confronting Anna? Without even listening to what Max has to say?"

He clasps his hands. "You've spent the better part of five years keeping everyone at arm's length. And that's worked for you, sure." He shrugs. "But ask yourself this—ten years from now, twenty years from now, which will you regret more? Taking a chance on something real that *might* not work out, or never knowing what could have been because you were too scared to try?"

Well, shit.

I know I'll drive myself mad if I don't give Max a shot, but the idea of confronting Anna floods my mind with all the worst-case scenarios. Will it make matters worse? Does she think I'm not good enough for Max? What if it gets nasty? What if she's so mad at me, she refuses to understand?

I want to believe our friendship is stronger than this, but if she *does* forgive me, can she ever trust me again?

"Take the rest of the day and tomorrow," Henry says unexpectedly. "You've worked hard these last few weeks and achieved amazing results. Go have a break. Enjoy April's wedding."

My body temperature plummets at the mention of April's wedding.

Max will be there.

My own heartbreak aside, I need to make things right between me and Anna. I can't stand between my two best friends and pretend that everything is okay. Regardless of whatever happens with Max, I can't lose Anna too.

I blink, surprised. "Are you ordering me as my boss or my friend?"

He smiles. "Both. And I'm sorry about Lance. Really, I am."

I acknowledge silently and stand to leave when he stops me. "And, by the way, Gemma?"

I peer at him over my shoulder, hand on the doorknob.

"I agree with you," he adds.

My brows furrow in confusion.

"Louise really is a miserable cow," he declares.

For the first time in nearly a week, I smile.

Chapter Fifty-Nine

Gemma

"**H**ey!" April greets, rushing toward me.

"Hey," I say, wrapping my arms around her.

She texted me just after work and asked me over for nibbles and wine. My response was immediate.

"Come in, come in," she says, stepping aside.

I follow her to the kitchen and take a seat at the breakfast bar while she pulls out two wine glasses and a chopping board, which she begins loading up with cheeses, sliced meats, and other goodies.

"James is at the studio, so we have the house to ourselves," she says, rolling the salami into neat little piles. I eye the cold cuts, aware of how little I've eaten this week but unable to fathom forcing food down my throat. I'm worried I'll heave it back up.

April pours two generous glasses of red. I stand and help her, carrying the board over to the coffee table. We settle onto the sofa, clinking our glasses and taking a long, much-needed sip.

"So," April says, and I can tell she's about to get stuck into me. "I spoke to Anna."

My eyes close softly. "When?" I ask.

"Sunday."

I gulp. My stomach folds in on itself knowing Anna's been speaking to April but ignoring me.

"What did she say?" I ask.

She shrugs. "Nothing I didn't already know."

I blink back tears, and she reaches forward, rubbing a soothing hand over my thigh. "She's going to be okay, Gem. She was just taken aback. Give her time."

"You should have seen her, April. She was ..." I search for the right words to articulate her despair, the broken look in her eyes when she saw Max and me together. "Inconsolable."

April sighs, turning her body to fully face me, balancing her wine glass on her knee. "She told me what happened. Why she was at Max's."

I perk up, straightening my spine. "Is she okay? What is it?"

Her expression turns sympathetic as she regards me. "She and Mason are getting a divorce."

My hands shoot up to cover my mouth and my eyes water instantly.

Oh my God. She came to Max's seeking comfort and found the two of us together instead. I shake my head, because how stupid could I be? How utterly and completely self-absorbed?

"What?" I whisper through my fingers.

April nods. "Mason decided against having children. They've tried to see if the relationship could work if they didn't go on to have a baby, and Anna can't do it. Mason doesn't want the pressure. He doesn't want to feel as though he's holding her back from living her life, from someone who can give her what she wants," she explains.

My hands fall to my lap. "Fuck."

"Hey," she says. "This isn't your responsibility to shoulder. It's not happening because of you and Max. It's just bad timing, that's all."

I avert my gaze. "All on the week of your wedding."

"It's okay. I'm still getting married, and you'll both still be by my side." Her lips tip up in a small smile.

What if this isn't resolved by then? I suck in my bottom lip, terrified that we'll be standing next to April pretending everything is fine.

"Anna told me that Max loves you," April says after a moment.

I swallow hard. "It doesn't matter. He's leaving."

She studies me, tilting her head slightly. "And if he weren't leaving?"

"That's not the point," I say, struggling to navigate the web of guilt and fear and want tightening inside me. "Anna needs me. I can't ... I won't choose him over her."

April sips her wine. "Gemma, this isn't going to be easy to hear, but I need to say it."

Our gazes lock. "I think you're hiding behind Anna."

"I'm not—"

"You are," she cuts me off gently but firmly. "Don't get me wrong—I know you care about her. But your feelings for Max frighten you, and I think you're using Anna's reaction as the perfect excuse to run away from him."

Heat blooms across my chest. "That's not fair."

"Isn't it?" She leans forward. "Gem, how many chances have you walked away from at the first sign of real intimacy? How many men have you kept at a safe distance so they could never touch anything real?"

I stare at her, stunned that she's bringing this up. "This has nothing to do with my dating history."

"Every time someone gets close, you find a reason to push them away," she utters.

I place my glass on the coffee table with a thud and stand abruptly. "If I wanted therapy, I would book a session," I snap.

She raises her hands in surrender. "I'm not saying this to be mean. I'm not trying to psychoanalyse you," she says, remaining calm. "I'm trying to be your friend. I want to be honest with you, hon. Which means I need to point out that you have a pattern."

A tear spills free. "Which is what, exactly?"

"You run from anything real because real means risk. It means there's a possibility of you getting hurt. And after Todd, you'd rather walk away first than give someone else the power to leave you. Someone hurt you, so this is how you've taken control."

Her words spear me and my knees buckle. I drop to the sofa, burying my face in my hands.

She's right. I flee at the first sign of vulnerability. I've been running from my feelings for so long that I've convinced myself it's the only way to avoid getting hurt. Aside from my best friends, I never let anyone close enough to matter.

Max is different. He refuses to be pushed away. He's seen all that I am and still wants me—not just my body—all of me. Ever since Todd rejected the intimacy I sought, I've been convinced I'm not worthy of love so I never allow it to be an option. But if I'm only desired, then I can't be seen. I can't be exposed. I can't be disappointed or heartbroken.

I build walls and keep men at arm's length because I need to hold all the cards, because giving someone else the power to hurt me feels like handing a stranger a loaded gun.

April scoots close, reaching for my hand and squeezing it once. "I'm sorry, hon. I know that's not what you wanted to hear, but I think you needed to." Another squeeze. "I love you *so* much. And you deserve more. You deserve happiness, and I think you've found that with Max, if you give him a chance."

"He sees me," I whisper.

"Then let him," she presses.

"What if I lose them both? It feels easier to sacrifice something I want than risk fighting for it and failing," I say, finally voicing the fear that's been haunting me since last Saturday.

"Anna's processing her loss, Gem. And when people are in pain, everything feels like it's falling apart—even when it isn't."

"She looked at me like she didn't even know me," I say, my voice low.

"I know, and that hurts. But that's not forever. She's reacting. She's grieving a future that doesn't exist anymore. She'll be okay. She's strong. And I know she'd want you to be happy," she says. "As for fighting and failing—wouldn't it be worse to never know what could have been?"

Deep down, I know I couldn't live with myself if I never gave Max a shot. He's fought to show me he's worth believing in.

"The regret would eat me alive," I confess.

Her answering smile is small and tender. "Maybe it's time you stop letting your past dictate your future. Give yourself some grace and allow the two of you a chance."

I muster a tearful smile, and as April wraps me in her arms, I feel a stir or hope—that this time, I might be strong enough to trust and let myself fall.

Chapter Sixty

Gemma

The morning of April's wedding arrives and I'm still shitting myself over the fact that Anna and I haven't spoken in almost a week. I feel sick.

April touched a nerve on Thursday night. As confronting as it was to hear her dissect my dating life, she was right. I've spent the last couple days thinking—properly reflecting—about the mess I've made of things instead of just drowning in wine, self-pity, and dick. Turns out I've been so preoccupied protecting my heart that I've forgotten what it feels like to be truly happy.

What a fucking revelation.

After rinsing off the spray tan I marinated in last night, I lather on a thick coat of vanilla and coconut lotion over my bronze skin.

April and James canned tradition—they opted not to have hen or bachelor parties—instead spending their last night as boyfriend and girlfriend together rather than apart. Anna and I are meeting at April's house to get ready.

Today will be the first time I've seen Anna since she discovered me and Max, and to say I'm nervous would be an understatement. That's like asking "Do you think the *Titanic* had a bit of a leak?"

The Suite Secret

Truth be told, I *want* to open myself up to the possibility that Max and I could have something magical together. I want to try. But I need to speak to Anna first.

I triple-check my day bag to ensure I haven't forgotten anything before jumping in an Uber.

Anna isn't there when I arrive at April's, so we indulge in celebratory coffee and brownies while we wait.

"How are you feeling?" I ask April, settling into her kitchen, cradling a steaming mug.

She inhales a sharp breath and her hands flutter to her chest. "It doesn't feel real." Her face glows as she speaks. "I'm so happy, Gem. I can't wait to marry him."

A soft smile spreads across my face as I watch her with such overwhelming tenderness.

My heart expands at the pure elation in every word. She's about to spend the rest of her life with the man of her dreams, and despite everything we've all been through this week, this moment is untouchable.

"He's the luckiest man in the world to have you. You're perfect for each other, and I'm *so* proud of you," I tell her.

It wasn't easy for April and James to get here. After Lucas broke her heart, I wasn't sure she'd ever trust someone enough to walk down the aisle again. But she did. She fought for love and won.

And if she can find her happily ever after following such a tremendous heartbreak, then maybe so can I.

The doorbell rings and I nearly soil myself.

April's eyes flick to me. "It's going be fine," she reassures.

When she opens the door, Anna stands at the threshold, bridesmaid dress in hand and dark circles under her eyes. Still, carrying the weight of the world on her shoulders, she smiles through her pain, wrapping an arm around April and pulling her in for a firm hug.

"You're getting married today!" She beams.

"I can't believe it," April says. "Oh, my phone's ringing. I'll be right back."

Anna frowns. "What? No, it's not. You don't even have your phone."

April plucks the dress from Anna's hand and dashes upstairs to hang it across her bedroom curtain rail with mine, leaving Anna and me standing in awkward silence.

Turd.

Anna and I stare at each other wordlessly, and when I can't stomach it anymore, I take a step forward.

"Hey," I say, my voice small.

Her mouth curves upward. "Hey."

"April told me about you and Mason." The words tumble out. "Anna, I'm so sorry. I wasn't there for you when you needed me most, and I should have been."

She shakes her head. "I kept it to myself. I didn't tell you or April because I think, deep down, I was hoping he would change his mind. Like if I avoided speaking about it with you and April, it wouldn't be real." She shrugs and straightens her shoulders. "I'll be okay. I'll get through it." Her eyes shine. "I have my two best friends."

"Anna, about everything else, I'm so—"

"Oh, that can piss right off," she interrupts. "Come over here and give me a hug." She opens her arms wide, and I rush forward without hesitation, squeezing her tight.

"I hate not talking to you," I whisper against her hair.

"Me too. I just ... I needed some time to process," she says, pulling back. When she looks at me, her eyes gloss over with emotion. "The whole thing weirded me out. I was scared that you'd push me away if things went wrong. I ..." She pauses. "He's my *brother*, Gem. You guys were sneaking around behind my back for weeks."

I hang my head, shame burning through me. "I know. We should have told you as soon as it started."

The Suite Secret

"I was upset with you," she says. "Both of you."

"I'll never go behind your back again," I say. "I promise."

She nods, gaze dropping to the floor. "Thank you."

"I love you so much, Anna. When you avoided me all week, I was so scared I'd lost you."

She lifts her eyes to meet mine. "From what I've heard, I'm not the only one who's been avoiding someone this week."

She raises her brows expectantly and understanding dawns on me.

Max told her I'm ignoring him.

"Anna—" I start, but she holds up a hand.

"We can talk about that later," she says. "Today is about April. But Gem?" Her face softens. "We're okay. And whatever happens, we'll figure it out. Together."

I throw my arms around her neck, and she holds me tightly. I don't think I've ever felt so much relief in my life.

"Oh, thank God that's over with," April says loudly, marching down the stairs. "Now, who's ready for champagne before hair and make-up arrives?"

* * *

Shoulders back, spine straight, arse out, I tell myself as we line up, waiting for our cue to walk down the aisle. Anna's leading the procession, I follow, and then, of course, April, who will be escorted by James's mum, Caroline.

The venue is perfect. The ceremony is in the heart of the Royal Botanic Gardens at Kew, surrounded by beautiful trees and vibrant flowers that wind around the altar. The reception will follow inside the glass house, where fairy lights have been strung between exotic plants. It's enchanting.

April is a total knock-out in her sleeveless ivory gown, wrapped in lace and flowing silk. Anna wears a burgundy dress with an elegant cowl neckline and thin spaghetti straps, and I'm in my dreamy purple halter number. Simple and sophisticated.

"You look gorgeous, girls," Caroline whisper-shouts from behind us, adjusting April's train.

Through the gap in the hedge, I watch as the sea of heads turns. James stands hands clasped behind his back with Oliver, Tom, and Will beside him.

Somewhere in that crowd sits Max, and despite my best efforts to focus on April's big moment, my stomach is having a rave at the thought of seeing him again.

"Ready, ladies?" the venue manager asks, ducking her head around the hedge.

We shoot her a collective nod, and she speaks into her earpiece before soft music carries through the garden.

Anna takes the first steps gracefully, and I suck in a deep breath and count to ten, just like we rehearsed, before following in her wake.

Heads turn, people gasp, and guests prepare their tissues as we walk down the aisle.

My gaze scans the crowd of faces until suddenly, it collides with a pair of ocean blue eyes that slam into me like a wave.

He's standing three rows from the front in a charcoal suit. His hair pushed back like the night of the launch party.

He's so damn handsome.

He stands with his and Anna's parents, his hands clasped in front of him.

I force one foot in front of the other and focus on making it down the aisle without tripping over my own nerves.

When I reach the end, I flash James a smile, which he returns warmly, and take my place just before April begins her walk down.

And when the guests gasp, all eyes turning to April, I follow suit. She looks like she's just stepped out of a fairy tale, all ethereal and shit. I can't contain my emotions. Rivulets of tears stream down my cheeks, and I say a silent prayer to the make-up artist for using waterproof mascara and a boatload of setting spray.

Out of the corner of my eye, I know Max isn't looking at April. I can *feel* his eyes burning into me and my skin prickles with awareness. And while everyone is captivated by our bride, Anna leans in beside me, her voice a soft, barely there whisper.

"He told me he's in love with you, you know."

My stomach drops so hard, I swear I could shit out my actual soul.

And for just one dangerous split second, I allow myself to look at him again, and I silently beg him to read everything I'm feeling but can't bring myself to speak. All the love, all the fear, and all the need I've been shoving down for the past week.

And the way he's looking at me tells me that I'm the only person at this entire wedding who matters.

Chapter Sixty-One

Max

That Will dickhead from the engagement dinner won't leave Gemma alone. I've had to watch that fucker slow dance with her three times already, and all I can do is grip my whisky glass and zero in on the way his hand rests against her back.

Whoever designed Gemma's purple dress is cruel. It's so sexy, it takes all my willpower not to rip it off her and trace a line down her spine with my tongue. The only reason I haven't knocked the guy's lights out is because Gemma looks like she's in physical pain every time he touches her, which she's clearly only enduring for April and James's sake.

I almost didn't come today. After calling her relentlessly for days, leaving voicemails for calls she never returned, I finally admitted defeat. I couldn't stomach the thought of sitting in the office all week surrounded by reminders of her, knowing she'd avoid me like the plague. There wasn't any need for me to return to the office, anyway—the launch is over. The campaign was a raging success. Gray Hotel has made an absolute killing in its first week, so now it's time for me to go back to New York.

Anna called me three days ago and begged me to attend April's wedding. And selfishly, the only reason I'm here is because I knew Gemma would be, and I needed to see her one last time before I fly home tomorrow morning.

Home.

I think of New York and how excited I was when I stepped off that plane two years ago. Excited for a fresh start, single life in a new city, working with my best mate. The apartment near Central Park, the new role that challenged me.

I was so desperate to escape London following my divorce that I started thinking about home as a place. But now, when I look around the room at Gemma and my sister dancing with their best friends, and my parents staring lovingly into each other's eyes, I realise that has changed.

New York might have my apartment and my career. But is that really a home? I don't know anymore. I'm starting to wonder if maybe home is a feeling—a person.

I came to London for work, to build something temporary, and instead, I'm leaving having found something I want to be permanent.

Gemma made it crystal clear that whatever we had is over, but maybe if I stay, if we had more time, she might come around to the idea of us.

Anna shimmies over and drops into the empty seat beside me where Mason would have sat, panting and sweaty. "Come and dance!" she says.

"I don't dance."

"Oh, come on," she says, slapping my back. "You look more miserable than I do, and my husband pulled out of coming today."

I smile at her, but it doesn't reach my eyes. "I'm sorry, weasel."

She swats the air. "Today's not about that."

A burst of laughter pulls our attention to the dance floor, just in time to see Dad take Mum's hand and twirl her around, her face lit with joy. Even after forty-two years married, they're still madly in love.

Anna watches them for a beat, then turns to me with a sad, soft smile. "I'm really going to miss you."

I throw my arm around her shoulders, pulling her in for a side hug. "Yeah. Me too."

When Gemma takes James's and April's hands, dancing with the both of them in a circle, my throat constricts.

She's so damn beautiful.

I want to go to her.

God, do I want to go to her.

But I won't. Not here. Not now.

Her head's thrown back in laughter and she's surrounded by people who love her. There's a time and a place to confront her, and her best friend's wedding doesn't fall into either of those categories.

But *Christ*, I miss her. I miss holding her. I miss kissing her. I miss tickling her and falling asleep with her. I miss undressing and tasting her. I miss threading my fingers through her hair and laughing with her.

So, I give myself three more seconds to watch her. To study her. To memorise her smile.

I stare at my phone for a long time before punching out a text and hitting send. Then, I set my drink down, hug my sister tight, and slip on my jacket.

And I leave.

Chapter Sixty-Two

Gemma

Guests clap and cheer as April and James disappear through the large reception doors hand in hand, blissful in love.

My gaze sweeps over the room, looking for Max, wondering if he left and I missed him. I look down at my phone screen, rereading his text.

Max: *I leave tomorrow morning, and the idea of getting on that plane without talking to you is killing me. I want you to know that I meant everything I said. I still do.*

"He left," a voice says behind me.

I turn and find Anna.

She tips her chin toward the door. "A little while ago."

I nod, pressing my lips together tightly, unsure of what to say. Both because this is awkward, but also because I might start crying again, and I've had enough of tears.

She rolls her eyes. "Oh, for fuck's sake, just go to him, will you?"

I blink. "What?"

"You both look so bloody glum," she says, crossing her arms. "He loves you, Gemma. Can't you see that?"

My brows draw together. "I ... I thought you—"

"I was angry. I was hurt. But watching you two dance around your feelings is *exhausting*. You're both bloody hopeless."

I stare at her, speechless.

"He's leaving tomorrow," she says. "So, if you've got something to say—say it. Don't wait until he's back in New York and you're left wishing you had."

My eyes well, overwhelmed that she's given me her blessing. "Are you sure?" I ask.

She lets out a sigh, nudging me. "Yes, I'm sure. I'm not completely heartless."

I fling my arms around her and give her a quick squeeze before pulling away.

Finally, I crack a smile.

And then ... I run.

Chapter Sixty-Three

Max

Without much else to do once home, I shower and distract myself by answering some work emails.

I only came to London with a couple of suitcases, so it didn't take me long to pack this morning.

Eventually, I sink onto the sofa, slipping my phone from my pocket, and open Instagram. I see Anna's uploaded photos from the wedding to her story, so I tap through—photos of Anna and me at dinner, a couple of Anna with Mum and Dad, and when I tap to the next frame, my heart stops.

It's a photo of Anna, April, and Gemma. All three of them in their dresses, taking a full body mirror shot in the bathroom, but I only see *her*.

Soft background lighting creates a halo effect around her golden locks and her eyes are crinkled at the corners from smiling so wide—*really* smiling.

This is the Gemma I fell for. Totally unguarded, radiant, and completely herself.

So gorgeous and happy and so painfully out of reach.

Closing the app, I open our text thread and reread my last message to her.

Read at 12.00 am. No response.

Fuck.

Gemma Clarke has thrown me. With her, my defences crumble to shit. I am everything I swore I'd never become again after Casey: irrational, emotional, and worse? Hopeful.

Because hope means I'm still holding on. Still waiting. Still desperate for a chance to breathe the same air as her. Still clutching to the idea that maybe she'll show up. That maybe she'll choose *us*.

I'm fully prepared to negotiate my work schedule. Grayson's a practical man, and if I tell him this really means something to me, which it does, I know he'll give me a chance to try working from London.

But if she doesn't come. If I don't hear from her ...

I could have shown up at her door with flowers, but that's not who I am. And that's not what Gemma needs.

My intentions are clear. She knows my willingness to fight for this. I've shown her my hand, again and again, and now the ball is in her court. The last thing she needs is me backing her into a corner. Pushing her now would be the fastest way to ensure she never speaks to me again. That kind of pressure will only make her run further. I won't make that mistake.

No. This is a conclusion Gemma needs to reach herself, and whatever she decides, I have to respect it. I'm playing the long game. If she needs space, I'll give it to her.

The rational part of my brain knows I should be relieved she hasn't contacted me. This is the kind of clean cut we discussed, that we agreed to. The kind of clean break we need to get our lives back on track. I can board that plane tomorrow and step straight back into my old life.

But deep down, in my heart, I know the truth—I don't want my old life back.

The buzzer cuts through the silence like a guillotine.

There's only one person who would show up to my apartment at this hour. Without thinking, I press the button to let them up, and that niggling *hope* surges through me.

I walk to the door, running a hand through my hair, trying to calm the staccato of my heartbeat.

When the sound of footfalls in the corridor floats through my apartment, I yank the door open, expecting to see jade green eyes staring back at me, when—

"Hello, Max."

Casey.

Chapter Sixty-Four

Max

"Casey." Her name comes out like a slap. "What are you doing here?"

The question hits her like a blow, her smile wavering. "You haven't been responding to any of my calls or texts."

"Because I blocked you, Casey." My grip tightens on the door handle. "How did you find me?"

She blinks, taken aback by my question.

"How did you find me?" I repeat, my voice low.

"Anna's Instagram stories," she supplies.

I frown, confused. "I don't understand. How did you—"

"She tagged the wedding venue," she rushes to explain. "And then I saw your car leaving, so I—" She straightens her back, lifting her chin. "Well, I followed you."

"You *followed* me?" My voice drops dangerously low as I fight to contain my anger. "Are you out of your *bloody* mind?"

I step forward and she retreats, her back hitting the hallway wall. "Max, please. We need to talk," she begs.

"You can't be here." I start to close the door, but she lunges forward, trapping her foot in the threshold.

The Suite Secret

"I needed to see you. Max, please." Her hands fly up to fist my shirt as she clings to me desperately.

Instinctively, I lift my hands to pry her manicured fingers off me when—

Ding.

The elevator doors slide open painstakingly slow, and I feel the ground beneath me dissolve.

Gemma.

She freezes, all the colour bleeding from her face as she takes in the scene before her.

I see the moment I lose her, her emotions switching off.

No.

"Gemma," I say, cautious.

Her arm moves as she jabs the elevator button once.

"No, Gemma, wait—it's not what—"

The doors begin to close.

I rip Casey off me and sprint, but I'm two steps too late.

"FUCK!" I roar as my fist smashes against the cool steel as it shuts between us.

Chapter Sixty-Five

Gemma

Just breathe, Gemma. Push aside the intrusive thoughts. You need to see him. Tell him you're sorry for being a coward and bailing when things got real. That you're sorry for being too damaged to let someone love you. Tell him you want to try.

The doors slide open and my heart implodes.

Her hands are fisted in his shirt, pulling him toward her, and his hands are wrapped around her wrists, the way they've been wrapped around mine so many times—but he's not pushing her away. He's holding her.

Casey.

The woman from the old photos I've tortured myself looking at online. Endless legs, lustrous black hair, and flawless olive skin.

She's not just beautiful, she's *striking*.

They're so close, almost like they're about to—

The air leaves my lungs in a violent rush as my eyes ping-pong between the two of them.

How could I have been so bloody stupid to believe that he'd still *actually* want me?

Max's eyes widen when he spots me. Of course he didn't expect me to show up after his text. Why would he? I didn't chase him after any of the others I ignored.

And why would he hang around and wait for me when he could have her?

Stay calm, Gemma. Stay calm.

Fight-or-flight mode kicks in as every worst-case scenario I've imagined floods back. Every insecurity. Every reason as to why I only let men have my body, standing right in front of me.

Get me out of here.

My heart rate spikes, and my blood turns arctic as panic rises. I'm unresponsive, physically unable to form words.

"Gemma," Max's voice cuts clean and fast.

But I can't hear it. I can't hear his excuses—I can't breathe, can't think, can't do anything but slam my palm against the elevator button, willing it to close.

Hurry up. Close, please just close.

"No, Gemma, wait—it's not what it—"

He pushes past her and starts running toward me.

"No! Gemma, please don't go. Let me explain!" he yells as the doors slide shut.

I collapse against the mirrored wall. "Gemma, you idiot," I mutter. "Stupid, stupid, *stupid*."

My mind spirals back to that message in the car on the way to the Harrington estate. He said he didn't want to speak to her.

But how does she know where he's staying? How did Casey know where to find him? Unless ... unless he told her.

Is that what he did the second he left my flat last Saturday? The moment I told him to leave, did he run straight to *her*? Invite her over to stroke his wounded ego?

Did he leave April's wedding to meet her?

The thought makes me physically sick. All those sweet messages when he begged me not to shut him out—was I just a backup plan?

But then why did he send me that message tonight? Why tell me he didn't want to leave without speaking to me if he already had her exactly where he wanted her?

My thoughts tear through me, transforming the hurt into something molten.

I'm out of the elevator before the doors are fully open, running through the lobby like my life depends on it. Yes, *me*, sprinting in heels like some maniac who's lost her bloody mind. Because I have—I've lost it.

"Gemma?" the doorman calls after me.

I don't stop until Max's building disappears behind me, until my lungs and muscles burn and the breath I've been holding whooshes out of me in a gasp.

I probably look like I've just escaped a psychiatric facility, but I couldn't care less. All I can think about is seeing them together.

Oh God. Here we go. More tears. Excellent.

This is exactly what I get for letting myself hope.

It's not until I make it home, kick off my shoes, and climb into bed fully clothed that I let myself fall apart.

Chapter Sixty-Six

Max

"LEAVE!" I shout at Casey, the words exploding from me as I tear open the fire escape door. My feet are already moving before I can comprehend what I'm doing.

I take the stairs three at a time as I race the lift.

The metal railing screams as I grip it, swinging myself down the next flight.

Twelve sodding floors between me and any chance of explaining this nightmare to Gemma.

My phone buzzes against my thigh but I ignore it, praying I'm not too late.

By the time I crash through the stairwell door into the lobby, my chest is on fire. Jim, the doorman, is already standing with the main door held wide.

"She went left, Mr Browne."

I nod without slowing down and barrel past him onto the sidewalk and into the night.

I'm not wearing any bloody shoes, the pavement is ripping at the soles of my feet and *burning*, but I don't stop.

My eyes scan every face I pass. None of them are her.

By the time I reach South Kensington, I stop, doubled over and gasping for air as reality washes over me.

Even if I could find her, even if I showed up at her flat pounding on her door like last time, it won't work. Not after what she saw.

She was giving me a chance, and it's completely destroyed now.

I straighten up slowly, my hands on my hips as I stare down the empty street.

She's gone.

And this time, I don't think she's coming back.

Chapter Sixty-Seven

Gemma

Bang, bang, bang.

The knocks at the door wake me. I groan, pushing the duvet back and climbing out of bed. I barely slept a wink. Instead, I sat in bed propped against my headboard with a tub of cookie dough ice cream and ate my feelings until I got brain freeze, then ate some more.

He leaves today.

I check my phone. Ten missed calls. Nine unread messages. I drop it back on the bedside.

I'm such a fool to have let myself get hurt like this again. The only way to have your heart broken this deeply is to feel this deeply in the first place. My heart isn't just crushed—it's shattered. Obliterated into pieces so small I'm not sure I'll find them all.

I was so naive to think it could ever work, that this would end any other way than one of us completely fractured. Only, it's *me* bleeding.

Look at Anna and Mason. They've been married for the better part of eight years. I thought they'd be together forever—Mason was completely besotted with Anna, he worshipped the ground she walked on, and that turned to complete shit.

We don't get to pick and choose the things that leave us beyond words. We don't get to select the hand we're dealt. So, it's easier to not feel. It's easier to bury those emotions deep, because if *this* is what I get for loving? Then I don't want it.

Is any love worth this kind of pain? The kind where it feels like someone's twisting a knife between my ribs until I can't breathe?

Twelve hours ago, I would have convinced myself that *yes*, it is worth it. But sitting here while my heart cracks open and spills all over my Egyptian cotton leads me to think *absolutely not*.

Bang, bang, bang.

"I'm coming!" I call out, my voice hoarse from crying. I grab my glasses from the bedside and shove them on, shuffling to the door. I look every bit as tragic as I feel. My eyes are puffy, and I have mascara smudged halfway down my face. And yet I don't have the strength to care.

At least I took out my contacts.

I swing the door open to find Anna holding two cups of steaming coffee.

"Thank God. Took your sweet time," she says, pushing past me. I follow her wordlessly as she strides through my flat and into my bedroom, where she immediately starts rifling through my wardrobe.

I rub my eyes, wincing as my fingers come away black with yesterday's make-up. "What are you doing?"

"Fixing this." She tosses a pair of jeans and a cashmere jumper onto my unmade bed.

I frown. "What?"

She huffs, spinning around to face me with her hands on her hips. "You heard me." She nods toward the clothes she's pulled out. "Get changed. Now."

"Where are we going?" I ask, even though I have a feeling I already know. Anna only gets this determined when she wants to prove a point or Costa Coffee has a two-for-one deal on banana bread.

"To stop you from making one of the worst decisions of your life."

"Anna, I already made the worst decision of my life. Remember? I told you about the time I let those guys use me as a human sushi board and they put wasabi—"

"Jesus Christ, not that!" she says, flapping her hands. "I'm talking about Max." Her eyes narrow as her gaze finally sweeps over me. "You look absolutely dreadful, by the way."

I cross my arms defensively, my eyes darting to the digital clock on my dresser. "It's 6 am."

"Did you sleep at all?" she asks, her voice softening.

I gawk at her. "Anna, do you have *any* idea what happened last night?"

Her eyebrows squish together, confusion clouding her face. "Yes. I spoke to Max. Which is why I need you to get changed and come with me."

Max didn't tell her?

"Anna, there's no point. He's with Casey," I say.

She freezes. "What are you talking about? Max isn't with Casey. The only person Max wants is *you*, Gemma."

I shake my head. "I saw them together. With my own eyes. Her hands were all over him and he was—"

"No," she interrupts firmly. "He's *not* with her. Last night wasn't what it looked like."

"I know what I saw." My voice cracks.

She steps forward, her hands gripping my shoulders. "Casey saw my Instagram stories. I stupidly tagged the wedding venue, and she *followed* Max home."

"What?" The word comes out as barely a whisper.

"She tracked him down like some unhinged stalker. You caught him trying to get *rid* of her, not reconciling with her."

I stare at her, my brain working overtime to process. "That can't be right ... her hands were on him. He was holding her wrists ..."

"Because she was grabbing him and he was trying to get her off!" Her voice rises. "For crying out loud, Gem. He chased after you, you know? He rang me as soon as he got Casey escorted from the building."

My eyes widen. "Escorted?"

Anna nods fervently. "She'd been trying to contact him for weeks—messaging *me*, calling him from new numbers when he blocked her. The doorman had to call the police when she refused to leave. She's been given a formal warning to stay away or face stalking charges. She's gone, Gem."

"Oh my God," I say, my hand flying to my mouth.

I drop my gaze to the floor, unable to speak. Afraid to believe that maybe I got it all wrong.

"He called me at two in the morning, totally distraught." She pauses. "In all my life as Max's little sister, I've never heard or seen him so cut up about anyone."

Tears burn behind my eyes. "Anna ..."

"He loves *you*," she says softly.

"I can't ..."

"You *can*, Gem." She drops her hands, her eyes flicking to the empty ice-cream box on my bedside. She sighs. "Look, I'll support you with whatever you decide to do, but you can either come with me or stay here and cry into your empty ice-cream tub."

I look up at her. "I've screwed this up pretty badly, haven't I?"

"A little." She smirks. "But we can fix this. You're going to put on some clothes, wash that raccoon make-up off your face, and get your arse out that door."

"Where are we going?"

Anna's responding smile is pure mischief. "The airport."

The Suite Secret

* * *

"Ouch!" I say, slipping a foot out of my shoe and rubbing it.

"That's what you get for wearing two right shoes, you tit," Anna says.

I huff in irritation. "What if he doesn't want me anymore? What if this is a bad idea?" I flip down the sun visor and pinch my cheeks, desperate to add colour to my death-warmed-up complexion.

Anna side-eyes me as she weaves through traffic. "Who are you and what have you done with Gemma Clarke? Since when do you not have any confidence?"

I throw my hands up in exasperation. "I know! This is exactly the issue! This is why I've only ever felt with my vagina for years—love is disgusting!"

She snorts. "No, it isn't, and I say that with my whole incredible double-D chest—love is beautiful. Even when it breaks you."

I'm taken aback. How can she sit here, after she and her husband agreed to divorce, and still tell me that love is beautiful?

"You really believe that?" I ask. "Even now?"

She laughs, but there's something raw in it. "Surprisingly, yes." She glances at me. "Don't you think that's what life is really about? Being completely wrecked by the things that happen to you—the good *and* the brutal? That's what makes us human, Gem. We *feel* everything so intensely."

Her expression softens. "I'm going to be real with you right now."

I lift my brows, bracing myself.

"April told me about Todd. About how selfish he was. And I'm so sorry you've felt like you've had to build these massive walls to protect your heart because that vanilla piece of shit couldn't love every part of you."

My posture slumps as the old wound tears slightly. "I wanted too much. *I* was too much."

She shakes her head. "No, Gemma. You were never too much. He was just too small."

I close my eyes.

"Here's the thing," she adds with conviction. "Loving is brave. And yes, when you feel something so strongly, and when your heart inevitably breaks, it doesn't just crack. It shatters into a million little pieces—"

"Anna, I don't know where you're going with this, but it's not sounding very hopeful," I interrupt.

"I'm not finished," she shoots back. "You might not get to choose who destroys you or how badly it aches, but you *do* get to choose what you do with the wreckage afterward. So, as you sit here crying over *my brother*—who I've watched fall apart for the last week because some twat named Todd broke you years ago—just remember this."

She takes a breath, her eyes burning. "The same heart that's breaking right now is the same one that's going to feel incredible happiness when you finally let the right person show up for you. And Max *will* show up, Gemma."

I stare at her, tears threatening again. "I'm scared," I whisper.

She shrugs, her eyes glistening. "Love, divorce, babies, taking risks, starting over—we're all scared. But none of us are alone. You, me, and April? We have each other. We always will."

And she's right. No matter what curveballs life has thrown at us, we've always gotten through them—together. When April's parents passed away in the car accident, Anna and I took shifts to cook meals and make sure she was eating, sleeping, and functioning like a human being instead of drowning in her grief. When Lucas broke her heart by cheating with women online, we held her while she cried herself sick and bought her a dildo (my idea).

We don't believe in "I told you so". We believe in being each other's constants, no matter how muddled and complicated things get. April and I are going to be there for Anna through every moment of her divorce, and if she's brave enough to walk away from her marriage because Mason can't give her what she truly wants—a family—then I can walk toward something that scares me shitless.

I can be brave enough to fight for Max.

"Besides," Anna says, swatting a stray tear away, "if Max screws it up and hurts you, I'll help you key his Mercedes."

We laugh, tears clinging to our lashes.

I squeeze her hand, sniffling. "Okay," I breathe, and something softens where I'd been holding tight. "I'm doing this. I'm gonna keep fucking your brother."

Anna yanks her hand away like I've burnt her, gripping the steering wheel. "Jesus Christ, Gemma. We were having such a nice moment!"

Chapter Sixty-Eight

Max

I learned to leave love out of my vocabulary. I didn't chase it. I didn't want it taking up space in my life again. I had everything I needed.

Then Gemma blazed in and derailed all of it.

Now, after seeing how terrified she is to let anyone in ... All I want is to love her back to life, back to herself, back to believing she deserves to be cherished so completely. But I can't.

For the first time in my life, I finally understand what the songs and poems are about. What drives men to madness.

It wasn't that I didn't want to believe in love again. It was that I had been waiting my whole life to find the woman worth giving it to.

And now I've lost her.

"Clear. You can come through, sir." The gentleman at airport security ushers me through.

My steps feel as heavy as my heart.

I slip my hand in my pocket, double-checking my passport and ticket are together. I collect my bag and head through the bustling terminal to my gate.

Heathrow Airport is chaotic, teeming with travellers.

The Suite Secret

An announcement echoes through the departure lounge. "Final boarding call for British Airways flight two-seven-eight to New York, gate thirty-three."

It's my flight.

I adjust the strap of my carry-on and head toward the gate. I'm in the worst mood.

Last night can't be how it ends—I can't erase the image of her, bereft, from my mind. Those sad green eyes will haunt me.

My phone feels like a dead weight in my pocket. Ten missed calls. Nine unanswered texts. The fact that she refuses to speak to me hurts like hell.

How do you convince yourself it's time to walk away from the person you love? That you need to accept that they aren't coming back?

Even now, as I'm about to put an ocean between us, I'm not sure I have the strength to admit it.

After a short walk, my gate comes into view and I see there's still a queue of passengers waiting to board. Families headed on holiday, people returning home, workers checking their emails—life just ... goes on.

I'm about fifty metres away when I hear a shouting behind me, and it's growing louder.

"Ma'am, you cannot pass without proper documentation—"

"I'm telling you, my brother's in there!"

Hold on. I know that voice.

Anna.

I turn and jog back into the terminal, my eyes scanning the crowd. Sure enough, about a hundred metres away, she's in the middle of a full-blown altercation with airport security.

She's yelling and swinging her handbag around like a mad woman.

What the fuck is she doing?

She spots me from a distance.

"For Christ's sake, he's right there. MAX! Maxwell Browne, you posh prick!"

"Ma'am, if you don't have a boarding pass—"

"I don't need a bloody boarding pass!" she shouts. "I need to stop my emotionally constipated brother from messing up his entire life!"

And that's when I see it. A blonde flash in my peripheral vision, darting around security unnoticed while Anna carries on behaving like a complete nutter.

Gemma.

She's running.

"Max!" she calls, her eyes scanning wildly. "Max!"

Behind her, Anna makes a break for it, dodging security's grasp and bolts full speed out of the terminal.

But I'm frozen. Because *she's here.*

Face streaked with tears, breathing hard. Her hair is unruly and—*is she wearing two right shoes?*

My bag drops to the floor with a heavy thud.

She doesn't slow down.

"Gemma!" I call, my body moving before my mind catches up. "Gemma!"

Her eyes lock on mine and a jagged sob breaks loose as we book it toward each other.

I stop just a few feet away, but she doesn't. She launches herself at me, full speed.

I catch her, my arms closing around her as she wraps her legs around my waist, burying her face in my neck.

"You can't leave," she murmurs against my skin. "You can't just leave," she pleads.

I'm holding her so damn tight, I'm probably crushing her, but I can't loosen my grip. I can't let her slip away.

"I'm not letting you go," I promise, my voice breaking.

She pulls back, cradling my face in her hands. "I'm an idiot. I'm such a bloody idiot—"

The Suite Secret

I lower her to the floor gently and she doesn't let go.

"No. No, you're not, sweetheart," I say, tucking her hair behind her ears.

"I'm so scared I won't be good enough for you," she whispers, her eyes closing. "Do you even know me, Max? You see the confident Gemma who knows what she wants and isn't afraid to take it. But that's not all of me." She peers up at me. "I've pushed people away because they couldn't handle what I need. I need to feel alive. I need someone who meets my intensity and doesn't make me feel like a freak for wanting more."

"I love every version of who you are. I've seen your intense side and I've seen your soft side. Both are real and both are beautiful. They're what make you, you." I search her eyes. "You feel this?" I take her hand and place it over my heart. "You feel that?"

She nods.

"That's for you. That's what you do," I tell her. "You're not just good for me. You're the reason my heart remembers how to beat properly."

Her breath hitches. "Max ..."

"I choose *you*, Gemma. Always."

"I choose you too," she whispers.

Her thumbs brush across my cheekbones. "I should have let you explain. I should have trusted you. But I saw her hands on you and I just ..."

"You always run," I say, pressing my forehead to hers. "You can't run, baby. You have to talk to me."

"I know." Fresh tears spill down her cheeks. "I've spent years running, but I can't anymore ... you're the first person who's ever made me want to stay."

I swallow thickly.

"I love you," she says, her voice quiet. "I love you so much."

I take her hand and gently kiss the back of it. "Then let me love you back. Properly."

She nods and rises to her toes. I don't wait. I meet her in the middle, slamming my mouth against hers.

The airport intercom crackles above us. "This is a final boarding call for Mr Browne on British Airways flight two-seven-eight to New York, departing from gate thirty-three. Aircraft is ready for departure."

We break apart, chests heaving, pupils dilated.

"They're waiting for you," she says.

"Let them wait," I say, cupping her face in my hands. "I'm not going anywhere."

"But your flight—" she starts.

"Fuck the flight."

"Max, your job—"

"I'm not going. I told you, I'll figure it out."

"Will Grayson be pissed?" she asks, wincing.

"Livid," I confirm.

She blows out a long breath, rubbing the back of her neck. "Max—"

"I'm staying."

"I might be a bad girlfriend."

"You won't be," I say without hesitation.

"I don't ever want children."

"I don't either," I return quickly.

"I'm emotionally unpredictable. I panic. I might shut down."

"I know."

"I'll probably push you away if things get hard," she warns.

"I'll still be here."

"I don't cook. I'll forget anniversaries," she says.

"I'll cook and remember important dates for the both of us."

She lifts her chin. "I'll never give up my work."

"I would never ask you to."

"I might get overwhelmed at times."

I step closer, cupping her jaw. "I'm not going anywhere, Gemma. You're mine."

The announcement repeats.

"Are you sure?" she asks.

"I've never been more certain of anything in my life."

Her face splits into a grin. "What happens now?"

"Now," I say, pulling her closer. "We go home, and I show you exactly how much I've missed you."

Chapter Sixty-Nine

Gemma

"Sorry sweetheart, but we need to make a quick stop at the hotel first. I just remembered something," Max says, his arm slung around my shoulder.

He quickly fires off the hotel address to the cab driver.

My brows furrow. "You've only just remembered *now*? I thought we were going back to mine to ... *you know* ..."

He smiles. "It'll be quick. Trust me." He takes my hand and gives it a gentle squeeze.

I lift my brows in surprise, but I don't argue.

Ten minutes later, we're pulling up to Gray Hotel.

Max pays the driver and gets out, offering me his hand as I try to—somewhat gracefully—step out of the cab.

The doorman beams at us. "Good morning, sir, madam. Welcome to Gray Hotel."

"Good morning," Max replies.

Threading his fingers through mine, he leads me through the grand entrance into the buzzing foyer. I take in the scene: reception checking in guests, concierge busy on phone calls, bellmen helping with bags, taxis pulling up outside—when my gaze lands on—

I stop dead. Blink once. Twice. My heart lurches.

I turn and smack his chest. "How? I thought ... "

Beside me, Max chuckles. The cheeky bastard.

My throat tightens and tears spring to my eyes.

I can't believe he did this. For me.

Max slides his hands into his trouser pockets, leaning in close. His breath tickles my ear, sending warmth down my spine. "Go and get your coffee."

I step forward, joining the busy queue. My face lighting up the moment the barista spots me.

"Morning, lass!" he booms.

A tear slides down my cheek as I whisper back, "Hi, Lance."

* * *

I didn't want yesterday to end. After catching up with Lance, the proud new owner of the Gray Hotel Coffee Cart, Max and I spent the rest of the day and evening in bed, tracing and tasting every inch of each other. And now, I wake to the feeling of Max's hard length pressed to my arse. I smile, arching my back, rubbing against him.

"Open your legs for me, sweetheart," he instructs.

I obey, exposing more of myself for him. I'm already impossibly wet and ravenous. Tilting my head, he captures my lips, and I sink into the feel of him. His thick thighs, strong shoulders, and chiselled stomach. Craving more, I turn in his hold.

He cups my heat, running his fingers through my mess.

"What do you need?" he asks.

"I want you to fill me," I breathe.

"Yeah?" His fingers glide lazily through my pussy, lapping tight circles over my clit. "Where do you want me to fill you?" He starts teasing my entrance with two fingers. "Here?" He thrusts his fingers inside me slowly before pulling them out and running them down to the hole between my cheeks. He smears my wetness over my arsehole. "Or here?"

A moan slips out. "Both," I say, dusting my thumb over his crown, spreading the pre-cum through his slit.

I grip him firmly, pumping a long, firm stroke up and down his shaft. He exhales shakily and I smile against his mouth.

He drives his fingers into me, scissoring and spreading me open until I'm soaked. We continue this way, working each other up with our hands before decreasing our pace, testing and teasing.

"Top drawer. Bedside table," I pant.

He breaks the kiss, reaching over and opening the drawer to peer inside. The moment he sees the contents of my bedside table, he smirks.

His muscles shift as he pulls out my eight-inch dildo and a bottle of lube. With a wicked glint in his eyes, he drops both items beside me.

"Get on all fours," he says.

I don't waste time, scrambling to my hands and knees.

He settles behind me, stroking each cheek and smoothing his hand up and down my spine. He snakes an arm around me, pulling me up on my knees so my back is flush to his chest. He's warm and strong, wrapping an arm around my stomach to keep me in place. A heat stirs in my belly as the hand holding me slides down to my clit, and I gasp. His other hand gets to work kneading my breast, pinching and pulling my nipple until I'm rolling my body into his, sinking against him.

"Are you ready?" he asks, his lips on my shoulder.

I nod. He drops his hand from my breast, rubbing his erection through my pussy, coating himself.

I fold my arm back and around his neck, pinning him close.

Slowly, he pushes inside me, sheathing himself.

We groan in unison as he begins to move and I rock into him, my hips slamming down as he thrusts up. The room echoes with every slick, filthy connection of our skin.

I widen my knees, granting him better access.

"Fuck, Gemma," he growls, plunging into me so deep I swear I can feel him in my throat.

I cry out as he grips my hips, slamming into me.

"Is this mine?" he pants.

"Yes," I gasp. *"It's all yours, Max."*

"That's right," he says, his voice all smoke and heat.

He drops a hand, and I hear the distinct click of a plastic cap right before a drizzle of cool liquid trickles through my crack. He rubs the lube over my arsehole.

"I'm gonna get you ready here, okay, sweetheart?"

I nod, whimpering and moaning, my body begging to be stuffed full of him.

"You have no idea what you do to me," he grunts. "I fucked you all day and night and I still need you. So. Fucking. Bad." He punctuates his last three words with a thrust, jamming into me until I see stars.

"More, Max," I cry.

A finger pushes into my arse.

He perfects an alternating rhythm, moving his cock and finger in tandem. I relax into the feel of him, coaxing me open. He slides his finger out, rubbing circles around my hole before plunging back in. He understands exactly what I need, reading my body as if it's written in a language only he speaks.

"I'm going to stretch you open," he declares. "And then I'm gonna fuck both your holes."

"Please ..." I sigh.

He adds a second finger to my arse, working me open with thick, slick circles until I'm shaking.

My pussy strangles his cock.

"So damn tight," he grits out. "So perfect."

I don't respond because I can't. I'm lost in oblivion as he pushes me closer to the edge.

"I'll come like this," I breathe.

He bites my shoulder. "Yeah?"

I nod frantically and he speeds up his movements. "Come for me," he says, and I lose control, coming apart all over his cock and fingers. I bear down, riding out the wave as long as I possibly can. My body trembles and convulses as he tapers back, prolonging my pleasure.

When the stars dissipate and I come back down, he pulls out and I whimper at the loss, the emptiness so profound. Dropping down to my elbows, I press my cheek to the bed, gripping the sheets as I anticipate more.

"I'm gonna fuck your arse with my cock and your pussy with the dildo now," he says.

I nod.

I hear the slick glide of lube and the low curse he lets out as he coats his dick, getting it ready for me.

"Breathe for me, baby," he soothes, and I do. "Show me how deep you can take it."

And then he's there, the dildo notching my pussy and his cock brushing my arsehole. He's patient and slow, breaching me inch by inch at the same time until I'm so *incredibly* full.

My mouth drops open and a broken moan escapes me. My thighs tremble, every nerve set alight. He's buried to the hilt. My hand curls underneath me, down to my core, and I hold his hand with the dildo in place.

"I want to do it," I pant.

He bends forward, planting a kiss to my back before giving the dildo up and gripping my waist.

I'm overcome with emotion—with the realisation that Max not only makes it his mission to satisfy me completely but to listen to what I crave.

Then, finally, we move. He works my arse over, matching the rhythm of his cock to the dildo.

"You like that?" he grits out. "Having every tight hole stuffed?"

I nod as he ploughs into me, over and over.

I can't speak; I just move.

He snarls, snapping his hips harder, and I scream his name, needing the burn so badly. His hands go to my buttocks, kneading and squeezing as he hauls me into his thrusts.

My tits bounce and the headboard bangs against the wall. I'm sure the whole building can hear every depraved and sinful noise we're making, but I don't have it in me to care.

Let them hear.

Let the world know that this man *owns* me.

"So—so good," I manage, my voice wobbly.

I'm barely holding it together as he fucks into me at a bruising pace. My pussy sucks the dildo inside me as I grind, and I feel my muscles tighten—that telltale flutter of an orgasm already building again.

"I won't last much longer," he growls.

This is my favourite part, when he can no longer hold back. My stomach flutters with pride knowing that I can strip away all his composure and drive him to the edge.

"I'm s—so close," I say.

"I'm going to come in this arse," he says, sinking his fingers into my soft flesh.

"Max," I murmur brokenly.

"Gemma!"

He chokes out my name. I detonate at the same time as he roars, his thickness swelling and spilling his heat inside me. I clench around him and he doesn't relent, thundering into me. This is it. This is nirvana.

Blackness clouds my vision just as he finishes and my body slumps, completely spent. My arse overflows with him, oozing down my thigh.

Finally, when we collapse together, he gathers me in his arms, breathing hard. He presses his lips to my forehead tenderly.

"I love you," he whispers, nudging my nose with his.

My eyes shine with affection as I take him in. All of him, flushed and gorgeous in his afterglow.

I used to think that letting someone in led to loss of control. But as I stare into Max's kind eyes, I realise now that running from love meant running from myself. Maybe we'll mess it up. Maybe we won't. But at least he's shown me that true love stays. That it isn't conditional or judgemental. It doesn't require you to be perfect or have everything figured out. It doesn't see your chipped edges and reject you. It exposes your most vulnerable parts and nurtures them. It doesn't ask anything more than to trust. It doesn't ask you to be someone else. It just *is*.

This man has earned my heart, and I'm finally ready to hand it over.

"I love you too."

Epilogue

Gemma

Six months later ...

"Bloody hell, this hallway goes forever. What's in here, anyway?" Anna calls out as she approaches the open door carrying a large cardboard box labelled MISCELLANEOUS. "It's so heavy!"

Today is moving day and the gang is in full force. I've even enlisted Henry to help.

Max and I got approved for a flat in South Kensington with a gorgeous view of Kensington Gardens. Our first home together.

We decided to lease out Max's penthouse and start fresh somewhere new. Somewhere unknown to Casey, close to both our jobs, and within walking distance to our friends.

Yes, *our* jobs.

After Max missed his flight back to New York, he had a heart-to-heart with Grayson. What began with Grayson losing his shit, quickly shifted to understanding when he realised how much Max missed London and his family. And how much he loves me, of course.

Max did need to return to New York for eight weeks to close out his apartment and transition his responsibilities to his replacement. Those two months apart nearly killed me, but Henry was brilliant and gave me time off to fly over and visit him.

There may have been lots of phone sex involved, too.

The hotel's opening exceeded everyone's expectations, so Grayson's solution to keep Max in the business was to promote him to managing director of the entire Gray Hotel chain. Max still reports to Grayson but runs operations from London, only needing to travel to New York every six to eight weeks. It's the perfect arrangement. By the time he's due to leave, I'm usually desperate for some quality time with the girls.

And the best part? I've got my own reading room with floor-to-ceilings shelves, all mine, and ready to be filled with every filthy, taboo, smutty romance I can get my hands on.

The place isn't as modern as Max's penthouse, but it's oozing character, which I love. It's big and bright, but it feels homely.

I'm standing on the balcony admiring the view when Anna shouts again.

"I'm gonna drop it!"

I spin on my feet and see which box she's carrying. I wrapped it with 'fragile' tape specifically to ensure Max and I could keep an eye on it. To make sure *we* handled it—my bad.

"Here, let me help!" I say, jogging toward her, but it's too late.

"We're losing him!" Anna yells as the box bottoms out, the tape ripping.

Max, Henry, April and James run out of the kitchen to see what all the commotion is about.

We all watch on in horror as a large pile of very obvious, very colourful sex toys spill all over the floor.

The Suite Secret

Shit.

For a moment, no one says anything. It's so quiet you could hear a fly fart.

Max and I glance at each other before he closes his eyes in slow motion, sucking in a breath.

Anna blinks down at the mess. "Oh."

Max whispers a tortured, "Jesus Christ."

There's my thick, purple tentacle dildo-slash-doorstop, two pairs of leather handcuffs, a spreader bar, a few butt plugs, variously-shaped vibrators ... and I'm pretty sure a bottle of something just rolled under the sofa.

Henry's gaze darts between Anna, Max and me, awkwardly waiting to see what happens.

April rests a hand over her five-month bump and covers her mouth with the other. "Gemma!" she says, lifting her brows.

The corner of James's mouth twitches as he tries to stifle his smile.

"Oh, you can talk," I say to April, gesturing to her round belly. "We all know how *that* happened."

"For fuck's sake," Anna whispers, glaring at the pile. "Why are there so many?"

She finally lifts her eyes to mine, and not knowing what else to do, I just shrug. "In my defence, you can't be surprised. You knew exactly who your brother was dating."

Anna turns away, unable to look at Max. "I'm going to go and get another box, and when I return—" she points in the direction of the pile, her face still turned the other way "—I expect this to be cleaned up."

"Go, Anna. Please," Max says, his voice steady.

Anna shakes her head before spinning around and racing out the door.

"Come on, babe," James says, placing his hand on April's swollen belly and steering her into the kitchen. "Let's start unpacking the kitchen stuff."

Henry shakes his head with a look of amusement. "Gemma, Gemma, Gemma," he says. "Why am I not surprised?"

"Oh, piss off," I snap.

"*Five* dildos?" he questions, raising a brow.

"Like you can talk. You love dick just as much as I do," I say.

Max's head snaps up, confusion painted across his handsome face. "What do you mean, *you love dick just as much as I do*?"

Henry's expression matches Max's confusion. "Because I'm gay?"

Max stares at him. "You're gay?"

"You haven't told him?" Henry asks, turning to me.

"Oh, shit," I mutter. My eyes latch onto Max's. "I forgot to tell you. Henry's gay."

"I've been with my partner, Nate, for three years," Henry explains.

Max's eyes narrow at me and I bite my lip, trying not to laugh at the look of betrayal on his face.

"You little shit stirrer," he says, fighting a smile and prowling toward me. "You mean to tell me that all those times you were laughing and flirting with him in front of me—"

Henry holds his hands up in defence. "I had nothing to do with that. If it helps, I was utterly repulsed."

"I wasn't flirting!" I protest, backing away as Max advances on me with that familiar predatory look in his eye.

"No?" He runs his fingers through my hair when he reaches me. "Then what were you doing?" he murmurs against my ear.

"I'm leaving," Henry mutters, heading for the door.

"Bye!" I call, still staring into Max's eyes.

Our lips are just about to touch when—

"Oh!" April pokes her head out from the kitchen. "I think I saw a vibrator roll under the sofa along with the lube."

Oops.

* * *

"Cheers!" we all say brightly, clinking our champagne flutes together.

We're seated around the dining table celebrating a hard day's work with a healthy spread of takeaway pizza, chips, and bubbles.

Henry left hours ago, the poor love. I think physically seeing my dildos might have been a bit much for him.

"Anna, how's your work going?" Max asks. "It's almost half-term, isn't it?"

Her face lights up. "Yes! Thank God. I'm hanging out for the break. The divorce has exhausted me."

"You deserve a proper rest. You'll finally have some time to catch up on all those monster romance novels I've been recommending. The minotaur one has an Irish audiobook narrator," I say, pumping my eyebrows.

"I'm not sure minotaurs are my thing," she replies, eyeing me sceptically. "Actually, speaking of Irish ..." She leans in. "There's this new Irish kid who just transferred to my class. He hasn't spoken a word to anyone in months, apparently."

Max's brows furrow. "Any idea why?"

"His mum abandoned the family for another man." Anna shakes her head. "His dad's some professional athlete who's struggling to cope. The female teachers are all losing their shit over him, but I feel for the poor kid."

Even though I don't have a maternal bone in my body, a wave of sadness floods through me.

"That's heartbreaking," April says, her hand resting over her bump.

Anna nods, taking a shaky breath. "But enough of that," she says, pushing back from the table to stand, champagne flute in hand. "There's something I'd like to say."

I set my fork down and turn toward her.

"I need you all to know how grateful I am." Her eyes find Max first, and I watch her composure start to crack. "Having my brother back home—God, Max. I didn't realise how much of myself I'd lost when you left. Family dinners felt so empty. London wasn't the same without you."

Max's jaw works, his knuckles whiten where he grips his glass.

"It was so hard not having you around." A tear escapes down her cheek. "Sorry, I don't want to make you feel bad about it. I'm just so happy you're here." She brushes the tear away. "And I know it's because of Gemma that you came home."

A lump lodges in my throat as her glistening eyes find mine.

"Gem, thank you for being brave enough to love him. I don't think I'll ever be able to thank you enough."

"Anna—" Max starts.

"Let me finish," she whispers, wiping her face with the back of her sleeve. She turns to me. "Gemma—you're my best friend. Seeing you and Max together gives me so much hope. I see the spark in both of your eyes, the love you share, and I'm so happy you gave each other the chance you both deserve. I know you're going to have a happy life, and I can't wait to see what you both do with it."

I shoot her a watery smile.

She turns to April and James. "And you two idiots are about to become parents." She points to April's bump. "That little boy is the luckiest kid on earth to have parents who love the way you do. Unconditionally."

"Oh, Anna," April chokes out.

"You're both so hot, and he's going to be such a little stud." April sobs into James's shoulder.

"I'm just so bloody happy," Anna continues. "For all of us. We've all been through hell in different ways, but look at us now. Look what we've built together."

Tears prickle at my eyes.

"I couldn't have gotten through the last six months of my divorce without you all. You guys are my rocks." She raises her glass in salute. "To new chapters. And to family—the one we're born into and the one we choose."

"To family," Max says, standing.

We all join him, clinking our glasses together and taking a sip.

"This sparkling apple juice is rank. I miss alcohol," April says, sighing dramatically.

Anna nudges April. "Excuse me, you're growing my precious godson in there. No booze for you."

"Are you okay, baby?" Max whispers against my ear, and I can hear the crack in his voice. Anna's toast got to him just as much as it got to me.

"I just have something in my eye," I say.

"I love you," he whispers.

"I love you too," I whisper back.

I look around the table at these incredible people and feel my heart swell. Anna's right. We've all been through hell, but it's led us to this moment. To each other. To this love.

Max smiles at me and when I look at him, I see my entire future reflected in his eyes.

THE END

Acknowledgements

First and foremost, thank you to every single reader and follower who's joined me on this journey. Your support has been everything. Without you, none of this would be possible, and I'm so incredibly grateful for each of you.

To my wonderful friends (you know exactly who you are) and family, thank you for your love and words of affirmation, especially during those niggling moments of self-doubt. There are times when writing can feel quite lonely, and you've been my anchor through it all. I'm so lucky to have you in my corner.

To my exceptional team—Sophie, Annie, Emily, Jennifer, and Susin—thank you for your expertise, brilliance, and for helping me bring Gemma and Max's story to life. Your feedback and care are so appreciated, and I'm truly grateful for everything you've done to help me mould *The Suite Secret* into the best story it could be.

A special thank you goes to Bec. You've been such an important presence in my life this past year. Your knowledge, encouragement, and friendship have meant more than you know. Thank you for the late night FaceTimes, putting up with my rambling text messages, offering your guidance, and for believing in this story (and in me) even when I didn't. I'm forever thankful for everything you've taught me.

Book Three in the
London Hearts series
is coming soon!
Discover Anna's story in ...

THE PLAYER'S PROMISE